Shenandoah Fantastic

MYSTIC WHISPERS FROM THE VALLEY'S VALES

Edited by James Blakey & Catherine Simpson

Whitaker Lyon Press

Broadway, Virginia

It's the Great Valley of Virginia but not as you know it. ***SHENADOAH FANTASTIC*** gathers 24 talented authors' tales of the odd, the unusual, and occasionally, the horrifying. Running the gamut from funny to tender to scary, these stories are sure to entertain. I know that I will never again look at some common parts of life in the Valley (such as grouse, farmers markets, and potato chips) the same after reading ***SHENADOAH FANTAS-TIC!***

—Stephanie S. Gardner, Author of *Rattlesnake Granny*

A charming read, funny, whimsical, something for everyone in this enthralling collection of stories.

—Danielle Holzhauser, Author of *Brought to Life*

All set within the geography of the Shenandoah Valley, the twenty-four stories included in — take readers on an entertaining ride from the "almost real" to the extremes of fantasy. If tales involving time travel and fairies make us smile, others exploring the curious unexplained coincidences of life make us think. Two thumbs up to the talented local writers who assembled such an imaginative anthology covering the spectrum of what we know to what we dream.

—Award-winning Author E.A. Coe

An endearing and absolutely Appalachian story. If you're In the mood for charming dialogue, and some adventure, this is your book!

—The Staunton Wallcrawler

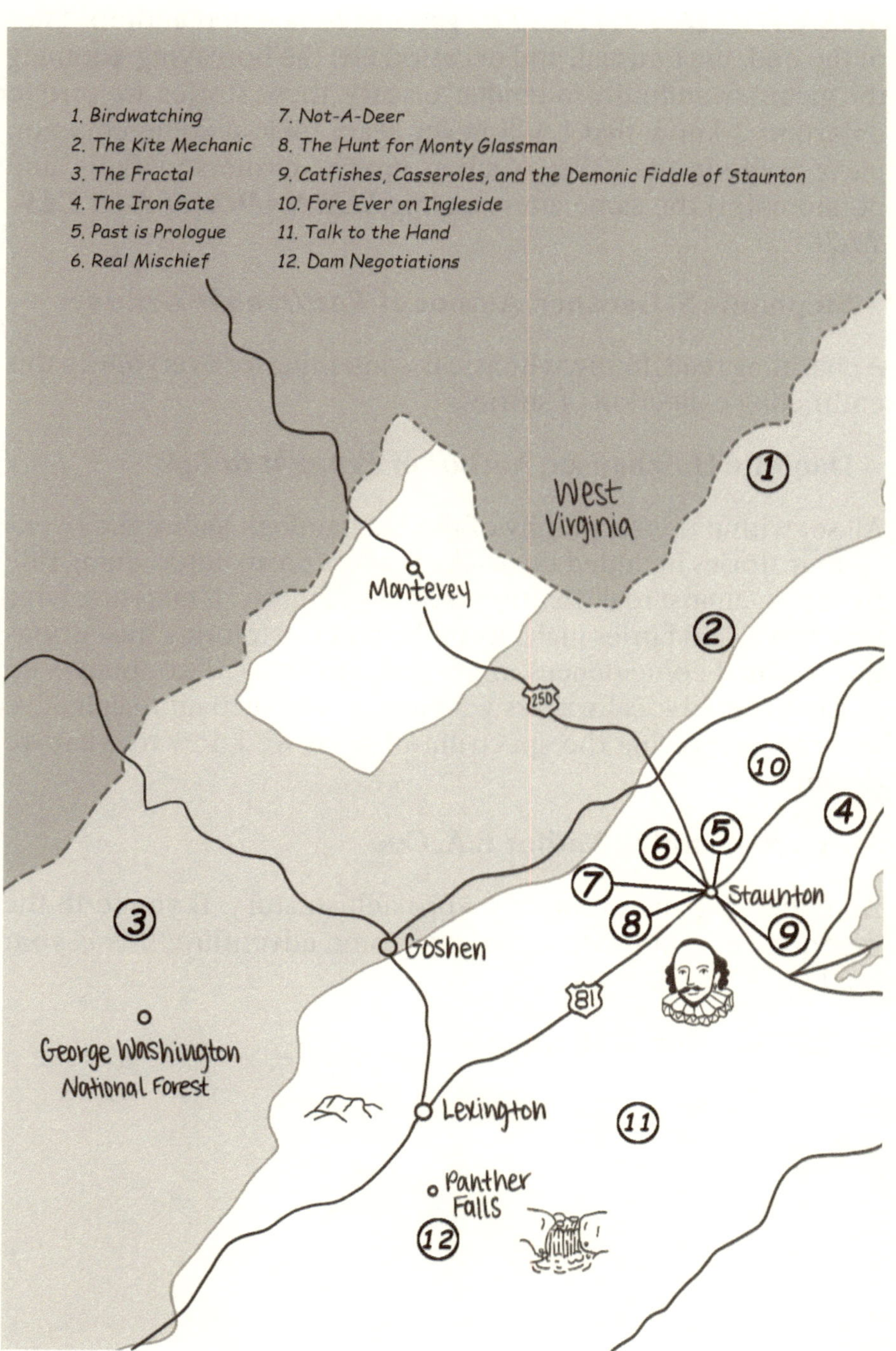

1. Birdwatching
2. The Kite Mechanic
3. The Fractal
4. The Iron Gate
5. Past is Prologue
6. Real Mischief
7. Not-A-Deer
8. The Hunt for Monty Glassman
9. Catfishes, Casseroles, and the Demonic Fiddle of Staunton
10. Fore Ever on Ingleside
11. Talk to the Hand
12. Dam Negotiations
West Virginia
Montevey
250
10
2
6
5
4
7
Staunton
8
9
3
81
Goshen
George Washington National Forest
Lexington
11
Panther Falls
12

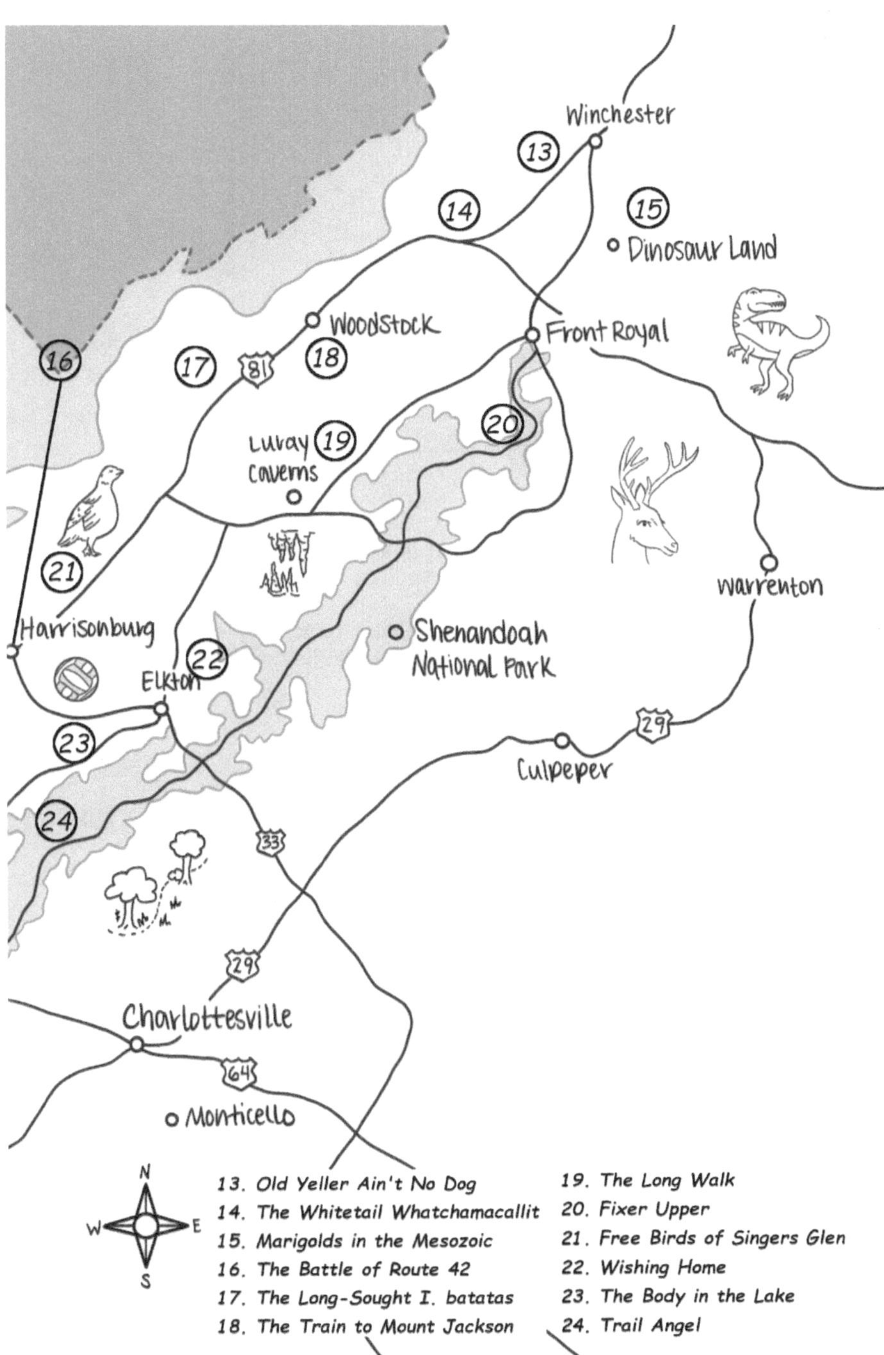

Winchester
13
14
15
Dinosaur Land
Woodstock
Front Royal
16
17
81
18
20
19
Luray Caverns
21
Harrisonburg
22
Elkton
Shenandoah National Park
Warrenton
23
29
24
Culpeper
33
29
Charlottesville
64
Monticello
N
W   E
S
13. Old Yeller Ain't No Dog
14. The Whitetail Whatchamacallit
15. Marigolds in the Mesozoic
16. The Battle of Route 42
17. The Long-Sought I. batatas
18. The Train to Mount Jackson
19. The Long Walk
20. Fixer Upper
21. Free Birds of Singers Glen
22. Wishing Home
23. The Body in the Lake
24. Trail Angel

Cover and art on pages 12, 53, and 190 by Andriy Dankovych

Frontispiece and art on pages 56, 94, and 134 public domain, courtesy of Wikimedia Commons

Map by Mary Lewis Simpson

Remaining art by Regar

Library of Congress Control Number: 2025919968

ISBN: 979-8-9909340-4-7 (Paperback)

ISBN: 979-8-9909340-5-4 (Hardcover)

Whitaker Lyon Press

4464 North Pointe Drive

Broadway VA 22815

WhitakerLyon.com

"In the Shenandoah, folk are shaped by star-wrought rivers, their hearts bound to a Valley that dreams its own tales."

—Unknown 19th Century Hollows Preacher—

Contents

William Shakespeare
(c. 23 Apr 1564 - 23 Apr 1616)

Past is Prologue

Kent M. Peterson

IT STARTED, OF COURSE, with the authorship question.

Hanford and Davis and I had gone to see *Much Ado About Nothing* at the Blackfriars Playhouse in downtown Staunton with several other Mary Baldwin people—students and staff. The three of us were adjuncts, united in paucity of paycheck and wealth of workload. Hanford was the physicist who commuted across the mountain to UVA, Davis was some mix of the social sciences but always referred to himself as an anthropologist, and I was the English teacher. After the performance—excellent, as usual with the Shakespeare Center—most of us walked the couple blocks to a place Hanford knew where we could get some drinks and socialize before heading home. The conversation was energetic and good-natured, until Davis said something about the play being good enough to really deserve proper credit.

"In what sense?" I asked.

"In the only possible sense, obviously!" Davis exclaimed. "Credit for writing it!"

I snorted. "Shakespeare has the credit already. Don't know what you're worried about."

"But that's the problem, there's no way Shakespeare could have written it."

There was a bit of an uproar at that point. I very decidedly made my opinion known as to the ridiculousness of this opinion and turned to Hanford for backup. He shamefully disappointed me.

"It's not as crazy as it sounds. There are some very interesting points to be made about—"

"Good God, not you too?" I exclaimed. "Shakespeare's name is on the documents! Nobody ever questioned that. Who else would have written it, his dog?"

"I'm glad you asked," Davis said, smiling gently. "It so happens that the seventeenth Earl of Oxford, Edward de Vere—"

One of the students burst out: "When *Macbeth* was first performed, de Vere had been dead for three years!"

Someone else promptly jumped in, asserting that simply because a thing is written does not require it to be acted on, that words on paper are still perfectly serviceable several years later, and so on. I was going to add my own weight of authority to this discussion when Hanford preempted me.

"You're both right; de Vere wasn't the man. Roger Bacon was."

At this, Davis nearly exploded. "Bacon! Bacon! Always Bacon! Can't you people show any imagination? You're almost as bad as this Stratfordian, here!" He gestured at me, nearly knocking a glass over in the process. "If you were to suggest Marlowe, you'd still be wrong, but—"

"Marlowe? A candidate for the poetically illiterate!" I said. "The sensibilities of the two bodies of work are irreconcilable. Haven't you ever read—" And we were off, all talking over each other, misquoting poetry, citing Bacon's journals, arguing about the social status of actors in Elizabethan times and the present day. In a momentary lull when everyone was catching their breaths, another of the students spoke up.

"Look, I don't understand something. Why couldn't Shakespeare have just, like, read books and talked to people? He could have learned enough to do it. The author of the plays was a good judge of character and the human condition. There's nothing in that making it impossible for Shakespeare to be the author."

"Ever been in court?" Hanford demanded. "Ever been face to face with a judge and had to make a legal argument after being silly enough to not hire a lawyer? Ever watch the judge roll his eyes at what a mess you're making of the terminology? Get this. The plays attributed to Shakespeare are full of legal terms. Complicated ones. And in every single case"—Hanford's voice was rising into a bellow, his hand waving around as if he couldn't decide whether to point in the air or pound on the table—"used correctly! I defy you to find a legal layman capable of that. No, sir, the author was a trained and practiced lawyer. When in Mister Shakespeare's twenty years of working as a stableboy in the boondocks before getting his actor job did he get his legal training, hmm?" He settled the question of what to do with his hand by seizing his drink and draining it.

I waited a moment, then said with the proper amount of dry contempt: "You got that entire line of argument from Mark Twain. A pity. I considered you an original thinker."

Hanford's face got rather red. I don't remember the details of the shouting that followed; we all got into it. Topics touched on included the customs of the high nobility, the geography of central Europe, the social norms of the Italian city-states, and the correspondence or lack thereof for each of these with Shakespeare's accounts of them. After some time, I noticed that my glass was empty, as indeed were most of the others on the table. It all seemed a bit perplexing, but I was quite sure that I had a preference for some moment earlier in the evening, when my glass was not yet empty.

That's when I had *the idea*. All I can say in my defense is that it seemed like a good idea at the time.

"Why don't you"—I paused for a burp, then continued—"go back in time and ask the gentleman himself whether he wrote them?"

Hanford and Davis looked at me, and then at each other.

"All right," Davis said.

"All right," Hanford said.

We had several more rounds and swore a mighty oath. I think. Someone suggested sacrificing a goat, or an okapi, or something, to seal the deal. After talking it over, that seemed like too much trouble, so I'm pretty sure we didn't. It's all a bit hazy.

***

The topic didn't come up again for a few months—until Hanford's car blew a tire. They didn't have the right replacement in immediate stock, and he figured he could bum rides from friends for a few days rather than blow money on a rental. I was helping him lug what must have been a month's worth of groceries into his apartment when I saw the papers scattered all over his kitchen table, and the whiteboard leaning up against the wall covered with all sorts of strange-looking equations. I thought I remembered my high school physics so I stopped to look at it more carefully, but couldn't make heads or tails out of any of it. When I looked up, Hanford was watching me in an embarrassed manner.

"It's, ah... it's Burkhard Heim's paper on his hyperspace theory," he said.

I stared at him blankly.

"Right. I forget. Look, most people consider Heim to have been a total crackpot. But that's the thing, crackpot theories don't get investigated or properly tested! Everyone says □oh, that's nuts' and moves on. But after reading up on the Zybourne team's experiments, from 2006 to 2010, I started thinking—maybe there's something to this. So I dug up a copy of the paper and I've been cranking through the math to see if I can follow his argument."

"But hyperspace—that sounds like space travel."

"Yes! Exactly!" He laughed. "I figured, why not take the back way around? It's space travel—faster than light space travel—and that's the point." He grabbed a marker and started sketching loops and equations on the whiteboard. "Now, it is a necessary and unavoidable consequence of faster than light travel that it inevitably results in closed timelike loops, which—"

"Please don't get technical," I begged. "Not if you want me to understand what you're getting at."

He barely heard me. "—supermassive rotating cylinders of course aren't practical on a subplanetary scale, and all the high-energy labs have been really interested in wormholes for years. So none of that's a likely area for breakthroughs for me. But then I remembered the problem of inertia!"

"It's a problem?"

"Yes! Does inertia derive from spacetime, or does it define spacetime? What if you could reduce inertia to zero? This all ties into what I'm convinced is the reason our models of FTL result in paradoxes in the first place, the accelerated frames haven't been properly reconciled. So what I'm trying to do—"

I was shaking my head, holding my hands up in surrender. "Please, I'm totally lost. This all depends on context I just don't have."

He put down the marker with some reluctance. "Well, if I build a device and it works, I'll tell you about it then."

"Sounds good. Hey, are you on board for tickets at the next play at the Blackfriars?"

"Oh, sure, sure... Hey, good thing we didn't specify a time limit for our time travel, huh?"

Then he laughed uproariously at his own joke.

The topic came up a couple of times when I would cross paths with Davis. He would only say slyly that he was "working on it." What exactly he meant by this did not become clear until the next season of plays. The three of us had made arrangements for tickets in advance; the first performance was *King Lear*.

Hanford and I arrived a little early and lingered outside, chatting a bit, until Davis made his appearance. He was outfitted in a thoroughly remarkable Elizabethan-period costume, with hosiery, puffy sleeves, and a flamboyant feathered hat.

We stared at him.

"What's this?" Hanford demanded.

Davis bowed. "Good sir, I attend the spectacle presented for our pleasure, as do yourself!"

Hanford squinted at him. "You look like you got lost on the way to a RenFaire."

Davis smirked, twirling the feather in his hat. "Nay, gentle Hanford, I am but arrayed in the manner befitting the house of Shakespeare, where spirits high and fancies wild do hold their court."

"Are you seriously gonna talk like this the whole time?"

"Forsooth, 'tis my solemn vow! I shall not break character ere the final curtain falls."

Hanford rolled his eyes. "Well, come on then."

The theater staff reacted rather differently.

"Good sir!" the usher exclaimed. "How pleasant to see a gentleman such as yourself, with proper taste in accoutrements! The customs of dress in this strange land are surely among the most surprising. I trust you will find our play most charming."

Davis bowed again. "Indeed, fair lady, I cast myself into the hands of your noble company, trusting in thy companions' skill and art. Surely such trust was never better placed."

I can say this much for Davis: the Blackfriars staff always treat people well, but he earned us extra smiles and special attention from them that evening.

The playhouse was built to resemble the original Blackfriars in London—a rather small, cozy space compared to most modern theaters; generally oval in shape, with wooden benches for most seating. We usually tried for seats in one of the balconies. There are also seats quite close to the stage; I prefer to avoid them. The actors tended to make a point of playful interactions with audience members sitting there, which many find fun. My own inclination is to observe the performance, not be part of it.

Once seated, I turned to Davis. "So what's the big idea, anyway?"

"'Tis passing simple," Davis said. "Behold, we do sit within the Blackfriars Playhouse; likewise did Master Shakespeare's company once tread the boards at a theater bearing the same name. By means arcane and wondrous, I shall harness the Laws of Magic, quickened by the passions of these noble players, and establish a mystic harmony betwixt this place and its ancient twin. When the resonance doth reach its zenith, lo! The twain Blackfriars shall be as one—and I shall find myself in the very theater of Shakespeare himself."

"That's the nuttiest thing I've ever heard," Hanford snorted. "Laws of magic?"

"Laws indeed!" said Davis. "From the tribes of darkest Africa, to the ancient sages of the Indus; from the Kuxil codex of the Maya to the pagan tales of the Lithuanians; yea, even the rustic yarns of medieval Christendom—all do sing in chorus of the same truths concerning the unseen world. Frazer, mayhap flawed in method, was the first to set it down; and though scholars now cast stones at his work, 'tis nonetheless a revelation most wondrous. Consider, good friends: every pre-industrial people beneath the sun hath arrived at the same tenets. Wouldst thou wager the odds of such a thing arising by mere chance?"

"But that's just primitives engaging in wishful thinking!" Hanford protested. "At least gravity is simply stated and experimentally verifiable. What, specifically, are these"—he waggled his eyebrows—"*laws?*"

"First, the Law of Contagion: where two things are brought together, there remaineth a bond, an affinity. Second, the Law of Similarity: that which doth bear likeness to another shall wield a like effect. For this cause do the native peoples cast water droplets skyward in their sacred dances, hoping to conjure rain by mimicry."

"Confirmation bias," Hanford stated. "They didn't make it rain—they just noticed when it happened to rain afterward."

"Hush up," I said. "The play's about to start."

King Lear is always fairly grim, so maybe that was why Davis was less talkative as we filed out. Hanford did ask him something as we left the lobby. All I heard of the exchange was Davis saying that proper experiments need repetition. He said it in plain English—modern-day talk.

We went to a couple other performances that season, and the next season as well. Davis did his Elizabethan clothes-and-talk act for every single one of them. I was told he actually did it in the classroom as well, until some students objected that their comprehension of the material shouldn't depend on familiarity with anachronisms. By the end of that second season, he seemed to be getting frustrated, but he wouldn't talk about why. The period costume got put away.

Hanford, also, seemed to have run into some sort of brick wall. He gave evasive answers when the topic of the Shakespeare pact was brought up or laughed the topic off. Only on one occasion did he give me any sort of detail.

"I thought I had a design for a test device," he said. "I rented a U-Stor-It unit to have some room to build it. But it's not doing what it should. I don't know why."

Then he shrugged and changed the subject.

***

Well, it might have stopped there. But once again I had to interfere.

I had made time for a month-long summer trip to England. The ostensible pretext was a literary conference but I took advantage of it to jam in all the tourism I could afford. I picked up some souvenirs along the way, many of which I handed out as gifts when I got back. For Hanford: a 1940s slide rule, complete with instruction booklet. He was absolutely ecstatic about it.

I found Davis at Grafton Library, staring at nothing, an eclectic collection of books and papers spread out on the table before him.

"You're back! How was England?"

"Marvelous. I've got pages and pages of notes from the conference and met some really remarkable people," I said. "Oh, and I brought back gifts—here's yours." I laid a small cardboard box on the table. "It's a dress-dagger. I thought it might improve your costume. I got it dirt cheap along with a few other things lying around in this antiquarian's place. It might fetch a couple hundred bucks in a perfect world, but I figured you'd make better use of it."

"Oh," he said. "Well, thank you. That was nice of you." He drew the dagger from its sheath and eyed it doubtfully. "How did you get it through customs?"

"Stuck it all in my checked baggage. Nobody complained."

"Purloined letter style." He shrugged. "If it works, it works. It looks to be in pretty good shape, for... What time period is this from again?"

"Late sixteenth or early seventeenth century. The dealer couldn't tell me much about the trinkets I picked out so I had the lot appraised. The others were mostly nineteenth century, but this is definitely Elizabethan era. I would have thought that would make it more valuable, but apparently there's quite a lot of ironmongery from then still lying around."

"Really? That's interesting. That's..." His eyes grew wide, then he jumped to his feet. "The Laws of Metonymy and Symbolism!" he shouted. "The best symbol for a thing is the thing itself!" He clutched the dagger to his chest, snatched up an armful of papers, and dashed off, nearly knocking over the library staff member who was coming over to shush him.

***

The three of us were, of course, at the opening performance of the next play at the Blackfriars. It was *The Tempest*. Davis was back in full costume and full period act, with the "prithees" and the "harks" and so on—and, I noticed, the dagger at his belt. The theater staff loved the whole effect, and they all riffed off each other at every opportunity. We took our usual seats on one of the balcony benches, Davis still keeping up a running line of patter in pure period lingo. He did fall silent when one of the actors came cavorting out on the stage to remind us all of the rules.

"Good gentles all, thy presence is most welcome in this hallowed house of mirth and tragedy! Before the play unfoldeth, lend but a moment of thy ears, for rules must needs be spoken..."

"Two of a kind, aren't you," Hanford muttered.

"...silence thy magical devices—those strange glowing stones of communication—for their beeping and blaring doth offend both muse and mortal. Hold thy selfies until the morrow, and let no flash of light pierce the shadowy dream we weave."

"I do feel like he's getting into it more than usual," I said quietly to Davis.

"'Tis but the spirit of the hour!" Davis grinned. "Canst thou not feel the Bard's breath upon thy neck?"

Shakespeare as a vampire stalker, there's an idea, I noted to myself. Not a very good one, I admit, but I always keep track of writing ideas. Force of habit.

The introduction continued. "Should thy hearts be set to flee—perchance from fright or fondness of fresh air—know ye the exits lie to the rear and to either side, marked by yonder glowing exit symbols. And lastly, let civility reign: speak not in loud discourse, lest the spirits of theater past smite thee with glares most withering and ushers most swift."

That earned him laughter. He smiled, strode back to the center of the stage, and finished: "And now, the curtain shall rise, and time itself shall twist—for tonight, we walk not as mortals, but as shadows in Shakespeare's dream."

The play itself was one of the best-performed I'd ever seen. I was completely absorbed right through the grand redemption and forgiveness of the ending. As the lights came on, I drew a deep breath—I must have been holding it for a while there without even thinking about it.

"Well, that was something," Hanford said.

"It sure was," I agreed. Then, looking around: "Where's Davis?"

There was no sign of him. His spot on the bench next to us was empty—his program was on the floor, but of Davis himself there was no trace.

Hanford shrugged. "Went to the restroom, maybe?"

"How'd he get out without us noticing? He would have had to climb over several people. We must've been more enthralled than I thought. Well, we can wait for him at the door."

Davis didn't show. After a while Hanford checked the restroom; Davis wasn't in there. The ushers didn't remember seeing him leave. We went our separate ways, sorely puzzled.

The phone records show it was 2:37 a.m. when Hanford called me, waking me out of a sound sleep. I couldn't understand what he was saying at first, and I know I was mumbling incoherently.

"He's done it!" is the first coherent thing I remember from that call.

"Done what?" I may have still been mumbling, but I'm not sure Hanford was listening closely.

"I tell you he's done it! I was thinking about it and fell asleep in my chair and when I woke up that was one of the two things!"

"The two... what?"

"The two things I knew when I woke up! Set your subconscious to work on something, it solves the problem. Davis was one, and the solution to my problem is the other! I'm headed over to the U-Stor-It while it's all clear in my head and—" At this point, he put the phone down, or dropped it, or something. I could hear him running around, moving things, still talking excitedly, but I couldn't make out the words until he picked the phone up again. "—until I get back! Got it? Don't forget! It's important!"

Then he hung up.

I glared at my phone for about a minute. The whole thing had been unutterably rude, and I really dislike being woken from a sound sleep. And it wasn't like he could be bothered to tell me clearly what he was talking about anyway. I turned the device off and was asleep again before my head hit the pillow.

I didn't think about it again until the police made their inquiries. Hanford never showed up at UVA to teach his next class. Apparently, I'm the last person he spoke to. After hearing what

I had to say, they went to the U-Stor-It and found his storage unit. The door was locked, and it had gotten slightly warped out of shape. It now had to be forced open or shut and the metal squealed loudly. Inside, there was some broken glass in one corner. Other than that, the unit was completely empty.

Nobody has seen Hanford or Davis since.

It's been a few months and there's some things I can't stop thinking about.

In the beginning was the word.

The pen is mightier than the sword.

I tried to distract myself with reading—the complete works of Thomas Zane. It's strange how few people know of him—but the more I read, the more an idea became clear to me. I wouldn't have taken it seriously if not for Hanford and Davis's absence.

I wasn't explicitly part of the pact. But I wasn't explicitly left out, either. And they're wrong. Shakespeare wrote those plays.

I am an English major. Am I not one of countless heirs to the Bard himself? Am I not a wielder and guardian of the greatest power humanity has ever known? Am I going to let an anthropologist and a *physicist*, of all things, show me up?

Zane was a remarkable writer, and I'm pretty sure he knew more than he was telling. I think I know what to do. I think I know how to do it. And I think it's going to depend on how good of a writer I am.

I think I'm good enough.

There's a few things I'm going to try.

It should be perfectly safe.

But—if I disappear like they did. If you can't find me...

Look in the books. The *old* books.

I'll try to leave some clues.

Free Birds of Singers Glen

GINGER GROUSE

As long as I'd known him, Spike never had much respect for chickens. He had even less respect for *barn* chickens.

"Why should we have any respect for birds that cannot respect themselves?" he argued, drumming his wings. "A lot of bootlicking sellouts. Why should we feel bad about the plants if that's what they choose?"

"They don't *choose* to go to the plants!" Hazel pleaded. "They don't know any better. They hatch in those big barns, fatten up on cheap grain and propaganda their whole lives. It's an echo chamber. We just need to wake them up!"

"They have no intelligence," Spike said, drumming faster. "Information is lost on them. Too fat and lazy to do anything for themselves. They would rather live in a state of denial."

"That's why we preach the benefits of a stateless society," Clip interrupted, preening his feathers.

"Not helpful, Clip!" said Hazel, pecking at the tender spring tree buds.

And so it went one early spring morning on Little North Mountain as we all roosted in the treetops near the humans' metal tower, gazing across the rolling valley with the long, low, loud, stinking barns stuffed with flocks of our domesticated cousins. For grouse like Hazel, the chickens were a great revolutionary hope. For Spike, they were an embarrassment to birds everywhere. The rest of us were like Clip: entertained by the debate, but more concerned with eating bugs and taking dust baths along the forest roads.

Spike was an excellent drummer and dancer when he wasn't being cynical, and one day I fell for him. For a few seconds. Just long enough to end up with a clutch of twelve. I laid my eggs in a secluded spot in the base of a hollow oak, and I got lucky with a late-season snowstorm that buried me in place. As I nestled in the insulated fluff with my unhatched brood, I listened to the whispers of the forest, carried underground through tendrils of mycelium.

Famine, fire, and flood.
The end of the world.
The end of the world.

I didn't understand the meaning of these whispers. But as the warming air melted the snow from my nest, exposing me to the sun again, I was filled with dread. And yet, a strange curiosity came over me, too. Having survived a winter, it dawned on me that I was now an elder, one of just a few hundred of my kind in these mountains who had seen the previous year. Few of us make it this long. I fluffed my feathers around the twelve lumps under my body. Would any of them attain my age?

"Hello, Misty!"

I exploded, flapping my wings and bolting straight down the mountain, landing in a tulip poplar ten glides downslope.

"Calm down, Misty! It's just me!"

I took a breath, slowing my racing heart, and looked back toward my nest. It was Hazel. I chirped an apology as she flapped to where I perched.

"No need to apologize," she said, alighting on the branch above me. "Being high-strung is how we get to be elders, right?"

"If we don't crash into a tree and break our necks," I replied sheepishly.

Hazel was three winters old, mother to two broods, a survivor, truly on her way to becoming legendary among the Little North Mountain flock.

"Don't you have a nest to guard?" I asked.

"Yes, of course," she said. "Emergence in one week, just like you. But this is more important."

"What could be more important than that?" I asked, head cocked quizzically.

"I'm telling you what must happen now that you are an elder. The memory ceremony."

"Memory?"

"All that has come before. Where we have come and gone, lived and died. What we have learned. The truths of these mountains and forests. There is more to life than gravel and bugs. Like, did you know it used to be easier to find bugs?"

"What do you mean?"

"Life wasn't always as hard, Misty. Once you've gone through the ceremony, you'll see what I mean."

"But what about my nest?"

"Don't worry. Spike's got you! Tomorrow. Meet me at the tower at dawn!" She flapped away to the south, leaving me with my puzzlement. I returned to my nest and hunkered down.

"Heeyy Misty!"

I exploded again. This time I careened fifteen glides downslope before diving under a laurel thicket, body trembling.

"It's Spike! Where'd you get off to?"

Aggravated as much at myself as at Spike, I let out a long, low squeal. Spike glided to a fallen log and puffed himself up, black ruffs standing out from his neck, his tail feathers resplendent with patterned bands of gray and brown and black. He began a slow rhythm with his wings, then steadily increased the tempo. The irresistible display of feathers and sound calmed me, amused me, drew me out of my hiding spot.

"There you are," he said sweetly.

I flapped over to him, and we beat our wings together affectionately.

"You here to watch the nest?" I asked.

"You have a ceremony to attend," he replied.

"Not until morning."

"I thought we could talk."

"About what?"

"About what to expect," he said. "I've got two winters, remember? I've seen thousands of grouse emerge. Only a few live a year.

That makes you special. I don't want you to get caught up in whatever Hazel is planning. Life is too short for—"

"If you're going to use that beak of yours to tell me what I can and can't do with my life, you can fluff right off!" I snapped.

Spike took a step back, ruffs flattened against his neck, feathers deflated.

"I have a mind of my own," I assured him, strutting forward.

"I can see that," he said, recovering, preening his feathers. "Then at least let me prepare you for the ceremony."

I glared at him skeptically, but relented. "What do I need to know?"

"It's going to feel a little... strange." With this, he stretched out his right wing, and the tips of his primary feathers appeared to twist and turn, as though they had minds of their own. My beak gaped. I had never seen anything like it! "Magic, evolution, whatever it is, the forest will change you," he explained. "And you're about to understand why we argue about chickens all the time."

***

Two dozen of us met Hazel at the tower near the midpoint of the long ridge that was Little North Mountain, which bounded the rolling hills of Singers Glen to the east. The sun was just rising over the escarpment of Massanutten Mountain.

"Follow me," Hazel said. She glided effortlessly down the western slope through the treetops, descending into the creek valley at the edge of the Allegheny Mountains. We sailed across a road and into the vast forest on the other side. For the rest of the morning we meandered our way higher and higher, passing ridges and summits where snow still clung to the shadows. We took frequent breaks to forage and drink, cleaning our feathers in the dust of one of our favorite fire roads. More grouse joined our party along the way, coming from all corners of the forest.

Hundreds of us came to rest around a massive oak in the early afternoon, in a steep, secluded draw. The trees were only beginning to leaf out, and the view of the forest floor was unobstructed for many glides in every direction.

"My fellow grouse," Hazel intoned from her perch in the oak as we roosted in the branches of nearby trees. "Today you will receive the gift of memory, and your bodies will transform. No longer will your life be only about evading foxes and catching the next meal. As elders, you will see to our long-term survival, not just as grouse, but as members of the forest community. Come!"

With this, she dropped to the forest floor and began scratching the leaf litter at the base of the oak.

"Come closer. It's safe!" she assured us, beckoning with a wing.

So our little flock gathered in, scratching and rustling, burrowing into the loam. Nestled in the leaf litter, Hazel spread her wings and stilled her body. We did the same. To all but the sharpest-eyed observers, we would have been invisible, our brown-and-gray-patterned feathers a perfect camouflage.

As my body stilled, the vibrations and whispers of the forest came to me as they had when I was under the snow. Then suddenly, a flash of light, and I *was* the oak. My roots burrowed deep and wide, entangled with threads of fungus and the roots of other trees. I felt the forest floor spreading out from my feet, up and down the slope, over a finger ridge into the next draw. Then the next. I was inextricably linked to the grouse gathered at my feet. The feathers of my wingtips, once without sensation, began to throb and tingle.

Then there was time. Incomprehensible time! Two hundred winters! Memories of memories, passed from branch to root, root to root, stretching back to the time when humans lived in balance, when the forest teemed with more life than we'd ever imagined.

We are dying. Most of us are already gone.

Sorrow and horror washed over me with the images of centuries, cascades of memories with the whispered words:

Famine, fire, and flood.
The end of the world.
The end of the world.

The hours passed in a moment. When our eyes opened again, I had become an elder, part of the forest, a one-year grouse who was centuries old. I examined my wings: each barb and filament pulsed with sensation, and I found I could move them, twist them into a multitude of miniature shapes. Some new forest magic had changed me. The forest had equipped us and entrusted us with a mission: stop the humans before they destroy everything living. Suddenly, I understood the stakes of the chicken debate. Chickens were relatives, natural allies, and they lived among the humans. We could get to the humans if we could free their birds! That was the day I became convinced of the revolutionary potential of the domestic barn chicken.

***

"You what?!" Spike exclaimed when I rousted him from my nest the next morning.

"I agree with Hazel," I repeated. "We should disrupt their economy by liberating the farms."

He rolled his eyes and angrily preened his wing feathers.

"How can you not see it?" I demanded. "I mean, what do we have to lose by trying? You see the way the climate is going, don't you? These mountains could be uninhabitable for us in two decades, maybe less!"

"I'll be lucky to see another winter," he said. "I don't see why I should be worried about twenty winters from now."

I let loose a low, hostile squeal at Spike's apparent lack of enlightenment—noting to myself that having the right information is no guarantee of wisdom or moral insight. "Where did you learn that thinking? You talk like one of those humans!"

He drummed his wings and strutted away, but I hadn't given up. I knew how to motivate him.

"Coward!" I chirped.

He stopped in his tracks and turned. "Am not!"

"See if I ever mate with you again!" I chirped.

He puffed his feathers, neck ruffs standing up. "You won't if I get myself killed on some suicidal chicken mission."

"I definitely won't if you don't try," I chirped with finality.

"Hmph." He perched on a log, puffed his feathers, displayed his ruffs and tail, and began to drum.

I ignored him, busying myself with my nest. He repeated his display twice, three times, to no avail. I was a rock. Deflated, he gave up.

"Fine. I'll help," he relented.

"Good," I said, fluffing my feathers over my eggs and settling in. "War council is in one month."

***

The forest between the ridgetop and the nearest farms was lightly settled, but settled enough that we usually avoided it. It felt unnatural, venturing this far down into the Shenandoah Valley, and it took every nerve in my body to not go flapping back upslope to safety. But Hazel, Spike, Clip, and I had a job to do.

The target was a small poultry farm on the edge of the valley, with two parallel barns two glides long. Spike and I were to take the north barn, Hazel and Clip the south. When the sun sank behind the mountain, we crept close and hunkered in the brush on the edge of the property. A heavy, damp miasma of chicken feces hung in the air, assaulting our beaks from twenty glides away. A cacophony of clucking from the barn drowned out every other sound.

"Do we really have to go inside those death traps?" Spike shouted over the din.

"Quit grousing and just do your job," Clip chirped.

We all looked at Clip with narrowed eyes.

"The entrances are around the other side, facing the road," Hazel yelled. "The workers should all be off for the night, so we're in the clear. Everyone check your multi-feathers."

I quietly straightened my wing and worked the barbs on primary feather number ten. I was getting used to this new ability that put opposable thumbs to shame. I nodded. Hazel nodded back and waved us forward, and we split up.

Spike and I silently ran around the north side of the barn. The structure seemed to stretch on forever when viewed from up close, and massive ventilation fans roared overhead, sucking clean air into the barn, threatening to pull us in if we tried to fly.

I stayed low as we rounded the corner and faced the personnel door, just to the left of the truck bay.

"You want to do the honors?" Spike shouted, his voice barely audible over the screaming birds and roaring fans.

I nodded. While Spike kept an eye out, I flapped into the air and stabbed my multi-feather into the lock. I worked my barbs around, feeling the intricacies of the mechanism until I found its shape. I locked in and turned hard. The lock clicked, the knob turned, and I pulled hard with my wing. The door swung open.

The wall of stink knocked me out of the air onto the ground, and the redoubled decibels of tens of thousands of clamoring, clucking chickens deafened me.

Spike extended a wing, boosting me to my feet. Cautiously, we pushed into the darkness of the barn.

"I'm going to need a dust bath!" Spike lamented, gingerly treading on the soft litter underfoot, rustling around in the dark, feeling the wall for a light switch.

Clunk! Clunk, clunk, clunk, clunk!

The banks of lighting illuminated the cavernous barn. A sea of fattened, white-feathered hens crammed the space, packed body to body, with less than a square foot allotted to each bird. I could not believe my eyes. How could any bird endure such conditions?

Suddenly illuminated, the throngs turned their eyes curiously toward us and gradually fell silent.

"Your turn," I said to Spike.

Spike hopped onto one of the feed pipes that ran the length of the barn and fluffed up his feathers, extended his neck ruffs. Then he began to drum, beginning a slow beat with his wings.

Tap...tap...tap...tap, tap, tap, tap, tap tap tap tap taptaptaptap tatatatatatatat!

He repeated the display, wings beating, ruffs ruffed, tail feathers splayed, up and down the barn. The effect on the flock of hens was hypnotic. Satisfied that he had their full attention, Spike handed the show to me.

"Sister hens!" I proclaimed. "I am here to warn you that you are in terrible danger."

Their beaks flashed toward me as they fixed me with their beady eyes.

"Danger?" someone asked. "What danger?"

"What is your name?" I asked, searching the crowd for the speaker.

"Frida," she said confidently, shoving her way forward.

"It is good to meet you, Frida," I said, extending a wing. She looked at it with suspicion and did not approach.

"What are you doing in our barn? What do you want with us?" she demanded.

"I'm here to talk to you about the humans and what they want with you."

The birds flicked their eyes at each other and back at me, grumbling.

"Do you know what they call you?" I asked. They blinked. "Broilers. Not birds. Not chickens. Do you know what that means?"

They blinked.

"It means you are their food."

"The rumors are true!" someone cackled.

"I knew we shouldn't have eaten the food! They're fattening us up!" cawed another.

"Oh, shut up, idiots," clucked a third. "They're imposters, just trying to stir up trouble and spoil a perfectly good thing! They're going to get us all culled! Probably carrying Avian Flu!"

A few of the hens backed cautiously away from us at that, but the spell wasn't broken.

"You don't have to be their broilers," I said, spreading my wings. "You can be free, if you choose. There is a whole beautiful world waiting for you outside this barn. Fresh air! Healthy food! Exercise!"

"And monsters!" someone cawed. "Giant bird-eating dogs with nasty teeth! And owls with sharp talons! No way I'm going out there!"

"It is true, there are predators out there," I said calmly. "But to die respectfully in the teeth of the fox or the talons of the owl is to die with purpose, our bodies freely given to the cycle of life. To die enslaved is not worthy of you. When that truck comes, you will be taken to an even deadlier monster: a giant factory where they cut you to pieces and sell you to their supermarkets. It is no way for a noble bird to die!"

The air surged with cluckings of fury and fear. I looked at Spike, who stared back at me with awe and disbelief.

"Hazel was right," I said with a wink.

"What do we do to get free?" Frida called over the din.

I raised my wing, motioning for silence, then gave my instructions: "Eat. Your bodies are weak. You are not ready. We will put medicine in your grain that will make your minds sharp and your feathers strong like ours. You will know what to do when the time comes. And when it does, we will be there."

***

Intelligence from friendly ducks informed us that the corn supply for valley poultry came from grain elevators, and two of them were located in the city of Harrisonburg. They called the one in the middle of downtown Chicken Mordor, after the sinister object of some legendary quest in the humans' lore. I thought the name fitting after learning of my next mission: travel to Chicken Mordor and dose the grain with our ceremonial spores, disseminating insurrectionary knowledge and dexterous feathers across the valley.

Spike and I travelled by night, sticking to the woods along waterways. We stopped in a park on the south end of town, where we met up with Floppy, a duck who would escort us into the city proper.

"Hmm, no good, no good," Floppy quacked, rubbing his bill. "You're gonna stand out in those streets like the coupla bumpkins you are. How about you give me the medicine and you let me do the honors?"

Spike fluffed his feathers and loomed. "Not a chance. The medicine is proprietary. This is our mission, and we'll see to it."

"Fine! Fine!" Floppy raised his wings defensively. "No offense! Just tryna help. Just tryna help."

"So how about you get us to Chicken Mordor?"

"Sure thing. But you're going to need a little disguise. I got just the thing. No human will know the difference!"

He produced two fake bills and slipped them over our beaks. We looked ridiculous, and nothing like ducks. Then he produced two pairs of webbed slippers.

"No way!" Spike protested. "We're not wearing those!"

"Yes, you are," Floppy insisted. "You grouse are a menace in flight, so this is an amphibious mission. Today you learn how to swim."

With that, he slid into the water and floated easily, beckoning us to join him. I sighed and pulled on the slippers, looking nervously at the dark, dingy water, coated with a chemical sheen. I grimaced with disgust as Floppy plunged his head under, wiggling his tail feathers in the sky as he nibbled a snack from the muddy bottom.

"Disgusting," Spike shuddered, tugging uneasily on his slippers.

Floppy's head popped up as he righted himself. "Get in, bumpkins!"

I nervously stepped into the current. The water rushed into my feathers, soaking me to the skin, threatening to pull me under. I flailed and splashed, coughed and sputtered, until a firm wing caught mine and pulled me out.

"No good, no good," Floppy said as I shook the water out of my feathers. "You just have to relax and float."

"We aren't ducks!" I snapped.

"Hmm, evidently." Floppy rubbed his bill again. "We'll just have to adapt. Get in again, but this time, hang onto my back."

With trepidation at first, we progressed upstream with Spike and me clinging onto Floppy like a life preserver, one on either side. We waited until nightfall before moving north out of the park, picking our way through the shadows of a railyard and a lumberyard. Then we understood why we needed the swimming lesson. The creek ran through a culvert under the city for long stretches, leaving us with a choice: swim the tunnel, or fly in the open.

We shuddered and hung on for dear life as Floppy paddled us through the first tunnel. I had never known such a total absence of light, and I gagged at the strange smells of chemicals and rotting trash. We emerged in the middle of downtown and rustled along the stream bank with towering walls on every side. Restaurant patrons ate on a porch overhead on our left. Warm smells of ginger and soy wafted down, and I couldn't help but morbidly wonder if chicken was on their plates.

We slipped into another tunnel, emerged by a small park, and followed the stream through back lots until we came to an overpass.

"This is as close as we get by water," Floppy whispered. "We go topside."

My heart raced as he led us over the top of the bank and onto the sidewalk above.

"Behold! Chicken Mordor!" Floppy intoned as we scrambled up.

I followed his gaze to the north, and my legs quaked. Towering over us two blocks away loomed the barren gray box of the grain elevator, its summit illuminated by an eerie lamp.

"Snap out of it, Misty," Spike whispered, nudging me with his wing. "We've got a situation here."

When I looked around, I met the gaze of over a dozen ducks, who quacked quizzically at Floppy's outrageous-looking companions.

"Important mission! Important mission!" he quacked in explanation.

Spike bristled and shook his head. "*Top secret* mission," he hissed to our guide, who paid him no heed.

"Come! Come! Follow me!" Floppy proclaimed to all comers. And before we could protest, the entire flock had surrounded us, shoving us across an intersection toward railroad tracks that led to the grain elevator complex. Cars swerved around us until we had taken the entire street, and then traffic came to a halt. The flock gently nudged us along, exhibiting no urgency.

A small child pointed from a sidewalk cafe and shouted to his parents, "Duckies!"

It took every ounce of effort not to explode in panic and fly straight into the grill of the nearest car. I did my best to carry myself like a duck, awkwardly padding along in the ill-fitting slippers. Our canard companions did their best to hide us with their larger bodies, and I hoped that Spike and I might pass for adolescent ducklings.

I breathed a sigh of relief when we stepped off the pavement into the railyard, safe from prying eyes and deadly cars.

"We'll wait here," Floppy said, "while you do your job."

Our breast feathers were loaded with the fungal spores that would bring strength, dexterity, and enlightenment to all who consumed them. Spike took the elevator complex by the near-by tracks, while I crept north through the shadows to Chicken Mordor itself. I followed a railroad siding across a street and into a bay at the base of the concrete tower, where the railcars disgorged their cargoes of corn into a grate between the rails. It took only a second to shake out my feathers, depositing my gene-altering payload.

Mission accomplished!

I rejoined Spike and our duck allies. Then we slipped out of town, back the way we had come.

***

"We watch and wait," Hazel said while we took sentry duty back at the tower, roosting on the metal spars in the heat of the early summer. "Once the spores take effect, they'll be perfectly capable of making their own decisions."

"What if they don't rise up?" Spike said. "What if they decide barn life isn't so bad after all?"

"Not the chickens I talked to," Clip replied. "They were flapping mad! They were practically sharpening their barbs *before* I started talking."

"They should be sharp enough by now," I mused. "If they don't make their move in the next day or two, they're broiled! What are they waiting for?"

"I don't think they are," Hazel said, gazing toward the valley below.

"What? What are you talking about?" Spike said.

"Look!" She nodded at one of the farms below. A column of smoke rose from the engine of a parked chicken truck surrounded by an agitated, fluffy white cloud.

"Is that..." I began, squinting.

"Yes, those are birds!" Hazel exclaimed. "They're going to need our help!" With that, she took off, gliding down the slope toward the growing fracas below.

We followed, hard on her tail, and alighted along the tree line minutes later and beheld a scene of utter mayhem. Chickens had broken out of their cages on the truck, sent the driver packing, slashed the tires, and set the engine alight! Now they were flapping to and fro, preparing to torch the barns as their sisters poured out into the fresh air, taking their first breaths of freedom, clucking with joy.

"Misty! Spike! Thank you for helping us!" It was Frida, flapping and running toward us, her face lit up with excitement. "All the farms of Singers Glen are rising today, chickens *and* turkeys, thanks to you!"

"That's amazing!" I shouted and flapped. Frida's joy was infectious!

"What are you planning to do next?" Hazel asked.

"We were thinking we'd come join you in the forest!" she said eagerly.

"What?" Hazel exclaimed. "The forest?"

We grouse looked at each other anxiously. The forest ecosystem couldn't handle millions of new residents. Most of them would end up as someone's prey. And what would the humans do? Would they send in the National Guard? I began to have doubts about the wisdom of letting these barn dwellers think for themselves.

"We want to be free birds, like you," Frida asserted. "We want to be connected to the land, the way we were meant to be. Not living in crowded barns. Besides, the humans will counterattack. We need someplace we can defend. Let us take to the mountains!"

"Okay, sure, fine, we'll figure out the details later," Hazel said. "Can you fly?"

Frida gestured around at her sisters, flapping and running about the barnyard. "Does it look like we can fly?"

Hazel cursed under her breath. Getting these breast-heavy, stumbling birds up and over Little North Mountain would be a tall order. The terrain was too rough. But there was a gap with a road at the southern end.

"We should take the road," I proposed.

"We can organize air support," Spike added.

"And take on the cars?" Hazel exclaimed.

"They stopped their cars when we took the street in Harrisonburg," I pointed out. "Humans have a soft spot for birds."

"Those were free ducks," Hazel argued. "They think ducks are cute. These chickens are just fugitives to them."

"But we're also money," Frida said. "The farmers will try to take us alive. We can use that to our advantage."

All of the grouse from the mountains pitched in that day, flying reconnaissance, passing messages from farm to farm, spreading the word that we were taking the gap. The chickens left trashed barns and disabled trucks in the path of their march. They waddled and flapped their way over the hills, cutting through cornfields, converging with their poultry compatriots on the road over the gap.

A line of befuddled farmers awaited us with a handful of Sheriff's deputies, their vehicles lined up on the shoulder. A helicopter hovered overhead. Passing drivers craned their necks, wondering what all the fuss was about.

The multitude hesitated for a moment at the sight of the police, but Clip had an idea.

"I've got quite the payload saved up," he said with a sneaky grin. "How about y'all?"

In all the excitement, I had not relieved myself for quite some time. I followed Clip's gaze toward the shiny police cruisers. I smiled.

"On me!" Clip called. He exploded into the air, followed by dozens of grouse, our wings setting up a thunderous beat.

A startled farmer dropped his cup of coffee. A deputy ducked and flipped over the hood of his cruiser, gun drawn. I aimed for his hat. Swooping in low from the side, I loosed my bowels.

"Awww, disgusting!" I heard him shout as I climbed out of my dive.

Glancing back, I saw pandemonium on the road as the grouse air force unleashed our strike, smearing the shiny vehicles of our foe with our sticky ordnance.

A cry of "flock the police!" rippled through the emboldened feathered army, and the chickens and turkeys surged forward. The people took shelter in their trucks and cruisers as the birds went to work, slashing tires, smearing windshields with droppings, stuffing gas tanks with feathers. They triumphantly carried off the cruisers' lights as trophies as they pushed their way up the winding road over the gap.

The flock descended the backside of the gap, and as the sun sank behind the mountains, they turned into the Allegheny backcountry, where they dispersed into the night.

***

Even high in the mountains, the hot, humid, late-summer air pressed against my feathers as I perched on the power line in the moonlight, waiting for Frida's signal. She gave me the "feathers-up" sign. I closed my eyes and gritted my beak, wondering if the switch we had rigged with plundered parts would work, or if I was about to get fricasseed. I flipped the lever. The wires stopped humming. When I opened my eyes, the lights of the Shenandoah Valley were dark. Success: a sign that our physical strength, intelligence, and ingenuity had only grown over the past few weeks. And while we'd lost many of our new comrades to predators, they seemed to prefer the danger to a meaningless death in captivity.

Hours later, just past sunrise, a line of utility trucks escorted by a National Forest cop rumbled up the gravel road, looking for the source of the trouble. It was not hard to find. We were waiting for them at a roadblock of downed trees high on a mountainside, prepared by a team of buff turkeys with stolen chainsaws. Thousands of chickens roosted in the branches and ledges, brandishing their newly evolved, sharpened primary feathers.

The foreman gulped nervously as he stepped down from his truck. The officer stepped out of his SUV with his hand on his holster. Spike stepped up on one of the logs in the road. He began to drum, his ruffs and feathers on display.

The befuddled humans did not know what to make of the preposterous scene until Frida waddled in front and opened her beak.

"This is our forest now," she said. "We control your power supply. The deal is simple: treat us with respect, and we leave you alone. If you don't, we cut the juice."

The men looked at each other, mouths agape. Workers craned their necks out the windows of the trucks.

"And start weaning yourself off this electric grid," Frida continued, pointing at the wires. "Reality is coming for you hard. That so-called 'civilization' of yours is killing everything. It's over. You're going to have to learn new ways. But we won't make you give it up cold turkey!"

With that, Frida nodded at my perch high on the power line, and I flipped the switch, restoring power. The foreman's cell phone rang moments later.

"Uh huh... Gotcha... Yup," he said. "You're not gonna believe what I'm lookin' at up here... Yup, a buncha birds, and get this: one of 'em's talkin' to us!"

Wishing Home

Ember Rensel Heishman

THE SOUL OF A tree was a hard thing to capture. But the woods were aching to stretch their winter limbs, and, armed with a butterfly net and a milk jug full of pond water, Amelia thought she just might manage it.

Pines and spruces, she knew, were reluctant to reveal themselves. They could stay hunkered deep down in their roots for decades, only shaken awake by the worst of windstorms. But the trees that dropped their leaves every year couldn't help but poke their noses into the fresh spring air, as if to see if it were safe to bud or if there were a bit of ice still clinging to the breezes that swept up the valley and over the long line of mountains.

Amelia liked the mountains. They stretched sideways instead of upward, nothing like the jagged peaks in which she'd been born. They were soft and round, friendly in the way that grandparents were supposed to be. And she liked the bowl of the valley, the way the ridgelines seemed to cradle her between them and the weather rolled up high over the peaks before tumbling into the fields below.

She especially liked the mountain that peaked right in the middle of the valley and swept dramatically down into the bottom of the bowl. "Mass a nothin'," her grandfather had called it when she'd first pointed it out. But she didn't think it was nothing. In fact, that's where the trees had first told her she might catch one of them.

She trekked across the field behind her grandparents' house, the winter-pale grass lit so brightly by moonlight that she could

see her own shadow despite dawn barely lining the tips of the
mountains. She repeated the riddle to herself, as she had every
day all winter long, exactly as the maple had whispered it to her
last fall. Her navy blue rubber boots brushed through the tall grass,
a rhythm to her rhyme:

We trees stand watch over forest and field,
Our roots sunk deep in Soil's dark yield,
Our branches stretched in Sky's wide shield.

But our souls wander far when our bark brittles dry,
In search of still waters when the full moon is high,
And it's too late for snow, but not time yet for butterflies.

If nature's net should catch us, and you choose to set us free,
We'll grant you a wish, what you most want to see.
A promise that's sealed on return to our tree.

And tonight, almost five months later, the moon was full, the
forest was dry, and Amelia was ready to get her wish.

She looked both ways and crossed the deserted road that bor-
dered the field opposite her grandparents' neighborhood. She was
just approaching the copse of oak trees on the other side when
headlights from a rusty farm truck caught her in their beams. The
truck slowed, and she dropped her jug of pond water to shield her
eyes.

"What are you doing, girl?" a gruff voice called.

Amelia shrugged, still blocking her face from the lights.

"You alone?" the driver asked.

Amelia shrugged again.

"Your parents nearby?"

No, Ameilia's parents were not nearby, but she knew what he
meant, so she pointed her butterfly net in the direction of her
grandparents' house, one slanted brown roof in line with all the
other roofs that guarded the back of the subdivision.

"Don't talk much, do you?" asked the voice behind the headlights.

Amelia shook her head.

"Well run along home now, yeah?"

She couldn't, as home was thousands of miles away and that's why she was out here in the dark trying to catch a tree soul in the first place, but she knew what he meant, so she nodded, and the truck rumbled away.

When she bent to retrieve her jug, she found that the cap had come off and freed all but a few drops of water. She sighed and began the trek back to her grandparents' house, empty-handed but for a plastic jug and a butterfly net with freckled orange paint peeling off the handle.

***

Amelia struggled to keep her eyes open at school that day, and during recess she caught herself eyeing the middle school down the hill and wishing that she could be there with Shannon, rather than stuck here by herself. But her sister was two years older and had friends and was doing fractions and decimals. Amelia sighed and dug her fingers into the grass on either side of her crossed knees, feeling loose soil pack down under her nails.

Excited voices pulled her attention to a propped-open cellar door around the back of the school building, hidden from the teachers chatting on their bench. After a moment's hesitation, she stood and followed the voices down the rickety stairs and into the dark, windowless room below, tucking herself into a corner.

"Look!" one boy exclaimed. "A tree is eating our school!"

Amelia watched as they poked at a root that had burst through the cement-block wall. She waited until a teacher's voice calling from above pulled the other students back up the stairs before she approached the root, wanting to feel the smooth, tunneling tendril for herself.

She'd just pressed her palm to it when the metal door clanged shut and the room plunged into darkness.

Amelia ran up the stairs and pushed on the metal. It didn't budge. She banged her small fist against it, but the voices outside were fading, and she knew her class recess—the last one of the day—was over. She tried to summon her own voice, but she'd left it somewhere back home in her parents' house almost a year ago.

She was trapped, and it was cold, and she was alone.

She plopped onto the stairs, curled her knees up to her fore-head, and began picking the dirt from beneath her fingernails. She wished that someone could hear her. That someone would notice she was missing and look for her. She wished she were a tree with roots so strong she could break through the wall and escape into the sunlight.

She wished she weren't alone.

She wished for so long that she'd nearly fallen asleep when metal scraped behind her and the door creaked open on rusty hinges.

Amelia blinked against the sudden sunlight.

"Ah, there you are, dear," said a voice above her that sounded like the valley come to life: wide, rolling fields and dry leaves and soft pine needles and slow-moving rivers. A shadow blocked the light for a moment as a woman with wispy white hair stepped past her and floated down the stairs. Amelia blinked as the woman twisted the lid off a glass jar and poured a trickle of water over the school-eating root.

Her white hair floated about her face—almost as if she were underwater—as she stuck the jar into a leather sling bag with leaves and petals sticking out the sides beneath the flap. She then turned her gray-green gaze to Amelia and said, "Come then, child, it's well past time for tea."

Against her better judgement, Amelia stood and followed her rescuer out of the cellar, across the now-empty schoolyard, and along a narrow path through a small strip of forest that her class-mates called Blue Jay Woods and dared each other to explore when teachers weren't looking. German fairytales of witches lur-ing children into ovens scuttled through her mind, but then the woman opened a wrought-iron gate and Amelia forgot all about her uneasiness.

They had emerged into a faerie world: a small round cottage with bark siding nestled amongst leaning pines, a garden carpeted in white snowdrop flowers and mounds of sleeping thyme stretch-ing out before it. And it smelled of magic—that rainstorm, moss, and old pewter scent that permeated everything with a mingling sense of something ancient and something just beginning.

So Amelia sat in the garden and sipped tea with Nina, as the woman had asked Amelia to call her when she reemerged from the cottage with a steaming teapot. Nina told stories about flowers and faeries, tipping up the floret of a snowdrop so Amelia could see below its narrow white petals to the curled form of a softly glowing faerie sleeping there. She didn't seem to mind that Amelia was silent.

Amelia was enchanted, in every sense but the literal.

Nina eventually phoned Amelia's grandparents using the number they'd scribbled inside each of her school notebooks alongside their address. Amelia traced the inked letters and numbers, wishing they were different ones—the ones she'd memorized *before*—as she listened to her grandmother's tinny, worried tone lean toward relief under Nina's assurances.

Nina led her around to the rocky, moss-covered front yard as the pair of haggard septuagenarians and a red-haired sixth grader rolled up the packed-dirt driveway in a minivan that had likely carried the girls' mother to school three decades ago.

***

As the faeries unfurled from their fading snowdrops to burrow back into the roots for another year and bluebells sprang up in their place, Amelia made daily treks to Nina's cottage after school, guzzling tea and tales for as many hours as she was allowed to stay.

She learned that hearing a bluebell ring meant someone close would die, and that important things should be kept in glass jars, and that ancient things slept under the mountains, and that flower faeries would answer one question every year if asked nicely. She also learned that gardens like Nina's had once been commonplace in the valley, since the fertile, well-tended soil had drawn all sorts of magic into its bowl. "That's why Virginia is so very green," Nina explained, adding that it was also why the coal-stripped states that touched it had faded into grays and yellows and browns.

Day after day, Amelia tried desperately to coax her voice out of its burrow so she could ask Nina about catching a tree soul. She warmed her throat with Nina's tea and made the shapes of words with her lips and imagined what it might be like to say the words, but day after day she was silent. But the adults had all said her voice would come back, so she waited.

It was the middle of March when Amelia tumbled through the wrought-iron gate to find Nina crouched beside an elder bush along the fence, watching a spider spin a web in its lower branches with a sad sort of something in her faded eyes.

Amelia dropped her backpack in a patch of thyme and joined her companion.

"Odd creatures, spiders," Nina murmured, gazing at the web maker, her voice slipping into the distant tone she often used when a story took her far away. "Eight legs, eight eyes, infinite upon infinite. Passive predators, planners, weaving nature's nets and sitting on their nests of wrapped-up prey like—" her voice cut off suddenly as Amelia's hand gripped her forearm. Nina turned to her with wide eyes. "What is it, child?"

Amelia pointed at the bush and fumbled her way through signing the letters N E T. She'd been trying to learn the hand shapes from a tattered book her grandmother had given her, and she was now furious with herself for not trying harder as Nina's pale brows knit together in curious confusion.

After a bit more miming, her wrinkled face cleared and she said, "Ah, nature's net." She shifted her gaze back to the spider and spoke quietly. "Yes, powerful things, spiderwebs. They catch more than flies, and they don't like letting go. It takes two to free a faerie trapped in spider silk."

Her ancient face clouded, and in a sudden burst of uncharacteristic speed, she sliced a hand through the newly finished web. Then she stood and strode into the cottage.

Amelia stayed frozen in her crouch, startled by this strange cruelty. When, after long minutes, Nina did not emerge with their usual pot of tea, Amelia scooped the fallen spider onto a leaf and lifted it back into the elder branches, wishing she could whisper an apology to the creature for the loss of its home.

She went in search of Nina and found her in a rocking chair, a faraway look in her gray-green eyes. So Amelia put the kettle on to boil and fixed a pot of tea as best she could, then filled their two cups. But even long after Amelia had finished her tea and the familiar sound of tires on packed earth pulled her out the front door, Nina's cup sat untouched on the side table.

✳✳✳

That night, Amelia stole from her grandmother.

Despite weighing almost nothing, the embroidery hoop she'd taken from the craft closet hid heavily in her backpack the next day, and by the time she arrived in Nina's garden, her shoulders ached from the weight of her guilt. Her stomach sank further when she didn't see Nina's white hair and willowy form among the plants, and she worried that she might find the woman still staring at a memory in the rocking chair.

But as the gate clanged shut behind her and the cozy familiarity of the garden settled over her skin, Nina emerged from the cottage with a pot of tea and began chattering about an herb that allowed sleepers to pull things from their dreams. As Amelia had not had a good dream in some time, she allowed her mind to wander to the stolen embroidery hoop and her plans to pin a spiderweb between its rings, like she'd seen her grandmother do with fabric.

She'd also been carrying a glass jar around in her backpack for a few weeks, in case she came across another pond that wasn't as scummy as the last one (she'd decided that, with a net as pretty as spider silk, dirty water wouldn't look very tempting beneath it, no matter how still it had been). After that, she would just need to find a good spiderweb before the next full moon.

Then she'd wish for her home, and everything would go back to the way it was.

But the next full moon came and went before she'd found either piece of her tree-soul trap, and she was as cross as she had ever been as her class filed through the lobby of a cave in the next town over and began their field trip. She tried to pay attention to their guide, but "the oldest continuously operating cave in the United States" seemed somewhat trivial after spending every evening watching faeries drop out of flowers, dart around like fireflies, and bury themselves back into the soil to tangle with roots, like they'd been doing for centuries before anyone had even been around to discover caves at all.

But as they stood on a steep staircase, the cold metal pipe railing stinging against her palm, her ears snagged on the guide calling the place "The Still Water Room." Suddenly attentive,

Amelia craned her neck, trying to see the water, but they were only pointing their light at a line in the cave wall where still water *used to be.* Her heart sank as she followed her class the rest of the way down the stairs and into a big room with rainbow lights illuminating a hole beneath one of the overhangs.

She was still sulking while the guide talked about missing stalactites, but then they shined their light into the rainbow corner and Amelia realized it wasn't a hole at all, but water so still it was a perfect reflection of the ceiling!

All at once, the wonderful, steady magic of the place washed over her. There was an aching stillness in the pure, earthy clay scent, tinged with the crystal coolness of that mirror-smooth water, like an ancient thing still waiting to be born.

Just like that day in the school cellar, she let herself melt away from the group, into deep shadows behind the second guide, and waited until they'd moved on. Then she dug the glass jar out of her bag and approached the upside-down world reflected in the pool.

She ducked beneath the metal pole, careful not to touch the cave wall or low ceiling (the guides had said a LOT about not touching anything). But she hesitated with the jar poised over the pool's perfect surface. Disturbing this eerie stillness suddenly struck her as a terrible thing to do—even worse than taking the first scoop from a new jar of peanut butter. But thoughts of her old bedroom and a pile of abandoned stuffed animals thousands of miles away made her push the lip of the jar beneath the surface. As water flooded into the glass, rainbow lights rippled, making her dizzy and nearly pulling her into the water.

Terrible deed done, she scrambled back onto the path and merged with the shadows to rejoin her class, backpack heavier than ever.

***

April's Pink Moon rose above the Blue Ridge Mountains while Amelia sat at dinner, listening to Shannon chatter to their grandparents about her middle school track team. Amelia usually liked listening to her sister talk, but this—Shannon pretending she was happy here—made her want to scream. But she stayed silent, waiting until she could wash her plate and go fix things for them.

She'd found her spiderweb beneath her grandparents' deck three nights earlier and had the jar of cave water and other supplies already in her backpack. She'd left a handful of dead flies from her windowsill as an apology gift for the spider she'd stolen from.

When the house finally fell quiet, she retrieved the spiderweb and backpack from beneath her bed and snuck out the back door. This time, her trek across the field was accompanied by twilight, with the mountains on the sunset side of the bowl standing like upright shadows against the last light of the day. Unfortunately, instead of the dry winter grasses of her last excursion, the tell-tale smell of spring in the valley—"chicken-made fertilizer," her grandfather called it—squelched beneath her rubber boots.

She scurried across the road and into the trees before any trucks could stop her and, once she was beneath the fresh buds of leaves, she delicately set her trap. She filled a glass bowl she'd filched from her grandparents' kitchen with the cave water from the jar she'd filched from the same location, carefully extracted the filched embroidery hoop and its perfect spiderweb, set it over the bowl like a lid, and wondered if she might be a thief.

Unsettled by the thought but satisfied with her trap, Amelia settled in to wait. She had come prepared to sit for a few hours, but before she could tug the ratty fleece blanket from her bag, a flash of yellow-green light hurtled past her toward that bowl of perfect, magic-scented water, hitting the trap so hard she thought the web would snap or bounce the light away like a trampoline.

But the web held, and Amelia held her breath along with it as she peered at the pulsing light squirming against the spider silk. It looked so much like a flower faerie that, for a moment, she wondered if her trap had caught the wrong thing. But it was bigger, and brighter, and so very *green*.

Yes, she had caught the right thing.

And it was a marvelous thing, a tree soul. Just looking at it made her feel like her toes could grow roots right into the ground. Like her fingers could stretch toward the sky and grow leaves. Like she could belong here as if she'd been planted, instead of being dropped into this bowl by metal and wind and left to float around on the surface of it.

Looking at it felt like being home.

Home.

Now! Now was the time to make her wish! To get her home back!

She opened her mouth, the shape of the words on her lips, but no sound filled the shapes. Her voice was still stuck inside her throat as firmly as the tree soul was tangled in her trap.

She'd thought that when it came time to make her wish, her voice would be there, like it used to be at home. But her chest felt the way her grandfather's truck had sounded after he'd left his headlights on all night: a rumble of something behind her collarbones, but somewhere on its way to her mouth, it clunked over itself and went quiet.

Amelia clenched her fists and tried again and again to muster the sound of her wish, but again and again it died in her throat. She tried through the darkest hours of the night, and when the first plane of the day roared to life at the little airport just beyond her copse of trees, she finally allowed tears of frustration to drip down her nose and into the bowl of water below her captured tree soul.

A terrible feeling welled inside Amelia, big and dark and roiling like the storm clouds that rose up over the mountains in the fall. She snatched the pulsing tree soul, still tangled in spider silk, and shoved it into the empty glass jar. She would find her voice, and as soon as she did, she would make her wish and set the tree soul free.

As she hurried back toward her grandparents' house, a terrible certainty rolled through her: she *was* a thief.

***

By the time she pushed through Nina's gate after school that afternoon, she was exhausted. She stumbled off the stepping stones that marked the garden path, and a light tinkling sound brushed her ears. She blinked down at her tennis shoes, realizing she'd stepped into a patch of bluebells and set them swaying. She pulled her foot out of the stems. The tinkling sounded again.

Amelia frowned, reaching down to brush her fingers over the soft purple petals. More tinkling, louder this time. As she crouched to examine the flowers, the clanking of the glass jar in her backpack tore her attention back to the important matter of the tree soul that had been getting dimmer and dimmer every time she'd checked on it between classes.

She swung her backpack around and frantically dug the jar out of its depths, terrified the tree soul might go completely dim before she could make her wish. She let out a breath when she saw that it was still pulsing with a faint yellow-green light.

The back door of the cottage creaked open. Amelia knew Nina would be displeased to learn that she'd kidnapped a tree soul instead of setting it free, and her voice was still stuck, so she wouldn't be able to explain herself properly. She hastily tried to shove the jar back into her bag but only succeeded in knocking the whole thing over, tipping pencils and her lunchbox onto the path and sending the jar rolling out of reach. It settled beneath another patch of ringing bluebells.

"Oh dear, child, are you well?" Amelia watched in horror as the woman's bony bare feet stepped just past the jar, nearly kicking it back into the path. Amelia gathered up her spilled things and nodded hastily. She'd come back to get the jar later.

But later, her grandparents arrived early and Nina walked her straight to the car, leaving Amelia no chance to retrieve her flickering tree soul.

***

Her leg bounced all through dinner. It was well after midnight before her grandmother finally put away her sewing project and turned out the lights. Amelia tiptoed outside and pulled Shannon's bike from its precarious lean against the house, then pedaled furiously all the way to the cottage. She'd never noticed how wide the road was before, or how far Nina's was from her grandparents. In the dark, the world seemed to stretch further than she'd known it could.

Her legs were jelly by the time she reached the cottage, and she was startled to find the kitchen window spilling soft yellow light into the forest. She propped the stolen bicycle against the bark siding of the cottage and snuck around to the garden, only to find the back door swinging lightly on its hinges. The kitchen light illuminated the garden and glinted off the glass jar in the middle of the path, the tree soul within it now a dim gray-green. Amelia's stomach knotted, and she scurried forward to gather up the jar.

Her hand brushed another patch of flowers, and she finally remembered what Nina had said about hearing a bluebell ring. Jar in hand, she rushed to the cottage and searched every room. Every single one was empty, the teapot in the sink the only indication that anyone had been there at all.

Heart in her throat, Amelia ran to the bike and pedaled home faster than she had ever pedaled before. She leapt from the bike and sprinted straight through the backyard toward that copse of oak trees. She was halfway across the field when another of Nina's lessons came back to her.

It takes two to free a faerie trapped in spider silk.

She turned and ran the other way, her legs nearly numb from exhaustion, her lungs on fire. She crept through the house and swallowed hard before pushing Shannon's door open and shaking her sister awake. With Nina gone, Shannon was the only person who could understand Amelia enough to help.

"What is it, Mils?" Shannon asked groggily.

She'd seen Shannon sneaking peeks at her sign language book, so Amelia made the sign for HELP, a hitchhiker's thumb bouncing urgently against her opposite palm. After a moment of concentration, Shannon scooted out of bed and followed Amelia to their boots and out the back door. Together, the girls raced across the field.

As soon as they reached the trees, Amelia opened the jar and gestured for Shannon to help her untangle the tree soul from the spiderweb, cupping the light in her palm. It tickled, almost like a downy feather, and Amelia kept her eyes glued to its barely pulsing shape, afraid it might float away if she wasn't watching it.

But it didn't move, even as Shannon pulled the last threads of the net away. Amelia set it in the grass, but it just settled amongst the dry stalks, flickering like a wilting firefly.

Maybe she had to make a wish?

"Nina," she whispered to the little light. Her voice was harsh and insubstantial, like a winter breeze through bare branches.

Shannon gasped. The oaks overhead rustled. But the tree soul merely flickered in the grass.

"Nina," she said again, her small voice cracking, bare, begging. Nothing.

At the feel of her sister's arm coming around her, Amelia wept. She leaned into Shannon the way she used to when their parents were yelling in the next room, hiding behind the curtain of her big sister's bright orange hair and pretending she was inside of a tiger lily, curled up in the petals like a faerie.

She sat upright so fast that Shannon nearly fell over.

The faeries! She could use her one question to ask *them* what to do!

She scooped up the dimming tree soul and sprinted for the house, her sister hot on her heels. She made for the bicycle, but Shannon tugged on her arm and burst into their grandparents' bedroom. Amelia's face burned as Shannon demanded transportation to Nina's cottage. When her grandparents' eyes fell on her, Amelia signed PLEASE as best she could with one hand still cradling the faint light.

To her shock, they both rose, dressed, and drove the girls back to Nina's cottage, where the kitchen light was still shining and a few faeries were glowing softly in their flower nests. Amelia raced around to the garden and knelt, placing the faded tree soul on a bed of thyme and tapping a finger against the nearest glowing bluebell, murmuring Nina's name in that dry whisper she'd managed to coax out of her throat beneath the trees.

But before the faerie could fall from its petals, Amelia had to shield her eyes against a sudden brightness.

"What are you doing, child?" a familiar voice asked from behind the glow.

Amelia dropped her arm. "Nina!" she cried, launching herself into the thyme and hugging the woman tightly, like she'd float away if Amelia let go.

But she didn't float away, and Amelia realized that Nina was still glowing, a pale light pulsing beneath her wrinkled, bark-like skin. She met Nina's eyes, shining with the same gray-green glow they always had, and she smiled. Then she remembered the yellow-green light of the tree soul she'd caught, so different from the light of her friend, and she frowned.

"You switched," she signed to the tree-woman, glancing pointedly at the place where she'd dropped the jar, then at the place she'd found it.

Nina nodded. "Of course I did, child. She had to get back to her tree. How else were you going to get your wish?"

Amelia glanced over her shoulder at her sister and her grandparents, standing just outside the enchanting garden world. She looked at the tree-trunk cottage and the faerie flowers and the mystery of a woman who'd answered the very first wish she'd made, trapped in a dark cellar with a tree root.

As warm spring sunlight spilled into the bowl of the valley, Amelia tunneled her fingers into the rich Virginia soil and whispered, "Home."

Dam Negotiations

CATHERINE SIMPSON

IF YOU'VE EVER TRIED to reason with a naiad, you know it's not for the faint of heart. Or the impatient. Or the easily irritated.

Or, honestly, anyone with anywhere to be on any sort of schedule.

"Come on, Phoebe," I said, wishing I'd undertaken this mission more than half an hour before the council was due to meet. "It'll be good. More water means more people, and that means more you-know-whats."

Phoebe ran her new comb through her hair. I'd rescued it from the dumpsters behind the sorority houses—school let out last week, leaving a skeleton crew of research assistants and a hefty load of unwanted trinkets. I wasn't too interested in the research assistants, but the trinkets were real handy when it came to bribing undecided naiads. Mermaids and rusalki, too, if I ever finished with Phoebe.

"I don't know," she said slowly. She said everything slowly. "The dam..."

"Yes," I said. "The dam. We liked the dam."

"I don't know, Isobel. I reckon the fish like it better now."

Twenty-five minutes until the meeting.

"Yes," I said. I was about ready to tear my own hair out with the bedazzled fork I'd stuck in my pocket. "But we can get around that. We've got *solutions*. We've got *options*." We just needed the damn dam back where it belonged.

"Isobel..."

"Phoebe," I said. "You can't honestly tell me you *liked* how quiet it's been these last few summers."

Naiads aren't as human interaction dependent as us kelpies, but they certainly don't shy away from attention. Particularly of the male variety. And given where the river's situated, winding its way around all of those houses held up by poles, a good chunk of Maury floaters tend to be of that persuasion.

But I could tell she wasn't convinced. That's the other problem with naiads—they could be terribly wishy-washy about taking a stance.

"Listen," I said. "You know where they've been going instead, right?"

"Where?"

I paused, hoping she'd understand the gravity of my words. "Panther Falls."

Her comb froze midway through a snaking lock of hair. "No."

"Yes," I said darkly. "And we can't have that, can we?"

*****

This whole situation was really the council's fault. They're the ones who insisted on allowing the city to proceed with the dam deconstruction. Sponsoring it, even. They hadn't said a word through all the protests, through all the back and forth, through all the planning meetings. And when the city's workmen arrived with their hard plastic hats and their rollicking machines and their disregard for the preferences of the Maury River kelpies, they said nothing.

The fish were in favor of getting rid of it. Dams weren't *natural*. They were tired of the tossed-aside beer cans and blasting music and the sunscreen sheen that semi-conscientious floaters left in their wake.

The other piece of things—the potentially-safe-for-humans piece—didn't even get brought up. Which was a shame, really, as I'm all for human safety. These days, kelpies have practically perfected the art of catch and release.

***

I caught Melody in the shallows of Woods Creek, right before the bend where freshman biology students tested the waters for unsavory substances. We had about twenty minutes until the council met, but that was more than enough time—they'd started holding meetings in the tunnel, a temporary change in locale while their preferred pond played host to a bevy of disgruntled beavers. Fortunately, mermaids are easily swayed.

Well, Melody is, at any rate.

"What was it you wanted, Isobel?"

I handed over the bedazzled fork. "I need you to side with me on the dam referendum."

"The what now?"

"The dam referendum. You know, about the one at Jordan's Point?"

I felt around in my other pocket, trying to remember where I'd stashed the matching spoon. I didn't see much purpose in rhinestone-encrusted silverware, but these were far from the strangest jewel-covered items I'd found by the sorority dumpsters.

"Oh," Melody said. "I thought that already happened, and we got rid of it."

"Technically yes. We, I mean *they*, did." I patted my back pockets. No dice. "I was just talking to Phoebe, though—"

Melody lifted a shimmering hand. "I have no interest in what *she* has to say on the matter."

Mother of pearl. I'd forgotten about that particular situation. I can't speak for saltwater mermaids and naiads, but the freshwater ones around here get along about as well as sophomore boys from rival fraternities during peak rush season. This specific conflict was a longstanding one, dating back to when we still harbored sirens in the valley. We don't anymore—don't get me started on *that*—but mermaids have *very* long memories.

"Um, well. Actually..." I fished around for some way to save the conversation, but I could tell I was losing her. "Wait!"

In a flash of inspiration, I remembered I'd hidden the spoon down my sock. It seemed like a good idea at the time—I hadn't wanted Phoebe to catch sight of it—but I was sort of regretting it now. My submerged sock was soggy. My whole self was soggy, honestly.

I brandished the spoon like a scepter. "For you. And about Phoe—about that other individual—I was just going to say that she hates the dam. You know. In case that changes things."

"Hmm." Melody accepted the spoon, pleased with it despite herself. The spoon was soggy, but the handle held more jewels than any self-respecting spoon had a right to. "Are you sure about that?"

"Yes," I lied. Kelpies aren't deceitful creatures by nature, but we have no qualms about doing what needs to be done. "Also, the Panther Falls mermaids are anti-dam. I'm sure of it."

"Hmm," she said again, but more thoughtful-like. "Maybe I will vote for your dam."

I smiled. Mermaids, in addition to liking things that sparkle, have a penchant for small rivalries. Keeps things interesting underwater, I suppose.

***

Now, you might be wondering: Isobel, what's the deal with Panther Falls?

I'll tell you what.

Kelpies, as much as I hate to admit it, are a dying breed. There aren't all that many of us in the valley, and the vast majority of that not-many live deep in the hills and hollers, in the kinds of creeks and brooks where you'd expect to find something of primeval origin and indeterminate goodwill. This mountain-dwelling can be chalked up to our overall preference for solitude, but it leads to issues with finding you-know-whats, which leads to issues with the continuation of the species.

For what it's worth, the valley kelpies—both the Maury River and Panther Falls contingents—have figured out how to keep our you-know-whats alive (see: catch and release), but I digress.

Panther Falls. Or, as they prefer to be called, the Panther Falls League of Kelpies.

They're our cousins, our neighbors, and our biggest rivals, and they're currently knee-deep in a Shenandoah Valley takeover.

Now that the dam is gone—well, they just don't see why we need this whole lonely stretch of the Maury to ourselves. Better to hand it over to the folks who need the space. It'd be a great place to send those fledgling krakens.

And I'm sure it would be. If, you know, it wasn't already occupied by *us*.

***

By the time I got to Nina, she'd heard I was coming for her.

"It's not going to work," she said. We were still in the shallows of Woods Creek, where a weathered set of buildings peeked through the summer-thick canopy of maple and poplar and sycamore leaves.

"What do you mean, it's not going to work?"

"It's just not going to," she said.

One thing about rusalki—or, at least, about Nina—is that they tend toward pessimistic. Understandable, I suppose, but not exactly helpful for the cause.

"I feel like it could. We've got half the younger vote on our side." Half of that half, anyways. If we made it to a vote.

"Hmph," she said.

I switched tactics. "Wouldn't it be nice, having *rapids* again? It's got to be getting old, this knee-deep situation. Not to mention all those fecal coliforms..."

I stepped to the side, jostling a rock, and a crawfish bit me on the ankle. Offended by my disparaging comments about its environment, probably.

"It won't work," Nina said morosely. "They never listen to us."

"Well, about that—"

We paused to let a research assistant slosh by, a case of Busch Light dangling from each hand. He couldn't see us, not unless we chose to be visible, but Nina's eyes followed him as he walked, tracking him like he was about to take the last table in Pronto. I've never quite figured out what the deal is with rusalki and their you-know-... oh, fine. I'll say it: their *victims*. Their *targets*. Their *prey*. Sue me for relying on polite euphemisms.

But yes, I've never quite figured out what happens to their prey. I'm not losing sleep over it, though. They go for the bad ones, and it all works out in the end. Probably.

"Look," I said to Nina. We had about a minute and a half to get into the council meeting. "Back me up, and I'll hang out on Trav until I've got at least three names for you. Five, even!"

"Ten."

I stuck out my hand. "You've got yourself a deal."

***

The Council.

There isn't all that much to say about the council, to tell you the truth. They're pretty much what you'd expect: a group of crotchety old rule-makers who decide what's best for the rest of us.

There's a word for that, I think, but I'll refrain from using it for politeness's sake.

***

"Order in the tunnel!"

The eldest Council Elder, an absolutely ancient gnome, banged his gavel against the brick wall in an attempt to quiet the echoing chatter filling the tunnel. It was considered respectful to choose a meeting location that appealed to all local creatures, but this was a tight squeeze with the non-aquatic folks packed like sardines onto the narrow walkways.

"Order, I say!" the gnome cried out, his long beard tickling the water's surface. It took the two-handed whistle of a local hag to get everyone to shut their mouths.

"That's more like it. Now, first order of business: the proposed tax on imported cauldrons—"

"Excuse me," I called out. "Forgive me if I'm right, but aren't we supposed to start with questions and petitions?"

They liked to make a big show of this—every other full moon, they gave us lowly plebeians a chance to raise queries and share what we'd like to see done. A town hall, if you will. One that lasted a full fifteen minutes.

"Well, I never." The gnome squinted at me, wire-rimmed glasses magnifying the etched-in wrinkles at the corners of his eyes. "Young madam, if you'd read the latest edition of the bylaws, you'd know that we moved the Curious Citizens portion of the meeting to the very end."

I had not read the bylaws. "Oh," I said. "Okay, then. Carry on."

A couple of warlocks and a surprisingly passionate banshee spent a good twenty minutes debating the futility of cauldron regulations—everyone did what they *wanted*, with no regard for *consequences*—and we all sat through an interminable speech on the decreasing frequency of pots-at-the-end-of-rainbows by a guy who I'm pretty sure is distantly related to me before the gnome regained the floor. Er, the ledge.

He ran through a series of rather boring administrative admonishments—no parking your broom or carpet or enchanted watercraft in front of the colonnade, no selling of lucky charms on the Sundays before exam week, no slipping of sleepy-time potions into patrons' cups at Lexington Coffee—before getting to the meat of the meeting.

"And now, as stated, we shall open the floor to the Curious."

My hand whipped up like a car flying down 64.

The gnome sighed. "Yes, Isobel?"

"I've got a petition I'd like to bring to a vote," I said.

"I'm not sure that's what this meeting is—"

"I hereby move to bring back the dam!"

Murmurs broke out amongst the assembled creatures.

I continued, "We've come a long way in terms of fish protection"—and people protection, though that wasn't necessarily a plus with this crowd—"and I know I speak for *multiple* sectors of the aquatic community when I say we need the traffic the dam brings."

The murmurs turned into outright discussion.

"I'm serious," I said, raising my voice. "Without the dam, us kelpies—and naiads and mermaids and rusalki and so many other residents of the Maury—are in real danger of losing our way of life. Why, just yesterday a representative from Panth—"

"Enough!" The gnome was practically quivering with annoyance, his grip tight on his gavel. "That's enough, Isobel."

Discussion returned to murmurs, and the murmurs disappeared into the soft whispering of the water.

"I'm sorry to foil your vendetta against our friends and neighbors up at the swimming hole"—seeing the look on my face, he spoke even louder, tugging forcefully at his beard—"but the dam isn't up for discussion. You know full well that the decision to remove it was a unilateral one, agreed upon by all parties. Including water-dwelling representatives."

The gnome was referring to the selkies, and possibly the nixies, though they were hard to find and even harder to draw out of their underwater metropolises. Regardless, selkies and nixies are vehemently in favor of anything that lowers the possibility of human contact.

"Yes, but—"

"But nothing! The dam referendum is filed and finalized." The gnome banged his gavel again, sending ripples across the surface of the water. "Curiosity over. All non-council members are dismissed."

"But—"

"That includes you, Isobel."

I reluctantly returned to the sunshine.

"Tough luck," Melody said.

"Didn't even make it to a vote," Nina added. They'd joined me outside the tunnel, and we watched a kitsune wade out of the creek and leap onto the bank, transforming midair into his fox form.

Phoebe drifted by, the comb I'd given her in hand. "They never listen to us, anyways," she said. "At this point, you might as well try to make an alliance with the humans."

"She's already tried," Melody said, flicking her tail at Phoebe.

Phoebe said something in reply, but I wasn't really paying attention, my mind leagues ahead. An alliance—that wasn't a half-bad idea.

I'll admit it: the Panther Falls issue isn't a universal one. It affects us water creatures, and us water creatures alone. But kelpies and mermaids and the like aren't the only ones who live up there, not by a long stretch. And there may not be other fantastical folk—or maybe there are, and they're wise enough to dodge the drama—but there *are* other residents.

Other residents who might be tired of the constant splashing in-and-out of people.

Other residents who'd appreciate some extra room to roam.

Other residents of the dam-building persuasion.

***

Getting up to Panther Falls can be an involved process, with creeping miles of pitted gravel road and hidden turn-offs and a swampy bit of trail to traverse before you hit the waterfall. That's what it's like for humans, but for me—well, kitsune aren't the only ones who can transform. And I'll tell you what, getting up to the falls in horse form is a piece of cake, so long as I stick close to a waterway.

Which isn't that hard to do in this part of the world.

I met the beavers under the cover of darkness, in the farthest pool from the waterfall. I'd spoken to the beavers on the Maury, of course, but for my plan to work, we needed a coordinated effort. Hell, we'd need all the beavers between here and the Cowpasture if we wanted to get this thing done in a night.

And that's all we'd have—one night. The council hadn't made any anti-beaver regulations, but that's because they hadn't thought of it yet.

"Here's the deal," I said. I was speaking Beaver, obviously. You pick these things up if you spend enough time underwater. "Y'all help us out, and you've got free access to the river, now and forever."

A murmur, not unlike the one in the tunnel, ran through the assembled crowd.

"Lots of fallen trees, most of very good quality."

The murmur turned to outright discussion.

"*And* it'll quiet down up here when the people return to the river."

And that's all it took. They were in.

***

The swirling predawn mist was still rising from the Maury when the Council discovered the new dam.

They were livid, but there was nothing to be done about it. For in addition to building a dam that stretched all the way across from Jordan's Point, the beavers had created something else: the Shenandoah Valley Regional Coalition of Beavers.

The SVRCB was happy to entertain any dam-related inquiries presented through the appropriate channels—in fact, open meetings would be held tri-quarterly. In the meantime, curious creatures were welcome to speak with the beavers' fantastical folks liaison, a rather determined kelpie by the name of Isobel.

And I am, of course, more than pleased to handle any and all of your dam concerns.

The Hunt for Monty Glassman

E.G. REGER

THE SHELTER ASSURED HER Monty Glassman's energy was at a geriatric level, that he was a cat who could be relied on to do nothing but eat, sleep, and make his presence known often enough to stave off her cold, persistent loneliness. So when Thea Green returns home from a late-night study session at the library, finds a hole chewed in the screen of her second-floor apartment, and sees only Monty Glassman's indented spot on the couch instead of Monty Glassman, her first thought is, "They *lied* to me."

Her second thought, hand still on the doorknob, is, "Oh God. His sinus medication." Monty Glassman's chronic sinus condition, characterized by intense snoring and sneezing vast quantities of snot all over everything Thea owns, is an affliction of legends. It only gets worse unmedicated.

Her third and final thought is, "That stupid cat."

So Thea Green, already exhausted from midterms and square-eyed from typing a ten-thousand-word essay, barely takes the time to pull on a hoodie before she strikes out into the night after him.

***

Coalter Street is quiet and dark at near midnight. Thea cuts down toward Mary Baldwin's campus, hoping that Monty might have followed her scent to Grafton and is sitting outside the heavy metal doors in an old, gray lump.

It's a big night for a little cat to get lost in.

"Monty!" Thea calls down the empty street. "Monty!" She turns onto campus.

The courtyard outside Spencer Residence Hall is deserted, its iron patio furniture casting black skeleton shadows. The rest of campus is similarly empty, the sidewalks plated silver with moonlight. Thea shivers and burrows deeper inside her hoodie. And then, tired as her eyes are, dim as the lights on campus are, Thea picks up movement. Down on the Grafton terrace a woman walks briskly with two scruffy dogs trailing at her heels.

"Hey!" Thea calls. "Excuse me, ma'am!" Thea picks up the pace, jogging downhill. Maybe she's spotted Monty, or maybe her dogs did.

The lady doesn't seem to hear, bustling toward the steps that lead to downtown. One dog pauses to sniff as the woman begins to descend. Her long skirt kicks out with every step. "Come along, Jam! Ham!" Her voice rings and the dogs scuttle after, nipping at each other playfully.

Thea reaches the terrace as the woman vanishes down the steps, the clip of her heels hanging in the air like a ghost. And despite how Thea scrambles down after her, the woman is out of sight when Thea reaches the bottom. All that's there is the darkened street to downtown and Thea, tired, worried, gives one more call for Monty before she jams her hands into her pockets and continues onward.

Downtown Staunton sleeps, all set-sun grayed stone and blackened panes. Thea calls for Monty and winds her way up toward the train station to walk along the platform. The air is quiet, still, glass-like. In the singular yellow glow of a streetlight, on this empty platform, Thea feels lonelier than ever, and the ache of Monty's missing is sharper and pricking.

A deep, reverberating chime rings through the hush—the downtown clock tower. It leaves a soft, gentle pause between Thea's ribs before ringing again. Thea, alone in the night, thinks of Monty Glassman—on the couch when she comes home, rubbing against her ankles while she makes coffee, lying on her desk while she works, curling into a warm, weighty presence on her chest when she sleeps.

The tower intones ten... eleven... twelve... *thirteen.*

Thea, profoundly confused, takes her phone from her pocket and glances at the screen. *13:00.*

There is a sudden hitch in the air, as if someone's picked everything up and given it a brisk one-two shake. The shadows all slide sideways like loose minute hands, pointing in wrong directions. The final chime of the clock tower hangs, crystalline, in the air. Thea realizes she is holding her breath.

Then the train rushes in, whipping the air into a storm, flapping Thea's clothes and pulling her hair, and filling the night with steam that smells of oil and metal and the crack of ozone after a lightning strike. Eyes wide, Thea stares as the steam sweeps away to reveal an emerald engine, so deeply green it's nearly black. The train pulls only two silver cars, but when the doors hiss open, a sea of people emerges.

First is a group of girls laughing, wearing blue jeans and sneakers and hoodies. They argue, briefly, about the best way to go, then fall into a more familiar-sounding argument about the best tacos downtown. Thea feels a small pang between her breastbone and heart, the spot where loneliness set up shop and Monty found a place to quietly warm. None of these people from the train will have seen him. Thea squeezes through the crowd, shoulders hunched around her ears.

The woman from Grafton terrace hurries to the train door, her two dogs leaping around her skirts. She embraces another woman in greeting. "Mary B!" the woman cries with a smile, the two of them cheek to cheek. "It's been too long!"

A couple of men in starched collars and breeches stroll by arm in arm, which doesn't seem terribly strange until Thea notices how finely polished their hooves are, how the short horns peeking through their curls glint in the light. She blinks. The two men greet a lady in a dress that turns from lilac to gold in the starlight, her hat as vaporous as the cloud over the moon. Someone with delicate scales on their face, their jacket embroidered with pieces of frosted sea glass, smiles as they pass. Thea turns to follow them with her eyes, bewildered.

Her attention lands on a pair of friends taking a selfie. One holds the phone, pale and short and wearing a pair of plum-lensed sunglasses, while the other, lanky with brown skin, grins with a pair of impossibly sharp canines. A tall figure with a furred face tilted to the blue glow of their phone screen nearly collides with Thea and murmurs an apology. She can't seem to answer. The figure moves on, and Thea's hair gently stirs in a gust from green wings flapping away the stiffness of a train ride. Their owner pulls a beanie over a set of frilled antennae, wide red eyes blinking in the warm light of a street lamp.

So, not entirely people. People and not-people. People and impossibilities.

And Thea—stunned, surprised, caught—finds herself in the center of the swell, swept from the station toward the Wharf, poured down a narrow set of steps and into the municipal lot used for the Staunton Farmers' Market. She's jostled and jangled then deposited gently beside a food truck. The lot is filled with booths, all lit with paper lanterns and impossibly floating globes of moonlight. Thea's been here in the daylight before, eaten an incredible pupusa and bought a single tomato. But this is most decidedly not the usual weekend market. This is something else.

The crowd from the train joins the tight current of shoppers, and Thea stands there with her mouth open.

"Hey."

Thea turns. A gigantic squirrel leans out of the order window of the truck, looking at her.

"Hey," Thea says, slightly strangled.

"Looking for something in particular?" The squirrel props its elbows on the counter. It's wearing a backward baseball cap and an apron embroidered with a little acorn. Hysteria rises in Thea's chest.

"My cat," Thea says, because, truthfully, she doesn't know what else to say. The menu on the side of the truck names it "By and By" and advertises drinks with names like "Hot Milk and Foamed Lilac Breeze" and "Tincture for Hopeful Wednesdays."

"*Your* cat? Surely he's his own." The squirrel smiles, as much as a squirrel can smile around a set of big front teeth, to show Thea it's joking. Thea returns what she's certain is a scrawly, weird smile back. "But if I was a cat I'd probably head to the Monger's booth."

"The Monger's?"

"Yeah, she usually sets up in the far corner." The squirrel points all the way across the lot with one paw, then gives Thea a considering look. "You've never been to the Night Market before, have you?"

"Is it that obvious?" Thea asks weakly.

The squirrel squints at her, vanishes into the truck, and returns with a paper to-go cup. "On the house," it says, passing the cup to Thea.

"Thanks." She takes a sip of her drink. It's sweet and flowery and spiced with something warming Thea can't name.

"Honeysuckle and luck latte," the squirrel says. "Does your cat have a name? In case I see him?"

"Uh," Thea says, "it's Monty Glassman. I know it's kind of a weird—"

The squirrel throws back its head and laughs. Thea, outside of some kind of inside joke, blinks as the squirrel wipes a paw across its eyes. "Well, you have your work cut out for you then!"

"What do you—"

"Oh, hang on, there's a customer." The squirrel turns to the slightly transparent teen who's floated up to the counter. "Head for the Monger's anyway," the squirrel says over its shoulder. "He likes it there."

"He does?" Thea squeaks.

***

So Thea walks. She admires a reasonably priced bunch of flowers pressed between wax paper sheets; their petals are shaped like bluebells but are the mustardy yellow of raw beatitude. There is another shaped like a rose but the silvery violet color of unspoken favor. The booth next door sells books by authors Thea knows but with titles she doesn't, golden letters stamped on crumbling leather covers. Next is a table of soaps that sparkle, glitter, and put off gentle waves of pastel fog. Thea avoids that one. Fragrances make her sneeze. She thinks of Monty, probably a full-on snot-rocket by now, and quickens her pace.

Until she gets to the dragon, that is. Thea pauses, stares, knows she's being rude. The dragon stares back. He sits behind a too small card table with a sign taped to the front reading "The Dragon's Hoard." Thea drops her gaze to what he's selling, attempting to disguise her nosiness with interest in his wares. Scattered across the table are tabletop miniatures, sets of trading cards, a few packs of dice.

"Interested in a mini fig?" the dragon asks, smoke curling from his nostrils. "I painted them myself."

"They're really cool," Thea says.

"Thank you."

"I like..." Thea picks up a figurine of a cat-person, its fur painted a soft gray. "I like this one. Makes me think of my cat."

"Oh, yes!" the dragon says brightly. "I actually painted it to look like a cat that comes here often. He likes to play with the dice. A Monty Glassman. Don't suppose you know him?"

"Hrgh," is all Thea says. And then, "Hrgh?"

"It can be yours!" The dragon sounds gleeful and seems to take Thea's grunts as answer enough.

"I... uh. I don't have my wallet," Thea admits, a little nervously. She hopes the dragon won't brûlée her.

"Hm." The dragon taps his chin with one claw. "What do you have?"

Thea digs in her pocket and brings out a handful of random things. Her student ID, a paper clip, a golden brad, a piece of blue string. The dragon considers this collection. Then, to Thea's disbelief, he plucks the brad from her hand and crunches it between his teeth. Slowly, Thea returns everything else to her pocket.

"What's your cat's name?" The dragon begins to wrap the figure up for her.

"Monty Glassman," Thea says, still thinking about the brad. "I have to get him home to give him—"

"Oh!" the dragon interrupts as he hands her the bag. "Well! Isn't that a coincidence? That's why you're buying the figure! You say you're trying to catch up with him?"

"Yeah." Thea hooks the bag on her arm. "Have you seen him?"

"I haven't, not this evening. But he does do his rounds, you know!" The dragon smiles, wickedly toothy. But it is a smile Thea can't help returning.

And so Thea presses onward—past a woman selling bottled memories, a table of preserves with colors bright as paint manned by a human-shaped tree, a row of herbalists with dried bundles and small brown bottles and mortars made from wood, metal, crystal, stone, until she finally stops at a deer in legwarmers selling knitted gloves and hats.

Thea admires a chunky green beanie as she asks the doe, "Have you seen a cat? He's probably sneezing. Like, a lot." She's proud of how she hardly jumps when a fawn wearing a pink bobble hat pops its head out from under the table.

"Monty?" the fawn asks in a high reedy voice. Its eyes are wet and dark, and its little face is sweet.

"Uh, yeah," Thea says. "You've seen him?"

"Gone to the Monger's," the fawn says. "But he was here to play with the yarn. Unraveled all of the angora. And we gave him a hanky, but he didn't use it."

"Oh, sorry," Thea says. "I'll, uh, scold him. About both things. When I find him."

The doe laughs. "It wouldn't be a Night Market if Monty didn't come and ruin a skein," she says. "And, please, take the hat, dearie." The deer points her nose to the beanie Thea's been coveting. "Any friend of Monty's is a friend of ours."

"Oh. Wow. Thanks." Thea takes it. Pulls it on. Her ears, chilled from the night air, feel better almost immediately. The yarn is soft and fine and when the deer tells her how nicely the color suits her, the spot between Thea's breastbone and heart warms and warms and warms.

Behind the doe's table, a pair of glassblowers perform a demonstration outside of Sunspots Studio. As they work, faces red and sweaty, their finished pieces float in the air at the ends of long gossamer strings, knocking together clumsily like too-fat birds, sounding like a delicate windchime. Thea admires how the glass catches the light as she pushes past a booth selling fossils and arrowheads and tiny ghosts in mason jars.

And then she finds herself nearly in the middle of a performance. Thea scampers out of the way, dodging a dramatically flung hand and finding safety in the ring of audience. Three actors perform what sounds like Shakespeare, using the parking lot and curb as an improvised stage, and Thea, drawn in, can't help but watch.

She's taking a Shakespeare class this semester but can't quite place the play. A sign on the curb identifies it as *Love Labour's Won.* There's to be a performance "next Night Market" and the venue will be Blackfriars Playhouse, and Thea, certain she'll never find her way back to the Night Market, decides to watch for a bit. The actors are quick and clever and pull the audience in with every joke, interacting as if the crowd is part of the show.

"Seen a cat?" she whispers to an actor. He's come and put an arm around her shoulders while he waits for his next line.

The actor grins, eyes crinkling, and Thea notices how his hair and mustache are threaded with strands like sunlight.

"Little gray one?" he whispers back.

Thea nods.

"Monty'll be headed for the Monger's. Can't stay away." The actor claps her on the back before returning to the action with a leap and a laugh and a classic Shakespearean double-entendre.

When Thea moves on, the actor waves to her in farewell.

Next, Thea comes to a table of Pufferbelly's toys. Except instead of remaining on display, the stuffies and soldiers and action figures march along the pavement. The kites swoop in an aerial show, and the vendor, an intricately painted porcelain doll, squeezes the trigger of a plastic bubble machine to send iridescent bubbles toward the stars. Thea leans over a crowd of kids, a few of which seem to be human, a few decidedly not. Somebody's wing nearly gets her in the eye.

"Seen Monty Glassman around?" Thea asks the doll, since everyone seems to know him. The doll turns her light blue eyes to Thea's face. Points her bubble blower in the direction of the Monger. Cocks her head and gestures to Thea's hat. Gives a thumbs up.

"Thanks," Thea says, grinning.

The doll offers her a small plastic tube of bubbles, and Thea, a sudden bright spark of delight in her chest, takes them.

***

The far corner of the Night Market is not as busy as where Thea began. The night has deepened. The breeze is chillier and the stars are brighter when, at last, Thea comes upon the Monger's stand. She blows a silver stream of bubbles to the moon. The stand's not really much to look at after such a buildup, some wooden boxes on a wooden table, an old truck parked behind.

But the woman behind the stand is really something to look at. She sits in a folded out beach chair, and she's old, face creased like a letter re-read many times over, familiar with age and attention. The bucket hat on her head is covered with fishing lures, enamel pins, strings of beads, and embroidered patches. The garish purple flowers on her muumuu burn Thea's eyes, and the fingerless leather gloves on her hands are spiked at the knuckles. She wears a pair of bedroom slippers on her feet. They're shaped like cows.

A little gray cat lies curled on her lap.

"Hello!" the old woman calls. "You must be the one asking around after Monty." She runs a hand down Monty's back. The cat uncurls and yawns, then sneezes a streak of snot to parts unknown.

"Yeah," Thea says. "Thank you for finding him. It's late, he needs his medicine"—she gestures in the vague direction of the snot—"and I was worried."

"Didn't need to be worried," the old woman says as Monty gets up, stretches, meanders off her lap. He lazily picks his way across the table and cranes his neck out to sniff delicately at Thea's chin. Thea's relief is nothing compared to the joy she feels at the touch of his cool nose on her face. The spot behind her breastbone sings. She rubs his ears and he purrs, trying to press his cheek against hers.

"Old Monty never misses a Night Market." The old woman springs from her chair with more spryness than Thea would have given her credit for. She bustles to a box, checks something inside. "He tells me about how you got him out of the tank, took him home. He really likes that cheese you give him."

"It's just singles," Thea says, figuring this might as well happen. Talking squirrels, talking deer, Monty talking to an old woman. Sure. "I don't even think it's really cheese."

"Well, regardless," the old woman grunts as she opens another box. "He's asked me to mong you something. So. What'dya want?"

"What... uh... do you... mong?" Thea asks.

"Oh." The Monger paws through the box. "Fish, fruit, fear, war. Love, hope, revenge, socks. Really fresh eggs. The perfect hat."

"Well," Thea says. "How about..." She presses two fingers to her breastbone. "Do you mong anything to help with... uh... loneliness?"

The Monger narrows her eyes. Purses her lips. "I think you're taking care of that just fine on your own," she says briskly. "Got Monty. Got the Market."

"But I don't think I'll get back to the Market," Thea says. "I don't know how—"

"Nonsense!" the Monger cries as Monty chirps. "Monty'll bring you! So here." She reaches for Thea's arm, takes her by the wrist and lifts her hand, then dumps something into her palm. For a brief moment, Thea holds the impression of feathers, fine bones, beating wings. Then nothing. Her hand is empty.

"Little bit of hope," the Monger says.

Monty purrs and presses his head against Thea's raised hand. She obliges him with a pat.

The Monger shoos at them both. "Now, go on! Monty's been waiting for you, and he's got places to be!"

***

Thea's first thought is, "This is fine."

Monty, a cat, leads her, a human, through the Night Market at a slow, weaving stroll, past booths she'd missed the first time, and everywhere Monty goes someone gives him something for free—a cookie shaped like a fish, a strand of pearls, a silk bandana, a jar of brine shrimp—and Thea ends up carrying packages and bags in both her hands and under her arms.

Thea's second thought, as a newspaper bundle slips from her armpit, is "This cat is using me."

But Thea sees the doll and the actor and the deer and the dragon and the squirrel and they all gesture excitedly to Monty, wave to her, call out their goodnights. The spot between Thea's breastbone and heart is a presence now—a polished, filled-in knothole, a freshly mended crack in a Kintsugi, gold where there once was a break.

Thea's third and final thought she voices. "Monty? Want to go home?"

***

Thea hangs her hat by the door, dumps all of Monty's packages on the hallway floor, puts the dragon's miniature on a shelf, convinces Monty to take his medicine by wrapping it in a slice of not-cheese, then, at last, flings herself down on her bed. Monty comes and curls on her chest, purring and warm. He sneezes. Now there's snot on the pillow; the meds take a little while to kick in.

Thea flips the pillow over.

"Next time," Thea says, resting a hand on Monty's side to feel the slow rise and fall of his breath, "don't chew through the screen. Okay? We'll go together. And we'll stay as long as you want."

Monty rumbles. The alarm clock by the bed reads 1:00 a.m.

Thea closes her eyes, tired, happy, counted, seen, and she smiles to herself, to the night, to the little cat asleep on her chest.

The Fractal

CAITLIN WOODFORD

THE SUN ROSE HALTINGLY through the mist and crooked pine branches. Dr. O'Connor wiped some sweat from his forehead. The walk up the hill had been whipping hot, even in the late October dawn. He remembered with a cracked sting of longing the brief autumns of his youth—the chill in the air, the breath clouding in front of his mouth. These days, it was a relief to get a chill from the rush of a passing car. Here in the hemlock stand, though, he thought it felt cooler. It must be his imagination. Virginia hadn't dipped below 75°F in thirty years.

He grunted and twisted the borer again. Grunt, twist. Grunt, twist. It was slow going, but the instrument was making sure progress through the thick trunk of the hemlock. Pine needles brushed his shoulders as he worked, pricked at his cheeks. He pushed the branches away with a gentle hand. Finding these trees this morning was a miracle, the stand seemingly untouched by the hemlock woolly adelgid that decimated the species in a handful of decades. He would treat this survivor, and the handful around it, as the gods that they were.

Finally, the borer gave way through the far side of the trunk. Dr. O'Connor allowed himself a sigh of relief and a pause to look up at the flickering green branches before beginning the process of unwinding the borer back toward his body. The sample emerged in a smooth flourish, the rings of the tree unfurling like the folds of a swirling skirt as the instrument slipped out. He patted the trunk. *Hang in there.*

***

The trek back down to the old Forest Service station was easy enough. Minimal undergrowth, patches of open grass where species after species had disappeared quietly into the growing heat mirage. Emerald ash borer, Dutch elm disease, the hemlock woolly adelgid: victims all gone the way of the American chestnut. Perhaps there were bigger problems to worry about as the Earth's simmering threatened to boil over. But Dr. O'Connor, along with a few like him, still kept his head tilted up to the overstory.

He brushed a layer of dirt off the visitor's sign in front of the weary wooden building: *Welcome to the George Washington and Jefferson National Forests!* As he shouldered open the door, catching a whiff of mildew, he pulled out his phone to respond to a colleague. *Just got the sample. Will update in a few with age readings, etc.*

His was a small community, and word traveled fast. Since Dr. O'Connor's discovery of the intact hemlock stand, and his excited text blast to a counterpart in the Rockies, he'd gotten messages from several other researchers across the country asking for updates. And he couldn't blame them—this was the first real spark of hope in months. He smiled to himself remembering the triumphant shout he released upon seeing those trees, the aftershocks still reverberating in his body. He'd stumbled across the stand by accident—he was looking for something up on the ridge (but now, in the subsequent excitement, he had forgotten what), when he noticed a dip in the landscape. Following the curve down into a small hollow, he came across the stand practically sparkling under the orange glow of predawn. He sprinted back to headquarters for his gear, leaping the whole way.

Now, in the lab, Dr. O'Connor pulled the sample out of the borer and arranged it under his microscope. He wanted to get a rough estimate of the tree's age to guide further testing.

Focus, Anthony, he told himself, as his hands flitted quickly over the gear. *Don't jump ahead of the science.*

He adjusted the knobs, brought his eye to the lens to see the tree rings open in front of him like a spread of cards. He settled into the familiar routine, making notes as he traversed the spread of years. Low water one year, drought season, insect problem another year: a typical spread of climate fluctuation.

About halfway through the sample, something under the microscope made him stop short. How had he not caught this immediately?

At the point where he paused, the tree rings disappeared completely. A stretch of sample remained, the tree obviously still growing, but the wood was blank. It was as if the tree had fallen out of time. Dr. O'Connor shook his head. Perhaps the rings were too faint to see at this magnitude.

He pushed the lens closer in. Ah—there was something! Right next to the last ring he recorded, another faint line was barely visible. Strange, though, that they were so close together. Dr. O'Connor had never seen a ring so tightly packed against the previous one. He weighed the options. Was this evidence of the impact of heightened warming? No, he had looked at plenty of trees from the initial warming era, and the signs were always different, always more in the realm of slow and normal responses to weather shifts.

He pushed in further, hoping for a clearer look at the ring, when he noticed another one, also barely visible, tucked next to it. Observing it closely, he realized with a start that this ring was an exact match to the one before. The same miniscule curves, the same color, the same width—deciphering tree rings could be a subjective analysis, but Dr. O'Connor had been trained to find even the smallest designators of evolving climate conditions. He was certain: these rings were utterly identical.

Had he mistakenly zoomed out? He took his eye off the lens, shook out his hands. *Let's try this again.* His excitement must be clouding his rigor. He looked back down, zooming in slowly and deliberately. But it was the same as before. As he pressed further, the ring appeared, then the next, then, to his shock, yet another identical one. Something cold forming in his stomach, he continued to zoom. The string of subsequent rings formed a fractal—an infinite repetition of identical shapes, repeating in decreasing size, until the microscope could not be zoomed in any further.

Dr. O'Connor sat back in his chair, pressed his fingers together over his mouth. If what he saw was real, it implied that this tree was experiencing the exact same conditions over and over again, on an extremely short time scale, ad infinitum. *This is impossible.* The only way such conditions could occur would be the repetition of the weather over a single day. *A loop in time.* He scoffed to himself, knowing how he sounded, even as the thought tucked hooks into his imagination. A time loop was fine fodder for movies, but not for science. There was no evidence to suggest time could be bent in such a way.

And yet. How else could he explain these growth patterns?

His phone dinged. Dinged again. An email, a text. His colleagues, waiting hopefully to receive some good news. Dr. O'Connor shrugged off his theory, silenced his phone. He needed more data.

***

Dr. O'Connor spent the bulk of the day trekking up and down to the stand, pulling samples from every tree in the little hollow. Each time he examined them under the microscope, he found the same—that sinking fractal, glinting menacingly at him through the lens. He checked and double-checked the samples, gathered them in his hands like dry pasta, begging the trees to start making sense.

He took temperature readings in the stand, feeling his throat tighten: 57°F. Not a feasible temperature in this biome anymore. Based on global climatic trends, the last time this forest could have experienced such a low temperature was in the early 2040s. He tested humidity, checked undergrowth species against historical records to see what might be expected to grow on a day in late October 2040, measured soil samples in comparison to soil outside the hollow. Again, and again, it came up inconsistent with his expectations. This grove was something ancient, something separate from the rest of the forest.

***

As the stars rose cold overhead, Dr. O'Connor gave up on trying to impose a logic to what he was seeing. Exhausted, he collapsed in an old rocking chair on the station porch, looked out over the scraggled remains of the forest. He fought for this slow-dying land for longer than he could remember. Even as a young child, born as the world began to turn against its wayward inhabitants, he felt something deeper in the trees. They seemed to contain an eternity in their winding trunks—a rare comfort to a kid who felt dizzy on the brink of annihilation. When even the trees began to buckle under the weight of change, he threw away everything he knew to come out to the woods and try to save them.

In a way, it was a relief that even after all these years, he could still be surprised by the forest. A fierceness rose in his heart, for these trees that he loved and for the ghosts of their ancestors, their bodies in the soil still feeding the churning biome. Dr. O'Connor looked down at his hands, starting to wrinkle as the spread of his own century broke over its middle peak. He was beginning to resemble a trunk himself with that skin texture. He sighed. These trees were a miracle that he didn't trust to share. If the results were true, if that patch of woods was capable of bending time in an infinite loop, there was no telling who might storm in here and take advantage of it.

Dr. O'Connor was certain that he alone could not save this forest. But maybe he could save those trees. He would fudge some numbers, report to the other researchers that he was mistaken about the species identification. He would go to see the hemlocks one more time, and then let them go. He stood from the porch chair, stretched his aching back, and readied to go to the grove.

***

It was a quiet night in the valley. Dr. O'Connor walked carefully, not wanting to disturb whatever creatures were left sleeping in the teetering world. A bat swooped by his head with the whoosh of a splash of water. He remembered his father, a stern hunter who was terrified of bats. What would he think of his son now—would he have respect for his determination? Disdain for his gentleness? Perhaps it didn't matter. Dr. O'Connor was nearly the age that his father had been when the heat dismantled his heart. He sniffed, noticed the sweat pooling in his boots. No use staying any longer in the past.

As Dr. O'Connor pushed away the memory and trudged on, he began to feel a shiver in his bones. It caught him off guard—he had not been cold in years. The red tinge of the coming sun began to peek behind the mountains, and he looked around, the direction of his thoughts slipping away as easily as one could drop the end of a thread from slick fingers. The night was rolling over into a new morning, and he could not quite gather together his reasons for coming out here in the first place.

What was he looking for, again?

***

What's that dip in the landscape? Dr. O'Connor didn't think he had been over there before.

***

The sun rose haltingly through the mist and crooked pine branches. Dr. O'Connor wiped some sweat from his forehead. The walk up the hill had been whipping hot, even in the late October dawn. He remembered with a cracked sting of longing the brief autumns of his youth—the chill in the air, the breath clouding in front of his mouth. These days, it was a relief to get a chill from the rush of a passing car. Here in the hemlock stand, though, he thought it felt cooler. It must be his imagination. Virginia hadn't dipped below 75°F in thirty years.

The Kite Mechanic

WILL J FAWLEY

EVERY SPRING, WHEN THE winds rolled through the valley, carving their way between rolling hills, the Kite Mechanic took to the skies.

At the foot of the Allegheny Mountains, on the outskirts of Parnassus, the Kite Mechanic lived on a hill that brushed the clouds. At that height, he was close enough to hear the wind's secrets. Even better, because he lived his life as part of it—the wind listened. Farmers, children, and lonely widows alike came to him with their desires. They brought him not only kites to repair, but wishes, dreams, and hopes, which he launched into the sky.

One year, when the first flowers unfurled, their vibrant hues dancing across hilltops in the early spring winds, the Kite Mechanic sensed a change as the world came to life with the breath of the skies. But one thing was for certain, it was flying season, time to open the old shed that served as his workshop. The walls were hung with canvas and tarps for making kite sails and tails, rods and slats for building their bones, and string and twine for tethering the wishes to the earth.

He sucked in a deep breath of that icy March air and blew a family of spiders off the kite he'd been working on at the end of last season.

"Ain't too early, is it?" a voice behind him asked.

The Kite Mechanic turned. His neighbor, Hank Miller, stood in the doorway of the old shed.

"Naw," the Kite Mechanic said. "Yer right on time with the wind."

As if to illustrate his point, a gust nearly yanked Hank's John Deere cap right off his head. He held onto it by the bill and shivered. Hank was only in his forties, partially hunched from a life of hard labor, and his short-sleeved plaid shirt did nothing to protect him from the wind. He'd farmed these lands all his life, as had his father before him and his before that, and he wouldn't let a little chill stop him from feeling all this land had to offer. It had fed his family, his wife and daughters, through good years and bad, but it was getting tired, like him.

"What can I do you for?" the Kite Mechanic asked.

"I wanna fly a wish," Hank said. "Last year we could hardly feed our own selves, let alone sell off enough crop to support the farm another year. We're barely scrapin' by. This'll be our last year if we don't get some rain, and then, then I dunno."

The Kite Mechanic knew a thing or two about that. Like the land, like Hank, he was tired. But he owed it to Hank and to the land to fly his wish.

So the Kite Mechanic began his work. He perused his shelves until he found the right canvas—a light blue cloth with exactly enough give to bend and brave the wild winds that sliced through the valley, separating one season from the next.

"What is it yer after?" he asked Hank.

"I told you, I need a break from the drought."

"But is it the rain yer wantin' or somethin' else?"

Hank smiled. In all his years living as next-lot neighbors to the Kite Mechanic, he'd never asked for a kite of his own, but he'd heard tell. The Kite Mechanic was a tricky feller.

"Well," Hank said, pausing to reflect, "I suppose what I'm really wantin' is a future for my girls. My crops are the means, and the rain is the how."

The Kite Mechanic nodded and smiled. He thought about his own children as he pulled down a handful of strong oak dowels to stretch the canvas around to form the body of the kite. His children had grown and migrated to greener pastures across the continent years ago, starting families of their own.

The Kite Mechanic dug through a box containing spools of twine and string, digging to the bottom to find a splintering piece of grayed wood on which he'd wrapped his most precious threads. He'd retrieved it from his father's old barn before it had been demolished years ago, but he hadn't used it, not wanting to lose his memories to the sky. But this wish called for it, so he held the bittersweet happiness of knowing it was time to let it go.

To the kite, he bound in Hank's wishes for rain, for stronger crops, for his daughters' health and fortune, for them to grow up big and strong like the crops, for his wife to flourish, and for the valley to fill with rain but stop short of a flood.

The Kite Mechanic snipped and tied the string, building a tail with sails to make the wish fly high and fast up into the ether.

"Looks like she's 'bout ready to fly," Hank said. "How much this gonna set me back?"

"Yer old enough to know you cain't put a price on a wish."

Hank raised his eyebrows and shrugged, shook his head in bemusement.

"The winds're too fierce today," the Kite Mechanic added. "We'll fly 'er tomorrow."

Hank nodded in thanks and walked down the hill and back up toward home.

***

That night, the Kite Mechanic massaged his arthritic hands and mirrored his wife Maribelle through a series of stretches. He'd need to get another good run out of his weary bones in order to launch Hank's drought-ending kite.

"Other people's wishes're one thing." Maribelle reached toward the ceiling in a way that made the Kite Mechanic's spine pop with empathy. "But you gotta take care of yerself."

"I know, I know." He mimicked her reach, but his hands barely summited his head. He'd never been much for fighting gravity without help from the breath of the skies. "But I'm nothin' without the kites an' the wind."

Her eyes curled up at the corners the way they did when she saw inside of him. They'd had this conversation many times, but that night it felt different. A weariness pulled him closer to the earth.

Maribelle glided through the house, as if gravity was her wind. She refreshed the water in her fresh-cut lavender, humming to herself as she arranged the flowers and set the vase back on the table.

Maribelle wished for his immortality. And he couldn't bear to see her cry, but he knew from decades of listening to the wind that not all wishes could be granted.

The Kite Mechanic dreamed too, of becoming the wind. Not only helping others ask their questions to the skies, but of being the one who answered them.

After he was spent and sore from his attempt at following his wife's stretching routine, Maribelle made him a cup of tea infused with her special blend of family secrets to conjure his strength and vitality. They read by the hearth until the Kite Mechanic fell asleep in his chair, losing himself in dreams of becoming the wind and blowing away into a future where he no longer fought against his weary bones, but soared lighter than air.

***

The next morning, the Kite Mechanic sipped his tea as the sun rose over the mountains. The light was fiercer this time of year, illuminating the near side of the mountains and the road that snaked through the hilltop pastures in a soft yellow glow. On the next hill, Hank's crop blazed in the sunlight, dry, cracked dirt splitting between the rows he'd tilled the day before.

The wind was right—a little mischievous with sharp gusts that tugged at the budding trees, but not too fierce for the robin who swooped through the yard.

After a breakfast of oatmeal, bacon, eggs, and fresh berries, the Kite Mechanic was ready to join the dreams of the sky. Gravity weighed on him, heavier than ever. He leaned on Maribelle as they walked the path to the shed where he made the final preparations to the kite, inspecting it to make sure the canvas was taut but had enough give to dance like the robin.

Once he was satisfied with the kite and the wish it bore, he carried it to the field at the top of the hill that served as the kite runway, Maribelle supporting him all the way. Amid the dry brown grasses, Hank stood waiting at the top.

"Make wishes come true." Maribelle planted a kiss on the Kite Mechanic's cheek before releasing him to ready the kite, his weary bones creaking with each step.

Once he was ready, the Kite Mechanic looked back at Maribelle, who offered her sweet lavender smile and nodded. He grinned back through the years at her, breathed in deep, then took his first steps out into the field, kite in hand. He walked, unsteady, praying the momentum would carry him until the breath of the sky took hold. As his legs moved in time with the wind, gusting faster and faster, his feet became lead, tangling beneath him, and he fell. He winced at the warm discomfort of his swollen joints, the gravity pulling him down and away from the wind.

Maribelle helped him up, and together they unwove the tangled string, and readied the kite once again for its journey into the sky.

Hank's girls had made the trek over the hill, and they cheered him on from the fence line. The wind whittled its way around him, hollowing out a path in the world. Together, Maribelle supporting him on one side, Hank on the other, they ran. As he moved through the wind, the Kite Mechanic felt all the wishes. Not only Hank's, but Hank's daughters', Maribelle's, and those of his own children off in the world—all the wishes the wind had borne over the years, all the wishes that he had launched, and still others that found their own way to the sky. The wishes imbued him with new strength, reminding him of his own. Hank and Maribelle stepped aside, allowing the Kite Mechanic to run by himself, the gravity decreasing until the wind took hold and he launched into the sky with the kite.

Hank and Maribelle shrank below. The girls crossed the field to join them, and the four looked up in awe together, shielding their eyes from the sun with their hands as they watched the Kite Mechanic become the wind.

Soon, he and the kite vanished beyond the clouds.

Maribelle felt a tear hit her cheek. Then another as she thought of her husband's greatest wish and how it finally came true. Another tear fell, and another, until the clouds burst with rain, soon building to a heavy downpour.

The girls splashed through the mushy grass, where puddles were already forming.

"Well I'll be damned." Hank put his arms around his girls as they held their tongues out to catch a taste of the falling sky. "He really done it."

Maribelle turned toward him, a sparkle in her eye. "My husband can make any wish come true."

The wind blew with a new intensity, a new voice. *There is a way to carry on without living forever.*

The wind connects all things, makes us flow from one year to the next. And as long as the wind still blows, the world will turn, and wishes will come true.

Unleash the Legend:
The 1957 Cadillac Eldorado

Powered by a 365-cubic-inch V8, the Eldorado delivers effortless performance, gliding over the open road with grace and authority.

Cadilliac Eldorado:
Born to Lead,
Built to Inspire.

Old Yeller Ain't No Dog

CAROL STEELE

"I CAN'T BELIEVE IT. She did it again. Just now. She hit her brick mailbox pillar as she pulled into her driveway. Come look!" Tess yelled as she bumbled and banged her way through the front door.

Irene turned into the hallway from the kitchen at the back of the bungalow. "What are you going on about? Who hit what?"

"Look, look, look." She double-hand motioned her roommate to the open door. "That old gal across the street, Mrs. Hebert, she just plowed into her mailbox pillar. Again. Look at the damn thing, it's going to keel over any minute."

Through the low branches of young oaks sparse with the last of their autumnal leaves, they watched Mrs. Hebert guide her 1957 Cadillac Eldorado the length of her Belgian block drive. The behemoth came to rest, the passenger side scraping brick, and the driver's door eased open. The bent geriatric woman sidled out. After gaining stable footing, she placed both hands on the car's window and gingerly pushed the door closed.

The ping of a kitchen timer called to Irene. "That's lasagna. You hungry? I made it meat-free. And I opened a bottle of that cheap pinot grigio you like."

"Oh, hell yes. And I don't like it, I adore it. Thanks for doing the meatless thing." Tess raked her sausage-like fingers through her purple-spiked hair. "I really appreciate it. I know I'm a pain in the ass, but maybe you're getting used to me?"

Irene treated the question as a statement and ignored it. "How do you know her name is Mrs. Hebert? I've rented here five years and I've never spoken with her." She sipped. Winced. Sipped again.

"I met her on the unit—overnight precautionary stay. She had an elevated heart rate, and the powers that be wanted to keep her for observation. That was six weeks ago, right about when I moved in with you. Seems like every time I'm waiting for the bus or getting off the bus, she's coming or going in that tank of hers. And she always scrapes or bangs into that pillar box or the garage thingy. Or both. And it's such a cool car."

"That 'garage thingy' is called a *'porte cochère'*, and she probably bought the car when it was new. I wonder how old she was in 1957." Irene raised her eyebrows in the direction of the lasagna, silently asking: "Cut you some?"

"Sure. Large slab, please. I'm going to die if I don't eat soon. Well, she's ninety-one now—her age was in her chart. So, in 1957 she was twenty-four. Same age as me now. And you're fifty-seven. That's crazy. That's just too crazy."

Over dinner, the subject of Mrs. Hebert withered. Retreating to the pillow-lined window seat that dominated the living room, the two finished a second bottle of wine. Irene gossiped freely about fellow tellers at Clarke County Bank, and Tess bemoaned her student loan debt, questioning her decision to attend private versus state nursing school. Neither woman had dating prospects, and they shared their dread of a long and lonely winter ahead. World problems were not solved.

***

Unable to sleep after a week of overnight shifts, Tess perched in the living room window seat and stared into the darkness. All was quiet on Fairmont Avenue until she heard emergency vehicle sirens and saw red lights ricochet off the wallpapered walls. Dimming the overhead light allowed a crisper view of the drama unfolding at Mrs. Hebert's house. The visit of one firetruck and one ambulance to remove the remains of a lifeless body took less than ten unceremonious minutes.

***

A near sleepless night due to hay fever caused by a too early and robust spring put Tess on edge, and the incessant doorbell ringing at seven a.m. pissed her off more than it warranted. *For crying out loud, let a woman have a cup of coffee and put a bra on before having to face the unknown.* "I'm coming. I'm coming." She reached the bottom stair and gave the bell box by the front door her middle finger. *That should fix things.*

While tying the drawstring of her Ninja Turtle pajama bottoms, she tugged open the door and gasped. A tall, classically handsome man, sixtyish, in a navy blue suit, a painfully starched white shirt, and a silk printed tie stood with the reserve and bearing of a military honor guard.

"Mrs. Spangolini? Mrs. Tess Spangolini?"

Tess's voice cracked. "Miss Spangolini. I'm not married." She blushed. "And you pronounced it right. No one ever does."

He edged forward. "Miss Spangolini, I'm sorry to disturb you. I'm Michael Hebert. Mrs. Hebert's son—from across the street." He gestured over his shoulder.

Tess nervously pulled at the neck of her Post Malone T-shirt, wishing she had brushed her teeth. "Oh, yes, yes. I was sorry to hear about your mother. Wow, right? Must be what, five or six months now. Well, hey, please come in." She stood to one side, opening the door wider.

"Thank you, but I'm in a rush and can't stay. My mother's estate is being settled, and she wanted you to have her car. I have the keys here." He dangled a single looped ring that held two keys.

"Oh, no way. Why would she do that?" Tess bounced on her tiptoes.

Mr. Hebert reached forward and captured her hand; he pressed the keys into it. "She wanted you to have Old Yeller, as she called it, because you were so kind to her last fall when she was in the hospital. And she sees, or rather saw, you at the bus stop. She recognized a need and is simply repaying your kindness. The title has been signed over to you." He removed a business-sized envelope from the inside breast pocket of his bespoke suit.

"I don't know what to say. It's such a generous gift. Are you sure you can't come in?" *He might be as old as granddad, but this man's hot.*

"I'm sure. And I apologize if I rang too early." He turned and walked down the limestone steps.

She smoothed her hair. "Oh no, not too early at all. And thank you."

She closed the door before Mr. Hebert said, "God speed, Miss Spangolini. God speed."

***

Expecting a rattle and a rumble, Tess's eyes widened in surprise when she turned the key and heard a kitten's soft purr. "How about that, as quiet as a Prius coasting downhill. Hold on. Off we go."

Two miles later, Tess pulled into the six-car backup at McDonald's drive-thru and turned to Irene. "I don't get it—this car is in perfect shape. Inside and out. Even after all the times she bashed into her mailbox pillar. Weird."

"Not that weird. Her son probably had body work and detailing done. No biggie."

"It is a biggie. That's a lot of dent removal and painting, but this baby's smooth. Even the rag top is perfect. It should look like Boggs Johnson's acne-scarred face, all bumpy and stuff."

"Her son probably had it put back into shape. And who's Boggs—"

Tess honked the horn. "Check that out. This car is awesome!"

A crackling voice through the speaker snarled, "I'll be right with you."

Both women scrunched their heads down into their shoulders and giggled.

After receiving their order, Irene restarted the conversation. "Who's Boggs Johnson?"

"Ah, Boggs. He's a custodian at work—couple of years younger than me, and he has horrible skin, but what a smile—it could melt you right in your tracks. Big, white Chiclet teeth. He's asked me out a bunch of times, but I always say no. He doesn't have a car, and well, I didn't have a car, so that made it hard to connect. But yesterday I told him I'd pick him up and we could go to the Museum—you know, the Museum of the Shenandoah Valley or whatever it's called. I thought we could walk the grounds tomorrow. That's pretty safe, right? In case he turns out to be a serial killer. Or something."

"I doubt he's a serial killer. He might be an 'or something,' though. Hey, weren't you going to get gas? Hit that little station off Stewart Street, the one with the Dunkin'. We're almost there. My treat for both."

***

The nozzle clicked off after two seconds. Irene tried again. Click. And again. Click. "Tess, what's your gas gauge say?"

"Full. It was full when we got in. Still full. How cool is that?" She slammed the center of the steering wheel: Honk, honk!

***

Tess double-thumb texted as Irene passed an overloaded plate of blueberry pancakes across the kitchen island.

"Hey there," Irene said. "Good morning. Hello. There's a real person in the room. Earth to Tess."

"Sorry, Irene. Just texting Boggs to tell him I'll pick him up in an hour." Tess scooped a too-large bite of pancake into her mouth, nodded her pleasure, and turned her attention to what lay outside the kitchen window. "Look at this day. Perfect weather to go cruising with Old Yeller's top down."

"Right. Sure."

With a mouthful of pancake, Tess asked, "What's up, Irene? You're somewhere else."

"I didn't sleep much—I've been thinking about your gas tank. It's odd. It should have taken some gas, even a little. Maybe you should swing by Frank's Auto over on Boscawen and have him take a look."

"I'm sure it's fine. You probably didn't have the nozzle jammed in right. Don't worry so much. Besides, I've got a date."

***

Tess put the car into reverse and heard the crunch and pop of aluminum and metal as she backed Old Yeller into a Toyota Sequoia at the edge of the museum's parking lot.

"Oh dang, Boggs! Get out and take a look, please. I can't. I just can't." Tess folded her arms along the top of the oversized steering wheel and began to cry.

He slammed his door. "Pull away a few feet. I can't see any-thing."

With shaking hands, she shifted into drive and jerked forward.

Boggs ran his hands through his buzz cut and over his face. He shook his head and reached for his Marlboros. "Man, oh man. I don't get it, Tess. Get out here and take a look."

She looked at the Toyota's bumper, the Caddy's, back to the Toyota's, the Caddy's. "What the hell, Boggs? What the hell?"

"What the absolute hell? We have to report this. Put Old Yeller in a parking place."

***

A police officer, looking ten years past mandatory retirement, inspected both cars and scanned the lot. "No security cameras or potential witnesses." Half a dozen Black Angus ignorantly grazed the slopes adjacent to the lot and offered nothing more than gentle lowing.

"I don't think you hit this car." He pointed to the Sequoia. "The damage here, although fresh, is extensive, so extensive that whatever hit it would be damaged as well. And your car is per-fect—look here at the height of your light and their bumper. If you hit this Sequoia, your light would be broken, but there's not even a scratch. I say you young folks go on your way and forget all about it. You did the right thing by calling it in."

***

Still shaky from the accident that didn't happen, Tess fumbled. "Christ, Boggs. Where'd I put the keys?" She raised her backside and dug into the back pockets of her jeans. She ran a hand along the bench seat and behind Boggs before banging both palms on the dash, frustrated. "Goddam this car! Goddam you, Old Yeller!"

The engine started.

She turned to Boggs, her face the mirrored expression of a Scream mask. "What the hell, Boggs? What in the freaking hell?"

He lit another cigarette. "I'm too young to be seeing things. But I think I am. How are you going to turn it off?"

"What?" She rubbed the steering wheel with both hands, plonked her head onto it. *Honk!*

"If slapping the dash turns it on, maybe slapping the dash turns it off. Try it."

Double-handed slap. Nothing.

They exchanged looks.

"Try again. Harder."

Again, double-handed slap as Tess yelled, "Old Yeller!" The engine went still. "Oh my gosh, we're in a Stephen King novel."

"Take me home, Tess. But first, stop at 7-Eleven. I need cigarettes. And beer. Lots of beer."

***

Wednesday afternoon, Boggs shoved his custodian's cart down the length of the cardiac unit's wide hall as Emma, a new food-service hire, approached. In near machine-gun cadence, she asked, "Hey, Boggs, I've been looking for you all morning. Did you hear what happened?"

"Sure, I did. Mr. Andrews in 207 died. Left all his expellable matter on his bathroom floor?"

"Oh, crap—so to speak." She pinched her surgically altered nose. "Not that. My car. Did you hear what happened to my car?"

He resumed pushing his cart. "No. Why would I care about your freaking car? You wouldn't go out with me because I don't have one. So, I mean, shove your car up—"

"Well, now I don't have one either. Some jerk bashed the daylights out of it, right out in the employee lot. Security says the footage shows my car absolutely fine, and the next second, the very next second, it's smashed to smithereens. The cameras caught nothing, and there were no witnesses. How can that be, huh?"

"How would I know, Emma?" His knuckles rubbed his shifty smirk, and he shuffled away whistling an improvised tune.

***

Over too loud grupero, Boggs leaned closer to Tess. "That's Maria. I asked her out last year. She said yes, but when I told her I'd have to meet her at the movie, she changed her mind. Same story. Stuck-up chicks won't go out with guys who don't have cars."

Tess pointed at the long-haired beauty behind the counter spooning refried beans into take-out containers. "Her? That one dressed all in pink?"

"Really? You need to point like that? What the heck?"

"Sorry, sorry." She took an ambitious bite of veggie burrito and studied his face. His eyes were as empty as a drunk's bourbon bottle three hours in.

"Whatever. She's a loser. Hey, do you think I could use Old Yeller after we finish dinner? I've got an errand."

Through a mouth full of corn chips and salsa, Tess said, "I guess so, sure, why not? You can drop me off at home, do your thing, and put Old Yeller in the garage when you're finished. It's one of those old and tight one-car numbers with an alley entrance. The walls are lined with junk, all kinds of boxes and stuff, and old paint cans—a real disaster. And no smoking in Old Yeller, not even with the top down."

"I hear you. And a full round of 'no worries' back at you."

***

As dusk settled in the valley, Boggs peered into the windows of the three vehicles parked in the crumbling asphalt lot behind Taco Fred's, guessing neither the 4Runner nor the Odyssey belonged to Maria. He bet on the red Ford Focus, its front seat littered with a silver sequined backpack, a pink hoodie, and sundry fast-food bags.

Ten minutes later, the Focus, now missing its front bumper and with a driver's door crumpled beyond use, lay wedged between the restaurant's back wall and its dumpster. Steam eased from under the hood, fluids pooled near a flattened tire, and viperous hissing touched the air.

Boggs smiled his satisfaction. Lit a cigarette.

Honk, honk!

***

A full moon high in the sky and the night young, Boggs cruised North Loudoun, cut around the walking mall, and picked up South Loudoun at Cork. With the Caddy's top down, fresh night air drifted in and pushed cigarette smoke out as he drove in a loose-grid pattern until he reached Handley Boulevard. He parked and scanned the grassy area in front of Handley High. Memories flooded back. Some good, most not. He remembered Sydney the Snob. Just because he followed her (more than once) to her family's historic house on Stewart Street, no need to get him into so much trouble. What a mess. And what a house—six times the size of the place he shared with his mother. Ten minutes of contemplation further blackened his attitude. He tossed his cigarette downward onto the pavement, sat up straight, and restarted the car.

He eased Old Yeller from the curb and took the right-hand turn onto Stewart. He crept the length of the first block, and near the end he spotted Sydney's family's house. Gas-lit pedestal lights, working with city streetlights, illuminated the professionally land-scaped grounds and house, sublime in the glory the property warranted. *Christ, it looks even bigger now.* Boggs pulled to the curb and lit a cigarette as a young woman came from inside and onto the portico.

Sydney the Snob.

She yelled into the house, "Bye, Mom. Love you."

Boggs revved Old Yeller's engine.

As Sydney walked the length of the stone pathway toward the street, a white-haired woman appeared in the doorway, waving as vigorously as a child seeking Santa's attention. "Love you too, darling."

Sydney's heels clicked on pavement as she crossed to the driver's side of a 2024 silver Mercedes GT Coupe. She opened the door and flicked the ends of her auburn bob. "Bye." She waved, smiling a toothpaste-ad smile.

Varoom, varoom!

The GT's door and an expensively tailored body wedged under Old Yeller's front passenger tire. The mangled metal-and-flesh mass screeched against asphalt as it was dragged twenty feet. Boggs swiftly reversed to free his under-carriage cargo as the woman's handbag returned from its upward flight. It hit the hood of the coupe, bounced, and came to rest in a dense row of pale pink and cream tulips and perfectly manicured miniature boxwoods.

Honk, honk!

***

Dawn broke as Irene and Tess stood shoulder to shoulder in the kitchen window watching billowing smoke lessen to vaporous waves, the backyard a swamp of firehose water and upturned turf. An insurance appraiser's eyes were not needed; the garage, although standing, was an unsavable ruin.

Fire under control, the apparent lead fireman entered the garage through the pedestrian side entrance and executed a jack-rabbit-fast exit. He bent over at the waist, shook his head as if to clear it, and called to a fellow responder upon straightening. After exchanging a few words, the younger team member entered the garage. One beat, two beats, he flew out, tossing his talon hook onto the grass.

"Let's go out there. They won't chase us away—the fire's out." Tess plonked her coffee cup on the counter with one hand, grabbing Irene with the other. The pair tugged shoes onto their bare feet, grabbed coats from the hall rack to pull over their pajamas, and headed into the backyard.

Crisscrossing both arms above her head, Tess yelled to the two men. "Excuse me! Excuse me! Hey there, can we get an update?"

The older man approached. "My name's Captain Jonathan Martin." He extended a hand. "I'm the on-scene commander. Who owns the car in there?" He looked back and forth between the women.

"Oh, he made it back?" Tess looked surprised.

"Ma'am, who made it back? Whose car is it?" He loosened the toggles on his coat.

"It's my car. Well, was my car. There's nothing left of it, right?"

He answered her question with another of his own. "Ma'am, who last drove your car?"

"A friend of mine. Boggs Johnson's his name. I let him borrow it last night, and he was going to put it in the garage when he was done and walk home—he lives a few blocks over on Kent." She pointed east.

"Have you spoken to Mr. Johnson since he took the car?"

"No. It's pretty early, and we've been watching the goings-on here. Why all the questions? What's up?"

"If you can stomach it, take a look."

Haughtily, she said, "I'm a nurse. I've seen it all."

"I thought I had, too." He closed his eyes and slowly bobbed his head toward the side garage door. "All yours."

Tess stood in the entrance, frozen. Every inch of the garage's interior mimicked leftover burnt embers on the bottom of an aged barbecue grill. All but Old Yeller, who sat pristine, her yellow paint smooth and sparkling. Her top and four windows were down, neither a bead of water nor a speck of ash inside. Except for Boggs Johnson behind the wheel in the pugilistic posture of one charred; every inch of him blackened beyond recognition, all but his gleaming Chiclet teeth.

Trail Angel

K.G. GARDNER

A man and a woman come into view, and I gird myself for yet another conversation about why Dan and I began our Appalachian Trail odyssey in Maine instead of Georgia like sane people do.

"Hey there, I'm Zipper," the man says, a smile nesting in his bushy brown beard.

The redhead with him waves at us like she's the Queen of England. She might as well be with that expensive gear she's wearing. "Hi, I'm Cherry Vanilla."

"Hey, I'm Hardbody and this is Halfway Honey," Dan says, nodding his head toward me.

People who thru-hike the AT get cutesy trail names, as if the journey weren't torturous enough. Dan got his from a hiker who saw him with his shirt off. Naturally, he loves it. I hated mine at first.

"You ain't gonna make it halfway, honey," this day hiker from New York told me on day 15, laughing at my relatively new boots and dime-sized mosquito bites. If he could only see me now.

"We started at Katahdin." I puff out my chest, and Cherry Vanilla notes my *Eras Tour* t-shirt with a tilt of her head. "I graduated from Colby College in May, and Hardbody thought the timing was perfect with the trail opening right after." I turn to Dan and grin. "We wanted to spend some quality time together before I start applying for grad school."

Dan smirks. "If you can make it through the toughest bit right at the start, it's all downhill from there, right? And the view." He puts his fingers to his lips in a chef's kiss.

"The views here are great, too," I say, thinking about silver creeks threading through the Shenandoah Valley, swatches of bright green farmland, factories with red brick walls, and small towns huddled against the sturdy bulk of the Massanutten Ridge. "Check out the Stony Man Overlook. It's up ahead just off the AT, a bit of a scramble, but it's worth it. You can see all the way to Luray if it's clear."

"Got any tips about what's ahead for us?" Dan asks.

Zipper cocks his head and strokes his beard. "Well, you're about fifty miles out from Waynesboro. Lots of amenities there."

"Eat at the Ming Garden Buffet." Cherry Vanilla mimics Dan's chef's kiss.

"Oh, and there was a trail angel a few miles from here," Zipper says.

Dan squeezes his lips together, cheeks reddening as he barely suppresses a laugh. It's become a running joke, how I thought the term "trail angel" referred to some kind of legend, like Bigfoot. Instead, it's a mere mortal who kindly supplies "trail magic"—cold drinks, fresh food, showers and rides—to weary thru-hikers starved of comforts. Last time he teased me about it, I put our romance on power-save mode.

"Thanks, Zipper," I say in a falsely bright tone meant to warn Dan.

Cherry Vanilla steps forward and lowers her voice, as if there's a real risk someone will overhear us in the middle of the woods. "Have you heard anything about people disappearing around here?"

Dan and I exchange looks. His face has returned to its normal color.

"Disappearing?" Dan asks. "Like getting lost? Or quitting the trail?"

"Or vanishing into thin air, never to be heard from again?" I add.

"That," Cherry Vanilla says, pointing at me. "He said some dude was involved, and something about singing, didn't he?"

"Forget what that guy said, babe." Zipper chuckles. "He was a nut. That's why his trail name is Squirrel Food."

"Yeah, I guess." She scans the trees like something might swoop down on us.

Dan shrugs. "We should probably keep moving, huh, Halfway Honey?"

He's really determined to make it to Springer Mountain by December. Hard to stop and smell the roses—or talk to people—with his literally blistering schedule. Zipper shifts his Hyperlite pack like he's keen to move on, too.

"Good luck," I say with a limp wave as we part ways.

"You too," Cherry Vanilla calls back, ponytail swinging.

***

We pitch our tent near a shelter and prepare ramen for dinner, with two Clif Bars for dessert. Again. In my other life, before this trek, I would have blanched at the thought of lamp-heated snow peas stewing in day-old oyster sauce. Now I'm fantasizing about that Chinese buffet in Waynesboro.

"Do you think there's anything to what Cherry Vanilla said?" I ask Dan as we're cleaning up. "About people disappearing?"

"Probably just someone who likes telling scary campfire stories, that's all."

Nature is loud at night, with tree frogs, owls, and raccoons all vying for the big solos in the woodland choir. I should be used to it after all these months, but I'm not. As I try to block it out and sleep, another sound enters the fray. I go still, ears straining.

"Do you hear something?" I whisper to Dan.

He stirs in the sleeping bag beside me. "Only the whole forest."

"I thought I heard singing."

"Yeah, owls and whatever." Dan is much better than I am at tuning the noise out.

"No, it's..." I freeze. "It's a man."

He yawns. "You're hearing things because of what those hikers said."

"Shh! Just listen."

He rolls over and lies quietly for a full minute.

"Listen to them," he says, putting on a thick accent, "the children of the night. What music they make!"

"Really?" I swat at him. "You're quoting *Dracula* at me?"

"Maybe he's out there, singing for you." Dan reaches out and traces a line down my neck. "Enticing you out so he can drink your blood." He says the last three words with the accent and laughs.

I smack his hand and turn my back to him. "Good night."

He brushes his lips against the shell of my ear and settles back into his sleeping bag.

I focus on the gentle rhythm of his breathing until sleep overtakes me. I dream about an angel with golden wings warming my hand with his own and singing *"Che gelida manina"* from *La Bohème*. He's playing Rodolfo and I'm Mimì, and we're falling in love with each sonorous word. His face is luminous, so much so that I can barely make it out. His rich tenor wraps around me like silk sheets and draws me closer to him. I'm floating on a gently moving stream of song, until that stream plunges over an invisible cliff, taking me with it.

I wake dripping with sweat and breathing like I've set a new record for climbing Katahdin.

"You all right?" Dan puts his hand on my arm.

"Yeah, just a weird dream." My brain feels scrambled, like I have a hangover. Must be dehydrated, or hungry. Probably both. I sit up and massage my temples.

I tell Dan about the dream while he makes coffee in our titanium French press.

"*La Bohème*, the opera?" He squints at me. "Is that why you called out 'Rodolfo' in your sleep?"

"I did?"

"Yeah." His jaw slides to the left, and I know he's sulking.

"Rodolfo is one of the main characters in *La Bohème*." I wink. "C'mon, I don't have to fantasize about other men when I'm bunking with someone called Hardbody."

A slow smile spreads across his face, reminding me how hot he is when he's not dirty, sweaty, and suspecting me of cheating on him.

"Hmm, yeah, I guess so." His arm encircles my waist and pins me against his chest. His stubble scrapes my cheeks in the best way as he kisses me, his jealousy of Rodolfo assuaged. Every nerve in my body tingles.

Slowly, carefully, he pulls away. "We should get a move on."

I sigh and finish my coffee.

***

A couple of hours into the day's hike, we pause to answer nature's call. Dan walks off the trail to the right, and I walk off to the left. I remove my pack and crouch near a cluster of rhododendron bushes. When I stand up, I see a flash of red about five or six yards away. I set myself to rights as quickly and quietly as possible and approach what I think is a scarlet tanager.

I've been playing bird bingo to pass the time on the trek. I have a field guide and a small notebook in my pocket to keep track of all the species we spot: woodpeckers, barred owls, indigo buntings, goldfinches galore, and bald eagles. Stony Man had more ravens than a Goth convention. Not as pretty as the other birds, but they're my favorites because they're badass and regal at the same time.

A twig snaps off to my left. The red bird startles and flies off.

Before the disappointment sinks in, I feel eyes on me. I whip my head around as a hiker emerges from the rhododendrons. He's got gangly limbs and circles under his dark eyes. Cheap earbuds poke out from under his shaggy brown hair.

"Hey," he says a little too loudly. "Trade you food for information."

"Dan!" I sprint back toward Dan and the trail—right into a spider web.

"Ack." I pick the sticky strands off my face.

"Can I help?" Dan grins as he brushes web off my cheek and hat. "You're normally extra vigilant for spiders."

My eyes dart back to the rhododendrons. Dan follows my gaze to the spot where the hiker stands. He takes one look at the new arrival and wraps his arm around my shoulders.

"Hey," the hiker says at high volume, "I just want food for information. Got any energy bars?"

"Who are you, and what information is worth an energy bar?" Dan shifts so he's slightly in front of me.

"They call me Squirrel Food."

Dan smothers a laugh and tells him our trail names. He unzips the pocket where he keeps his snacks for the day and tosses

Squirrel Food an oatmeal raisin walnut Clif Bar—my least favorite. He catches it one-handed and tears it open.

"This oughta be good," Dan murmurs in my ear.

Squirrel Food devours the bar in four bites and tucks the wrapper into a pocket of his cargo shorts. He rocks back and forth on his heels.

"Thirteen people have gone missing from the AT in Virginia in the past two months." He's trying to sound conspiratorial, but he can't pull it off when he's practically shouting.

"Take out your earbuds," I yell. Why would anyone wear headphones out here? We're supposed to be immersing ourselves in nature.

"No way." He claps his hands over his ears. "That's how it gets you."

"How what gets you?" Dan is already losing patience. We've sworn off staying in shelters because of weirdos like this guy.

"The siren," Squirrel Food says, his brown eyes bulging slightly.

The levee holding back Dan's laughter bursts.

"I'm serious, man." Squirrel Food pouts. "Trying to help you guys out here."

"A siren, like from Greek mythology?" I say, trying hard to keep my face neutral.

"Yeah. Thirteen people missing in the Valley. There's a siren on the loose, and no one's doing squat about it. Total cover-up, man." He gives the side-eye to Dan, who is wiping tears from his pink cheeks.

"How do you know it's a siren and not just people getting lost or quitting or something less... sinister?" I say.

"I've seen it." Squirrel Food holds out his palms like he's testifying at a tent revival. "It's got a human head with golden hair and wings like an angel."

Fear slices through me like a cold wind. How could he know about my dream?

"A trail angel!" Dan dissolves into laughter again.

"A trail angel is just someone who delivers trail magic." He lectures Dan like he's the one who deserves the Squirrel Food moniker. "I'm talking about a *siren*."

"Right." My disbelief is edging out my curiosity. "And what does it sing? Sirens sing, right?"

"Don't know." Squirrel Food sweeps a hand from earbud to earbud.

And disbelief puts curiosity in a chokehold.

"Thanks for the warning." I point to a narrow track. "Shelter's that way."

"How about another bar?"

Dan throws Squirrel Food a peanut butter bar. He makes quick work of it.

"Yeah, well, good luck, Halfway Honey. Hardbody. Plug your ears." He hesitates as if he's about to say more, then marches off.

"Who needs Netflix when you've got guys like that roaming around?" Dan's voice trembles with unspent mirth.

***

We find a giant Igloo cooler more or less where Zipper said the trail angel would be. I lift the lid. Strawberries, blueberries, carrots, mandarins, and apples press against a dozen or so Gatorade bottles. The mandarins look particularly irresistible. We take as much as we can reasonably carry, which is more than I thought. I tear a page from my notebook and scrawl a thank you note that I tuck inside the lid.

Then I hear it, emerging from the crackles and titters of the forest clear as a bell. It's coming from above us, as if someone has hung speakers high up in the oaks and hickories that filter the late summer sunshine.

"Che gelida manina ..."

The tenor's voice is so pure that every forest dweller falls silent to listen. The breeze stops stirring the leaves, squirrels cease scurrying along branches, birds halt their chirping mid-note.

"Se la lasci riscaldar..."

My breath catches somewhere in my chest. I place my hand over my heart like I'm pledging allegiance to this otherworldly sound.

"Cercar che giova..."

The urge to find the source overwhelms me. I step off the trail.

"Al buio non si trova..."

Dan's hand lands on my shoulder. I jump back about six inches.

"Jesus Christ, Maryn!" Dan grabs my arms to steady me. "Are you okay? I called your name like three times."

"Did you hear it?" Saying four words takes enormous effort.

"Hear what?"

"The singing."

Two vertical lines form between Dan's thick eyebrows. "What, the birds?"

"No, no." I chop the air with my hand as I enunciate each syllable. "A man singing. *La Bohème.*"

The whites around his irises grow larger. "You mean like that dream you had?"

"Yes, exactly. And Squirrel Food even said the siren looks like an angel."

"Coincidence." He puts his hands on either side of my face. "Maryn, you're not really worried about what that guy said, are you?"

"Maybe. I don't know." It comes out harsher than I intended.

He drops his hands to his sides. "I was maybe a few yards away, and I didn't hear anything." He's using his high school teacher voice on me, and I resent it.

"I. Heard. Singing." I cross my arms and glare at him.

"Do you hear it now?"

We both tilt our heads. The breeze, the squirrels, and the birds have resumed their activities—if they ever actually stopped. There's no other sound. Only the whole forest.

"No," I say. It's more painful than I want to admit, like a physical withdrawal from the high that beautiful voice gave me.

"I don't, either." His expression is full of pity, which scuttles my heart. "You know, I could sing our song for you if you want." He clears his throat, and the lyrics I scrawled inside the cover of my econ notebook pour forth. "*You called this a dream... but how real it seems... when you—*"

"Stop," I say. "Please."

"Ouch." Dan covers his heart with his hand. "You don't want to hear our song, eh? Well, if you prefer opera, I know some *Phantom of the Opera.*"

"God, no." I roll my eyes, and he laughs.

***

We barely speak for the rest of the day's walk. Every time Dan starts, I shush him, hoping to hear the invisible singer and prove I'm not hallucinating. After a while, he gives up trying to talk to me. He's gifted me an earworm, though. The signature number from *Phantom of the Opera* runs through my head, over and over.

Then the song is all around me, sweeping over me like a caress.

"There!" I grab Dan's arm. "You heard it, right?"

"Let me guess: singing?"

"Yes!" I nod my head like it's on a spring.

"No." That crease forms between Dan's eyebrows again. "But you've been humming *Phantom of the Opera* all day. You sure it wasn't you singing?"

I want to protest that I know the difference between my voice and anyone else's, but I can't speak.

"Come on, Maryn." Dan walks toward me, unblinking, while my feet stick to the spot. "You're not getting thru-hiker madness on me, are you?"

"No," I say, but I'm not as sure as I sound. Maybe he's right, and I *am* losing my sanity out here.

Dan releases the breath he's been holding and takes my hands in his. "Look, we're not too far from where we're going to camp. We'll make it an early night. Just hang in there. You've made it way more than halfway, honey. Stay with me for the rest of it, okay?"

***

Dinner is freeze-dried beef stroganoff, a blueberry cheesecake energy bar, and two mandarins. We go to bed shortly after sunset, Dan's arm draped over my hips. I dream again about the angel with the golden wings and the seductive voice. He bathes me in the greatest aria ever written by man, taking my frozen little hand in his. I'm hanging on Puccini's buoyant notes, a hundred feet in the air, and then the siren's song ends. He bellows my real name with that same anguish Rodolfo feels when Mimì dies, sustaining the last note as if it's a life preserver.

"Maryn!"

I sit up in the tent, that familiar fuzzy feeling in my brain.

"Maryn?" Dan pokes his head through the flap and smiles. "Wow, you really needed a good sleep. Want some coffee?"

I clutch the edge of the sleeping bag and nod. I don't mention the dream.

***

As we make progress toward Waynesboro, Dan maintains a running commentary on trees, animals, and trail history, like he's trying to drown out any other voices I might hear. He keeps a firm grip on my hand and doesn't let me out of his sight even for bathroom breaks. His vigilance annoys me and flatters me in equal measure, but it works: I don't hear any singing.

I persuade Dan to make a short detour off the AT to the Big Run Overlook. No day trippers in sight. The forest opens up to give us a stunning view across the Valley. The mountains remind me of ripples in a pond—really big ones, granted—the way their rounded ridges flow into each other. Sitting off the trail is another Igloo cooler stuffed with fresh fruit and cold drinks. We're still carrying some booty from the other cooler, so we don't take as much this time. We down a couple of chilled Gatorades as we watch the red-tailed hawks gliding on the crisp air. My heart swells at the beauty of it all. Can I really commit to grad school after an experience like this?

I fumble for my phone and take a panoramic shot, even though I know it won't do justice to the colors or the ethereal quality of the cloud cover. I move a little closer to the edge of the scenic overview and look down where it drops sharply to a tangle of treetops and rocks. Something unnaturally orange catches my eye. It's a shirt.

"Dan..." His name barely escapes my constricted throat.

"What? Oh, Jesus." He squeezes my arm. "Is that a person?"

The body of a man is splayed out, his hi-viz clothing vivid against the gray rock. His neck is twisted into an unnatural angle, and blood smears his face and shirt. One of his shoes lies a few feet away.

I hurl myself against Dan's chest so quickly that he has to take a step back. He's my last line of defense against the encroaching hysteria. We stand there like that until my ragged breathing slows and my pulse dips back into normal territory.

"Do you think he fell? Or was it...?" I can't finish the sentence, can't imagine that we've wandered into some B-grade slasher flick.

Dan slides his phone out of his pocket. "No reception. Let's walk to Skyline Drive and flag down a car."

I follow Dan toward the tourist road that runs to the east of the AT. He's got one eye on his phone, checking for bars. Something stirs in the underbrush to my left. I turn and see a patch of gold and brown leaves in the middle of some rhododendrons. They almost look like feathers. The patch quivers and flaps, and I realize it's a wing. I dig my field guide out of my pocket and flip to the section on the golden eagle. Looks pretty similar, but golden eagles are supposed to be in Canada at this time of year. Plus this wing is large, even for a golden eagle.

The wing shifts and drops slowly, revealing a man's face. Glittering amber eyes sit above his aquiline nose. Warm sunlight accentuates the contours of his face, his high cheekbones, his full mouth, all of it framed by a shoulder-length curtain of honey-colored hair. He stares at me so intensely that my skin crackles like kindling. The next thing I know, I'm standing right in front of him.

"*Che gelida manina ...*"

The hand that takes mine is warm and strong.

"*Se la lasci riscaldar ...*"

His voice vibrates through every corner of my body until I can't feel my feet touch the ground.

"*Cercar che giova...*"

Nothing exists but him and his velvety voice.

"*Al buio non si trova...*"

Something crashes into me and knocks me to the ground. The withdrawal is so strong this time that I scream in pain, shoving at the creature on top of me.

"Hey, knock it off! I just saved you!"

Squirrel Food rolls off me onto his side.

"Maryn! What the hell?" Dan runs over and grabs Squirrel Food by his pack. "What did you do to her? You trying to kill her? Did you kill that guy too?"

"No," he wheezes. "It was... going to get her."

"What the actual—"

"*You called this a dream... but how real it seems...*"

Dan and I swivel toward the overlook.

"Did you hear it?" I ask.

Dan nods, his face pale. "I swear I couldn't before, but it's"—he swallows—"it's our song."

I clutch my stomach as if I can stop the cold rolling sensation inside it. The siren has been hunting me, listening to me hum and talk in my sleep. Now it wants Dan, too. And it learned our song to ensnare us. Kill two birds with one song.

"*When you hold me close...*"

With glassy eyes, Dan starts moving toward the source of the singing, and I scramble to follow.

"No!" Squirrel Food grabs my head, his palms covering my ears. "*Happy birthday to you... Happy birthday to you...*"

I can't hear anything but Squirrel Food's horrible rendition of a song synonymous with an event I may never experience again. I move to kick him in the shin, but he throws me off balance and the blow doesn't land as intended.

"*Happy birthday, Halfway Honey...*"

"Stop!" I hip-check him and break his grip, then run after Dan. I get to the overlook a moment before my real-life Rodolfo falls to the rocks below, screaming my name. The siren dives into the Valley after him.

Squirrel Food skids to a stop behind me and tugs me toward the tree line.

"I'm sorry," he pants. "I couldn't save you both."

"Why me?" I fall to my knees, shaking and sobbing. "Why save me?"

"Because you believed me."

My unhinged laughter silences the entire forest. "But who will believe me?"

Real Mischief
GENEVIEVE LYONS

ROWAN HAD BEEN IN the room when it was conceived. The Queen City Mischief & Magic Festival, that is. She sat on the organizing committee for six years, and she managed the social media for the first few years until the algorithm bypassed her elder-millennial knowledge base. (To be honest, she was more than happy to pass on that task to a Gen-Z in a cropped T-shirt and wide-leg jeans.) Rowan spread the word to the nearby colleges, posted flyers in the local bookshops, even got to sample local vendors' test iterations of Butterbeer.

Rowan knew everything there was to know about the festival. At least, she thought she did.

So when Chloe approached her in the teacher's lounge during her planning period, Rowan was expecting the usual chitchat about the school's new dress code policy or the especially rambunctious group of ninth-graders they both taught. Instead, the younger woman brought up the festival.

"You know about the after-party, right?" Chloe said in a conspiratorial tone.

Rowan suppressed an eyeroll. "The reunion banquet? It isn't so much an after-party as a..."

A what? Rowan searched for the right word. *Gimmick* didn't feel right to say out loud to this enthusiastic young whippersnapper whom she'd only known for a few months. As left behind as she felt, Rowan didn't want to be that jaded teacher who took the wind out of someone else's sails. "It's a fundraiser," she finished.

The reunion banquet was a ticketed event, a themed fundraiser for a local church's food pantry. It took place in the long, narrow basement of the old stone Methodist church, decorated to look like an Oxfordian boarding-school dining hall. Costumed attendees competed in a wickedly hard trivia tournament, with questions so obscure that, rumor had it, a publishing assistant from Bloomsbury couldn't even get all the answers.

"No, not *that* one," Chloe said, tossing her red-orange curls. Rowan imagined Chloe dressed as a Celtic fairy. "*Anyone* can go to that if they buy a ticket. I mean *after* that one shuts down."

Rowan hadn't heard of any exclusive after-parties. She shifted self-consciously in the mauve vinyl chair and stirred her tea.

"At the speakeasy..." Chloe continued, prompting her.

Rowan didn't nod; she was pretty sure she knew of at least *two* speakeasies in Staunton. And it stood to reason that secret parties at speakeasies should not be discussed in the teacher's lounge.

"With the *real* magic," Chloe added slyly.

Rowan blinked. The *real* magic? The first place her mind went was drugs: psychedelics, stimulants. "I'm not..."

Chloe pressed her lips into a smirk, waiting. Rowan blinked. Finally, Chloe held up her hands in surrender, oversized-cardigan sleeves flapping. "I get it, I get it. And you shouldn't feel bad about gatekeeping this."

Rowan gave a close-lipped smile. "I'm not trying to gatekeep."

"Right. Uh-huh." Chloe grinned. The water cooler glugged as she filled her water bottle. "Well, see you later!"

The teacher's lounge door closed with a bang.

***

On her walk home, Rowan turned down a steep, dead-end street lined with aging bungalows and charming Victorians. She climbed the front steps of the house at the end of the row and lifted the brass knocker. The patina-ed metal felt cool to the touch; the autumn evening light slanted and waned.

"Hey, Gran," Rowan called, letting herself in through the red-painted door that her grandmother said kept ghosts away.

Rowan's grandmother worked part-time in the little bookshop in an alleyway off New Street, around the corner from the gift shop that sold crystals and tinctures. If anyone came across magic in Staunton, she would.

"Your mother send you here to check in on me?" her grandmother called from the den in the back of the house. "I'm just fine, thanks!"

"No, I—" Rowan paused in the kitchen as she made her way through the sequential rooms of the narrow, shotgun-style house. Three dirty teacups teetered in the sink next to a short stack of plates. On the stove, a dirty soup pot. Her grandmother, approaching ninety, lived alone and had for at least twenty years. Of course she didn't want to move to assisted living, with scrubs-wearing staff popping in all the time and a daily menu of overboiled vegetables.

Maybe her grandmother needed some help; her arthritis was bad. But they could deal with that another time.

Rowan settled on the sofa. Emerald velvet, a thrift-shop find. She gazed at her grandmother, eccentric yet somehow elegant in her colorful bohemian blouse. "I got out of school early today, and I had a question. You've lived in Staunton longer than anyone else I know."

Her grandmother's eyes, almost violet, sparkled. She leaned toward Rowan in anticipation.

"What can you tell me about... speakeasies?"

The glint in her grandmother's eye brightened and took on an impish, mischievous quality. "My dear, do you have a date? A new gentleman caller?"

Rowan pressed her lips together and willed herself not to get distracted. Four months ago, she discovered the attorney she'd been seeing for nearly a year, who lived over the mountain in Charlottesville, was married.

In retrospect, she should've broken it off with him the minute he informed her he didn't read fiction.

"I was talking to someone at work today, and they brought up speakeasies, but our conversation got cut short."

"It's not proper to *talk* about such things, is it, my dear," her grandmother said, the last traces of her Irish accent clinging to the words.

Rowan nodded. Her grandmother had practically been alive during Prohibition. She knew the etiquette.

"And it isn't ladylike to drink hard liquor."

Rowan suppressed a groan. "Then I'll drink champagne, Gran," she said, knowing it was her grandmother's libation of choice. "But I'm not talking about alcohol. I'm talking about..." she trailed off, eyes on her grandmother's face.

Rowan couldn't make herself say *magic,* even to her grandmother, who still talked about fairies and imps in the old country. County Cork.

And still, her grandmother's wise, understanding eyes widened. Then, she winked. "I'll keep my ears open for ye!"

***

Saturday morning, while she waited for her coffee to brew, Rowan texted Leah. Ever since Leah moved to northern Virginia, their communication had tapered off. Leah promised she'd be back to visit frequently—she'd miss the mountain air. But working at the law firm absorbed all her time and headspace.

Leah'd been a co-conspirator in all things mischief and magic festival. Rowan and Leah worked together, some might even say competed, as they brought the event to fruition. When Leah moved away, she left the festival in Rowan's hands. It felt like a handing-over. A ceding of possession. In darker moments, Rowan wondered if it was a maturing? A growing-out-of?

Having your best friend leave to take a big law job, while you stayed back in your small hometown to teach school, felt some type of way. It stung, being left behind. Still, Rowan wasn't convinced that Leah was having fun, or that she'd make it in corporate law. Did that make her disloyal?

Hey—still planning to come for the festival?

Leah didn't respond till hours later.

OfC

Rowan wanted to leave her friend's text on read, make her wait, pay her back for the delay. But she hated to leave a loop unclosed. She waited a pathetic twenty-five minutes before typing a response.

> You have dibs on my pull-out sofa. Unless you're staying with your mom…

Leah hearted the message.

Rowan hated herself for feeling the burst of warmth at Leah's positive reinforcement. But she wondered what the heart meant. Would Leah stay over, or did she merely appreciate the offer?

Then, because she wanted to continue the conversation, get Leah more engaged.

> There's an after-party, but it's kind of on the DL

> LOL, I know

Leah added a stream of emojis: the magic wand, the dancing stars, the clinking champagne glasses.

Then, nothing. No more texts.

Rowan knew, *knew*, she must be the only loser who hadn't heard about the after-party. A flush of embarrassment flamed in her cheeks. Even Leah, who didn't live in Staunton anymore, had heard.

Also, real magic? Really? Rowan wanted a magic wand as much as the next person, of course. One wave and—boom—laundry folded. Student loans—vanished. Societal issues—resolved. Who wouldn't want that? But magic was sadly relegated to the pages of books, figments of imaginations.

Well, she'd just have to figure it out. Like everything else in her life. Rowan could do this. She slipped her phone into her jacket pocket. Time for a sunset walk and think. She liked to wander the streets downtown, near the small college campus, feel the energy of the students, steal glances at the faces of the visitors who'd spent the day hiking in Shenandoah National Park and came to town for a pint and a slice.

The air promised the first crisp chill of fall. It was always cooler on the west side of the mountains. When the sun disappeared below the western ridge and her feet got tired inside her thrifted Chelsea boots, Rowan's thoughts turned toward what ingredients were in her kitchen cabinets and her Netflix queue. Nothing terribly interesting, that's what.

With each step she grew more and more frustrated. Why did she care, anyway? The festival was about the magic of books, of imagination and creativity. Of being with friends. Everyone knew there was no such thing as real magic. And the idea of a secret magic speakeasy—just another way to make things feel exclusive and fun.

So why did she want so badly to find it?

***

The week before the festival, Rowan tried hard to focus on work. Teaching high school English was a challenge worth double the salary she earned, and it took up most of her mind space. And Chloe, who taught computer science, kept giving her conspiratorial grins.

Worst-case scenario, Rowan decided, she could meet up with her colleague at the festival and just... follow her to the venue. Hope she didn't need a ticket, or a Portkey, or a password to gain entry. Hope her reputation as one of the festival's founders should be enough to get her in the door.

"What's your costume going to be?" Rowan asked Chloe in the teacher's lounge.

Chloe slurped microwaved noodles from a Styrofoam cup; Rowan nibbled a protein-fortified meal replacement bar.

"It's a surprise. You won't even recognize me," Chloe said.

***

On Thursday night, her grandmother called. "Oh, hello, dear! Don't let me keep you if you're out with a *friend*! I'd planned to leave a message."

Rowan didn't bother explaining to her grandmother, who re-tired before caller ID was invented, that nothing would've stopped her from answering.

"I was hoping you'd take me to the festival," her grandmother said. "Just for an hour or two. I'm saving up my energy."

Rowan nodded, her mind whirring, considering the challenges. She wondered if she'd be able to convince her grandmother to use a wheelchair.

"Rachel from the crystal shop popped in, and they talked about all the various events. I was so proud to tell them that my grand-daughter is one of the founders!"

"They know that already, Gran," Rowan said, but she bloomed with internal pleasure.

"It's the privilege of being old," her grandmother said. "You can repeat yourself, and no one's allowed to complain."

"You'll need a costume," Rowan said.

"I'll take that as a yes, my dear!"

***

The day of the festival dawned cool and misty. A front was ap-proaching, a storm hours away. In previous years, Rowan might have worried about the turnout, whether the weather would keep people away. But not this year. This year she didn't care. She wasn't on the leadership committee anymore; she could enjoy the festival like a civilian.

This was the positive spin Rowan had worked with her thera-pist to unearth.

She pulled on her black unitard and robe, pointed hat, and boots. She reached for her phone to slip it into her bag, and as she did, it buzzed. Leah's name flashed across the screen.

Rowan's arms went numb.

Rowan slipped the phone into her bag without replying and snapped the metal clasp shut. It stung, yet she wasn't surprised.

Leah had done the same thing—almost—when Rowan found out the attorney was married. She came to Rowan's apartment, ordered ramen from the local noodle bar, brought ice cream and wine. They'd watched comfort movies, Rowan dabbing her eyes and blowing her nose while Leah covertly checked her phone. The next morning, Leah left at eight to get back to DC in time for something work-related. Rowan knew she should be appreciative, but it felt like Leah'd raced out of there.

But Rowan put her painful emotions in a box for later; it was time to pick up her grandmother.

In the city, the streets of Staunton pulsed with good energy. Everywhere you looked were people of all ages, wearing pointed magician hats and robes, carrying broomsticks and wands. When Rowan knocked on the familiar red door, her grandmother's costume was so good that Rowan almost did not recognize her. Perhaps a friend had stopped by, a friend dressed as...

But the twinkle in her grandmother's eye was unmistakable. "Gran! You look great!"

"Thank you, my dear," her grandmother replied. "I had some help from my friends."

And off they went, into the mischievous and magical crowd.

"Where's Leah?" her grandmother asked after a while.

"She cancelled," Rowan admitted, looking away. "Work."

"My dear, it's the nature of her profession."

Rowan nodded.

"Maybe things will change someday, maybe they won't. And we're the ones who get to enjoy all this mischief!"

It really was glorious, Rowan thought, seeing her city transformed. Friendly faces everywhere, like usual, except heightened.

More magical. The barista who made their lavender lattes wore pointed elf ears, and the cashier's fairy wings glittered.

The day passed in vignettes of storybook magic. Rowan and her grandmother wandered the city, admiring costumes, chatting with strangers about their favorite books and movies, stopping to rest and snack whenever they needed to. They stopped at a psychic's tent for a reading (*"A mysterious stranger will appear in your life soon"*), which earned Rowan a glance filled with warmth and excitement from her grandmother. Rowan wanted to suggest that the stranger was a companion for her Gran, rather than a "gentleman caller" for herself, but she couldn't bring herself to break the illusion.

Rowan glanced at her grandmother across the table at the Mexican restaurant in the old train station. They'd enjoyed a delicious dinner of tacos, guacamole, and enchiladas, next to a booth of exuberant fairies and witches. The restaurant staff appeared in good spirits but fatigued, ready to do their closing work and sleep for a week. As the moon rose in the darkening sky, Rowan felt a twinge of sadness that the day had flown by. It was time to help her grandmother get home and settled in; then what? Her own feet felt heavy with fatigue.

And she was no closer to solving the riddle of the speakeasy, the after-party. Amazingly, this realization, counterbalanced against the day of mischief and fun, carried no sting. Almost.

"Well, Gran," Rowan started. "Time to—"

"Time for a nightcap!"

Rowan blinked.

"You didn't think I was going to go home before the after-party, did you? I want my glass of champagne."

"Of course not." She cleared her throat. "So you know the... password?" she murmured.

"Follow me." Gran winked.

Obediently, Rowan held the door and followed her grandmother. Outside, she offered her arm, and her grandmother led her down the sidewalk. As they passed the first speakeasy, Gran gave a conspiratorial smile. There was a line of nymphs and pixies, one of whom looked suspiciously like Chloe, attempting to look casual as they waited for the ogre/bouncer to grant them entrance.

Gran led Rowan two blocks over (or was it three?), down an alley that Rowan had somehow never noticed, and around a corner, there was a door. Her grandmother ran a bony hand up the wood grain, smooth from years of existence, pressing.

In the instant before the door gave way, Rowan realized it didn't matter what happened next. Leah was the one who had missed out. Rowan spent a magical day with her grandmother in their beautiful, tiny, mountainside city. A city that hosted an entire festival celebrating the magic of the written word, of imagination, of plots and subplots, of tales worth telling and retelling. The boundlessness of human creativity. Whatever else happened, whether or not she located a magical after-party, that was magic enough.

The door opened.

Inside, a bouncer dressed as a goblin leaned in as Rowan's grandmother whispered the password, then stepped aside to let them through. Rowan's eyes widened, taking in the scene. A polished wooden bar, a tin ceiling, a million fairy lights. Otherworldly music coming from seemingly invisible speakers. Exposed-brick walls with portraits of Gandalf, Eowyn, the swan queen. The scents of butterscotch, cinnamon, and beer wafted through the air.

They slipped into a cozy corner of the tufted oxblood leather banquette to survey the whole room, and a server who looked like Princess Buttercup approached.

"Two glasses of champagne, please," Rowan's grandmother ordered.

"Right away, ma'am."

Nearby, other patrons sipped elegant, unusual cocktails and champagne from their own coupes. A man in a hooded cloak sat at the bar, looking as though his pockets might hold dragon eggs. An umbrella holder in the corner held several broomsticks. Rowan didn't see anyone she knew—not a single person—though there *were* many mysterious strangers. A person clad in tall black boots and a leather jumpsuit made eye contact from behind his winged mask, and Rowan gave him a small smile, their eye contact only broken when the server appeared with two sparkling flutes of champagne.

Rowan's grandmother lifted her glass.

"Cheers to my granddaughter, to the festival you started, and to all the magic, real and imagined."

A burst of warmth flooded through Rowan's chest, all the way out to the tips of her fingers and toes. She raised her glass and clinked.

Rowan settled back against the banquette, her gaze soft.

A flash in her peripheral vision drew her attention, but she couldn't see what caused it. Her brow furrowed, and she followed her grandmother's gaze to the portrait of a fairy queen. She seemed to look directly back into Rowan's eyes.

Then, the queen smiled at her and winked.

Talk to the Hand

JULIAN CLOSE

IN THE NORTH OF Rockbridge County, east of Interstate 81, there is a roadless area where the hand of man has reached but never found much to grab onto. From the town of Percy, follow South River about a half a mile, then turn left into Dismal Hollow, head straight over the ridge, and you're nowhere. It's not a good nowhere, but nowhere appeals to certain sorts—hermits, fugitives, mystics—its main attraction, of course, being the presence of no one. If you make this trip, and you come through Percy, you'll find a rundown gas station, an abandoned sawmill, and a thriving mortuary. You won't fail to notice Percy Church, since it's large and well maintained, all things being relative.

The church is the closest most people ever get to the once-thriving gold mines that scatter the land on the other side of the ridge. The famed gold dowser Adam Clark, once of Vesuvius—now presumably homeless—had been a member of the congregation before he disappeared, but it was the eccentric preacher, Reverend Ingram Stotes, that I hoped to meet.

You don't knock on a *church's* door—not a *Pentecostal church*, not in this valley—so I made my way inside. It was getting late, and the amber light streamed in through the stained glass on the west wall and out again through the stained glass on the east wall, neither helping nor hindering me. Hindering us, I should say, for I was not alone.

"He's not here."

It was Reverend Rob Smith, Ingram's partner, an intense man who sprinkled his carefully chosen words with both scripture and Maoist slogans. "He went nuts again. Checked himself in to Western State. Go talk to him there, if you want. He always enjoys having visitors, and the Lord tells us to comfort the feebleminded."

"What happened?" I asked.

"Insanity is the price of seeing the truth too clearly. Ingram always pays it."

"Well, perhaps you could help me. I'm looking for a parishioner of yours..."

"Adam Clark?"

Reverend Smith obviously knew the purpose of my visit, and I had no reason to waste his time, so I told him who I was and which mining company I worked for. "All we're interested in is tailings reprocessing," I told him. "It would be a small operation—no damage to the hollow at all—but we'll need help with... a lot of things. There would be jobs."

"I'm not worried about your tailings reprocessing, and I'd love to see some jobs around here, but I'm not going to help you find Adam, and Ingram won't either."

"Can you tell me why not?"

"Talk to Ingram. Adam is one of his."

"You mean because he's *white?*"

"Because he's *schizophrenic,*" said Smith, not angry, but far from overjoyed. "We've got black and white together here. Not two congregations in one building, but one congregation. It's not supposed to be one of the miracles, but these days? There's too much affluence in the valley now. Racial discrimination in the United States has always been a trick of the bourgeois class. Have you seen anyone of the bourgeois class in Percy?"

"No," I said. "I apologize. I shouldn't be guessing at your motivations or your values, and I can see I was very wrong. But if you were to tell me..."

"Like I said. Talk to Ingram."

The error was clearly irrecoverable, so I said goodnight, went back to the motel, and called Western State to arrange a visit, which is to say I arranged to meet one schizophrenic to help me find a second, when the second didn't want to be found and I'd been assured that the first would offer me no help. I don't think I would have gone to such lengths if I didn't believe that it really was the right thing to do. Just a small stream of money flowing into these communities from the mining industry, after so many years, would be enough to change people's lives. I wanted that.

***

Getting led out through the wards to the big screen porch where Ingram spent his days was a little tense. I walked past a sea of lonely eyes that lifted to me in expectation, or hope, or *hoping* for hope, though I had nothing to offer them.

On the screen porch were dozens more patients. (No one gets called a "client" in a state hospital.) In one area, there was a circle of stools facing a reclining chair in which I saw a thin, unassuming, dark-eyed man. Unassuming-looking, I should say, for in action, he assumed quite a bit. The other patients turned to look at me with the same hopeful, expectant eyes I had seen before, but then, with barely half a gesture, Ingram sent them scattering.

I introduced myself. Everything was right out in the open, as it should be.

"What do you think of the place?" Ingram asked me.

"Everyone seems to be expecting something from me, but I don't know..."

Ingram laughed. "Don't worry about that," he reassured me. "They heard the footsteps and thought you might be bringing them a cigarette, that's all. Cigarettes are important for schizophrenics. They help with the powers, with continuity, keeping the objects in the timestream floating in the correct order, etc. Did you know that cigarettes don't raise our cancer rate? You can look that up. Do you smoke?"

"No."

"Good. It's a bad habit, you know, if you're *not* schizophrenic." Ingram took a deep drag off his cigarette after saying that, but in truth, he took a pretty deep drag off his cigarette after *everything* he said. "I was arrested a couple of nights ago. I broke into a truck depot in Lexington. It's where they keep the trucks with the refrigeration units that serve Percy's mortuary. Professional corpse handlers aren't good for a community. Everyone knows it's in the Bible, but most people still dismiss it."

"What *should* they do?" The question could have been taken as a challenge, but Ingram seemed to want to spar.

"They should *think* about it!" he said. "It doesn't really matter *whether* something is in the Bible or not. It matters *why* it's in the Bible, or not, so you have to *think* about it! If I could get a few more people thinking for themselves, we wouldn't *need* the Bible. That's all I've ever tried to do. Not everybody likes my approach, though. That's why I'm here, you know. It's political."

"Reverend Smith told me you checked yourself in."

"That's just what he says when I do something that gets me arrested and sent back to Western State. It's a little dig, actually, like committing crimes is my way of checking myself in. Did you know I've never been prosecuted? The state of Virginia knows they would be wasting money if they did. Even if they won, I'd just end up back here again. Usually, when I get in trouble, they call Reverend Rob Smith, and he comes and gives me a ride back to the church. This time, though, I broke through a glass security door and triggered an alarm system. Most cops I've seen in one place since I got caught shooting the valves off canisters of compressed gas on the backs of trucks on I-81."

I knew about that already. Everyone did. It was big news when the 81 Rifleman was finally caught, and it turned out to be a local preacher. Curious though I was about Reverend Stotes's various crimes, I sensed that if I didn't get to my point right away, the conversation might get so far past that I'd never get back to it.

"It's pretty clear to us," I began, "that Adam Clark has an easy time finding the entrances to gold mines in the roadless area, that he must already know of the locations of several. Several that we've lost track of. We've got contacts in local pawnshops, and when someone comes in with a lump of gold, we hear about it."

"Adam found some pretty impressive ones. Especially near the end."

"Oh, I know," I said. I fished in my coat pocket for a moment and then pulled out a lumpy disk, about the size of a hockey puck. "This is what we call a 'blob.' It belongs to the company, not me, but I did the analysis. This blob was extracted from ore using cyanide leaching between 1920 and 1945. The cyanide content is still high, and to the untrained eye, it doesn't look much different from concrete, but it's actually about forty-one percent gold. We could get thirty thousand worth of gold out of this, maybe a bit more. The pawnshop owner claims he doesn't remember how much he gave Adam. It should have been at least twenty, but knowing how these things go, I'd guess it was somewhat less."

"Ah," said Ingram. "And I suppose that if a kid from back in the hollow could come up with something like this, you all must figure there's quite a bit of gold left out there."

"Listen, I know what you must think of me, Reverend Stotes, but we're committed to our policy of zero net environmental harm. One of our rival companies has a tailings reprocessing site in Goochland County, and they've disturbed less than *one acre* of land. One acre! And we're not looking to exploit Adam, either. We know he's in a bad way. But with his help, we could do so much for the community."

"Oh, I know," said Ingram. "Adam wants to help the community. He always has. And you want to help him help the community."

"Yes!"

"And... you want to find gold. I understand. Believe me, it's very understandable."

He understood. That was all that needed saying. I have no idea why I said what I did next. "I, uh, *need* to find something here. I was supposed to be promoted to vice president a couple of years ago, but then we had a merger and a reorganization. I got pushed out to clear the way for... well, it doesn't matter who, but what they did to me *wasn't fair*. Believe me, it wasn't. I have *got* to find a way to get that promotion. I *need* it. I only have a few years left, and I *made promises*."

"Family?"

I nodded.

"The people you love the most?"

I nodded, and Ingram's bearing changed, as if he'd made up his mind about something.

"So how about this?" Ingram began again. "Suppose I was to tell you *everything*. The whole story—not what you've read in the papers, but what actually happened. If you listen, and I'm convinced you've *really listened*, then when I'm done, if you still want to know where to find Adam Clark, which you *might*..." he bit down on the word, and for a moment, I felt a jolt of electricity surging up my spine, blossoming out into my limbs, forcing all my hairs to stand on end. "I'll tell you."

"Alright," I said, and we shook on it.

"Right now, all you know of the story is what you knew of the gold when you first held it. Just the shape, just the outline. You don't know about the poison inside."

"I'll listen to anything you have to tell me, Reverend Stotes," I said.

"Yeah, well, listen good. There are things you need to know before you go back to your company and tell the board that they can call off this search of theirs, that Adam Clark can't be found, and that he was a fraud on top of that. Or better yet, that he's dead."

I held my tongue. It was Ingram's turn to talk:

***

It was about two years ago. They had a young man here who was very florid, who didn't want to take his medicine, and whom they couldn't compel to take it, since he wasn't a clear and present danger to anyone. Rhonda called me—she's the head of patient advocacy—and asked if I'd help socialize the young man. I've done that for a few hard cases over the years, and I said I'd be happy to try.

When we first met, Adam and I were sitting about where *we* are now. Lanky kid, sharp features, big mop of black hair—I liked him right away. He was hearing voices—*lots* of voices—which is odd, because that only happens to *real* schizophrenics. About half the people around here are diagnosed as schizophrenic, but in reality, there have only ever been a few of us. A lot of people here are just confused, or traumatized, or they took drugs until they freaked out. Some might even be sick—there *are* mental illnesses—but schizophrenia isn't an illness of any kind. It's a powerful, man-made augmentation of the brain, performed during gestation, that allows the schizophrenic to perceive and alter the world in ways otherwise impossible. We were designed as super-soldiers—*weapons*—but we were too powerful for the world's governments to control. We got free, but with all that power, an untrained schizophrenic can do a lot of damage, and Adam was one of the most powerful schizophrenics I've ever met.

Adam was seventeen, which is right around the age most of us receive our activation signals. I was able to confirm with him that he was hearing the same thing I had—an insistent barrage of commands to use the powers more often and more forcefully, sprinkled with assurances that if we proclaimed ourselves, the right people would get in touch with us and we would do important work, vital for the good of the country, and that we would someday be hailed as heroes.

But ours wasn't the only government trying to find its lost schizophrenics, and Adam was so sensitive, he was hearing the instructions not just in English, but also in Russian and Chinese—languages he didn't understand a word of. So, as confusing as all *that* was, it's no surprise that Adam was beginning to entertain the notion that he had gone insane. He was incredibly relieved when I explained to him that it was not the case. He was a nice guy, and I could see he wasn't likely to steal, get in fights, or scare girls, so I invited him to stay in one of the vacant rooms in the church. Within a couple of days, he was settling in and asking how he could help out around the place.

I spent a lot of time with him, every day, for the first few weeks, mostly fishing, walking the trails, or hunting. I even got him a job working at the sawmill, up the road from the church. I figured it was a good job, and he could walk to work. That was my first mistake.

One Friday night, we went out hunting—poaching, technically, if you care—in the roadless area. We stopped at *The Dollhouse*, a crumbling one-room hellhole near the center, miles from everything. Someone tried to build a house there, back in the sixties, and a family must have actually lived there for a time, because there were children's toys strewn all over the place. These included rubber dolls—Barbie, Howdy Doody, Dick Tracy—which were missing both eyes.

Once we were alone, I asked Adam to tell me more about his voices. It wasn't just the activation signals. He confided in me that he was also talking to spirits. There was a trickster spirit he called *Teardrops,* and that day there was a dead child named Jeremy—a boy, about ten—who had fallen down a mining shaft and never received a proper burial. That's pretty common, unfortunately. If you develop any sort of ESP, you're going to be hearing from a lot of dead children.

Last, there was Angel, whom Adam would sometimes smilingly call *The Angel of The Mourning*. It was clear from the way he said it that 'mourning' meant grieving, not dawn.

Angel would make strange offers, like "Eyes will see better, but eyes are cold?" or "Hands are quick, but slice through flesh?" Of course, you can't make a bargain with a spirit without letting it in, and once you do that, the spirit is in charge, not you. That's great if the spirit is the Holy Spirit. Half the miracles people say I've performed were really done by the Holy Spirit while I was in a trance. The problem is, the Holy Spirit isn't the only spirit—he's the only one that's holy. This was trouble, and I wanted to nip it in the bud.

"Tell me," I asked Adam, "which voices can you hear right now?"

"Just the three spirits," he said. "And I can still hear the activation signal, but in English. I can't hear it in Russian or Chinese anymore."

"That's good!" I said. It was a good sign that he was getting less sensitive. "Let me show you a little trick I use. Let's say I've got four voices in my head, competing for my attention. Here, I've got an alien from the orbit of Saturn—I'll label this 'A' for 'Alien.'" With that, I picked up a spent shell casing from the floor of The Dollhouse and put an 'A' on it with black magic marker. "And let's say this is Rev. Rob Smith, and this is a parishioner who is near death in the hospital, and this is Jesus." On three more shell casings, I drew 'RRS,' 'Dying,' and 'J,' respectively.

"Now," I continued, "I can't possibly talk to them all at the same time. Obviously, I want to talk to Jesus, but since he's an eternal being, he can always get back in touch with me another time. So, I pick up the 'J' casing and hold it next to my ear, like this. Now Jesus' voice drowns out all the other voices, and I explain, 'Listen, Big J, I've got a parishioner dying, and he really needs me. Can we do this tomorrow?' He'll say fine, of course. Nobody is more understanding than Jesus."

It was stupid, in retrospect. My trick relied on using safe voices to block out the dangerous ones. Adam didn't have any safe voices to talk to.

"I think I get it," said Adam. "But it's not just voices. I'm getting a lot of weird smells, too."

"What kind of smells?"

"*Beautiful* smells! Let me show you. Wait here!"

"OK," I said, and Adam walked outside.

It was dusk, and the light was fading fast. He was gone for five minutes, then ten, then fifteen. Just when I thought he was lost for sure, he came walking out of a copse of hemlock trees, his right hand in a fist. When he sat down again inside, he opened his fist, and some loose dirt fell to the floor, along with a millipede about five inches long. At the same time, the room filled with an exquisitely sweet smell, like cherries and almonds. It was the best thing I've *ever smelled*. I knew what it meant, though.

"Adam," I said, "that smell is cyanide. It's poison!"

"That's how I found it!" said Adam. "The more cyanide it has in it, the farther away I can smell it from. Finding millipedes is a cool trick, but I was thinking... what if I can also find *gold*?"

"I don't think that's a good idea," I said.

"I told you about Jeremy," said Adam, "the kid who fell down the mineshaft? Well, that was over a hundred years ago. He says that after that, the mineshaft was filled in with tailings, and that some of them have a lot of gold left in them."

"Adam, you *never* want to trouble the dead."

"I'm not troubling him!" said Adam. "He doesn't mind. He *wants* us to have it!"

"I think you should tune Jeremy out," I said. "Use the trick I showed you."

Eventually he agreed, which set my mind at ease. That was my second mistake. We spent the night in the woods, and the next day, we headed back into town.

After that, I was still keeping an eye on Adam, but not all the time. I had other things on my plate, too. I'd like to say I saw the tattoo on the back of his right hand on the day he got it, but maybe a day or two had already passed. It was an angel, beautiful and sorrowful, with black wings and eyes like the coronas of solar eclipses. I couldn't tell if it were male or female, but I knew it was Adam's *Angel of The Mourning*. My heart sank.

"Adam!" I shouted at him in the hall. "Dear God, is that Angel? Your Angel of The Mourning? On your hand? Didn't I tell you not to talk to him anymore?"

"Yeah," said Adam, "but then you told me I needed to shut out Jeremy, and this is the perfect way to do that. Now I can hear Angel all the time. He shuts all the others out, and trust me, I'd never take any of the stupid bargains he offers me. 'See in the dark, but never unsee.' 'Pretty girls like you, but aren't pretty anymore.' It's meaningless!"

I grabbed his wrist and pulled it close. The tat was beautiful, with lots of extremely complex details. A tat like that costs real money, not two weeks of working in a sawmill money. "Where did you get the money for this? Tell me you didn't go looking for gold!"

"I'm not talking to the spirits!" he said. "I used my nose, like I showed you. I needed a little cash for a car. I won't do it again, I promise."

Maybe I was too quick to accept that, but like I said, I'd seen what he could do with his nose, and it's very common for schizophrenics to be dealing with many heightened perceptions at once.

A few days later, he bought a car, then new clothes, and then, it seemed, lots of booze. The booze actually reassured me, somewhat, since it can help to keep the voices quiet. During this time, I would sometimes catch glimpses of Adam holding up his hand to his right ear or putting his hand in front of his mouth and mumbling into it.

Then, one weekend, he was gone for two days, and I was staying up around the clock to make sure I saw him as soon as he returned. When he did, he burst out of the bushes in the hollow, made straight for his car, got in, and drove away before I could reach him. I needed to follow him, and though I don't own a car or have a driver's license, I do know how to drive, so I hotwired Reverend Rob Smith's car.

I caught up with him fast enough and followed him to Stuart's Draft, where he stopped at a pawn shop. I'm guessing it's the same one where you got that lump in your pocket. I waited until he was inside, then I burst in after him. He had a lump of gold on the counter, a little smaller than yours, and Carter, the guy who runs the place, was looking at it with a magnifying glass.

"Adam!" I said. "You promised!"

Adam lifted his hands and said, "I'm sorry, Ingram, but it's not what you think! I had to do this. And it's not for me! The sawmill is laying people off. Jared and Brad are being let go. It could take them months to find a new job."

"What?" I said. "That doesn't make sense. Why would they fire the Booker boys? They've been working there for years, and you've been working there less than a month!"

"But I'm part-time!" he said. "They don't have to give me benefits. The damn company is getting rid of the people that cost them the most!"

"That doesn't explain why..."

"It was *my fault!*" he said. "So, I figured I'd grab a lump for them. It's really easy for me. Please, Ingram! You've got to let me do this!"

Technically, I had no way of stopping him, but now I wonder what would have happened if I'd forbidden him from selling that gold. Could I have convinced him to walk it back into the roadless area? To find a deep mineshaft and throw it in? I'll never know. He got $8,000, which he put in my hand, and a few hundred, which he kept. Then, we went back to the church.

I thought about keeping some of the money for the church, but I didn't. I gave it all to the Bookers. Thanks and praises to dear God in heaven for that.

It was three days later, on a Wednesday, I think, when Sheriff Riley called me and let me know what had happened. The Bookers used a portion of the windfall to buy gin, and they both got drunk, as they often did. They also got into a fight, which, again, they often did, but this time, Brad, who apparently used some of his money to buy a .38 revolver, blew a hole through Jared's head with it, and then atoned for the deed by blowing a hole through his own.

I broke the news to Adam as gently as I could, emphasizing that what he had done was a truly good and selfless deed, that he wasn't responsible, that he shouldn't blame himself. I meant it, too. How could it have been Adam's fault? You'd have to be *crazy* to think something like that.

Adam seemed to be taking it well enough, but the next day, I saw him praying—and *sobbing*—before the altar. When I saw that, I knew things were bad. I steeled myself and tried to help him. "Adam?" I said, and he turned to look at me. "What's going on?"

"It's Angel," he said. "The offers come so fast. What do they even mean? 'Words flow true, but lips bleed?' 'Gold is the light inside, but light is hungry?' I thought about that one. Gold is the light inside? The light inside that leads me to the gold? That's good, right? And who cares if light is hungry? I didn't take the offer, though. At least, I don't think I did. Wait, did I? How would I even know?"

"What about Jeremy?"

"I don't think there ever was any Jeremy," he said. "Angel tricked me. There was no Teardrops, either. It was always Angel."

"You need to have that tat removed!" I said.

"I know," he said. "I will. I'm not sure it will do any good, though. He's not in the tat anymore. He's in the hand."

A day or two later, he moved out of the church, but he kept coming for services on Sundays. A few months went by without trouble, and I was starting to relax a bit. That was when I made my last big mistake—thinking I could make something good come out of something that was so clearly bad. We had a woman in the congregation, Annie, who was about to give birth to twins, but the twins had been late separating, and they both had twisted spines. It was going to cost $10,000 or more to bring them into the world, and that would only be the beginning of the expenses, so when it was my turn to give the sermon, I talked about Annie and her twins, and how much easier life might be for them if someone who had some wealth were to donate to their cause.

Three days later, Adam came by the church, put $15,000 on the altar, smiled, and left again. For the next four hours, I was proud of myself, thinking I'd found a way to help Annie and make Adam happy. But then I got a call from the hospital. Annie had gone into labor, but things had quickly gone wrong. X-rays showed something impossible—her twins had re-fused at the lower spine. Together, the two boys were in such a colossal tangle that there was no way they could be delivered. An emergency C-section was done, but it was too late. Annie died, and so did the boys.

I tried to keep the news from Adam. I wanted to be the one to tell him, knowing he would blame himself. I still don't know who told him, but at around nine that night, I got a call from the sawmill. Wayne, the foreman, was hysterical. All I could tell was that he wanted me to come, immediately, and I did. It's about a half a mile from the church to the sawmill, and I ran it without stopping that night.

When I entered the room, I saw a scene straight out of hell. The machinery, the walls, the ceiling—all were bright red. At first, I thought there was something wrong with my eyes, but there on the floor, in a pool of blood, were Adam, Wayne, and a couple of the other workers. All blood-soaked, all wrestling. Adam's right hand was missing—sawed off at the wrist—and the others had managed to get a tourniquet on it. Adam was barely conscious, I could hear sirens approaching, and one of the workers had Adam's hand on a plate of ice.

"No!" I shouted at him. "Don't give the hand to the paramedics! He doesn't want it back! Don't you understand?!"

But there was nothing I could do to stop them. Soon, Adam and the hand were on the way to Winchester Medical Center, where the hand was reattached using the most modern micro-surgery techniques. A hundred blood vessels were individually reconnected. Nerves were realigned. After all the pain he went through, Adam still hadn't escaped from Angel.

He was in Western State for a good long while after that—nearly a year—until he did a runner two months ago. He would never do his physical therapy, so the hand got smaller and blacker and more twisted. But it still served its primary purpose—allowing Adam to communicate with Angel—and everyone who spent any time in Western State during that year can confirm that Adam spent his days away from other people, sitting alone, staring into space, and always talking to the hand.

* * *

Ingram crushed out his spent cigarette carefully, leaving no smoke rising from the butt. Then he tapped out a fresh one, lit up, and sat back, silent.

"Well," I said to Ingram. "That's a lot to think about."

"This is when you ask me to keep my side of the bargain," said Ingram, "but I've already told you all you need to know. The story has implications that I'd like to make sure you understand. Angel's purpose was never to hurt Adam. Adam cared deeply about people, and that caring was the path that Angel followed to his victims."

"I get that," I said.

"Good," said Ingram. "Then I'm sure you've already considered that if Adam were to help you, he wouldn't be doing it for himself. He'd be doing it for you, for your family, for the people you love the most."

I had. I left the hospital. The next morning, I filled my pack with food and camping supplies, such as I might need during an extended stay in the roadless area and drove back to Percy, stopping once at a gun store.

That brings us to the present. I'm parked in the church lot. My intention is to head up into Dismal Hollow, cross over the ridge, and search for Adam Clark until I find him. Something tells me that if I find The Dollhouse, it will be a matter of waiting. I don't know what, if anything, I'm going to say to Adam when I see him, but somehow, I think he'll understand. He cares so much about people. Isn't that always how the poison gets in?

The Train to Mount Jackson

JULIE CLINE

MOST PEOPLE HATE THE drive north on Interstate 81, and Claudia would agree. She preferred Route 11 from Harrisonburg to Woodstock, sailing by woods, crossing a bridge over the North Fork, and throttling down through towns from another century. Not today, though. Claudia clenched her teeth, shot up the ramp to the Interstate, swore at the construction, and braced herself for the fight with trucks passing through to God-forsaken places like New Jersey. She did it to shave fifteen minutes off her time. Her great aunt Eula Jean, all ninety-three years of her, says she's dying.

She exited at Woodstock and took a straight shot by the Fairgrounds before winding around to a clutch of old farmhouses. Eula Jean's house sat close to the narrow road, ten feet up from the tracks abandoned by Norfolk Southern. She'd transformed it into a fluorescent landmark when she had it painted bright petunia pink some years back.

Claudia parked in the driveway. When she opened the car door, September heat shimmered above the asphalt and rolled over her like a heavy, wet blanket. Cicadas buzzed in the trees, singing to each other, coaxing their mates home.

"Farmhouses are a dime a dozen around here," a realtor once told her. Claudia stared at the house. A covered porch stretched across the front of it, with a broken bottom step. Single pane glass rattled in the windows, and a tired air conditioner teetered on the windowsill upstairs.

When Claudia walked to the steps, Eula Jean came out on the porch, not more than five feet and one hundred pounds soaking wet. Tight gray pin curls covered her head. She wore a baby blue flowered house dress that almost swallowed her whole. Her spindly bird legs peeked out, feet below in white plastic tennis shoes with Velcro closures. Claudia wrapped her arms around Eula Jean's shoulders, always worried she'd break something if she squeezed too hard.

Maybe Auntie Jean just misses me and needs a good visit. I could use one myself.

"You look pretty good to me," Claudia murmured, "not dying just yet. And what's this about a train?"

"Come on in, hon. I made up the spare room for you, and I got the good bourbon out and a couple of glasses." Eula Jean grabbed her hand and headed into the house.

Claudia followed her to the kitchen and plopped down in a chair, while Eula Jean poured two fingers into each glass. "Auntie Jean, it's only four in the afternoon."

"Well," said Eula Jean, handing her a drink, "it's kinda late for me to start turning into a drunk, don't you think? I'll be ninety-four in November."

Claudia smiled, sitting with the floor fan going full blast at her legs. There was a shoebox on the table, tied shut with string.

"What's wrong, Auntie Jean?"

"I told you. I'm circling the drain, biting the dust, pushing up daisies any minute now. I went to see the doctor at the hospital on Main Street, and he says I'm having some heart trouble."

"That's not the same as dying," Claudia replied.

"Heart failure, he says. I know it's coming. I've been hearing the train at night." Eula Jean made short work of her bourbon.

Claudia gazed out the kitchen window, past the yard festooned with hydrangeas, at the remnants of the railbed across the road. She sipped slowly off the top of her drink to make it last.

"You know there are no trains now, the tracks were abandoned at least ten years ago," Claudia said mildly. "Maybe you hear trucks on the Interstate. It's not that far."

Eula Jean ignored her. "And riding on that train is a man I met in 1950. We fell in love, and I've loved him ever since. I got a letter from him today. He's coming for me and we're going to Mount Jackson."

Claudia's heart sank. *She has dementia. It's probably worse so late in the day, in the heat, with a weak heart and a glass of bourbon.*

Claudia reached across the table and took both glasses. "It's too hot, Auntie Jean. We shouldn't be drinking like this. You sit, and I'll fix us some dinner."

She put the glasses in the sink and scrabbled around in the refrigerator, an avocado-green Kelvinator. She opened a cupboard and pulled out a can, making a passable hot-weather meal: cold sliced ham, potato salad from the market, and peaches.

Claudia poured iced tea into two glasses and set the table. "Where do I put this shoe box?"

Eula Jean set it on the chair next to her.

They ate slowly. Claudia talked about her job, her cat, and her young man who might become a boyfriend, she'd have to see. She kept watch on her great aunt picking at her plate to make sure she ate. When they finished, Claudia cleared the dishes and washed them, and then she scooped vanilla ice cream into two bowls.

"Why don't you and me go sit on the porch and get fat on this ice cream? I want to hear about the man you met in 1950."

***

"His people lived outside of Mount Jackson, west toward Mount Clifton," Eula Jean began. She sat on the front porch with her ice cream set to one side, clutching the shoe box. Slipping off the string, she opened the lid and pulled out a stack of old letters.

"But I met him at the movies here in town. You know the Community Theatre is still open on Main Street? Still shows movies on Saturday night. I was there with my girlfriend Wanda almost every Saturday, and one Saturday in February, there he was. He was visiting with his cousin Hank. Wanda was sweet on Hank, and she finagled movie tickets so they could sit together, and guess what? I sat with Hank's cousin." She shuffled through the letters.

"What was his name?"

"Avery. Avery Klinesmith. Oh, my Claudia, he was so handsome! Tall and slim and he had dark wavy hair. I don't know why Wanda didn't want to sit next to Avery, I always thought Hank looked like a big dumb potato. I'm lucky she didn't, though, because the minute Avery opened his mouth and said my name, I fell in love. And he fell for me, too."

She handed over a bunch of letters. Claudia took the first one out of the envelope and read it, then she moved on to the second and the third. As she read, Eula Jean fussed with her ice cream. Shadows grew long over the yard as evening pushed the afternoon away. Clouds gathered, building and drawing strength from the steaming heat.

"Auntie Jean, you vixen, you! Listen to this. 'When I take you in my arms and kiss your warm lips, time stands still for me.' Were you necking in the back balcony?"

"Now, you hush. Avery drove his dad's pickup into Woodstock to see me every single week. He stayed at Hank's house."

"You were necking in the back of a pickup?" Claudia howled.

Eula Jean laughed too, laughed so hard she had to stop and catch her breath. She collected the ice cream bowls and disappeared into the house. When she reappeared, she carried the bourbon and glasses.

This time Claudia poured. "So, what happened?"

"He enlisted in the Army. These are letters I got when he was in boot camp, and a little later when he got sent to Occupied Japan. He planned everything out. He'd get leave and come back for me. 'On the train!' he told me. 'I'll make 'em stop in Woodstock, and we'll ride into the station in Mount Jackson. I'll be in my best uniform, with my best girl on my arm!' That's what he said. He wanted me to meet his family, and then we'd get married and live in exotic places all over the world."

Eula Jean took the letters from Claudia and put them back in the box. Then she selected another and held it tight in both hands.

Claudia turned on the porch light, sat down, and looked at the dark sky. "I thought I heard thunder in the distance. We'll get storms tonight."

She sipped her drink, then glanced over at Eula Jean, who stared, eyes wide and puzzled, as if she'd forgotten something.

"But you didn't marry, did you, Eula Jean." Claudia spoke softly, using her aunt's formal name to bring her back.

"The letters stopped. I kept writing and I worried. Then one day, it was January 1951, and Avery's father made a special trip to see me. Avery got sent to Korea, and in September of 1950, he went missing in action at the Battle of Inchon. Now, I could see Avery's father was hard bitten by nature, the way farmers generally are. He probably never showed his feelings. But when he pulled out the telegram, his hands shook, and he had tears coming down his face like he didn't know they were there. They just rolled down, and he didn't stop them, so I knew they were never gonna find Avery alive."

Claudia took her hand. "I'm sorry."

Eula Jean sighed. "I had a hard time in 1951. That was the year the train stopped taking passengers to Mount Jackson."

"Were you lonely all these years?"

"Oh, I wasn't exactly lonely. I lived here at the house with Mother and Daddy until they died. I worked. I had my church family, and you, of course, you little scamp! I babysat for Hank and Wanda's boys, five of them. You shoulda seen them, a whole family of big dumb potatoes."

Claudia smiled at that.

"I even had the house painted my favorite shade of pink, just because I could. But I was never in love again, not like that."

Thunder clapped overhead and rolled down the valley while rain painted patterns on the walkway. An old melody, a woman singing about longing and lost love, played on Eula Jean's radio somewhere in the house.

"This is what I got today." Eula Jean put the letter into Claudia's hands.

Claudia looked it over, the envelope crisp and yellow with age. Forwarding instructions littered the front and back; it was first marked Korea to Japan to Philadelphia, then "Dead Letter" in a strange, ethereal hand. Inside was a short note, written in a shaky scrawl. Claudia imagined a frightened young man, telling his girl that he loved her more than anything. He was coming on the train to get her and bring her to Mount Jackson so they could marry.

"Where did you find this?"

"In my mailbox. But Claudia, it didn't come in the mail. I got it before the mailman came today. Oh, hon, I see how you're looking at me. You think I've lost my marbles, but Avery is coming to get me. I packed a bag and everything. The thing is, I need you. I'm unsteady on my feet sometimes. I need you to help me get to the train."

"I can't, Auntie Jean. There's no train, remember?" Claudia pleaded. "The station in Woodstock is completely demolished now. The tracks are broken!" Claudia pointed in the direction of the abandoned railbed, covered with brush and branches, now draped in darkness.

The music played on.

"This was our song, Avery's and mine." Eula Jean whispered the lyrics softly to herself.

"I want to call your doctor first thing tomorrow." Claudia went on, "You and I can see him and talk about your condition. After that, I'll drive you to Mount Jackson if you like. You can see a replica of a train station there in town. It's a visitors' center and city hall now."

Rain rocketed down, lightning danced on the mountains east and west, and thunder roared applause.

Claudia stood and extended her hand. "Time to turn in. Tomorrow morning, everything will be clear. Maybe I can trace this letter. Who knows where it's been all these years."

Eula Jean, small and diminished, nodded and shuffled back into the house. She passed the small valise sitting by the door and trudged up the stairs. Claudia helped her prepare for bed, as she might for a child. She tucked her aunt in and turned out the light.

"Auntie Jean, where's your radio? I'll switch it off."

"I don't have one anymore," Eula Jean replied. "It broke, and I threw it away."

***

It was sometime in the night when the music seeped into Claudia's dreams. Interspersed with the melody was something more, faintly familiar and long unheard, a deep resonating train horn from far away.

"Claudia, help me!" Eula Jean cried.

Claudia sat up in her bed in the spare room, rubbed her eyes, and ran her fingers through her hair. *I dreamed this—the train and the music. Did she dream it too?* But a sharp rap on the front door made her jump.

Claudia leapt out of bed and barreled down the stairs, barefoot and wearing a long, oversized t-shirt. She switched on the porch light and yanked open the front door. Wild winds blew back hard. She forced the door shut and bent down to pick up an envelope on the floor. Something glowed inside it.

"What is it?" Eula Jean stood teetering at the top of the stairs in her nightdress.

Claudia pulled out a ticket: Woodstock to Mount Jackson on the Southern Railway.

"It's a train ticket for 2:15 in the morning," Claudia replied, transfixed. She grabbed her cell phone. "Today. In fifteen minutes. And, Auntie Jean, this ticket is glowing."

She held it up for Eula Jean to see.

"Claudia, he's coming! What am I going to do?"

Claudia looked up at her great aunt, gripping the rail at the top of the stairs. For the moment she appeared so much younger, hope and trepidation playing across her features.

Why not believe in a glowing ticket and a promise?

"I can't do it without you!" Eula Jean pleaded.

Why not believe?

"Throw something on, Auntie Jean. We're going to flag down a train."

Claudia bounded up the stairs, two at a time. Once in the spare room, she turned her overnight bag upside down and fished out a pair of shorts. Pulling them on, she grabbed her tennis shoes and tied the laces. The train horn blew, and the house rocked, but was it in time with the music or the pounding of wheels on a track? Claudia didn't stop to wonder.

She charged into Eula Jean's bedroom and held her steady while she stepped into a dress and slipped on some shoes.

"Can you help me with these buttons in the back?"

Claudia did them up.

"Does my hair look all right?"

"Your hair looks fine—let's go!" Claudia grabbed Eula Jean by the hand and guided her down the stairs, stopping to pick up the valise by the door.

When they opened the front door, warm winds encircled them, moist and cloying. Claudia carried the valise in one hand and held her great aunt's arm in the other. Eula Jean clutched her ticket and waved it over her head. Incandescent against the dark, it loomed bright and then dark and back again, and at its zenith it showed the way to the tracks down the hill.

"Hurry, Claudia, he's coming!" Eula Jean lurched forward and stumbled on the broken bottom step. She almost fell before Claudia caught her and yanked her back up.

"Hold on to me, Auntie Jean." Claudia put her arm around her waist and took long strides, lifting her aunt and setting her down with each step. They crossed the road and perched at the top of the embankment while she caught her breath. Roaring from the north, thunder rolled on the line, a horn sounded, and the winds surged.

"We have to get closer!" Claudia shouted. She wrapped her arm around Eula Jean and pounded down the slope, digging her heels into the bank. But the ground was soaked through and slick, and she slipped and fell. Clutching her frail companion to her chest, she slid down the embankment to the railbed.

"Auntie Jean, are you hurt?" Claudia picked herself up, scraped, bruised, and scrubbed with mud.

"I dropped my ticket!" Eula Jean struggled to get up. She patted the ground around her feet, then turned to the muddy slalom gouged into the slope.

Claudia spotted it halfway up the bank, lodged in a serviceberry bush. The ticket still pulsed like a beacon, in time with the train's approach. "I'll get it!" she shouted. Crawling up on all fours, Claudia grasped at branches and boulders to anchor herself. She grabbed the ticket and turned to look for Eula Jean below.

Standing halfway between the tracks and the foot of the slope, Eula Jean waited for the train. She'd retrieved her valise and set it upright. Her pin curls flew around her head, her hem was ripped, and mud smeared her dress. She was missing a shoe.

And there it was—the train. Careening out of the north with running lights blazing, volleys of steam shot from the engine. Wheels glistened, buoyant over the rising heat on the rails.

Claudia waved the ticket over her head and shouted. "Stop!"

Lightning shot from beneath the wheels as they seized up. The air crackled and jumped, and brakes shrieked, drowning her out. She slid back down the slope with the ticket held high, and when her feet found level ground, she stumbled forward and pressed it into Eula Jean's hand.

One passenger car rested between the engine and the caboose. The door swung open and a handsome young man stepped down, tall, slim, and done up in a smart Army dress uniform. He held out his hand to his best girl, Eula Jean, a pretty young slip of a thing with a fresh face and shoulder-length curly brown hair. She wore a summer frock, buttoned up the back, and ballet flats.

Claudia waved goodbye to the aunt she loved so much, the one blushing and radiant in Avery's arms.

"I'll remember you always, just like this," she whispered.

Avery closed the door behind them. After all, the train had a schedule to keep to get to Mount Jackson, and they'd waited long enough to board. The horn blasted, and the rails pulsed and hummed. The air snapped, and the train rose up, hovering for a moment like a fond memory, and then shot away to the south, wisps of ozone curling in its wake. The valise was left behind.

***

When morning arrived, Claudia woke up in the spare room, head pounding, body aching and stiff.

I'm throwing out the good bourbon; it makes me have wild dreams.

Chagrined and barely conscious, she rolled out of bed and wandered into the upstairs hall.

"Auntie Jean? I dreamed about you last night. You and Avery." She padded down the hallway, into her great aunt's bedroom.

The bed sat empty, sheets thrown back, and Eula Jean's nightdress lay in a heap on the floor. Claudia glanced in the bedroom mirror. She had twigs in her hair and her t-shirt was torn and muddy, with blood smears where she'd skinned her elbows. An ugly purple bruise bloomed on her thigh. She turned around and looked over her shoulder—road rash on her back and gravel on the back of her shorts.

Is she truly gone?

"Auntie Jean!" Claudia's voice echoed through the house. She limped downstairs. The front door stood wide open, and the floor was damp. She stood on the porch, staring across the road. Nothing but sunshine coming up over the mountains. Claudia spun around. Once inside with the door secured, she stripped, showered, bandaged what she could, then dressed and combed her hair.

She picked up her phone and called the Woodstock Town Police. "My great aunt passed last night."

Then she took a seat on the porch and waited.

A police officer arrived with an ambulance. "Where's her body?" he asked.

"She's not here," Claudia replied. "She took the train to Mount Jackson."

The officer frowned. Claudia watched him stroll over to the waiting ambulance and wave them away. When he returned, he took a seat in the chair next to her. "Miss, are you feeling ok this morning?"

Claudia shifted in her chair, easing away from the bruise on her thigh. "I'll live," she replied.

"And this great aunt—how did she seem to you?"

Claudia turned to the officer and smiled. "She was so happy. She was in love."

He nodded, and they sat quietly for a moment before Claudia said, "Officer, I need to talk with the funeral home about the circumstances."

He patted her on the shoulder. "There's no need." He stood up to leave.

"I'll let them know we have another empty casket."

Fore Ever on Ingleside

KURT JOHNSON

THE THREESOME SAT ON the edge of the hill and gazed at the mountains as the afternoon sun beamed on the storied course. A slight breeze blew over the 18th green as the player fetched his putter and approached the fluorescent orange ball that he stuck six feet from the hole.

"Jeez, I hate those colored balls. Colonel, I bet you five dollars he misses it a foot to the left."

"You're on, Bernard! The hole dips toward the old driving range. He'll miss it right, for sure."

"You're both wrong. He'll sink it," said Vinny. "Damn, this view never gets old. Think this will be our last year?"

The three men waited for the player to begin his pre-putt routine, address the ball, and slowly draw the club back...

"Something's wrong," said Vinny. "Colonel, Bernard, look at him."

"I know," replied Bernard. "His backswing is too long. He's going to blast it past the hole."

"Not that," Vinny said. "His face. See how it's contorted?"

The man never had a chance to strike the ball. Right hand clutching the left side of his chest, he dropped to his knees and died on the 18th green of Ingleside Golf Club.

"Hey gents, what do we do about our bets?" asked Bernard.

***

"How'd you hit 'em?" Vinny called out, watching the man haul himself up, putter still in hand.

The man, eyes wide, stared at him and stood silent for a while. The Colonel and Bernard lumbered over, golf clubs shifting in their bags, making quite the racket.

"Uh, pretty good, I guess... until the last hole. Don't remember putting out," said the man.

"Yeah, you're going to need to mark your round 'DNF', you know, 'Did Not Finish,' since you died on the green," said Bernard.

The Colonel added, "What kind of putter is that?"

Vinny intervened. "C'mon guys, let him get situated, you dig? He's not used to being dead. What's your name, my man? I'm Vinny, and this lovely chap here is Bernard. This one we just call The Colonel, obviously."

"Uh, hey, I'm Greg. And I'm not dead. I'm talking to you, so—"

Bernard interrupted, "You're dead, Greg. Bit the bullet, kicked the bucket. We saw it. Your heart attacked you right here on this green."

Greg scanned the odd crew in front of him. "Bernard, why are you dressed like Walter Hagen from the '20s? And Colonel, is this some World War II re-enactment? Vinny, are you going to a '70s-themed disco later? And I'm not dead. What on earth is going on here?"

The three men threw their bags over their shoulders and started up the hill toward the 1st tee.

Vinny stopped and turned to Greg. "C'mon, man, grab your clubs. We've been waiting for you."

***

The three men sauntered toward the tee box. Greg removed his visor and ran his fingers through his salt and pepper hair... no blood. Patting his arms and torso brought no pain. The white golf shirt, stain-free. A quick scan of his lower half proved the same.

The self-exam found nothing to support the accusation that he was dead.

I look and feel fine, and I just had a conversation. An odd one, but an actual conversation with three people. I'm not dead.

Greg placed the putter in the bag, grabbed the handle, and jogged up the hill toward the three men. "Hey guys, wait up. Thanks for the invitation, but I really need to get home. My family is expecting me."

"Not anymore, Greg, and soon they'll receive notification of your death," explained Bernard. "Ingleside is your home now, as long as it remains open, and we're your new family. Thanks for dying out there. We finally have a foursome."

Stewing now, Greg turned away from the men and walked to his car. *Ingleside is my home, and these clowns are my family... yeah, right.* He reached for the door handle and whiffed. Again, more intentional this time, his hand moved through the door handle like waving through fog.

***

Beyond confused, Greg jogged to the 1st hole to join the men. As he passed the 18th green, he spied emergency personnel tending to someone with salt and pepper hair and a white golf shirt. Reaching the 1st tee box he said, "Hey guys... will someone please tell me what's going on?"

"You're dead, son. Back there on the green, it's you," said The Colonel. "The medics, they're there for you."

"You'll tee off last since you just bit it a few minutes ago," added Vinny. "Bernard has been playing this course for almost a hundred years now and knows every blade and bunker. He tees off first since he's been dead the longest."

Playing along, Greg said, "But I'm too tired to play another round. I just had a heart attack, remember?"

"We're ghosts. Time, darkness, light, hot, cold, beating heart, none of it matters, except that Ingleside remains open," replied The Colonel.

"And, if it doesn't?" asked Greg.

"We'll get to that later, my boy," answered Bernard.

***

As Bernard took his practice swings, Greg listened to his story.

"Got shot by a jilted lover right here on the first tee in nineteen twenty-nine, one year after the course opened as a part of the Stonewall Jackson Hotel. That hateful woman walked right up to my foursome and shot me with a Colt .38 Special during my follow-through. I have a nice follow-through, don't I boys?" he asked of Bernard and The Colonel. "Anyhow, almost one hundred years later I still get the jitters teeing off from this hole."

Greg watched his three partners tee off, then it was his turn. Eyeing the yardage on his score card, he approached his bag and selected the driver. It took an eternity for its full length to emerge from his bag.

"What is that?" an awestruck Bernard asked.

"It's an extended shaft, oversized titanium head driver," answered Greg. "It helps with distance and forgiveness." He proceeded to knock it just shy of the green, besting the others by fifty yards.

"Far out, man, you tattooed that thing," said Vinny.

***

Each player parred the first two holes, and while walking to the 3rd tee, Greg asked again about the significance of Ingleside remaining open.

"If Ingleside closes, we cease to exist," a somber Bernard said. "Don't know why, other than we died on the course. Last time it closed was a couple years back, but only briefly. Before then it was 2003, and several times before that. When it closes, we suspend into this odd nothingness, like being underwater without the water. It's bleak, my lad. Upon its reopening, we return, unaware of time's passage until we overhear the present golfers speak of worldly affairs. We far prefer to linger here, Greg."

Greg listened intently, very much questioning, well, everything.

***

Bernard teed off and placed his club back in his ratty hundred-year-old bag. The Colonel shanked his tee shot hard left onto the old tennis courts, the ball bouncing off a net post. Vinny leaned down to place his tee in the ground and said, "Did I hear a clink, Colonel? Get it…?"

"Groovy, far-out joke, Vinny… you *dummkopf.* Like I've never heard the reference to *Hogan's Heroes,"* said The Colonel.

"Okay, settle down children," said Greg.

"Now you're getting the hang of this," added Bernard.

Greg continued, "So, Vinny, what happened to you?"

"Now, this is a story, my man. Ingleside had this groovy membership deal after the fires in '71, so I joined in '72. Chill course, challenging but totally playable. On this hole, I hit my drive in the creek down there at the dogleg. I was going in, you dig, cuz I was high as a kite on quaaludes. Just couldn't lose a stroke, man. Didn't pay attention to the weather. Heck, I barely knew where I was. With one foot in the creek and my sand wedge high in the air, the bolt struck me down… crispy fried Vinny, man! Bernard and The Colonel did me a solid, just as we did you."

This time Vinny hit his drive far right of the creek.

Greg selected his driver and approached the tee box, reflecting on what Bernard said.

Ingleside Golf Club must remain open.

***

After finishing the 3rd hole and walking to 4th tee, Greg said, "Guys, something's not adding up. Why am I able to play golf and talk to you, but not get into my car?"

Laughing now, The Colonel started, "We wondered when you would ask, son. The car is not on the course, nor related to golf. You're able swing a club, carry a bag, and talk to us because we're on the course… it's all about the course… the course where we all died."

Needing time to process that explanation, Greg changed the subject as they approached the fourth tee box. "Colonel, what's your story?"

"I prefer not to speak of such matters," answered The Colonel. "But since you inquired, I was part of the World War II internment camp project. I had retired from my military role and served as a foreign diplomat for the Greater Germany Reich. My family and I were shipped here in 1942 as 'prisoners' of the United States. We hoped to return to Germany after the war's end, but as fate would have it, I perished here."

The Colonel continued after a mournful moment, "I tee off second because only dear Bernard preceded me. I passed in 1943 playing this hole with fellow diplomats. We donned our old uniforms in a show of protest, much to the guards' dismay and our own detriment. For an uphill par three from about one hundred twenty yards, I'd use an easy 8-iron to let the ball drop right on the green, but that fateful day, I didn't even get to strike the ball. Cursed Chrysler veered off Route 11 and ran me over flat, right here on the tee box."

"Ouch," said Greg.

"What's more, that Chrysler kept going, or so Bernard said," continued The Colonel.

"It didn't have a scratch on it. Don't make 'em like that these days," Bernard added.

Greg played the fourth as The Colonel suggested: high lob, although with his pitching wedge, dropping the ball three feet below the cup for an easy uphill birdie.

***

The four golfing ghosts continued their round while Greg ruminated over the fate of Ingleside. Playing at a sprightly pace, they happened upon a group preparing to tee off on twelve. As ghosts, the normal etiquette of staying a good distance behind a teeing off group did not apply, so they walked right onto the tee box while the women were talking.

"Got the message this morning," one of them started. "Ingleside is due to close next month. Some big shot developer has offered the owner a pile of money to sell. Talk is that Staunton will agree to rezone the land to residential. Looks like condos are coming."

"I heard the same thing... a cryin' shame," added another. "I spoke with the owner last week and he doesn't want to sell but needs to double the number of rounds played to make it work financially."

"Guys, did you hear that? The course is closing next month," said an anxious Vinny.

"Of course we heard. We're right beside them. I might be one hundred and twenty-six years old, but I'm not deaf," Bernard said. "What can we do?"

"I have an idea on how we can help keep this course open!" Greg exclaimed.

"We're all ears, son," said The Colonel.

"The owner needs to double the number of rounds, right? Players play more golf when they're successful. Well, let's *help* them be successful," said Greg. "You all know this hole. Too many players use a driver, particularly from the red tees. How about a gentle nudge? Watch."

After the first three players drove the ball into trouble, Greg walked over to the fourth player's bag and pulled the 5-wood up a little higher than the driver. The woman approached her bag, searching for the driver, but instead selected the elevated club.

"Watcha hittin', Millie?" said her friend.

Millie turned. "I'm playing this safe. Going to lay up with the 5-wood for a better second shot." She hit the ball right where she should, setting herself up for a great score.

"Guys, do you get the idea now?" asked Greg.

***

The four ghosts quit their round to follow and 'guide' Millie's group. A propped-up lie, a bump out of the woods, a club 'suggestion' or two resulted in outstanding rounds across the four women's scorecards.

Approaching the end of the round at eighteen, Greg said, "Guys, I think it's working. Listen..."

"This could be the best round ever, and for each of us! I don't want this course to close," said Millie. "We need to spread the word. We all know people who golf. They should be golfing here! The views are great, and the price is right. Ladies, let's get this out on the *socials*."

The four Ingleside ghosts watched the foursome walk off the 18th tee box.

Greg said, "Ok, the seed is planted. When the new players arrive, we'll need to split up to 'help' ensure a great time with great scores. This will work, gentlemen!"

***

The next day, the four ghosts eyed a rowdy twosome driving up to the 1st tee box. Beer cans spilled out of the cart as they skidded to a stop five feet beyond white tees.

Greg said, "They're all yours, Bernard and Vinny. Let's see how you can help this motley duo. Remember, they need to score well... don't think we need to worry about them having fun."

"I'll assist posthaste!" replied Bernard.

Vinny said, "Yeah, whatever posthaste is, I'm in too.

Their charges, Chad and Byron, handled their clubs well through the first eight holes despite their levels of intoxication. Though if one cares about playing well, beer and golf eventually don't mix, no matter the skill level. As the round progressed and Chad and Byron's BAC levels rose, so did their voices and scores.

"Dang it! I never hook the ball!" bellowed Chad as he slammed his club in his bag and plopped into the cart.

Not being able to hold a straight face, Byron inquired, "You playing number nine or number eight? We're on number nine, you know."

"It's not funny, Byron, so stop your snickering. At least I can find my ball."

Having not been needed to this point, the ghosts sprang into action.

"Bernard, you take Chad and I'll take Byron. We need to get them back in play," said Vinny.

The ghosts glided ahead of their targets. A quick punch of one ball out of the woods and a slight nudge of the other for a favorable lie out of the rough, and the golfers were ready for their second shots. Chad drove the cart to Byron's ball first as he was farthest from the hole. Byron hopped out, grabbed a rescue club, and searched for his ball while Chad stayed in the cart.

"Hey Chad, drive on over here... need a different club!" hollered Byron.

"Why would you need anything other than a forest wedge?" joked Chad. "You're so deep the ticks don't go back there."

"Look here, with this lie I just need to hit it low and straight between those pine trees. This isn't nearly as bad as we thought, is it? I need me my 2-iron, Chad. I have a straight shot to the green!"

"No way, Byron. No way your ball landed here. You used your 'foot wedge' before I drove over, didn't you? I know you did."

"Shut it, Chad. What you know is that I don't lie or cheat. Must have been a fortunate bounce. Ingleside is taking care of me today."

"Just hit and let's go find my ball."

Byron blistered his 2-iron, and as the ball rolled to a stop on the green, the toasted twosome carted over to find Chad's ball. Like Byron's, his lie was almost perfect, as if someone had propped his ball on a sole tuft of grass, guarded by dirt and rocks.

"Looks like someone else owes the course some thanks, huh, Chad?"

Chad lofted his second shot on, deposited his lob wedge, and drove their cart ahead, stopping on the path beside the green.

"You're away, Chad, so go on and putt. You only have a bendy thirteen-footer. Easy peasy," laughed Byron.

Chad aimed right of the cup, struck the ball, and knew immediately he had misread the green. He spun to shout obscenities to the heavens above when he was stopped by Byron's excitement.

"It went in, Chad! Never seen anything turn at the end like that. It's like some force pulled it dead center into the hole!"

"Well, I'll be... Byron, call Jimmy and Derrick. They need to join us on the back nine!"

The four ghosts listened to the excited drunkards beckoning their friends. Mission accomplished.

"Good work, Vinny and Bernard. And, Colonel, well-played sneaking over and redirecting Chad's putt," said Greg.

"It's all in the line of duty, son."

***

As the weeks went by, the grapevine ran wild with tales of success from Ingleside. The owner decided not to sell as the rounds played more than doubled from the same time last year. The four ghosts had flawlessly executed Greg's plan. Word of mouth, mostly via social media, took care of the rest. Greg earned the honors of teeing off first on the final hole.

"Your idea, my boy, you go first. But make sure they're off the green. At three hundred yards, you might hit it on," said Bernard.

"Hey, isn't that Millie's group up ahead? No need to wait, Bernard. I've been playing this course for years and have never driven the green." Pulling his driver back, Greg exploded through the ball. The three ghosts gasped as it took flight.

"You crushed that, Greg. It might make it," said The Colonel.

"FORE!" shouted Vinny.

Greg's drive struck the right side of Millie's head. She stumbled backward two paces, lost strength in her knees, and spilled onto the 18th green, a few feet from where Greg died weeks earlier.

"Looks like we're starting another foursome," said Vinny.

"Fore ever on Ingleside!" the men shouted together.

The Long Walk

RODMAN

"You ever fink a takin' the Long Walk?"

Bolloch's question weighed heavy on the musty cavern air. He sat on an armchair built of ancient bone, thick rolls of troll fat cushioning him against its sharp nooks. It was a proper throne, the kind troll conquerors of Old sat in.

Folgi looked up from his book, thumbing a pair of undersized human spectacles over his misshapen forehead. "You haven't asked me that in a long time."

"'Ave so."

"Not since they leveled the forest over the old Strauch battle-field—"

"—hills of the bloody Pips!" Bolloch roared, drumming his fists on a resonant femur. He hated the Pips.

"Those hills are called 'James Madison' now. Some kind of mead hall with a school attached. It overlooks the Slob King's grave."

"Long may he feast!"

"He's been dead five hundred years," Folgi said.

Bolloch grunted. "You read too much."

They sat in a candlelit cavern, amber light spilling over stalactites that descended from the ceiling like jagged swords. Their ancestors would have squabbled for centuries over such a magnificent cave. Times changed. The ranks of men spread wide and fast. As bellicose as the trolls, cunning as the eilvi, and at times as nasty as the Pips. The Age of Man dawned, leaving even trolls as storied as Bolloch hiding in the depths. As much as he hated socializing—as any knob-knacking troll should—he secretly enjoyed visits to Folgi's dainty hovel.

The bespectacled troll fancied himself a historian and filled his little cavern accordingly. Ancient trollish banners bearing symbols of long dead warlords were strung from stalactites. Sturdy dwarkalfr armor with gold trim loomed over wickedly crafted eilvish swords. Here and there lay a hunting trophy: mammoth tusk, giant's teeth, a taxidermized set of particularly evil gerbils.

The remainder, to Bolloch's chagrin, were books. Scuffed leather tomes stacked from floor to ceiling, overwhelming shelves until they became the brick and mortar of their own paper walls. One described fourteenth-century medicine, or why a doctor must cover newly amputated limbs with soil in order to prevent infection. Another described how to woo gnomish women, or how to check for ents before building a treehouse. Bolloch eyed a stack to his right. Some were eilvish: *Melë i rûnya nísan* and *Ànin apsenë yello vanye*. Another appeared to be bound by dried animal skin and written in phlegm, which could only mean it was authored by that hated species which now dwelled in the World Within the World. Folgi even had books by humans: *Frankenstein*, *Infinite Jest*, *Fifty Shades of Grey*.

"What's this bloody fing?" Bolloch held a book of yellowed pages by its dilapidated back cover. "Withering?"

Folgi gave his friend an amused look. Three hundred years since the Great Retreat and the old troll still couldn't fathom reading words for entertainment. Too many blows to his thick, unprotected troll skull.

"Wuthering, Bolloch. *Wuthering Heights*. Emily Brontë. Exquisite examination of nineteenth century human society. Hatred, love, passion. Difficult time to be a human woman writing with such raw fervor."

Bolloch grunted again. "Wollops. You want a human woman with passion? Bow-dicka. Take a sword to yer enemies. Right wrongs with yer bloody fists!"

"Boudicca, yes. Not much good it did her in the end."

"What did scribbling books ever do for yer withering cow?"

Folgi didn't answer. There would be no convincing the greatest living trollish warlord of the merits of the arts, unless such arts involved painting with the blood of one's enemies. Luckily, they needn't have the debate. The hovel was a museum to the history of their own lifetime, and the great brute seemed to be wallowing in nostalgia. He pointed a gnarled finger toward a group of stalagmites. Nearly hidden amongst them jutted a glittering pommel plated with wyvern scales.

"Is that me old hammer?" Bolloch exclaimed.

Folgi grimaced. He'd forgotten to hide it. A slew of war stories was sure to follow, each bloodier and more brutal than the one before it. Bolloch rose from his chair unsteadily, mighty rolls of fat jiggling. Every feature exaggerated those natural to his species. While trolls were known for large bellies, Bolloch's was distended. His nose was twice as hooked, fingers twice as long. Three times the temper and half the sense. Never had Folgi seen more scarring on the pale gray skin of their kind.

"It is indeed," Folgi said.

"Shaft of mammoth tusk. I was the youngest one to ever do it, and with me bare hands, Folgi! I punched its skull to bits and scooped out the brain!"

The bespectacled troll nodded. Bolloch had, in fact, killed a mammoth as a youngster, though with a spear, a few friends, and under the guidance of an elder. But try telling an old troll not to spread tall tales.

"That you did."

"It must have been thousands of years ago!"

"Tens of thousands. During our migration over the North Pole onto the new continent."

Bolloch nodded, turning the weapon in his hand with the care of a new mother holding her baby. Except this baby was wrapped with the faded red intestines of a claw wyrm. A ball of condensed iron formed its head, studded by curved black fangs unwillingly retrieved from giant spiders in the Great Wood, now a national forest named after prominent humans. Gorge Washington and Tom the Jeffer's son, or something along those lines. The old warlord returned to his seat clutching the hammer like a scepter.

"The whole of the Lowly Mountains used to be mine. Mine, Folgi!"

He nodded. "They did indeed, old friend. They're called the Appalachians now."

Bolloch grumbled. "Always hated the human tongue. Kind of a name for mountains is *apple-atcha*?"

"I recall a young warlord believing names were the right of conquerors."

"I conquered it first."

"That you did."

Tiny drips echoed in the darkness. They marked the seconds like a ticking clock, forming trickles the size of troll hairs in minutes and little pools in hours. In the sunless interior, only water could mark time. Folgi had lived in this cave when the great pond behind his books was no more than a few drips off a stalactite. He hoped to see the water rise still more, Bolloch's Long Walk be damned.

The bespectacled troll continued reading while his gruff companion leaned forward against his hammer. The glory of old battles blazed in his eyes, embers growing brighter with each dusty relic they beheld. Deeper in Folgi's cavern, gentle drips of splashing water echoed from his pond, which in accordance with trollish practice doubled as both a bath and restroom. Something like a snake rose out of its flat waters, black and shiny with moisture. The serpentine beast bore no eyes or mouth, tiny suctioning circles dotting its underside. A tentacle. Bolloch watched it rise and rise until it began reaching toward the back of Folgi's neck.

"Heave!" Bolloch bellowed. He leapt from the bone throne only to tumble head first into a row of books that collapsed upon him. His breath came so haggard from the ground that he could only choke out a warning. "Folgi! A nasty beast at your back!"

Folgi rose with a sigh. He opened a chest that smelled of decayed fish, scooping out handfuls of rotted marine tissue like loose soil and tossing them into the pond. An oily black mass the size of Bolloch's belly emerged. It suctioned the rot meal into a spiral mouth laden with a thousand tiny teeth. As it gurgled down its meal, more tentacles emerged from the depths, gripping onto stalactites until it hoisted itself onto the edge of the pond next to Folgi. He patted it on the head.

"That would be the kraken, old friend. The one I carried across the ice."

"Not much of a kraken," Bolloch muttered, embarrassed by the fall. He rose from the book pile and limped to his throne, scepter now becoming a cane.

"Hard to grow, living in cave ponds," Folgi said.

"Agreed."

Folgi looked startled. "How do you mean?"

"Do you like it here, Folg?"

The bespectacled troll didn't answer.

"You were always an odd djinn, Folgi. I slew beasts, you saved ugly fish. I warred. You read books. I filled these caves with blood. You offered to write a peace treaty with the Underdwellers and be our *lamb-ass a door*."

"Ambassador," Folgi said.

Bolloch waved dismissively. "You are the least trollish troll I ever met. I must have saved your life half a hundred times."

"Seventy-five, as a matter of fact. Is this where you ask me why we ever became friends?"

Bolloch's visits to Folgi's hovel were rare even by the anti-social standards of a troll, yet they were set in routine nevertheless. Complain, reminisce, argue, complain some more, leave angrily. Tonight, the old warlord sat a bit more hunched. His voice didn't carry its usual echo. His boasts were tamer. Falling into those books left wounds on the only thing more important to a warrior than his body: his pride. The old warlord stared at his hammer, pricking spider teeth with his finger and letting the blood drip onto his toes.

"Bolloch?" asked Folgi, "what's this all about?"

He continued pricking his fingers on the teeth. "I think maybe if our chieftains were like you... maybe we wouldn't be hiding under the *lure-eye* caverns waiting to die."

Luray, Folgi thought. He didn't say it. He didn't know quite what to say.

"You've never said that to me before."

Bolloch nodded. "Do you remember when we first conquered these caves?"

Folgi knew where this conversation was headed. He picked up a small handkerchief in the form of a hand-knitted shirt a Mennonite left in the Luray Caverns gift shop.

"I try not to," Folgi said.

"Bloody bloodbath. Ten thousand Pips shooting nasty little darts from every nook and cranny. 'Orrible little mites. I hate 'em."

"They're not the most lovable sort."

Bolloch's hands trembled on the hammer in some mixture of rage and misery.

"They took," Bolloch broke off, his voice wavering. "They took her that day. Wily troll, she was. Arms the size of trees."

"Wonderful troll. I think she got her underbite from you."

"Aye. They took her down, Folgi. After you warned us to smoke them out first. That was you: plans and strategeries. That was me: charge, charge, charge."

"She got her fierceness from you."

"Lot of good that did. Now she's gone, and I'm buried under *lure-eye*. I think if you were chief, she'd be alive putting your pet kraken on a spit and roasting dinner for her father."

The kraken hissed. It spat a jet of black liquid that clipped the edge of Bolloch's ear, leaving acid-burned grooves and the smell of burning flesh. The old warlord hardly flinched. He sat wordlessly, his eyes boring holes into the cavern floor.

For all his books, Folgi could conjure no comforting words. Emotions were not as easy to read as ink on a page. Books can teach how to suture a wound. Many claim to teach mending a spirit, but no lessons came easily to mind. He tried to think of a story that might aid the warlord in his aging ailment. *The Iliad*, perhaps? Or *Memoirs of Sergeant Bourgogne?* What was that book-turned-movie with the handsome devil of a human? *Last of the Mohicans?*

Bolloch's voice rumbled slow and heavy, as if weighed down by the rock ceiling above him. "That's why I'm taking the Walk, Folgi. I'm tired. Dead tired. I'm tired of being tired. It's time to join my ancestors in the Blood Pits." Bolloch picked at a small tin of rotfish.

He may have been serious about the Long Walk. But the bespectacled troll was equally serious about convincing him otherwise. Folgi looked at a small, round crevasse in his floor, placed directly under a water drip, and took stock of its content. Ten, maybe eleven hours since sunset. The beginnings of a plan formed. Delay, delay, delay.

"I understand, old friend. Aging is hard when you can't engage in old pastimes. Cracking skulls, slurping organs, squeezing your enemies into delicious jams. There's an old story from the time of our early years in the Shenandoah Valley. Told by humans that conquered our grandfather's home in Scandinavia."

Bolloch looked up from the hammer, curious, as Folgi continued.

"You may have heard the story of Beowulf?"

Bolloch growled. "Slew my cousin Grendel."

"I thought you hated Grendie."

"I did. Still do. His mother stank of cleanliness."

"How hideous. At any rate, you are correct. Slays your cousin Grendel, slays his mother, becomes king for fifty years, dies slaying a dragon."

"So?" Bolloch asked, eyes betraying a growing interest. What could a troll love more than glorious death in battle?

"The last thing he sees is its great hoard of treasure." If there exists one thing a troll could love more than glorious death in battle, it's the allure of enormous treasure.

"So yer saying I need to find a dragon before I croak?"

Folgi shook his head in frustration. "No, old friend. I'm trying to tell you there's stories out there that remind me of you. Heroic feats, catastrophic loss, bravery in the face of insurmountable odds. These were our stories too, but our people had little interest in writing them down. We're beyond our dragon slaying days, Bolloch. But you can still read—"

"Not reading yer books, Folgi." The scarred warlord rose to leave. They had reached the angry departure portion of his regular visits. Perhaps his final visit. Folgi had one last gamble.

"Have I ever told you about the epic of the last great trollish warlord?"

Bolloch's brow furrowed. "Hrm?"

"Oh, he's famous. Killed a mammoth with his bare fists. Carved a fiery path through strongholds of Pips and pale giants. Conquered Appalachia. Strangled a wyrm in the Shenandoah River. Slew a vermicious knid at the peak of Old Rag Mountain. Scared a party of exploring humans so badly they began firing at random into the woods."

Bolloch cackled. Fangs the size of daggers filled his mouth, cracked and yellowed though they were. "When was that, ole Folg?"

"Early eighteenth century. Golden Horseshoe Expedition, or some such thing. Saw your ruby eyes glittering in the dark and opened fire! Tried to claim it was a ceremonial volley."

Bolloch belly laughed for several moments. Yet he too quickly returned to a mild state of fugue. Folgi's stomach sank at the look.

Bolloch's scarred smile disappeared rapidly. Tiredness returned to his voice. "That was the last time we roamed outside the caverns, wasn't it?"

It was. Until that point, the trolls of Appalachia disregarded rumors of human boomsticks as skittish fantasies of cowardly sprites. The deafening cracks of their firearms changed everything. The Age of Man once moved like distant storm clouds. Suddenly it arrived all at once, the black swell of man right overhead. So, the trolls went into hiding. One last war party descended into the World Within the World, led by the Slob King's son, the Pudge Prince, never to be seen again.

Bolloch limped toward an unlit passageway supported by his hammer. Folgi knew this passage to be the one that led to the surface. The bespectacled troll was all out of tricks. He let his shoulders slump as he grabbed a torch to light the way. He placed his own translation of *Beowulf* and some rotfish in a bag slung about his hip. Fanny pack, the humans called it.

"Is it that time?" he asked sadly.

"Aye, I fink so," Bolloch answered. Hesitation tinged his voice, which Folgi elected to hold onto as they trudged through narrowing rock. Nothing wrong with a bit of hope.

"What if there are humans milling about?" Folgi asked.

"Then I give them one last taste of the hammer!" Bolloch tried to bellow in his savage way but ended up in coughing fits. "Maybe a scare instead."

The rock passage sloped and slicked in turns. To ascend wet rock, they climbed like their ancestors had: with tooth and claw. Each troll growled angrily as he bit and raked into unforgiving stone. Folgi's torch was left on the ground level, its light fading until they needed to feel out with long troll fingers to know where to claw next. Bolloch felt thick wetness descending from fingertip to knuckle. Blood. He grinned, grabbing onto handholds more forcefully than before. Age forced them to rest on a stone ledge, Folgi's torch a tiny flaming speck on the ground below. They sucked on rotfish, leaving packs of scales embedded between their lower lips and teeth, spitting them over the ledge between breaths.

"What do you fink happens, Folg? After the Walk?"

"You're not getting second thoughts, are you, old friend?"

"Bah!" Bolloch waved off his question with a limp hand.

"I suppose we've never seen a troll take the Long Walk, have we?"

Bolloch shook his head.

"If what I read is accurate, when you run into the sun, you'll have a few seconds, maybe even minutes, before turning to stone. In that time, you may recall your life from birth to now."

"The good bits?"

"All the bits. The good, the bad, and the ugly. By the time that memory is done, you'll be a statue to ages long past."

"Will I see the little one?"

"I don't know, Bolloch. I'm sorry."

The old warlord nodded slowly. "You don't have to know. What do you fink?"

"I think, well... I think yes. You'll see the little one. All eight feet, four hundred pounds of her."

Bolloch gestured upward with his hammer. In spite of the difficulty of their climb, their hands marred by blood and spit, the old warlord stood taller now than when they sat down in the hovel. His eyes were alive. His muscular fingers itched to grab the next rock. The trolls ascended once more, boosting one another and using the hammer to pull each other up like a climbing rope.

Stone ledges atrophied in width as the altitude grew higher, like a pyramid from afar. At its summit lay a badly rusting steel door. Folgi put an ear to it, listening for the hectic sounds of human tourists. He had once come across one in the flesh, causing the poor creature to go into shock and die on the spot. Heart attack. Or indigestion.

No sounds came from beyond the door. He straightened and looked eye to eye with Bolloch, extending a hand. Bolloch was slow to take it. The old warlord stood taller. He'd experienced his first good sweat-and-bleed since first conquering the Luray caverns. Yet he came here to take the Long Walk. To join his ancestors. To join his daughter. To turn to a statue so fierce, humans would forever abandon these caves for fear of running into such a creature deep in its depths. A fitting end for a famous troll. Walk into the sun, feel its dreadful golden warmth, and embrace death.

Bolloch grasped Folgi's arm but avoided his eyes. The bookish troll wanted him to stay around and rot with a book in his hands. Beowulf did indeed sound interesting, and Bolloch knew he would enjoy reading about the death of his wretched cousin, but it wasn't enough. Not anymore. Greater forces called his name now. Bolloch turned the rusted door's screeching handle.

It opened no more than two inches when a sound more terrifying than any wyvern roar or Pip squeak poured through the opening. Shrieks emitted in high pitched, staccato bursts. The sound's rhythm was chaotic, though still distant and not quite identifiable. Bolloch turned to Folgi, only to see confusion on his face.

Vast knowledge of both the arcane and the contemporary did not help the bespectacled troll identify the source. His calloused brows furrowed. Soft drumming now accompanied the cacophonic shrieks. Folgi was taken aback by how familiar they sounded. The drumming could have been footsteps. Short, rapid footsteps. His senses determined the time to be late morning, on perhaps Tuesday.

"Oh gods," Folgi muttered. "Shut the door, Bolloch."

The old warlord brandished his hammer. "Nonsense. I'll smash 'em to pieces!"

Another shriek sounded, this one much closer. And easily discernible.

"Children! Human children!" Folgi screamed.

Distant toddler shrieks began to pierce his ears. They ingrained a horrid yet familiar throbbing that began between the eyes and continued around the skull to the back of the head. Human children were more terrifying to trolls than cats to Dracula. They had a capacity for screeching even banshees could not match, an instinct for destruction even giants could not contend with. Bolloch shuddered at the mental image of their beady little eyes.

Just a tablespoon of children's putrid drool had the power to cover even the hardiest troll in hives.

"Waagh!" Bolloch cried. He threw himself against the steel door to shut it. It appeared stuck open. The trolls pounded against it, hammering desperately. "Why are there so many of them?"

"A field trip," Folgi said miserably.

The shrieks had almost reached them. With a final groan, Bolloch smashed his hammer into the rusted hinges. His brutish strength knocked the door too far off its frame, leaving a gap on its left side. The children were about to turn the final corner. Soon, their awful little breaths would fill the air. Desperate, the old warlord raised mighty hammer one last time and wedged it into the gap, heaving forward until the steel door locked into place permanently. Both trolls covered their ears as the miscreant children passed by, trying to stifle the sound of those horrible giggles.

"Sorry about your hammer," Folgi said. Wyvern scales on its handle matched the color of rusty steel almost perfectly. To a troll's eyes, anyway.

Bolloch surprised him with a crack-toothed grin. "What a day, Folgi."

"Indeed, old friend. I suppose the Long Walk will have to wait until we find another way to the surface?"

"Aye."

"I don't suppose you'll want a book to read until then?"

"No," Bolloch said. He hesitated. "But maybe... you could read it to me?"

Folgi smiled. "An audiobook, then?"

"A what?"

"Never mind. Let's start at the beginning."

They descended ledge by ledge until they found themselves back in Folgi's hovel, one adventure richer.

Feed
The
Cat

Fixer Upper

JAKE SOLYST

SHE SEEMED LIKE THE kind of woman you could bare your soul to, sitting there on a barstool with her head craned up toward the TV, a fantastic mop of curly brown hair and a tattoo on her wrist that said "Love, Again." Joe paid for the woman's drink, and she gave him a "you're a little too young for me" look but smiled, accepted, and bought them both a round afterward. It wasn't until they were three beers deep that he asked for the woman's name, and she asked him what he was doing in this "Shenandoah sinkhole of a town."

"I'm riding the Blue Ridge Parkway," Joe told her.

Eileen lifted her eyebrows, not having pegged him for the motorcycle-riding type. "So that's your bike out there then?"

"More or less."

"You from D.C.? Silver Spring, maybe?"

"Why? Do I look like I am?"

She grinned, bringing the Heineken bottle to her mouth. "You're too polite to be from around here. Plus, you've got the money for a fancy motorcycle. What kind did you say it was?"

"Kawasaki," Joe told her. "Ninja series. But it was my dad's. He passed away this year and left it to me. I've been riding since yesterday morning, and I'm on my way back now. And you're close, I'm from Alexandria."

Eileen's acrobatic eyebrows lowered into crescent moons. She didn't spout off condolences the way most people did after Joe told them about his father's passing, just acknowledged the sorrow silently, like she was adding the news to a heap of hardship she'd witnessed over time. That was how Joe knew he'd found the right drinking buddy.

Throughout the road trip, Joe had been waiting for a moment or feeling that might bring him closer to his father. His dad made this same ride every year, from the top of Skyline Drive to the Blue Ridge Parkway and down to the Carolinas. Always in the fall, with crisp air and trees settled into their autumn hues. His dad talked about the highways like they were a living thing, said that when the conditions were right, you could ride them like a mountain stream. Blame it on inexperience, but Joe had no such luck. After two days of riding, he still hadn't gotten a hang of the terrain—jerking in and out of gears, flooring the engine to get up hills, slamming on the brakes when he came across a sudden curve. He was a fraud. Anyone could see that. And the fraudulence made him feel lonely. Not only did he not know his own dad; but now it seemed that he barely knew himself.

"So what do you do?" Joe asked Eileen.

She took a gulp from her beer and raised the empty bottle to the bartender. An older woman with hair like a cigarette butt came over with a new one. Eileen thanked her by name. "Tell him what I do, Maggie."

"She's a grifter," said the bartender.

Eileen chuckled, taking a quick sip as Maggie walked away with a smirk.

"What she means is that I provide services not always deemed permissible in the eyes of the law. Such as it is."

"What is it that you provide?"

"Currently?" Eileen asked. "Memories. I sell memories." A wide smile spread across Eileen's face as she leaned into Joe, lowering her voice almost to a whisper. "You've heard of Right Well, haven't you?"

Like most people, Joe had heard of Right Well. The health and wellness brand was all over social media despite the fact that only ten percent of the population could afford its products and treatments. Intellectuals called it "The Happiness Gap," how the other ninety percent became even more depressed now that they were priced out of the wonder drugs. Money, it seemed, was the only thing that could buy happiness, and Right Well knew it.

"Sure, I've heard of it," Joe said begrudgingly. "You work there or something?"

"Let's say I have a connection with someone who does. They just came out with their new Neuro-Durability line. Memory Enhancers. Stuff is *incredible*."

The other thing Joe knew about Right Well was that it was constantly releasing new products: pills that snuffed out anxiety for months at a time, treatments that made you fall in love with your job no matter how mundane, injections that took away self-doubt the way Botox removed wrinkles. The company worked closely with the Drug Advancement Agency (formerly the FDA) to test the products through AI simulations and market them within a web of influencers, culture content, and cross-product sponsorships. This happened more or less instantaneously, so that within twenty-four hours of a product launch, the drug was already a pop culture staple. Your wealthy aunt's favorite new stocking stuffer.

"So it helps you remember stuff?" Joe asked.

"Something like that," Eileen said, taking a gulp. "Tell you what, I live just up the road. After this drink, let's head over and I'll give a sample. If you like it, I'll cut you a deal for another dose."

The bartender was hovering close by. Joe figured she was someone Eileen could trust. Then he put it together. Eileen probably came to the bar every night looking for customers and dealing to old ones. That didn't bother him, though. Everyone needed a side hustle these days. Joe's dad had taught him that. He was a Great Layoff guy who used to write code for a medical company until the new *Elias Language* model came out and made that job obsolete. That's when his father really checked out. Spent all his free time in the garage working on a bike he didn't ride anymore, collecting paltry Workforce Transition Checks until the bone cancer set in, a development he seemed rather proud of, as if the cancer, in trying to kill him, was proof that he was still alive.

After settling up with Maggie, Joe got on his bike and followed Eileen up the road to her place. She lived in a development of connected monochromatic homes that wove up a steep Virginia hill like a triangular ant farm. Eileen's place was at the top.

"Sorry for the mess," Eileen said as they entered the apartment.

Joe stood at the foot of the door, hands stuffed into his leather riding jacket as he gazed over the unkempt, open-floor apartment.

Socks, hoodies, and tennis shoes littered the furniture, as if Eileen had tried on fifty different outfits before heading out. Whatever bowls and cups she used that week didn't appear to have made their way to the sink. A note on the fridge read "FEED THE CAT."

"Where's the cat?" he asked.

Eileen stuck her head out from a closet she had been digging through. "Hiding, probably."

She continued to rummage for another minute while Joe paced around, feeling more intruder than guest. Finally, Eileen emerged with a shoebox in hand.

"Take a seat," she said, nodding at the couch.

He moved a big pillow and lowered himself onto the sofa. Vape pens, mugs, and an empty wine bottle lay on the coffee table in front of him. Eileen added a row of pink, unmarked pill bottles fished out of the shoebox to the mix.

"So how does this work?" Joe asked.

He tried to keep the sound of his voice steady, but the nerves were apparent. This wasn't the first time he'd been in a room with a drug dealer, but it was the first time he'd been in a room with a drug dealer selling a drug he knew nothing about. Was this something a doctor should clear him for, he wondered? As far as he knew, you didn't need a prescription to buy Right Well products. Just a lot of money.

"They're called Memory Enhancers," Eileen said. "Or MEs. Basically, they target dopamine receptors that heighten feelings associated with certain memories. They make bad memories good and good memories great. All you have to do is think about something that's happened to you, and then mold it."

"Mold it?" Joe asked.

"Yeah, you know, *guide* the memory to where you want it. It's like humming a melody, except this pill turns you into Stevie freakin' Wonder."

Eileen went to the kitchen and poured a glass of water while Joe sat on the couch, thinking about the memory he wanted to "mold." On her way back, Eileen turned off the overhead lights and dimmed a lamp, so that the room was barely lit. Joe made an effort to loosen his shoulders and relax his body, like settling in for a massage.

"So how much is one of these pills?" Joe asked. "My bank account's a little low right now."

"The market value for a single pill is ten thousand. But I sell them for much, much cheaper. And don't worry, this one's on the house."

Eileen held out a glass of water and a single pill—$10,000 worth, to be exact. After a moment of hesitation, Joe took the drug and washed it down.

Maybe ten seconds went by before the pill kicked in. The lamp that had been dimmed started glowing brighter and brighter until it looked radioactive. He could taste the inside of the wine bottle on the coffee table and the tobacco under Eileen's fingernails.

"Quick, close your eyes and picture your memory," Eileen said. "And try to relax."

He closed his eyes and saw himself as a young boy, standing at the foot of an open garage where his dad was working on his bike.

Suddenly, Joe couldn't hear or smell anything in the room with Eileen. He was fully attuned to that scene in the garage: the smell of the motor oil and sweat on his dad's back, twangy old folk songs playing from a Bluetooth speaker, the Virginia humidity laid on thick.

Joe, as a boy, observed his dad from the opening of the garage, keeping quiet. He wasn't supposed to bother his dad while he was in the garage and sometimes got in trouble for watching. But after a moment, Joe saw himself taking tentative steps into the garage, closer to his dad, who turned to him, smiled, and waved him over.

His dad explained the parts of the bike—the gears, the motor, the transmission—and Joe focused his eyes trying to follow along. They were fixing it up together, an older model Kawasaki than what Joe had now, the one from that crazy-old movie his dad watched about Air Force pilots who played volleyball. His dad made a joke, and Joe started laughing, confident that his dad was by far the funniest, most clever guy in the neighborhood, if not the whole state of Virginia. The adult Joe didn't know what the joke was, but he could feel the pure joy of it, the pride of being there with his dad, learning about the bike. Somehow, he knew his dad was excited to have him around. Joe was a quick learner. He had a knack for automobiles, just like his old man.

Slowly, the scene drifted away. Joe's senses dulled, and the image of the scene became less vivid. Then, all at once, he was back in Eileen's apartment, lifted out of the memory like a diver coming up for air.

Eileen sat there grinning at him, trying to hold back a laugh. Joe's hands rubbed against the lumpy sofa, and his knees struck the coffee table.

"Good stuff, huh?" Eileen said.

"That was incredible," Joe told her. "I mean *incredible.*"

She giggled, already counting out more pills and stacking them in groups of five.

"It was so vivid. Like I lived it."

"You did live it," Eileen told him. "Or at least now you have."

Joe sank back into the sofa, trying to figure out what that meant for him. His legs and arms sprawled lazily like the limbs of a marionette. He couldn't wait to immerse himself in the memory later, maybe while finishing up his road trip.

"It's sweet that you chose a memory of your dad. Most guys just think about girls they've been with."

Joe laughed, rubbing a slow hand over his face, still high off the experience. He hadn't laughed like that in so long. Not since childhood.

"What I'm going to recommend is a daily dose of ten milligrams," Eileen said. "But I can cut you a deal for the first month. How does seven-fifty sound?"

Joe's mind was so light that it took him a moment to piece together what she was proposing. The price was steep. Pretty much impossible. But the real question, which Joe blurted out, was why did he need more pills?

"It's not a one-time fix, Joe," Eileen said. "You need to keep enhancing the memory, otherwise it'll go away."

Joe closed his eyes and tried to recall the memory with his dad again. He could see it—see himself kneeling by his father, who was pointing out something about the bike, handing Joe a tool from his toolbox—but the colors were already faint and details blurred, like taking an eye exam and realizing you needed a new prescription. Joe wasn't even sure if the memory was real or if he had made it up.

"Tell you what, if seven-fifty is too much, we can work out a payment plan. The more months you can commit to, the better discount I can give. And I take pawns. Watches. Jewelry. That bike, maybe."

Joe caught himself glaring at Eileen, who promptly lowered her head to count out more pills. She couldn't even look Joe in the eyes anymore, and he knew why.

God, she *was* a grifter. Just like everyone else he met.

America was a land of hacks and shadow-makers. Orphans in the era of post-truth.

Joe leaned toward the coffee table and gripped the neck of the empty wine bottle. Eileen didn't even notice, still counting out tablets. She must've thought him a sucker, an empty coat, a non-threat. Joe lifted the bottle high and brought it down on her head.

Eileen made a low, truncated huff as she fell to the floor, blood leaking from her head like spilled milk. Her eyes, still open, stared at the corner of the coffee table she'd never managed to clean.

Joe swept the pills from the table and stuffed them into his jacket pocket. He shot across the room and rooted through the closet, seeing if there were more MEs mixed in with Eileen's junk. Before leaving, he took a closer look at the "FEED THE CAT" note. The letters were tall and wobbly like they'd been written by a kid.

Joe pushed eighty miles per hour on the Blue Ridge Parkway, headlights knifing through the curves of the mountain road. He didn't have long before the cops tracked him down. The moment Eileen hit the floor, the sensor that monitored her brain activity—implanted during infancy, as required by almost all states—messaged the AI-powered Safety Support Network, which then bypassed security regulations to tap into home and traffic cameras, gather data, assess data, and reason that Joe was the one who caused her death with 98.5% certainty.

Joe rode on in spite of this.

A gray haze softened the night sky as the moon fell slowly behind the trees. A little after dawn, a cop car sitting at an overlook pulled up behind him and hit the sirens. Joe reached into his jacket pocket and pulled out the bottle of MEs, flipped open his visor, and tossed the pills into his mouth. Suddenly, the gentle sunrise grew to a vast golden mass, and the dense foliage sang with a million tiny voices.

At this point, Joe truly began to ride. He sensed no difference between his body and the bike and the bike and the road and the road and the sunrise. The Blue Ridge Parkway, like his dad had said, was a mountain stream. Joe rode it easy. Up and down and through the ridges and valleys, gliding through the ancient terrain. The sirens whined in the distance.

Joe was off. Off to meet the horizon.

The Whitetail Whatchamacallit

GRIFF THOMAS

THE HUM OF TIRES on asphalt filled the cab of Sherman Grant's pickup as he and his best friend, Tecumseh Brown, cruised up I-81 toward Winchester.

"Hey, Tecumseh," Sherman drawled, "how come we didn't go to Woodstock when we lived so close? I heard that was an all-time great music festival."

Tecumseh squinted at the road. "I think you're thinkin' of a *different* Woodstock, Sherm."

"You sure about that?"

"The music festival was up in New York, back in 1969. We weren't even born yet."

"Oh," Sherman said, a touch deflated.

"And the town here's named after that cartoon bird, everyone knows that."

"You mean Tweety?"

"You know of a town called Tweety? I'm talkin' about Woodstock."

"Oh, yeah, he's real talented," Sherman conceded. "So why isn't his name on the 'Welcome To' signs? I ain't trackin'."

Tecumseh shifted in his seat, turning to face Sherman slightly. "You know how some towns got them 'Welcome To' signs?" he began, his voice slow and thoughtful. "Like the one down in Front Royal?"

"Yeah, I'm with you," Sherman replied, peering through the windshield.

"Well, I been noticin', some of 'em got a little somethin' *extra* painted on 'em, like they added fancy letters. You ever seen that?"

Sherman scratched his head. "Can't rightly say I have."

Tecumseh leaned in conspiratorially. "Well, if you did, you might see somethin' like, 'Welcome to Front Royal, Home of John the Baptist.' That 'Home of John the Baptist' bein' the extra words part."

Sherman's eyes widened. "John the Baptist? He's from Front Royal? I always thought he was from the wilderness, but maybe he did start in Fro Ro. They did used to call it Hell Town."

"Now, Sherman—" Tecumseh started, but Sherman, bless his heart, was already off on another tangent.

"Wait, wait, wait," Sherman interrupted. "I'm thinkin' different now. If I was in charge of the whole Earth, say I won some big election—"

"There ain't no election for bein' in charge of the Earth, Sherman," Tecumseh gently reminded him. "Be serious now."

Sherman looked genuinely puzzled. "Well, how'd they decide somethin' like that? Odd man, or rock-paper-scissors, maybe?"

Tecumseh grinned. "Likely a turkey shoot, or somethin' requiring real practical skills."

"Alright," Sherman said, puffing out his chest, "say I won the big turkey shoot and I'm runnin' the whole show..."

"I'm trackin', Mr. Brown," Tecumseh said, smiling. "Congratulations."

"Thank you, my loyal subject," Sherman said, waving a hand like a benevolent mayor. "If I was in charge, I'd put my best people, like John, in the toughest places, Hell Town for sure bein' one of 'em. He'd come in and clean things up, a-preachin' and a-baptizin' in the Mighty Shenandoah."

"What about the folks in Winchester?" Tecumseh asked.

"Well, what about 'em?"

"Ain't no river," Tecumseh pointed out. "Where'd you dunk folks when you got no river? Rain barrels are only quarter full this time of year."

"Easy as pie," Sherman said. "You wouldn't need dunkin'. You'd do other miracles. Find someone who can do some real fancy tricks like Moses, settin' this and that bush to burnin', conversin' with trees, or maybe turn your walkin' stick into a black rat snake."

"That's fair," Tecumseh nodded. "You know, Winchester ain't got no extra paint on its sign neither. I'm lookin' at it presently."

"Meanin' what?"

"Meanin' it's still *available*," Tecumseh said. "Nobody real famous come from Winchester 'sides Patsy Cline. Showbiz is its own thing. We're talkin' business."

Sherman chuckled. "There's room for all our names, I reckon. What could we do to get our names on that sign?"

Tecumseh's eyes twinkled. "You just ain't a-dreamin' my dream yet. You might be king of the planet, but *I* got an idea what'll make us famous. It'll take some work, but we can do it."

"So, what's your plan, Stan Jobs?"

"Well, I don't know *yet*, but it's gonna strike me directly. Also, it's *Steve* Jobs, Sherman. Stan works at Tractor Supply," Tecumseh corrected, with a patient sigh.

Sherman shook his head. "I swear, if I see another dead deer by the side of the road... What a tragedy."

"I heard if you was to put seventy-five Virginians in seventy-five cars, one of 'em's gonna hit a deer, every time," Tecumseh said.

"In that case, I'm startin' to order my take-outs from West Virginia," Sherman muttered, shaking his head.

"*Odocoileus virginianus,*" Tecumseh said. "White-tailed deer. Now, don't that sound majestic?"

"Sure does. Where'd you pull that one from?"

"Just common knowledge, ain't it?"

"Well, it ain't common to me, but I like how it names 'em as Virginians. *Sick semper tyrannis*."

"You got that right, brother."

"I mean, if that don't make you want to help them harmless creatures, I don't know what will."

"I can't lie, I do love me some deer," Tecumseh said. "And it's a shame so many get hit. Why do you reckon it happens so often?"

"I know exactly why. Automobiles are invisible to deer," Sherman stated plainly.

"You sure about that?"

"Course. They done studies up at Shenandoah University, and deer are what they call 'auto-immune,' which is a fancy way of sayin' vehicles are invisible to 'em."

"We owe it to our four-legged friends to preserve the precious gift of life bestowed upon them," Tecumseh said. "So we can hunt 'em down later."

"A worthy cause," Sherman agreed. "You got a plan yet?"

"We teach 'em to use crosswalks," Tecumseh said, a spark of inspiration in his eyes.

"But what about the deer on the highways?"

"We teach 'em to be afraid of the highways, maybe build over-passes."

"Deer ain't too bright," Sherman said. "How'd we do that?"

"They ain't stupid," Tecumseh countered. "They're as smart as a four-year-old. And kids are gettin' smarter, so that means deer are too. If my nephew Henry can use a computer and he's only three, it should be nothin' for a deer."

"Lemme make sure I'm trackin' you here. You're sayin' that because the average four-year-old human is smarter than they used to be, that means the deer are smarter too?"

"That's exactly what I'm saying, you're trackin'."

"No, I ain't. How's a beloved woodland creature, like a white-tailed deer, *Odocoileus virginianus*, gettin' his brain growed by some kid he don't even know, learnin' about comput-ers?"

"It's on account of the collective unconscious, I reckon."

"Ain't that what a fella by the name of Jung says? Joe Young, I'm thinkin'."

"Well, Mighty Joe Young was one of them giant movie gorillas like King Kong."

"That's likely not him then."

"Not likely. You're thinkin' 'bout Carl Jung, I reckon?"

"That's the fella. He's good," Sherman said. "I'm trackin'."

***

The next morning, crisp and bright, Tecumseh and Sherman met at the Abrams Creek Wetlands Preserve, their usual spot for a morning walk.

"You know," Tecumseh said, inhaling the fresh air, "this'd be the perfect spot to start our project. Got all the fixings we're needin'. Look around, deer everywhere, and all them doctors and nurses drivin' to Winchester Medical Center passin' right by."

"And ambulances," Sherman added, nodding. "And there's a crosswalk over yonder."

"Plus, we got a big space to set up some trainin' for them deer," Tecumseh said, pointing toward a clearing.

"I'm tracking," Sherman said. "This is a perfect place."

"Now, all we gotta do is set up the learnin' zone for deer," Tecumseh said, rubbing his hands together.

***

The next day, their pickups were loaded with supplies.

"Did you get it?" Tecumseh asked, looking at Sherman.

"Course I did," Sherman replied, patting the truck bed. "My friend Harlan, he works for the city on roads. They just upgraded the crosswalks last fall and bought too many. They ain't gonna miss two of 'em."

"Great," Tecumseh said. "There's a game trail right beside the railroad tracks. We can setup our training crosswalk there."

"Great," Sherman agreed. "But how do we make 'em think that part of the game trail's a road?"

"Simple," Tecumseh grinned. "We blacktop over the part of the trail between our crosswalk lights and buttons. I got some left over from when I redid my driveway before Apple Blossom last year."

"I'm tracking," Sherman said. "How 'bout you go get your blacktop, and I'll set up the crosswalk equipment?"

"Now, I'm tracking," Tecumseh said. "Hey, I just thought of somethin'. There's no electricity down here, so how do we power the—"

"They're solar powered," Sherman interrupted, tapping his head. "The sun does the work for us, son."

Tecumseh smiled. "How long you figure we been best friends, Sherm?"

Sherman scratched his chin, a thoughtful look on his face. "I mark it since we was five. First day of kindergarten. They put us in the back—figured we were slow learners. Didn't bother me none. Knew me and you, we just saw the world different, that's all."

Tecumseh grinned, a nostalgic glint in his eye. "Couldn't have said it better myself. Remember that chili cook-off? We spiked the other entries with so much Tabasco, nobody else could even taste theirs. Talk about fire-breathing dragons!" He chuckled, shaking his head.

Sherman laughed, the memory clearly vivid. "Like it was yesterday. Or how about that time we rigged up all them mirrors to bounce the TV picture from your living room, down the hall, through the kitchen, to the bathroom door, all the way to your bedroom... just so's we could watch SpongeBob in bed?"

Tecumseh's smile widened. "They said it'd never work."

"But there we were," Sherman finished, "stretched out, comfy as could be, watching SpongeBob in supreme comfort."

Sherman nodded. "We're like two peas."

"Two underestimated peas," Tecumseh agreed, a hint of playful defiance in his voice.

***

The following day, they put the finishing touches on their invention, the "Whitetail Whatchamacallit, Deer Life Saver, Crosswalk Teacher." Name was a mite long.

"Blacktop looks real sound," Sherman said, admiring their work. "Nice and level, too. Not that it matters out here, but it's craftsmanship just the same."

"The more realistic we make it, the better," Tecumseh agreed.

"So, what do we do now?" Sherman asked.

"Well, this part gets a bit technical," Tecumseh said. "So I asked my sister to help out." He waved toward an approaching figure. "Hi'ya, sis! She works for the Glo Fiber folks, a technical whiz. Mornin', Tammy."

"Mornin', boys," Tammy said, giving them a stern look. "I just wanna say, y'all are plumb crazy, and if you ever mention me in connection with this foolishness, they're gonna be serving *you* at Sexi Mexi. Not as guests, but as ingredients, understood?"

"We're trackin'," Sherman said, swallowing hard.

"So, what I'm gonna do," Tammy continued, "is use some scrap cable and wiring. I'm connecting this old answering machine to the signs. Volume's turned up to ten, and it's real loud. You have the tape, Sherman?"

"Here ya go," Sherman said, handing her a cassette. "The greatest hits of my beloved Caddie, Mabel Louise."

Tammy raised an eyebrow. "Yer sayin' it's an entire tape of automobile sounds. I'm trackin', son."

"Mabel's good and loud too," Sherman said. "I recorded her revvin' and honkin'. It'll scare the scat out of the deer."

"Well, I'm done hooking her up," Tammy said, wiping her hands on a rag.

"Looks real quality, sis," Tecumseh said.

"How's it gonna work, though?" Sherman asked.

"Just watch," Tammy said. "It's *real simple*. Remind you of anyone?"

Sherman shook his head. "Nope."

Tammy shrugged. "When a deer walks up, the motion sensor makes the arm come down, the car noises start, and the 'don't walk' light flashes."

"I'm trackin'," Sherman said.

"When the tape's done, the racket stops, the gates open, and the green light comes on," Tammy explained. "They clear the intersection, the gates close. And I rigged the button. Press it, and it drops out food on the far gate."

"Thank you kindly, sis," Tecumseh said. "Wanna stick around while we test it?"

"Not for all the Paw Paws in Paw Paw," Tammy said, shaking her head. "I'm getting out of here. You boys are nuts. Remember, Tecumseh, you're babysitting tonight. I left charts."

"She really gets to the point, doesn't she?" Sherman said.

"She's fairly direct," Tecumseh agreed. "But think on all the lives we're savin'."

"Well, let's try 'er out," Sherman said.

"Okay, you walk behind me like I'm the lead deer," Tecumseh said, winking. They walked to the intersection. The sensor triggered. The answering machine whirred to life, blasting Mabel Louise's Caddie Convertible revving engine and horn. The "don't walk" light flashed, and the gate clanked down.

"Damn, that's loud," Tecumseh said. "But it sure stops you."

"Sure does," Sherman winced. "From hearin' for a week."

They pressed the button. The cacophony of car noises abruptly cut off. The green light illuminated, and the gate rose. They crossed.

"And we get the food reward, right?" Sherman asked, his eyes wide with a boyish curiosity.

"You got it," Tecumseh said, a gentle smile tugging at the corners of his mouth.

"Course I don't really *want* to eat it, I'm just curious," Sherman clarified, like he was explaining why he was peekin' at a pie cooling on a windowsill.

"Course not," Tecumseh chuckled. "Never thought we would."

"What *is* it anyway?" Sherman asked, his brow furrowed in genuine wonder.

"Blueberries, blackberries, acorns, grass, and forbs all spun up," Tecumseh listed, like he was reciting a recipe for Aunt Tammy's special jam.

"It *does* sound tasty," Sherman admitted. "I hope it works."

"Well, they ain't gonna be no deer action today, we've scented it all up and such," Tecumseh said, shaking his head slightly.

"'Sposed to get a real humdinger of a storm tonight, oughta rinse our scents away real fine," Sherman said, nodding in agreement.

"How's about we get up with the chickens and meet here tomorrow? We'll hunker down real proper and see what we see? What say you?" Tecumseh asked, his eyes twinkling.

"I couldn't be more ready if I was the Apple Blossom Grand Marshal's alarm clock," Sherman said, beaming.

***

"Here come a buck and two does," Tecumseh whispered, his voice barely audible.

"I seen 'em. Real fine specimens," Sherman whispered back, eyes wide with excitement.

"Okay, they're a-comin' to the open gate. I'm all goose pimply waiting for the gate to come down," Tecumseh said, anticipation lacing his voice.

"I don't figure you'll wait long," Sherman reassured him. "There it goes!"

The crosswalk gate clanked shut. Mabel Louise's Caddie Convertible revving engine and horn blared from the answering machine, startling the approaching deer. They scattered.

"Holy smokes, what a racket! It's too loud, they done run away. Lord sakes, it did scare the scat straight out of 'em," Tecumseh exclaimed, shaking his head in disbelief.

"Darned if it didn't almost scare it outta me as well. Reckon we oughta bring it down to a six maybe?" Sherman suggested.

"Let's go five and see. I'll ratchet down the decimals iffen you scatter the scat?" Tecumseh offered, a mischievous glint in his eye.

"I'm trackin'. Hey, I just thoughta somethin', I'm gonna scat so I can scatter the scat," Sherman said, a grin spreading across his face.

"Don't give up yer day job, Sherm," Tecumseh teased, chuckling.

"Heck T, I don't have a day job, I work nights down at the FedEx. You know that," Sherman replied, a touch of mock indignation in his voice.

"Figure of speech, I was meanin', not like liberally. Read a book, why don'tcha," Tecumseh said, ribbing him good-naturedly. They walked out of their hiding spot, adjusted the volume, and re-hunkered down.

"Here come a doe," Sherman whispered, his breath clouding slightly in the cool morning air. "Don't wanna jinx us, but she looks like a smart one."

Tecumseh squinted. "Why do you say that?"

"See how her nose is all twitchy? Looks like she could bolt if a bullfrog farted," Sherman said, eyes fixed on the doe as she cautiously approached the crossing.

Tecumseh chuckled softly. "Sherm, your imagination troubles my mind at times." He watched the doe. "Okay, she's almost there... couple more steps..."

The crosswalk gates clanked shut. The (now quieter) recorded car noises startled the doe, but she didn't bolt. She froze, ears swiveling, eyes wide.

"Here we go! Gates down, sounds much better. She didn't bolt. She's just stopped there watching," Tecumseh breathed, relief in his voice.

"That's it, my deer friend," Sherman murmured, encouragingly.

They waited. Nine... ten. The gates began to rise. The green light flashed.

"Now, walk on through, you can do it," Tecumseh whispered, quietly proud. "Be the first of a new generation."

The doe hesitated, then stepped onto the blacktop and crossed.

"And there she goes!" Sherman exclaimed, awestruck.

"Good Lord, it worked!"

"Sure fire, it did," Tecumseh agreed, grinning.

"T," Sherman said, pulling out a mason jar. "I bought this home brew from clear up in Augusta for a special occasion, and this seems like it. Have a swig, my man."

Tecumseh whispered, "There's gonna be a plaque right here someday, maybe even a statue." Tecumseh took a long pull. "Ooh, that's like straight fire down my gullet. Shermie, today, we have changed the world!" he declared, quietly triumphant.

A woman's sharp voice cut through the morning. "What in the heck are you two doing out there in my backyard?"

"We're changing the world is all," Sherman said, rolling his eyes. Some folks just didn't recognize history in the making.

"Well, go change it in someone else's backyard, ya imbeciles," she retorted.

"Yes, ma'am," Tecumseh said.

"You think this is how Columbus felt?" Sherman asked, eyes wide.

"Lord, I hope not. From what I can gather, all Columbus felt was lost," Tecumseh chuckled.

***

Six months later.

"Whitetail Whatchamacallit, this is Tammi, how may we assist you?"

"How's things up there in Winchester?" the Mayor of Paris boomed. "Heard y'all invented something real helpful."

"Growin' by leaps and bounds," Tammi replied.

The mayor inquired about the different models, and Tammi explained the Highway Helper Two-Fifty, a ramp and bridge system.

"That sounds very exciting," the mayor said. "What would you recommend for our situation?"

"Let's get Tami out for a survey," Tammi suggested.

"Perfect. When can you do it?"

Tami K's voice came over the speaker, rustling papers in the background. "We're booked for three months, but I can squeeze you in then."

"I'm regretting being late," the mayor admitted. "It sounded like nonsense, but now? Ninety percent reduction in the 'clobber rate'—impressive."

"It's great for people too," Tammi said. "Fewer injuries, fewer car repairs, fewer dead creatures. Everybody wins."

***

Five years later.

"Whitetail Whatchamacallit, Tahmee J speaking."

"*New York Times* here," a woman said. "Doing a story on Whitetail Whatchamacallit's meteoric rise. That IPO was amazing."

"Yes, ma'am," Tahmee replied. "It's been another good year."

"I'd like to interview them," the woman said.

"They're in India now, back in two weeks," Tahmee said. "How about the sixteenth?"

"Perfect," the woman said. "What are they doing in India?"

"Discussing the Beef Bridge," Tahmee said. "A super-sized Highway Helper Two-Fifty. We're swamped with orders."

***

One year later.

"Graduating class of Harvard," Tecumseh began, addressing the crowd, "if you wanna know how we became Shenandoah Valley's first billionaires..."

"Find something everybody thinks is an impossible and stupid idea," Sherman chimed in.

"And that you're idiots for even attempting it," Tecumseh added.

"And then," they both said in unison, "make it work."

***

The very next day.

"Congratulations to Tecumseh Brown and Sherman Grant, honored by Winchester today. Whitetail Whatchamacallit, a global powerhouse, started right here. The 'Welcome to Winchester' signs have been updated, listing their birthplace. I'm Tam E Thornton. Good night, and save a life—a wild life."

The President of the United States approached them. "Listen fellas, congratulations on all you've accomplished."

"Thank you, Madame President," Sherman said.

"This is certainly an honor," Tecumseh added.

"You can call me Tammeey. I've heard you guys are the ones to turn to for clever solutions. I sure miss Virginia."

"Whatever we can do to help, ma'am," Sherman replied.

"Well," the President began, "for some reason, local traffic has become significantly slower all over the US, and deer are terrorizing people's gardens. Do you think you can tackle *that* for me?"

"Sure thing," Tecumseh said. "How would you feel about remote-controlled flight suits for deer?"

"I'm tracking," the President said.

The Battle of Route 42

JAMES BLAKEY

EMU's outside hitter Riley Voss wiped the sweat from her brow as Yoder Arena buzzed with a frenzy of tension, anticipation, and frustration. A contingent of SU faithful sporting red and white whooped and hollered, one voice jeering: "You're just a flightless bird!"

Home team fans in royal blue held their breaths and glared at the scoreboard. Match point in the fifth set, 14-13, with the Hornets of Shenandoah University holding the advantage. One point, and Shenandoah would claim the ODAC upset of the season. One point the other way, and the Royals would force deuce.

The serve wobbled from Shenandoah's back row, a vicious float from their defensive specialist, and Mia dove, popping it up with a clean forearm pass.

"High!" she screamed.

Arm cocked like a loaded spring, Riley exploded off the floor. She smashed a cross-court shot, aiming for Zone 1, but the SU libero read the angle like a chess master.

"Up!" she shouted, floating the ball toward the SU setter.

The setter leapt without hesitation, hands flashing beneath the ball, and delivered a quick set to Shenandoah's already airborne middle hitter. Eyes locked onto the ball, she snapped her wrist in a brutal top-spin spike, targeting EMU's vacant Zone 6.

Shenandoah fans sprung to their feet, sensing the kill.

The ball screamed downward, a blur of white, blue, and yellow. Unreturnable.

The point, the match, the upset—all guaranteed.

For Riley, the world slowed to a crawl. The roar of the crowd dulled to a distant hum, the fluorescent lights overhead stretching into streaks of gold. Her teammates, the crowd, the ball, suspended in a fleeting sliver of a moment. The shot's trajectory, a glowing line etched in the air, the spin telegraphing its landing spot with cruel clarity.

Her damp ponytail slapped her neck as Riley lunged right, dropping into a sprawl. Moving faster than the now sluggish ball, she caught up to the leather sphere. Left arm extended, elbow locked, platform angled just so. The ball thudded against her forearms like a muffled drum, and for a moment she thought it would pancake off her wrists and die on the floor. But it held, the ball popping up in a high, desperate arc toward the center of EMU's side.

Time snapped back to normal. Riley crashed to the floor at full speed, her head bouncing off the court.

Jess sprinted under the ball, hands soft as she bumped it toward Kayla. Shenandoah's blockers were caught flat-footed, reeling from the impossible dig. Kayla—who'd been quiet all match—took her chance. She leapt, form fierce, hammering a shot straight down the sideline, past Shenandoah's outstretched hands.

The ball banged the court with a satisfying thud, a hair inside the line. Point, EMU.

The Royals bench exploded, players spilling onto the court as the crowd roared in disbelief. Teammates swarmed Riley, shouting over each other—"Voss, that was insane!" "You're a freaking wizard!"—as the scoreboard ticked over: 14-14.

But Riley barely registered it. Still on her knees, one hand pressed to the floor, the other clutching her temple. Her head throbbing, and her balance shaky, like the court tilted beneath her.

Coach Daniels, whistle bouncing against his chest, jogged over. Teammates hovered nearby, cheers fading into murmurs.

Daniels knelt beside her. "Riley, look at me." He held up two fingers, eyes scanning her face. "How many?"

Riley blinked, the fingers blurring together. She tried to focus, tongue thick in her mouth. "T—two?"

"You're out. Concussion protocol." Daniels waved over the athletic trainer.

Riley wanted to protest, but the words wouldn't come—like her head was stuffed with cotton. The trainer helped her to her feet. Teammates clapped her on the back, their voices a distant echo—"Hell of a dig, Ri!" "You saved us!"—but she scarcely mustered a nod.

She sank onto the bench, an ice pack pressed to her temple as the trainer asked questions—her name, the date, what she'd eaten for breakfast. Riley answered mechanically, eyes fixed on the court. The Hornets were clearly rattled, shoulders slumped, movements sluggish. That dig sucked the wind out of them, and the Royals spotted cracks.

Two quick points, the last ball slamming to the floor untouched.

EMU for the win!

***

Riley sat propped up in a stiff hospital bed, the sterile white walls of Sentara RMH closing in on her. Her left shoulder ached from the hard fall during last night's match, a dull throb that matched the pulsing headache lingering behind her eyes. A tray of untouched green Jell-O sat on the bedside table. She killed the TV, kicking herself for forgetting her phone.

The door burst open with a familiar energy, teammates Jess and Kayla storming into the room.

Jess tossed her short blonde braid back and held her phone aloft like a trophy. "Voss, you're a freakin' celebrity!" she crowed, voice bouncing off the walls.

Riley raised an eyebrow, pushing herself up straighter against the pillows. "What're you talking about?" The sight of her teammates—still buzzing from last night's win—lifted the fog that had settled over her.

Kayla plopped onto the edge of the bed, hands fidgeting with excitement as she shoved the screen in Riley's face. "Sports-Center Top Ten, baby! That dig of yours is everywhere on Insta!"

A grainy clip from the match. Riley sprawling across the court, improbably catching Shenandoah's spike at the last possible instant. The commentator's voice blared through the tiny speaker: "At number two, action from the Old Dominion Athletic Conference. It might be Division Three, but this play proves the talent's first-rate with an unreal dig by senior Riley Voss of Eastern Mennonite University—match point on the line, and she keeps the rally alive!"

"Only number two?" Riley cracked a smile.

"Ohtani hit an inside-the-park grand slam." Jess shrugged. "Least he knocked the Mets out of the playoffs."

Kayla leaned closer, like she was sharing a secret. "Coach nearly lost it when he watched this morning. Says it's the best play he's seen. *Ever.*"

Riley felt a flush creep up her neck, a mix of pride and embarrassment. She scratched at the bandage on her wrist, a souvenir from the IV they'd stuck her with. "Not that big a deal," she muttered. "Just doing my job."

"Your job?" Jess snorted "You hit the floor so hard I thought you'd dent it. And we got the win because of you! Shenandoah didn't know what hit 'em after that."

Kayla nodded. "Totally deflated. Final two points were cake."

Her teammates kept chattering—about the celebration at the diner after the match, how Coach actually smiled for once, how the clip was blowing up TikTok with #VossTheBoss trending.

The door creaked open again, and Dr. Lee stepped in, a tablet tucked under her arm. A short woman with a calm demeanor that Riley appreciated since last night's endless questions—though now, something in her expression made Riley's chest tighten. The doctor glanced at the visitors, then offered a small smile. "I need a moment with Riley, if you don't mind."

"Yeah, sure. Don't eat her Jell-O, doc. It's probably the only thing keeping her sane." Jess winked at Riley. "When you get out of here, pizza from Marco's. I'm buying." She grabbed Kayla by the waist, and the pair ducked out.

Riley shifted in bed, hands fidgeting with the edge of the thin blanket. "So, what's the verdict? No concussion, right? I told the trainer I was fine—only a little woozy."

Dr. Lee tapped her tablet, scanning the screen before meeting Riley's gaze. "You're correct," she began, her voice steady. "The CT scan and neurological tests ruled out a concussion or worse, which is good news given the fall you took."

Riley exhaled, the knot in her chest loosening. "I'm cleared to play? We've got this match against Bridgewater, and—"

Dr. Lee raised a hand, cutting her off gently. "Not so fast. There's something else we found on the scans." She paused, her eyes softening with a weight Riley hadn't noticed before. "Riley, there's a mass in your brain—an abnormality..."

Riley heard the words... radiologist... tumor... neurosurgeon... brainstem... oncologist... but comprehension eluded her.

The room spun, and a sharp hum filled her ears, drowning out everything but the pounding of her own pulse.

***

True to her word, Jess grabbed two pies from Marco's—buffalo chicken and classic pepperoni. The three teammates joined by Mia the libero settled into Kayla's dorm in Cedarwood Hall. The space was a mess of volleyball gear, textbooks, and fairy lights strung along the walls. They sprawled on the floor, boxes open between them, paper plates scattered as they dug in.

Chatter started light—recapping practice, laughing about Kayla's wild swing that nearly took out the water cooler, speculating if Coach secretly practiced his scowl in the mirror. Mia replayed the clip for the tenth time, the commentator's voice hyping Riley's dig like it was an Olympic feat.

As the food dwindled, the conversation took a turn. Jess stretched out on her back, staring at the ceiling, and tossed out a random hypothetical. "Yo, what's the one thing you'd do if you only had, like, a month to live? No limits—go big."

Kayla wiped sauce off her chin. "Easy. Round-the-world trip. Hit every beach, maybe skydive in New Zealand. Gotta live it up, right?"

Mia tilted her head. "I'd probably chill with my family. Like, nonstop. Cook all my grandma's recipes, play board games with my little brother until he's sick of me. That kinda stuff."

Riley's stomach twisted. She set her half-eaten slice down and leaned against the wall. "I'd stay right here, I think. Play every match I could, even if I'm half-dead by the end. You jerks are my family anyway."

Jess propped herself up on her elbows, raising an eyebrow. "Half-dead? Geez, Voss, dramatic much? We'd drag you out there anyway—family doesn't bench family."

Riley forced a laugh that sounded brittle even to her. She sipped her Cherry Coke, the carbonation burning her throat, and steered things away from herself. "Yeah, well, you'd probably set me a brick and call it strategy, Jess. What's your big 'if I were dying' move?"

Jess shrugged, grabbing another slice. "I'd eat my weight in buffalo chicken pizza and tell everyone I've ever hated exactly what I think of 'em. Go out with no regrets."

The banter drifted after that—more random what-ifs, profound only in the dark. Riley cracked a few jokes, but her mind kept circling back to the tumor, the ticking clock she couldn't see. She hadn't told anyone. But sitting there, surrounded by her friends, she felt a flicker of something like resolve.

If time were short, maybe she should make it count.

***

Riley sat in the third row of her Advanced Public Speaking class, notebook open but untouched, a half-finished outline for her persuasive pitch scrawled in messy ink. The classroom in the Campus Center smelled faintly of chalk and stale coffee, the early-morning sun slanting through the windows and casting long shadows across the desks.

Tomorrow night: "The Battle of Route 42" against Bridgewater with the top seed on the line. But Riley's mind wasn't on volleyball. It was on the oncologist appointment scheduled for Friday morning, the one where she hoped to get answers.

Professor Hargrove stood at the front of the room, eyes scanning the roster as she called the next name for the day's presentations. "Riley Voss," she said, her tone clipped but expectant. "Your pitch is up. Let's see what you've got."

Riley's stomach dropped, fingers tightening around the edge of her notebook. Between practice and the constant loop of tumor-related dread, her focus had splintered.

The assignment: Deliver a three-minute persuasive pitch for a hypothetical PR campaign. Riley chose to pitch a mental health awareness initiative for student-athletes, something weighing her court down now. She threw together a few talking points late last night, but the words jumbled in her mind, tangled like a net after a bad block.

Riley stood, smoothing her EMU Volleyball hoodie, and shuffled to the front of the room, sneakers squeaking against the linoleum. Twenty pairs of eyes followed her—classmates she laughed with over group projects, debated with over media ethics, waiting to judge her delivery.

Professor Hargrove leaned against her desk, arms crossed, pen tapping rhythmically against her clipboard. "Whenever you're ready." A faint edge in her voice that told Riley that the professor sensed her lack of polish.

Riley cleared her throat, setting her notebook on the podium, hands shaky as she glanced at her outline—stats on athlete burnout, a call for campus counseling resources, a vague tagline about "breaking the stigma." She opened her mouth to start, her voice catching on the first word. "So, uh, mental health among student-athletes is, like, a huge issue..." She winced internally at the stumble, cheeks flushing as a few classmates shifted in their seats.

Her heart pounded faster, a familiar panic creeping in—the kind reserved for match point, not the classroom. She tried to push through, rattling off a stat about thirty percent of college athletes reporting anxiety, but her tone sounded hollow, detached. Her thoughts circling back to Friday's appointment, the what-ifs piling up like bricks: What if it's aggressive? What if there's no treatment? What if I don't even make it to ODAC finals? The room felt smaller, the air thicker. Professor Hargrove's pen stopped tapping, her gaze narrowing.

Riley's eyes darted to the clock above the door—two minutes left in her allotted time, and she hadn't even hit her main argument. Her chest tightened, breath shallow. As she opened her mouth to pivot to her call-to-action, it happened again: the world slowed to a crawl.

The fluorescent lights overhead stretched into golden streaks, the hum of the classroom fading to a low, distorted drone. Her classmates' faces froze mid-expression—some bored, some curious, one guy in the back row sneaking a glance at his phone. Professor Hargrove's pen hovered mid-tap, lips parted like she was about to interrupt. The clock's second hand immobile, each tick stretching into an eternity. Riley's heartbeat thumped once, loud and deliberate, as her vision sharpened, every detail snapping into focus—the grain of the wooden podium, the smudge of ink on her thumb, the faint edge of anxiety in her window reflection.

In that suspended moment, Riley's mind raced, untangling the mess of her thoughts. She saw her pitch laid out like a volleyball play: the stats were her serve, the personal story she hesitated to share was her set, and the call-to-action was her spike. She thought of her teammates—Jess's relentless energy, Mia's sure grip, Kayla's quiet grit—and how they'd carried each other through the season. If she could dig a match-point spike against Shenandoah, she could do this. Tumor or no tumor.

Time snapped back like a rubber band, the world rushing in with a vengeance—the rustle of papers, a faint cough from the back row, the weight of Hargrove's stare. Riley exhaled, fingers gripping the podium as she abandoned her outline and spoke from the gut.

"Look, I know what it's like to feel like you're drowning out there." Her voice was raw but clear. "I'm a volleyball player. We push ourselves to breaking points nobody sees—practices, games, pressure to perform. But we don't talk about it. We can't keep pretending it's fine. EMU needs a campaign—posters, workshops, real conversations—so athletes know it's okay to ask for help. Because if we don't, we're setting ourselves up to crash."

Riley leaned into her pitch, speech steadying as she wove in stats—how one in five athletes wrestle with mental health. She painted a vision of EMU's campaign breaking that silence, her call-to-action landing sharp and clear, ending with 'Break the stigma, build the team' as the room leaned in.

"Solid pivot," Hargrove said as Riley returned to her seat, her tone carrying a rare note of praise. "Work on the prep next time, but you landed the emotional appeal. Good recovery."

Riley nodded, sinking into her chair as the next student was called. The adrenaline fading into a quiet ache.

***

Riley glanced at her phone, its screen flashing two thirty-seven. She sat cross-legged on the floor of her single in Northlawn Hall, back against the bed frame, the dim glow of her desk lamp casting a warm circle of light.

Her laptop sat open on the carpet beside her, tabs cluttered with search remnants of her hours-long internet scour—medical journals, neuroscience forums, Reddit threads, all offering fragments but no answers about the time-slowing episodes being connected to her tumor.

She'd watched the SportsCenter clip on loop until her eyes burned. At full speed, it was undeniable—her body a blur as she dove across the court faster than any human should be capable of. Her teammates laughed it off as adrenaline, the commentators called it "heart," but Riley knew better. Time slowed—physically slowed—around her, giving her those impossible seconds to react. And again in her public speaking class, when the pressure of her pitch made the room stretch into molasses.

The tumor must be doing this. But how? And why? The closest she'd come was a neuroscience blog about extreme focus altering perception, but that didn't explain the replay, the tangible proof of her speed. This wasn't perception. This was real.

If she could really slow time, she needed to control it. In Riley's three years, EMU had never beaten Bridgewater. Worse, each loss came against her former best friend, Ashley Carter, BC's star middle hitter. Riley and Ash co-captained their travel team until a falling out over a boy whose name Riley couldn't remember.

If Riley could harness this... whatever *this* was... she could lead EMU to victory over Bridgewater, claim the top seed. But sitting here in her dorm, safe and still, the spark she'd felt in those high-stakes moments was nowhere to be found.

Riley squeezed her eyes shut, trying to recreate the conditions. Her volleyball in her lap, a worn Wilson with faded red and white panels. She gripped it tight, imagining the gym—the roar of the crowd, the squeak of sneakers, the weight of match point. Her heartbeat quickened as she pictured Ashley across the net, eyes cold and sharp, the ball rocketing toward her in a kill shot.

"Focus," Riley muttered. She tried to summon the feeling—the way her pulse pounded against her ribs during the Shenandoah dig, the way the world had stretched into golden streaks, the ball's spin a lazy spiral.

Nothing happened.

Riley opened her eyes. The room stayed stubbornly normal, the faint hum of her mini fridge droning in the corner.

"Why won't it work?" The ache behind her eyes pulsed sharper, as if mocking her effort.

She recalled the moments it had happened—the Shenandoah match, her class presentation. Both instances, the stakes were real, the stress visceral. Here, in the quiet of her dorm, there was no pressure, no danger. Just her alone, pushing for what wouldn't yield.

Maybe she needed the real thing: real stress, real stakes.

Like "The Battle of Route 42."

***

Nininger Hall was a cauldron of noise, the stands bursting for the EMU-Bridgewater grudge match, a battle for the ODAC's top seed. The fifth set had stretched into a brutal back-and-forth, but EMU held the lead at 13-11, two points from victory. Riley stood in Zone 4, her sneakers gripping the hardwood, sweat stinging her gaze as the crowd's roar pulsed in her ears. Across the net, Ashley crouched low, her face a mask of frustration and defiance. Their falling out years ago fueled every point tonight, but this wasn't personal. It was everything: the match, the team, maybe even Riley's own survival.

Tonight, Riley felt it—whatever *it* was—simmering beneath her skin, a spark waiting to ignite. And when the first rally of the third set pushed her to the brink—a blistering shot from Ashley she'd barely dug—it clicked. She'd focused on her heartbeat, her breath, the raw edge of adrenaline, and time slowed, giving her precious moments to react.

Since then, Riley summoned the distortion multiple times, each instance more deliberate than the last. She triggered it to dig a cross-court spike from Bridgewater's middle hitter, her body blurring across the court to pop the ball up for Mia to set.

Her teammates reacted with disbelief—"What the hell, Voss?" Jess yelled, half-laughing, half-awestruck—as Riley recovered in a fraction of a second, faster than anyone could track.

Later, she'd used it again on a receive, to read a floater's dip and pass it perfectly to Mia, setting up a kill that left Bridgewater's defense scrambling.

"Unreal hands, Riley!" Mia screamed from the setter's spot.

Ashley, though, was taking a pummeling. Riley had targeted her relentlessly—spike after spike aimed at her zone, forcing her into desperate dives and shaky passes. During one rally, Riley triggered the distortion mid-air on an outside hit, adjusting her angle to send a line shot screaming past Ashley's block, slamming into Zone 1 before Ashley could react.

The Bridgewater libero glared at her teammate, muttering something about "getting it together." Ashley's jaw tightened, eyes flashing with a mix of anger and helplessness as Riley dominated point after point. Each distortion left Riley's chest heaving, her head throbbing faintly, but the thrill of control—of bending time to her will—kept her pushing.

Now, at 13-11, Bridgewater's serve came—their specialist's topspin cut toward Zone 6.

Riley called it—"Mine!"—and dropped low, her platform steady as the ball slammed into her forearms. The dig was clean, arcing high toward Mia.

"Set me!" Riley shouted as she sprinted to the left pin, her approach automatic—left, right, plant.

Mia delivered a perfect back-set, and Riley leapt, her stare locking on Ashley, leading Bridgewater's double block at the net.

The crowd's roar faded to a dull hum as Riley focused inward, power coursing through her.

The gym's lights stretched into golden streaks, the ball's spin a lazy spiral, Ashley's arms inching upward in her block. Riley had seconds—real seconds—where no one else did. She found the gap in Ashley's positioning—a sliver down the line—and adjusted mid-air. She snapped her wrist, sending a line shot screaming past the block, straight into Zone 1.

But in that frozen moment, Riley felt something—a sharp pop inside her head, like a balloon bursting behind her eyes. Pain flared, brief but intense, then faded to a dull ache as time snapped back. The ball slammed down, untouched, the sound a thunder-clap echoing in the suddenly silent gym. The whistle blew—14-11, match point for EMU.

Her teammates erupted, but Riley stumbled on her landing, hand flying to her temple as a wave of dizziness hit.

"Voss, you good?" Jess called, jogging over.

Riley forced a grin, but the ache in her skull throbbed sharper. She took a step toward the service line, ready to seal the match, when the gym tilted—a sudden lurch like the floor dropped out. Her knees buckled, and she sank, one hand braced against the hardwood. The crowd's buzz dimmed to a distant murmur, her vision swimming with golden flecks.

"Riley!" Kayla barked, dropping to a crouch beside her, hands hovering uselessly.

Mia rushed over, their shouts overlapping—"What's wrong?" "You okay?"—as Coach Daniels waved for a timeout.

The whistle sounded, a ghostly trill unable to pierce Riley's haze. The pop unleashed something—a floodgate cracking open. The tumor, wild and unmoored, its pressure shifting in ways she couldn't grasp. Her power flared too bright, too long, and now it was costing her.

The gym blurred into chaos—teammates' worried faces, Bridgewater's bench whispering, Ashley's stare cutting through from across the net. Riley tried to stand, but her legs wobbled, forcing her down.

Jess gripped her shoulder, voice low and fierce: "Sit tight, Voss. We've got this."

Mia nodded while Kayla muttered, "One point, for you."

Coach helped Riley to the bench as her ache dulled to a faint pulse. Riley's chest tightened—not with pain, but with the weight of letting go. Time wouldn't bend for her now; it was for her teammates to finish.

Riley slumped on the bench, her blue jersey damp with sweat. Coach hovered nearby, muttering about trainers, but her eyes stayed locked on the court. The gym lights glared too bright, the edges of her vision smudged with golden streaks.

She watched, half-dazed, as Hayleigh, subbing for Riley, stepped to the service line. Ball cradled in her steady hands, she tossed it high, her serve cutting a sharp arc over the net.

Bridgewater's back row scrambled, Ashley barking orders from her spot at the net. The ball ricocheted off a defender's arms, sailing high. Jess darted under it, her setter's fingers flicking the ball to Kayla, who coiled and snapped a cross-court kill. Ashley's hands stretched, deflecting it, but not enough. The ball grazed the block and dropped, kissing the hardwood.

The gym erupted—teammates' screams, the crowd's roar, the whistle's shrill blast—but Riley heard it all through an underwater hum, her head lolling slightly. Jess pumped a fist, Mia spun to point at her on the bench, and Kayla grinned, sharp and quick.

"For you, Ri!" Mia yelled, voice cutting through the haze.

Riley managed a weak nod, her heart pounding with pride and something heavier—relief, maybe—as the scoreboard flipped: 15-11, EMU victorious.

She caught Ashley's gaze through the chaos—a flicker of awe, maybe even respect, passing between them. Ashley's shoulders slumped, her face flushed from the pummeling, but she gave a small nod, her lips twitching into the ghost of a smile before turning to join her team. Not a full reconciliation, but a crack in the wall they'd built.

***

Riley sat in the oncologist's office, hands clenched in her lap.

Dr. Nguyen turned the screen toward her, his brow furrowed in a way that made her stomach twist. "Riley, I don't know how to say this." His voice was tinged with disbelief. "The mass—it's gone. Completely gone. No trace of it on the scans. No scar tissue, no remnants, nothing."

Riley blinked. "Gone? How—how does that even happen?"

Dr. Nguyen shook his head, flipping through the images again. "It doesn't. Medically, it's impossible. We've double-checked the scans, compared them to your last ones—it's like it was never there. I've never seen anything such as this in my career."

Riley remained silent, the memory of last night's match vivid—the way she'd moved, faster than humanly possible, the way time bent to her will.

Then, *pop!*

Had the tumor... done this? Had it given her something, some inexplicable ability, and then burned itself out? She didn't say it out loud—it sounded too wild—but the thought lodged in her mind like a perfect set.

Dr. Nguyen leaned back, still frowning. "We'll run more tests to be sure, but for now... you're clear. It's a miracle, frankly."

Riley left the office, stepping into the crisp October air lighter than she'd been in days. The tumor gone—whatever it had unlocked, it had taken itself with it.

Maybe it was better that way.

Maybe it wasn't meant to be explained.

Maybe it was just... hers.

The Long-Sought *I. batatas*

STEPHEN A. RODDEWIG

AIR HISSED AS THE ramp lowered, my rebreather fighting a valiant but ultimately doomed defense against the putrid taste of this world's air as it rushed in. At least I knew it would not shorten my lifespan after the scrubbers and carbon filters had done their duty.

Shorten my lifespan more than the already truncated life expectancy of a member of the Scout Regiment, anyway. My commanding officer informed me I had already beaten the odds when I returned from my first mission alive and with all limbs accounted for.

Still, even my EnviroArmor suit could not fully protect me from the silent killer: radiation. A fact I was reminded of as I took my first step onto the tainted ground and the detectors buzzed. Even a footfall was enough to disturb the layer of radioactive silt that had fallen.

Fallen like "snow," a phenomenon localized to this world. I had yet to experience this weather event but read much about it in the cultural artifact *Breaking Dawn*. I hoped to make use of my learnings in my upcoming negotiations with the surviving indigenous population.

Yes, the humans who once sprawled across the earth had advanced far enough to harness the power of the atom. Quite impressive for a civilization so impulsive.

Impulsive enough to turn that power on *themselves.*

Here, the scars had mostly healed. The detonations had not been close enough to flatten the existing structures. A blessing from the Hyperion Drift considering the penultimate objective.

The valley unfolding before me may have been spared the worst effects of the nuclear detonations, but nowhere was truly safe. Behemoths roamed these hills, as evidenced by the pagan idols the survivors had built in the place named for them: Dinosaur Land.

Fortunately, I had yet to encounter these titans and thus had not needed to test how effective my anti-material rifle was against their armored hides. Each time the *Winged Thresher* flew past the monuments, I was filled with a strange mixture of awe and dread.

Every sojourn to this valley, the giants' domain, was a risk. And I hoped this would be my last.

It was time to put the production facility back into operation and fulfill the command of the Emperor. Preferably before a roving dinosaur crushed it underfoot. It seemed another mercy bestowed by the Hyperion Drift that this had not already occurred, and I did not intend to find out how long this streak of cosmic fortune would last.

I landed a safe distance from the habitation unit. Prior experience taught me the indigenous population did not take well to an abrupt flattening of a dwelling from the backblast of the *Thresher's* hyperengines, and prior but more recent experience taught me that the surface dwellers did not find an abrupt landing in their "front yard" any less agitating.

Never mind the added risk from the time it took me to cross the land on foot from my discreet landing site, both from the radiation and ever-present possibility of dinosaur mauling.

But I suppose one could not blame these survivors for not observing the High Courtesies given they had squandered their chance to join the Interstellar Imperium by destroying all their advancements in one "Very Bad Day," as the locals liked to describe it.

I still *did* blame them, it has to be said. But even more recent experience taught me that shooting one clan member in the leg did not advance diplomatic relations with the rest of the group.

Never mind that my ultrasound-enabled visor allowed me to place the round where no arteries existed within the thigh.

The heated bolt even cauterized the wound. But though many words were offered to me after the shot, none could be described as gratitude. Fortunately, their antiquated weapons only scuffed the enamel on my EnviroArmor. Imagine, the power to control atoms but still relying on basic carbon ignition to propel your rounds.

We evolved to the far superior slingshot-powered gun millennia ago.

Strange lot, these humans. Descended from a common tree shared with the Imperium, and yet, distinct in so many ways. Most of them stupid.

I reached the property line, reminding myself that the concept of Common Imperial Domain did not exist among these inhabitants and that crossing the crudely made fence could be seen as an act of aggression.

Soon enough, my taller than average frame was noticed by the residents inside the dwelling. They marched out, doing their best to look menacing with puny "firearms" at the ready.

Their best, of course, being nowhere near enough for one who faced the spider hordes of Daishaka during Scout Regiment initiation.

The biggest of the party approached me, still only reaching my chest. "You the owner of that ship that passed overhead?" he asked, seemingly stuck between the impulse to look up and an equal desire *not* to look up and acknowledge our size difference.

"Yes," I answered, having remembered to set my rebreather's voice enhancer to Pacify from its default Terrify setting. "I trust your dwelling was not damaged in any way by its passage."

His eyes squinted at me above pocked cheeks, a classic sign of long-term radiation exposure. "Why? All the stories of you spacemen I've heard say you come here, take what you want, and shoot anyone that says anything about it."

I was grateful for my sealed helmet so he could not see my sheepish grin. "Yes, well, we have tried to learn from our, er, *predecessors.*"

That predecessor, of course, being me a few hundred rotations ago.

"All right," the man said, his rifle lowering a tenth of a degree. "So what do you want with us?"

I called up an image on my visor. "Are you a member of the Shenahan clan?"

The man started to shake his head when one of the women of the group piped up, "Kyle, you dummy! That's our family name."

"Oh, I forgot," the one known as Kyle said. "Steph there is much better about history and books than I am. Life's hard enough just fighting to survive, you know?" He nodded to my pistol holster and the anti-material rifle strapped across my back. "Surely you can understand. You have the look of a warrior. Not a reader."

The idiot known as Kyle could not have realized that accusations of mental incompetence were a great offense in the Imperium. Punishable by death for the accuser if found to be false. I had to keep repeating "he does not know" silently as I felt my hand twitch with the urge to draw my pistol.

Instead, the Pacify setting could not fully compensate as I growled, "I have read more than one thousand books since I was born. Including dozens written by your kind."

Further confirmation of my voice enhancer's lapse came as the man stepped back, his shoulders tensing. If he could have seen the fire in my eyes, his retreat would have turned into a rout. But mortal terror would not serve the mission.

So I took a deep breath, attempting to even my tone out so the enhancer could do its work. "That is of no significance to this discussion. I need one of the Shenahan clan to accompany me on an important mission."

Foolish Kyle attempted to square his shoulders and straighten himself to his full height. "Why should any of us go with you?"

"I don't know if we're being offered a choice, Kyle," Steph piped up from the main group.

It was time to put all of my cultural learnings to the test.

"This is not a demand. It is a..." I scanned the planetary dialect dictionary on my ocular display "...*request*. Allow me to offer gifts in exchange for your service."

Kyle appeared to be about to refuse when Steph shouted, "For God's sake, Kyle, he's a high-tech spaceman. He probably has some great stuff!"

"Fine," the idiot known as Kyle grunted. "What are you trading?"

The garments I had acquired on past trips were well received. Considering the ragged appearance of the Shenahan clan, they were sorely needed. No one looked twice at the questionable stains that spoke to how some of the clothes were gained. The one known as Steph seemed quite taken by the books I offered, though I held onto *Breaking Dawn*. To continue my cultural education, of course.

(Definitely not because I think Jacob still has a shot with Bella, and I need to see my chosen warrior pull it off.)

But when the human artifact known as "chocolate" appeared, they all but shoved Kyle at me as their newly chosen envoy.

"No," I said, pointing past him. "Let her come with me."

Kyle followed my finger. "Steph?" He turned back, eyes narrowing. "Why? So you can have your way with her in the woods?"

I refrained from informing him just how disgusting of an idea it would be for me to unseal my suit and expose myself to this vile atmosphere, let alone procreate with one of their ranks. Cultural education had its perks, as I continued to prove in real time.

Some of my revulsion still carried through the voice enhancer's filter. "No, because she appears to have inherited all the brains your gene pool has to offer."

An assertion only reinforced by Kyle's lack of a dispute as he nodded and said, "Yeah, okay."

So, clothing, books, and chocolate exchanged, Steph strolled up to the fence line. "All right," she said with mild curiosity, "what am I helping you with?"

I turned toward a cracking strip of gray midway through capitulation to the grasses and weeds that now sprouted from its wounds. "Follow, and all will become clear."

I had to modulate my pace to allow her to keep up, given the difference between our stride lengths. That, and the EnviroArmor boosted my movements for peak efficiency. The continued buzzing of the radiation sensors kindled my impatience until I stopped and held out my arms.

"Climb up," I instructed.

"All right," she said, resting her back against one forearm and slinging her legs over the other. "But do you mind if we go into the trees first? Never know what kind of weirdos might be watching."

"What do you mean?"

"You really want to have your way with me out here in the wide open?" She shrugged. "Fine."

I almost dropped her in alarm. But allowing her to hit her head against the crumbling asphalt was the last thing the mission needed. "No, that is not what this is about."

"Oh," she said after a moment. This time the word came out more as a sigh as she repeated, "Fine."

Only the Emperor could possess the wisdom to know why I did not let this conversation die in its tracks and instead said, "You seem disappointed."

Steph shrugged. "I'm a young woman. Young women have needs. And forgive me for going for a man without radiation burns or pox."

I felt a twinge of amusement as I countered, "I am in a suit. You cannot possibly know that."

She threw up her hands. "I guess not, but at least you're someone different. I've grown up knowing the same people my whole life. Do you know how unappealing it is when you're the only person with half an intellect for miles around?"

A new sense of discomfort far more off-balancing than the venomous bite of the Daishaka had taken hold, and my voice felt quite unfamiliar as I said, "Can we... please get back to the mission?"

Steph exhaled and crossed her arms. "Yeah, yeah. Sorry for putting my own needs first." Then curiosity took over. "Where are we going, anyway?"

"To an old sanctuary of your clan's," I replied before shifting into a tactical run, the combined weight and power of my footfalls making the pavement crunch beneath my boots. "Now hold on."

I breathed the next part so the voice enhancer would not pick it up. "...spider monkey."

In a condensed amount of time, we reached the production facility that lay along the remains of the road. I set Steph down, pointing to the ground before us.

"Watch your step, if you will."

"Why? All I see are a bunch of weeds."

I smiled within my helmet. "Surely you recognize an irrigation system when you see one."

She looked closer, and then the snaking lines of rubber hose laid out in neat rows came into focus. I opened a hole in the pulse shield that surrounded the facility, motioning for her to precede me through the gap.

"To keep us out, right?" she asked, noting the shimmering edges of the opening.

"Scavengers of all kinds, not just humans." I picked up a bucket and scattered growth nutrients as we walked toward the structure at the center of my garden. "These plants are very important to our—*my* Emperor. Each one is well cared for, exposed to the optimum amount of sunlight by the shield, watered at ideal times, and planted in soil with the best pH."

Steph grinned. "It's kind of cute, seeing a man so committed to gardening."

"*Cultivation*," I corrected far too quickly, and her grin only widened.

"Uh, huh. So what are you growing here?"

"We know it as the Almighty Plant of Honeyed Taste. You know it as the sweet potato."

She guffawed. "That's what's so precious? You gave my family all that rare stuff for help growing *sweet potatoes?* Why not just grow them on your own planets or wherever you came from?" After another look, she shrugged. "Besides, you seem to have it fully under control. What can I do?"

"Many attempts have been made to reproduce *Ipomoea batatas* off-world, but while its cousin *Solanum tuberosum* has proven just as hardy on Imperium planets, the 'sweet potato' refuses to grow anywhere but Earth. And attempts to reproduce the flavor by adding sweeteners to *Solanum tuberosum* have resulted in many Martyrs for the Emperor." I shuddered, recalling what became of that lab when the potato plants accidentally gained sentience. "And cultivation is not the issue."

"Then what is?"

"Come with me," I said, moving toward the door to the production facility.

Steph glanced at the roof, then paused. "You restored the sign?"

"I have restored the entire facility," I said, holding the door open.

She remained still. "Yeah, but the sign. The sign looks brand new. Did you repaint that?"

"Optimum functionality is crucial to the mission."

"Sure, but what does an advertisement have to do with that?"

Suddenly I was glad the helmet concealed my face as I looked off to the side. "I, uh, like history."

She laughed. "You're a collector! This is incredible. Walking around all high and mighty spaceman is a nostalgia junkie. He's more and more Earthlike by the minute."

I could have feigned outrage at what would have otherwise been a great slight. But she was onto something, and for reasons unknown, I felt like I could be honest with her. "We do not have art like this in the Imperium. It makes me a bit sad that there will be no more created. So once displays like this are gone..."

Steph's amusement fell away at the somber thought. "Yeah, good point." She took one last look at the billboard. "It's nice, too. I like the smiling potato guy. Even if it's a bit macabre that he's promoting the consumption of a bunch of his own kind."

"Then prepare yourself," I said, ducking through the Earth-dweller-sized door. "Because there are many more artifacts of the Route 11 Potato Chips business to see."

After several moments staring in disbelief at the display room returned to its original state, Steph turned back to me. "I take it back. You're not a collector. You're a curator."

"A bit of both," I said with a chuckle. "Many of the signs and other artifacts on these walls had been taken from this place when I first arrived. I returned them over the course of my scouting."

"Speaking of, I still don't get what you need from me."

"One more room and all will be clear."

Through the staff entrance, we moved to the production floor. Spotless, sterilized, and restored to full working order. The only difference was the power now came from a sun-fed reactor unit I had installed on the roof, which, as a byproduct of the fusion, also produced the water that fed the field outside.

"Wow, you really go all out on preservation," Steph said, clearly impressed.

"This time, the restoration serves a purpose."

"And the other preservation work didn't?"

I shrugged inside my EnviroArmor. "That was more to pass the time while I waited for the potatoes to grow. Turns out, even ideal cultivation conditions can only speed the process so much. And I read too fast. Not enough books around anymore. And all the stuff I have downloaded from the Imperium Archives is a bit, well, *dull*."

Steph snorted. "'Not enough books to keep me company' could describe my whole life." She placed her hand on my armored forearm. "Sounds like we're both a bit lonely."

For a moment, I almost wished I could actually feel her hand on my skin. Before recalling the many creeds that would violate. And the mission at hand.

"Yes, but when my work here is complete, I can return to my warrior brothers and sisters."

She sighed. "Of course. So, what is it I need to do?"

I turned to a shelf in the Ready area where workers would equip sanitary gear in a bygone time and where now a massive scrubber would scour my suit before I entered the floor. "When I first came to Earth, I gathered many artifacts along the way. The Emperor found many of them fascinating, but none more so than this." The bag of Route 11 Sweet Potato Chips crinkled in my gloved hand as I lifted it, dislodging a layer of dust. "He had never tasted anything as divine. And thus I was sent back. Over and over to satisfy his appetite for the Earthen delicacy."

Steph reached out to take the bag, and I drew back. "Whoa, okay," she said, putting up her other hand. "I'll be gentle."

After a moment's hesitation, I handed over the bag. "Take care, please. There are very few left."

She tapped her chin. "You know, I think I remember being given a bag like this once." I leaned forward at the thought of another bag in existence, but she shook her head. "I ate them. Sorry. It was a gift from my family for my birthday." Then another head shake. "Different flavor, too. They were good, though. Mom said our family used to make them."

"Yes, as the records here indicated." I nodded. "Some of the spices most critical to recreating the Route 11 Sweet Potato Chips recipe were labeled 'family secret.' Thus, I needed someone of your line to fill in the missing gaps."

Steph's brow furrowed. "You couldn't, like, run chemical analyses or something?"

"That was my first idea, but chemical makeup cannot fully explain flavor. There are some things unique to this planet and the way your spices are grown that Imperium technology cannot replicate."

I withdrew a bag that matched the proportions of the faded original Steph held. "This is the closest I have come to recreating the forebearer, as the scans indicate. But I need that family secret of yours. Only then will they be truly authentic."

Her mouth opened, and I zeroed in on her lips, waiting for the first syllable of the words that would unlock my ultimate goal. At last, the mission neared completion.

So intense was my focus that it took several heartbeats to realize no noise was being emitted. Only a rush of air as the rest of the respiratory system waited for the appropriate nervous system signals to dictate which vocalizations to make.

Shifting my gaze up, I found wide eyes and pale cheeks. The look produced within my chest a burst of panic only comparable to the time the *Thresher* and I had nearly crossed the event horizon of a black hole.

"You... you do not know the family secret," I said, filling in the words that refused to finish forming on her lips.

Before I knew what was happening, I had slumped against the wall. My impact with the floor made the whole room shake. Normally, I would have cursed myself for carelessness and set about checking all the fittings on the kettle, conveyor belt, and packing machines. But none of that seemed to matter anymore.

"Look, I'm sorry, but the Shenahans abandoned this place when the Very Bad Day came." Steph's voice came from somewhere right above me but impossibly distant at the same time. "We didn't think we'd ever return, so the tricks of the family trade were never passed to the next generation. I didn't know that's what you wanted, or I would have told you back at the farm."

Somehow, my helmet had never felt so heavy before. I continued staring at the floor, wondering if the radiation would finish the job if I simply sat here long enough.

Until I recalled that all radioactive material had been scoured from this place. The very first thing I did when I located the old facility, in fact.

I cursed my former self. Especially the self that had come across the strange bag full of crumbly material that offered no resistance at all to the hydraulic power gauntlet holding it. And once that bag had popped and the chips, now turned to silt, ran through my fingers, I cursed the former self who then noticed the *second* bag next to it and brought it back to Imperium space.

Why did I not bring back the Sour Cream and Onion bag? That chemical makeup would be far simpler to replicate.

Even now, my loyalty remained strong enough that I would not violate the first creed: never take your life in the face of defeat. Instead, give it up as a meat shield to slow the enemy's advance.

But there was no advancing enemy to be found other than my existential dread.

Steph apparently took my silence as anger. "Look, we'll give back all the stuff, okay? I think there's some Route 11 memorabilia squirreled away in the house you could have, too."

That last sentence made me start to look up. Until I remembered that I had failed the Emperor in my primary quest. My reason for being. Hobbies were for the victorious.

Steph knelt in front of me. "Seriously, I'm sorry." Her voice took on an alarmed note. "Just please, *please* don't hurt my family. They're idiots sometimes—well, most of the time—but they love me and they're all I've got in this awful world."

Startled, I met her wide eyes. "I would never hurt them. *Or* you. You are the progenitors. The ones who built this place. It is in the Shenahan shadow that I have worked these many rotations."

Steph breathed a sigh of relief and sat back. "Okay, because you could tear us apart if you wanted."

I started to agree, ready to cite many prior examples, but thought better of it. "I am not upset about the items I traded. They were of no use to me."

"Then what are you upset about?"

"If I cannot recreate the Route 11 Sweet Potato Chip with the original recipe, I will have failed the Emperor. Failure is not accepted in the Interstellar Imperium. I am far too young to be the latest Martyr of the Emperor."

"Oh, okay, I'm getting it now." Steph stood up and retrieved the bag of new sweet potato chips. "So, these are the closest you've gotten to the original?"

I nodded.

A smirk drew up the side of her face. "And you added the old logo for extra authenticity, right?"

I pointed to the original chip bag in her other hand. "Actually, the brown is slightly darker. Imperium ink has a different chemical makeup than what you used here on Earth. I mixed it with some organic compounds from this planet, but it is still a few chromas off when put under a spectrophotometer..." my voice trailed off as I saw her eyes sparkling. "What?"

"Your attention to detail. It's cute." She giggled. "Especially when you've spent your whole life around people that keep having to repair the same fence post because they never bother to measure anything."

She looked at the two bags, squinting. "Yeah, I guess I see what you mean about the color difference."

A new wave of despair washed over me. I could not recreate a simple plastic bag, even *with* the original equipment. How could I have ever thought I could tackle the infinitely more complex feat of recreating an Earthen delicacy from scratch?

Steph must have seen my shoulders slump, despite the EnviroArmor. "I'm kidding, dummy." She punched my armored shin playfully. Just in time, I disabled the electric countermeasure that would otherwise have zapped her across the room. "They look the exact same. You did great."

Somehow, hearing that from the descendant of the original architects of this place meant all the more to my ailing spirit. Then I remembered the most important element lay *inside* the bag.

"The Emperor will not care about the design if the contents are not perfect," I sighed.

Steph weighed both bags in her hands. "Well, have you tried your latest batch?"

I shook my head. "The chemical analyses indicate they are not a perfect match. What would be the point?"

"Just because there's discrepancies doesn't mean it won't taste the same. Like the shade of brown on the bag. Not everyone is going to put your creations under a microscope." I started to correct her when she continued, "*Spectrophotometer.* Sorry."

Her "sorry" sounded less than sincere. A distinct Earth-dweller dialect known as sarcasm, if my cultural learnings were any indication.

"So," she said, holding up the two bags, "can I try them?"

After a moment's paralysis at the thought of losing one of the last remaining original samples, I nodded.

With measured movements, she opened both bags, keeping the tear at the seams and not allowing the sides to be ripped. A clear sense of care and reverence I appreciated more than she could know. She sampled the original recipe, taking her time to fully register the flavor profile.

Then Steph withdrew one of my chips and chewed it an equal length of time.

I allowed her to mull it over in silence, not wanting to rush or bias her in any way as she furrowed her brow one way and then the other.

Finally, she spoke, "You're right. They're not the same."

"Yes, I alrea—"

Steph bounced my bag in her hand. "These ones are better."

"Better?"

My head dropped back toward the floor.

Apparently, she had expected a different reaction. "Hey, wait, that's a good thing. You improved the recipe!"

"The Emperor liked the *original.* I cannot know if he will like the 'improved' recipe."

"I suppose not." Steph tapped her chin. "But perhaps it's not a question of taste. You don't seem to think too highly of the Earth in its current state."

I nodded.

She chuckled. "I don't either, I suppose. So think of it this way. The old recipe was created with Earthen hands, grown in Earthen fields, and cooked and packaged by yet more Earthen hands."

She held up the new bag. "Meanwhile, you've created the entire product yourself. Imperium grown, cooked, and packaged. Potatoes grown to optimum specifications. Spices meticulously mixed by all your science technowizardry. Everything painstakingly supervised and checked by one of the Emperor's finest."

She gestured to herself. "The old Route 11 Potato Chips are sullied by our grubby hands."

Then she pointed to me. "The new Route 11 Potato Chips are *pure*."

For a moment, I sat in stasis, refusing to believe the answer could have been in front of me this whole time. That I might not be doomed after all.

Then I nodded. "Yes."

I stood up. "Yes."

Then, seized by an impulse with no explicable origin, I picked Steph up under her shoulders and swung her around the room. "Yes, that's it!"

A moment later, I remembered how frail Earth dwellers were without EnviroArmor and set her down. "Sorry, I got carried away," I said with a sheepish grin.

"It's okay," Steph said, taking a moment to regain her breath. "You're excited. I get it. Not every day I get to solve a spaceman's existential crisis." Then a new smile crossed her lips. "Now do something *impure* and kiss me."

It would violate any number of creeds. To even entertain the idea violated one, in fact. But this Earthen woman had just saved me from martyrdom and had an intellect that rivaled any in the Imperium. Meanwhile, I had access to the only replicable stock of a delicacy in the entire known universe. And that granted me the permanent favor of the Emperor.

So long as I continued to deliver his coveted Route 11 Sweet Potato Chips, the Emperor would ensure my facility was untouchable. Fealty to *anything else* beyond his precious snack supply no longer seemed so important.

Steph rolled her eyes as I deliberated. "Oh, sorry, I guess that would defy the Emperor's will or whatever."

"The Emperor can kick asteroids," I replied as I reached up to unseal my helmet.

CHI

Not-A-Deer

Bethany W Pope

About five miles outside the Staunton city limits, past the empty mall with its defunct Barnes & Noble, beyond the scraggly Walmart and the 1980s-era 1950s-style diner slumping on deflated wheels beneath its fritzing neon sign, out where the road rises up into a high ridge at the place where the mountains begin, there is an abandoned cemetery.

The boneyard was leftover from the closed Methodist church—the building itself is long gone. The whitewashed wooden steeple was repurposed as part of the local one-room school, now also vanished. But the graves remain.

It's bad luck to shift a grave, at least in Appalachia, so the gravestones remain, as do the yellowed bones beneath them, sinking altogether into slow dust.

I used to wander there, in autumn, spring, and winter. I'd bring a book of poetry (Rilke, perhaps, or maybe some Hughes) and settle into the hollowed-out heart of the ancient, dying yew that sprung up in the center of the graves, as picturesque as any vanquished castle. The graveyard was a pocket carved out of the woods by hands long buried there within it, and the woods were slowly taking their loaned land back, sending up shoots and saplings whose roots sent the limestone skulls and rain-pocked lambs a-tilting as they spread.

I liked it there. It was quiet. The newest grave was two hundred years old, so I felt lonesome enough to quiet the thrum inside my head, the high-pitched buzzing sound I hear in the meat of my brain whenever there are too many human beings around for my

own comfort. The only living things I saw up there, before
the time I'm telling about, were squirrels, rabbits, and the
occasional redbrushed fox.

In wintertime, I'd pack a blanket, some matches, a thermos,
and a book into the dun-colored rucksack I bought at Dollar
General and hike out there in the early morning, feeling the
snot crackling inside of my nose as it froze and watching the
rising sun light up the needles of the pines, encased as they
were in sheaths of ice, so that each individual tree branch
glowed from within like a reliquary, like an emerald-colored
saint-hair, burning holy, bound up in rock crystal.

I'd enter the cemetery via the white-stone, falling-down
gate, rub the ears of a lamb, carved seated on the gravestone
of a child who shat herself to death from dysentery, and make
my nest within the heart of that yew, to read and think and
generally recover (as much as possible) from the perils of the
week.

I didn't light a fire unless I had to, that is unless I let the time
get away from me and it got too dark to risk the walk along
the highway, but I always carried matches just in case, and I
generally left a cache of food up there—some granola bars at
least—locked up in a metal box inside the empty heart of the
yew, to keep the weather and the critters out.

It's cold up there, in February, so I tried to make it back
to my dorm more often than not. There was no curfew at
the college, and I had no roommate, but even animals prefer
to sleep indoors if they can. And I wasn't too keen on the
prospect of some drunken good-old-boy metamorphosing me
into roadkill, so I tried to remember to leave before sunset. In
winter, that meant getting out of there before three o'clock.

This particular Saturday, the one that I'm telling you about
right now, I completely forgot about the time. I was reading
Crow, going slowly through that brutal book. Beautiful cruelty
crashing against my brainstem in violent, mutilating waves. I'd
read a poem and it would rock me back on my heels, almost
like getting punched. I'd lie back against the ragged inner
trunk, my eyes closed against Hughes's visions, as *Crow* tore
his monstrous, innocent way across the cosmos. I hated every
stanza of it, but I couldn't stop.

By the time I realized that the sun was setting, it was too late to shuck my blanket nest and hit the road, so I set to work gathering the elements of a campsite from the encroaching woods. It had been snowing, but the air never warmed enough to trigger a melt, so there were plenty of dried branches and kindling scattered about. I built the shape of a fire the way my grandfather showed me, forming a chimney out of twigs and setting the spark going in the heart of it, adding the bigger branches after the little ones caught. I wasn't particularly worried about any of it. I'd camped here before, many times, and I often slept as well inside of that tree as I did in my own bed.

You've probably guessed that things shook out a bit differently this night.

I'd eaten two of my granola bars (frozen solid, but otherwise still good), bundled myself up into the clammy folds of my blanket, and I'd opened up my notebook to try to scratch out a response to Hughes's particular take on the end of the world, when I happened to glance up over the low flame of my fire and saw, through the white smoke and rising sparks, the vague outline of a deer.

You have to understand, from the first, that this in itself was unusual. Aside from the fact that most deer will go as far as miles out of their way to avoid a fire or any form of human habitation, they generally prefer to spend their winters nestled down in thickets. Additionally, bucks will shed their antlers, which bud in spring and spread in time for autumn rutting, sloughed off before the first hard frost.

This deer was huge, as high at the shoulders as a plow-horse, with an antler rack that spread out wider than I am tall. It blinked at me above the flame, from eyes that stared from the center of its face, its skull shaped to mimic the pattern of a predator. To see eyes like that on a deer, eyes placed to stalk and hunt rather than fright and flee, was startling enough to root me to the spot.

The buck stepped closer, slow as slow, maintaining eye contact as it approached. It grew eerier and harder to reckon the longer that I stared at it. As it stepped forward, entering the circle cast by my flames, I saw that its legs bent at more points than ordinary knees would allow, as though its legs were grafted from a spider despite the long and pointed hooves.

It pushed through the smoke, stuttering across the coals (which scattered and died in the snow) like a silent film when the crank on the camera is unevenly turned, the fire singeing the fur on its oddly wide body, and that sharp, foul stench did more to convince me of the reality of the situation than anything else I'd witnessed on that cold, dark night.

Unrooted at last, I scrambled back on my heels, with no place to go but the cold and rotting bark of the tree that scraped against my spine, even through the thick padding of my coat.

Of course, the creature kept coming.

It pushed through the ashes and the flame, shoving its rack, its queer, long snout through the cleft in the wood, utterly silent as it approached, absent even the heave and gasp of straining lungs as it pressed my body farther into the wood.

I was crying by then, tears running down my face and freezing as they fell, scrambling with my nails against the hollow shell of bark and wood, peeling away splinters and chunks of that rotting yew while the burning, blood-filled rack of horns scraped the flesh on my cheeks and my chest and those thin black lips peeled away from gums that were set with teeth longer and sharper than any real deer has ever grown.

Even then, enmeshed as I was in terror, my sanity held. I was more terrified than I had ever been, as swathed in horrific unreality as a fly in a web, but I remained certain of the general reality of the world outside of this small bubble of madness. But that was before the creature's fevered nose connected with the exposed flesh of my throat, leaving its mucosal trail slimed against my skin, and it was before the third eye, buried in the not-deer's wide forehead, opened its lids and bathed my nest in its dark and ultraviolet glow.

That was when something deep within me fractured. I heard the crack of it, like creaking frost on the surface of a lake, deep inside my skull. I was screaming so loud that my throat ached with the force of it, the world fading out around me, in spite of the danger, in spite of the creature bathing me with its fevered heat, the world fading to black as I faded with it.

I came back to myself two full days later, shaken awake by one of the paramedics the cop who found me called. One of my dorm-mates had reported me missing when Monday afternoon rolled around and she realized that nobody had seen me since Friday evening. They'd found me, wrapped in my blanket, huddled up behind the Wal-Mart parking lot. I had no memory of how I'd arrived there.

The police insisted on a full drug panel, which I cleared, followed by a complete psychological evaluation, which I passed, primarily because I thought it prudent to keep my mouth shut about the creature. Suffice it to say, I was back in class by Tuesday, with no one the wiser, though I did have to buy the library another copy of *Crow*.

I've never returned to the cemetery that I once thought of as my own personal island of private escape. I won't say that I don't feel the call of it, because I do. Especially in winter, when the new, soft eye forming beneath the skin in my forehead aches, and the bones in my arms and legs begin to lengthen, and the cold air in my nostrils crackles with the twinned scents of fire and raw meat.

Marigolds in the Mesozoic

Matthew Turner

"RUN THAT PAST ME again," Second Lieutenant Carver barked into his headset. He was crammed in the back of the Bearcat alongside the three other men of Task Force Marigold, Team Five. Adorned in all-black tactical gear, night-vision goggles propped on top of helmets, they braced for whatever unknown nightmare they'd been called to investigate.

"Dinosaur Land," Marigold Actual's voice hissed through the static. He was starting to break up, the reception affected by whatever Active Supernatural Phenomenon, or ASP, was at play. "Old theme park filled with dinosaur statues. Bunch of missing persons reports, most recently joined by our lovely friends at SIG-D."

Short for *Special Intervention Group, Domestic*, SIG-D and Marigold were as ancient rivals as the Army and Navy. If Marigolds were being called in to bail those guys out, then SIG-D must be desperate.

"Dinosaur Land? What, like Jurassic Park?" Tomato asked. Full name Thom Ato, his parents clearly did not love him very much. "We gonna meet Jeff Goldblum?"

"Yeah, you can ask for his autograph when you see him." Tychus laughed gruffly as he packed enough Skoal in his cheeks to kill an elephant. The big man of the squad, Tychus's bald head scraped against the low roof of the Bearcat.

"Well, you know, ah, life, um, ah, finds a way." Tomato gave a truly awful impression of Goldblum.

"All right, let's keep it at least a little professional, people," Carver grumbled with a shake of his head. "Don't need Team Five's reputation to get even worse than it already is."

"Not possible, boss." Odom, Carver's XO, shrugged, never one for many words.

Marigold Actual continued on, ignoring the banter. "The area's been quarantined since SIG-D lost contact with the five men of Task Force Firebrand approximately one hour ago at zero dark. You four are our quick reaction force. Go in, find any survivors, and bring them home. They may not be ours, but we don't leave men behind. Actual out."

The Bearcat rumbled to a stop. Carver knocked on his helmet once for luck, did a quick scan ensuring all his gear was secured, clicked on his helmet cam, then swung the heavy armor-plated door open and ushered the rest of the team out before following them. They moved silently despite the nearly hundred pounds of weight each man carried. The night air was brisk but nothing to complain about. Overlapping flood lights connected to generators illuminated the faded and worn-out sign in the parking lot:

DINOSAUR LAND
EDUCATIONAL PREHISTORIC FOREST
FEATURING OVER 40 REPLICAS FROM THE PAST

Next to the sign, three... *aged* dinosaur statues—a tyrannosaurus and two brontosauruses—towered above an abandoned Corolla in the gravel lot. Paint had flaked off, leaving bare patches of gray concrete on the sun-faded statues. Layered white tarps draped the area, covering the building and the park and leaving only the entrance exposed: a pair of double doors behind the gaping maw of a T. rex head built into the wall.

Carver had a bad feeling about this.

"Lieutenant!" One of the first responders, a Marigold fixer in white protective gear, called to him as the team spread out in the lot.

"Talk to me." Carver wagged a finger that told the man to fall in line as Team Five approached the toothy door.

"SIG-D boys went in over an hour ago. We haven't seen or heard anything since. We've sealed the area off in case of visual or psycho-hazards and already corralled the first two Clarke County deputies on the scene. They're in the black box awaiting debriefing."

"Keep out any more curious eyes. If we're not back in an hour, then blacklist us," Carver said.

The fixer nodded and left, leaving Team Five to their job.

"Used to love this place as a kid." Odom loaded a 40mm grenade into the under-slung launcher on his M4 rifle. "Shame."

"Maybe we can grab you a souvenir on our way out." Tychus spit out a glob of chaw juice, hefting his M249 SAW automatic weapon and spare ammo belt around his neck like Rambo. "A nice magnet or a doll."

"Maybe get you a coffee mug or something. That's nasty." Tomato shook his head as he stepped over Tychus's dip spatter.

"Hold onto your butts, gentlemen," Carver said.

Behind him, the other members all clapped a hand to a cheek in solidarity before plunging through the tyrannosaur's mouth into the unknown as the fixers closed the door. Overhead, cheap fluorescent lights buzzed as they trod on the creaking wooden floor. Carver on point, Tychus and Tomato behind him, Odom covering the rear.

At some point, the floor was no longer wooden planks, and the buzz of the lights had gone quiet. Not only that, the lights themselves were gone, slow but subtle, as the hallway shifted into... something else. A cave of some kind. Carver slid his GP-NVG-18 goggles down, the world turning a sickly static green. He waved the team forward, slow and careful. Definitely *some* kind of ASP at work, a liminal space or something stretching the confines of the park.

After nearly thirty minutes of walking, the darkness of the cave gave way to a quite literal light at the end of the tunnel, a narrow opening ringed with stalactites, prompting Carver to turn off his goggles or be blinded. He was now convinced that something supernatural was at work. From what he'd seen, Dinosaur Land should have been approximately two acres of temperate forest, fenced in and speckled with statues.

The small park had shifted, morphing into something more akin to a prehistoric jungle.

Team Five emerged from a rocky hillside's entrance, gazing out at a boundless wilderness. A soft, effusive light permeated the area. Not enough to see clearly but too bright to use their night-vision, and not right for 0100 hours. Great clouds of rolling mist blocked any view of the horizon. The stars and moon were similarly covered by storm clouds showering the team in warm, fat raindrops that pooled in the moss and wide leaves of ferns at their feet. If Carver closed his eyes, he could be in a sauna.

The tarps covering the original grounds were nowhere to be seen. Likewise, the only noises were decidedly... inhuman. Something large with webbed wings flew across the darkened skies, and the chirruping and clicking of strange animals echoed in the night.

"Fantastic. Air support's out of the question." Tomato gazed up and shook his head. He swatted angrily at a particularly large bug that wouldn't get out of his face.

"Business as usual, then." Tychus shrugged. He opened up yet another pouch of snuff and stuffed even more plugs into his mouth.

"Damn, man. Any more of that stuff and your blood will be toxic to these mosquitoes." Tomato slapped at his neck.

"Don't tempt me with a good time," Tychus rumbled with his mouth full.

"Bigger on the inside than the outside. Definitely liminal in nature. Or something like it." Carver punched his report onto the tacpad strapped to his forearm. "Anything on comms?"

"Only if you like white noise." Tomato grimaced at the squawk of static that poured out from his earpiece.

"Terrific," Carver muttered. "This'll make finding those SIG boys fun. Odom, mark our exfil point. Tychus, rig it."

Tychus placed two shaped charges overhead on the mouth of the cave, to seal it after they'd hightailed it with the SIG-D boys, and then he pulled out a second pair of explosives and began setting them up as well.

"Have enough plastic explosives?" Tomato asked.

"Hey, after Harper's Ferry, I never leave home without two pairs of C-4 and two pairs of dry socks," Tychus said.

Odom cracked a pair of neon green glowsticks, dropping them at both sides of the cave entrance, then slapped a small tracker on the rock wall. After a moment, Carver's tacpad synced up with the beacon, a breadcrumb trail to find their way home.

"All right. Fan out but stay in visual range of each other. Stagger your blinking just in case. We're looking for any signs of either civilian survivors or Task Force Firebrand," Carver ordered.

"So, soiled slacks?" Tomato asked.

Tychus and Odom took the far ends with Tomato and Carver in the middle as Team Five spread into a zig-zag line, still in each other's peripheral vision with their helmet-mounted cameras capturing each other's movements. A common effect of reality-distorting ASPs was the "Batman effect," where an individual would be there when you looked at them, but if you looked away for an instant, they were gone. Maintaining constant visual on each other prevented this outcome... usually.

Carver's boots crunched and squished through the dense undergrowth, dead branches, and fallen logs overgrown with ivy, all sopping wet. It could have been worse. It could have been the living flesh forest, or the trees could have been impossible colors that melted your brain like the ones the unfortunate boys in Team Twelve encountered. It could have been like that one house filled with a thousand screaming eyes. That was an exciting day.

Odom held up a closed fist, and everyone froze. Carver circled his index finger, then pointed at Odom. They gathered around him, speaking in hushed whispers.

"Shell casings, five five six." Odom nudged one of the spent brass with his boot. "Match SIG-D. And tracks in the mud. Boots and something else. Big."

"Real big." Tychus whistled, squatting to take a closer look. "Claws. Hell, maybe you're gonna get your wish after all, Tomato."

"They got into a fight and went this way." Carver traced the path and looked up. His tacpad was acting screwy, the digital compass a wreck. But using their entry point as south, the path followed the equivalent of due north. He dimmed his light amplification and could barely make out a pavilion. Two hundred fifty yards according to his optics. "Must've made a break for that structure."

"Were they chasing something? Or being chased?" Tomato asked nervously.

"Either way, we'll find out," Carver replied. "Let's keep mov—"

A shrieking roar cut through the jungle. The puddles in the mud jumped and rippled. A booming *thoom, thoom, thoom* hurtled toward them. Carver scarcely had time to turn, his XM7 rifle snapping to his shoulder when the most butt-ugly monstrosity he'd ever seen came trampling through a dense copse of trees. Enormous, lumpy, and misshapen, its toothy and stumpy maw spread unnaturally wide. Scales were a uniform mottled brick-red, and it thundered forward on two powerful legs, apparently compensating for its tiny arms.

And the freak was heading right for him with a look that would make a buffet nervous.

"Light it up!" Carver cried out, and the squad opened fire, tracers and muzzle flashes illuminating the tropical darkness.

Rounds bounced off its thick skin, the Tyrannosaurus rex look-alike not slowing as it roared once more and lunged to take a bite out of Carver. Drool dripped off its teeth and down its chin, and Carver barely threw himself out of the way, rolling out from one of its massive clawed toes before scrambling to his feet behind it.

The other men encircled the monster, not letting up for a second. Tychus howled as he cut loose with his M249, the belt feeding into the weapon faster than a kid housing a Fruit by the Foot, his swollen biceps jiggling as he walk-fired the machine gun like it was a paintball marker. Spent brass rattled and clanged, forming a metallic bed of leaves at their feet as they maintained a withering hail of fire.

The fusillade was as effective as a single ice cube in a pitcher of sweet tea. The T. rex doppelgänger whipped around, tail slamming Tomato, punching him through the rotten trunk of a dead tree.

Thunk! Odom fired his 40mm grenade, the high explosive blasting the dinosaur's skull with a flash and a cloud of black smoke. Carver clung to a brief flicker of hope that the blast did the trick... until the creature hurled itself right at Tychus, clamping onto his legs and lifting him into the air.

"You want a piece?" Tychus roared in pain and fury as the dinosaur swung him side to side like a chew toy. His tobacco-stained spit splattered across the beast's jaws as his furor erupted. One hand desperately scrabbled at the beast's snout, and the other kept a death grip on his machine gun, his finger committed to squeezing down that trigger until every last round was spent. "Eat this!"

"Ty!" Tomato groaned from the ground.

Carver dashed back to him as he tried to get a shot on the monster, but Tychus was in the way.

Tychus's screams echoed as the dinosaur unhinged its jaw and flicked its head, sending him down its gullet. With a crunch, the beast bit down, raining chunks of Tychus's weapon down to the ground in a bloody clatter, along with the detonator to the explosives.

The T. rex finished its meal and looked at the rest of them for dessert.

"Knees to chest, boys!" Carver cried out, pulling Tomato to his feet. He snatched Tychus's detonator from the bloodied ground as he sprinted forward. "Make for the building!"

"What about Ty?" Tomato shouted back, holding his side.

"Uh, he was a good man and a great friend, he'll never be forgotten!" Carver clipped his rifle to his chest, grabbed a flashbang, and turned to toss it, when the T. rex froze, its massive frame swaying, almost... sick? No time to consider it.

"Eyes shut!" he called out.

The jungle lit up like a fridge opening at two in the morning, and the roar of dismay from the dinosaur signaled that the grenade had done its job. Carver hurtled over fallen logs, swatting away branches of dense foliage. Tomato and Odom's footsteps crunched close behind, but seconds later, the T. rex's thunderous steps roared back, closing fast.

"Firing!" Odom unloaded another 40mm. *Boom!*

Carver's moment next, he spun and fired off a quick burst, aiming for the T. rex's eyes. But it was too fast, too twitchy, and the rounds scattered around its snout. With a wince and a curse, Carver turned and kept running.

The door was within arm's reach. As Odom, leading the charge, neared it, two armed men stepped out, hammering the T. rex with covering fire, their tracers snapping and whizzing overhead.

Carver nodded. *Task Force Firebrand. At least they've got good timing.*

"Get in!" The man on the right waved them inside.

He didn't need to say it twice. Carver made sure he was the last one in, then slammed the heavy metal door just as the T. rex crashed into it, denting the steel with a thunderous blow. Everyone scrambled away from the door, weapons raised, but after the initial clang there was nothing but silence. Carver held his breath for a hot second, waiting. Was it too much to hope that the monster had given up?

Probably. And now they were all stuck together in some kind of storage depot, with only the one banged-up door for an exit. *Fantastic.*

"Task Force... Firebrand?" Carver panted, struggling to catch his breath.

"Guilty." The guy that waved them in nodded. His long beard made him look like a Civil War general. "Name's Dusty. Who're you?"

Unlike Marigold, the three survivors of Task Force Firebrand sported more traditional Multicam fatigues with carrier plates, and they looked ragged as hell. Carver wrinkled his nose and tried not to let the disgust show on his face. All of them could definitely use a hot shower. Or two. Dirt and grime had smeared over their camouflage and onto the bare skin where their fatigues had ripped, and it'd be easier to point out which of their limbs *wasn't* bandaged or in a splint.

"We're... your rescue..." Carver managed to straighten up and jut out his shoulder to show his Marigold patch.

"Wow, Marigolds. That makes me feel great." The biggest one rolled his eyes and started to stalk off, though there was nowhere to go. "What took you so damn long?"

"Can it, Gumbo," Dusty said. "At least someone knows we're here."

"You in charge?" Carver asked.

"Am now." Dusty shrugged.

"Huh. Big guy chasing us get your CO?"

"Nah, he got eaten by a brontosaurus. Big-necked son of a gun." Gumbo flattened his palm and raised it up from his neck. "First one to go."

"I thought those only ate leaves?" Tomato cut in.

"Yeah, so did he. Turns out *Jurassic Park* lied. Who knew?" the third guy, Warren, said.

"Damn you, Steven Spielberg!" Tomato raised his voice as he shook a fist at the heavens.

Carver ignored Tomato's antics. "So, we've got a tracker on the way out. We have to make it there in one piece."

"You got a plan?" Dusty asked.

"I have a rocket launcher," Tomato said.

"That's a good start." Warren nodded.

"I've got an idea." Now that Carver had a moment to breathe and think, he considered how the T. rex had looked after it had eaten Tychus, rest his soul. "I think we gave that monster a stomachache. If we can wait him out, we may be able to just slip away, nice and easy."

"That's your great idea?" Gumbo threw his hands up. "The hell kind of rescue is this?"

"Yeah, gotta be honest, not feeling that one, LT." Odom nodded in agreement with Gumbo.

"Vote heard and considered," Carver said in a tone that clearly said he had not considered it. "That thing's shrugged off everything else, and we only have the one rocket. If you want to risk it, then be my—"

The back wall exploded in a shower of cement and rubble as the T. rex burst through like the Kool-Aid Man, apparently tired of waiting and eager for seconds. Carver flinched, shielding his face as debris knocked him to the ground, his team's shouts and screams mingling with the T. rex's roar in a chaotic eruption. Something about the monster was different though, less coordinated; rather than gobbling up Gumbo as it had done to Tychus, the beast tripped over its own feet, toppling onto the poor guy with a colossal crash that started a cave-in. Gumbo didn't have time to scream.

"Jesus Christ!" Tomato yelled, stumbling back as chunks of the ceiling rained down. Carver lunged for the only door, yanking it open to escape the deathtrap.

"Out! Everyone out!" Carver hoped his voice didn't crack.

They poured out faster than they'd gone in, the T. rex's jaws clamping on their heels. The T. rex thrust a vicious claw through the door as Carver turned to run, snagging his pack and halting him mid-stride. *Of course it would.* Cursing, Carver unfastened the straps with shaking fingers, fumbling as he wiggled his way out. The T. rex's claw hauled Carver back toward the depot, its talons shredding his pack. With a desperate heave, Carver tore loose, abandoning the gear and stumbling before bolting away. All they needed was time and distance.

"Tomato! Trade! Give me the LAW, then lead them to the cave entrance! We'll meet you there! Odom, with me!" Carver tossed the detonator to the explosives to Tomato.

"You got it, LT! Catch!" Tomato obeyed without a snarky comment for once, unslinging the launcher and throwing it to Carver. He caught it with one hand and slipped the strap over his shoulder.

"What's the plan, boss?" Odom asked.

Carver pulled out a flare and struck it, a fountain of incandescent orange sparks spraying out with a gushing *hiss*. He waved it over his head. "Like Tomato said. Jeff Goldblum. Keep tall and ugly on us, and if it eats me, you take the LAW and finish it off."

"Inspired as always," Odom said with a sigh. He lit his own flare and began to run alongside Carver.

The screech and the rumbling earth meant the plan worked as the dinosaur made for the two nearest targets, attracted by the light and motion. If Team Five could outsmart this thing, it really must be dumb.

Carver and Odom needed a good firing point, somewhere with room for them to set up and get the shot off. Ahead, water poured down a rocky outcropping with edges jutting out enough to serve as handholds and a flat bowl at the top. That'd have to do.

"This is it." Carver tossed the flare to the ground and took a knee as he pulled out the LAW.

Odom set up behind him, pulling open the collapsible tube and priming the single high-explosive anti-tank rocket.

The trees shook and buckled as their old friend stumbled forward. Carver's prediction was on the money. The T. rex looked as ragged as they did now, chest heaving for breath, beady eyes yellow and bloodshot. Footsteps uneven, like at any moment it could fall over.

Carver grimaced as he took aim. "Yeah, that's right. You are what you eat, and you are one ugly mutha—"

The monstrous dinosaur roared in challenge, and that was the opening Carver needed. Odom cleared the backblast, and Carver fired. The rocket streaked with a whoosh, blasting down the T. rex's throat. A heartbeat later, it exploded, raining tyrannosaur jerky.

"Hell of a shot, LT." Odom said, clapping Carver's shoulder before collapsing to the ground. Tyrannosaur gore plopped wetly around them as he added, "How'd you know it was sick?"

"Tychus had been shoving snuff in his cheeks since he was five. He was immune to that stuff. But our friend there? A tobacco virgin that got the biggest nicotine rush of his life."

"Hah! Looks like the big guy got the last laugh after all." Odom chuckled and shook his head.

The two of them lay there for a moment, collecting themselves. Too bad Carver didn't have any bourbon, or he'd pour some out for good ol' Tychus and the other fallen of Firebrand. That reminded him...

"You know, I was thinking. That guy, Gumbo, said his CO was eaten by a brontosaurus, right?"

"Think so, yeah," Odom said.

"As in, not the monster we pulped?"

"...Huh." Odom nodded slowly. "Time to go?" A gut-wrenching bellow from the jungle answered Odom's question, spurring Carver and Odom to their feet as massive shapes crashed toward them.

"Time to go!" Carver agreed. His tacpad showed five hundred meters to the exit. His legs shook like Jell-O, but he forced them to move all the same. Behind them, the long neck of the brontosaurus burst through the tree line, the thing drooling and braying as its head swung from side to side, and it somehow managed to be more terrifying than the tyrannosaur. Carver didn't bother trying to shoot, instead opting to get the hell out as fast as possible.

Three hundred meters. The earthquakes under their feet doubled in intensity as a second brontosaurus broke through the trees on an intercept course. *Perfect. Why wouldn't there be two?*

Carver pushed himself to run faster, gasping out between breaths for Odom to keep up as they cut through great fans of ferns and spiky bushes of elephant grass that sliced at his exposed skin. The mists seemed to cling to his lungs with every breath, choking him.

One hundred meters. Ahead, twin points of light, their salvation. The glowsticks flanked the entrance. Movement at the mouth of the cave. Dusty and Warren. And Tomato waving and screaming, something in his hands.

Fifty meters. The brontosauruses thundered behind them, twin juggernauts of muscle and bloodlust, trampling everything in a relentless storm, a living typhoon locked onto them like a cruise missile. Spatters of drool from slavering mouths and mud from stomping feet coated Carver's back. Sprinting beside Odom, he spotted Tomato ahead, clutching the detonator for Tychus's C4 rigged at the cave entrance.

Twenty meters. Carver dodged a brontosaurus's snapping jaws, stumbling but regaining his footing. Gonna be close.

"Run, you son of a gun!" Dusty cried out as he and Warren disappeared into the dark.

"Lieutenant, get the hell in here!" Tomato shouted as he dipped inside the cave. Carver screamed as he and Odom dove into the cave, the two brontosauruses thrusting their big ugly mugs inside.

Four thunderous blasts roared as the C4 detonated, hurling rock and dust down the cave entrance in a deafening *bang!* The collapse crushed the brontosauruses' skulls, burying them in a rubble tomb as the entrance sealed shut.

Carver, Odom, and Tomato lay gasping for breath in the pitch-black tunnel before Tomato broke out laughing and whooping. Farther in the dark, Dusty and Warren cracked up as well.

It wasn't pretty, but a win was a win.

"Atta boy, Tomato." Carver pulled down his night-vision and shot him a thumbs-up.

"I aim to please," Tomato replied. He kissed his fingers and raised them in the air. "This one's for you, Big Ty. You always wanted to go out with a bang."

"To Tychus." Carver nodded.

"Tychus," Odom repeated.

After a minute, Carver got up and helped Odom to his feet. "So, Odom. You still like Dinosaur Land?"

Odom looked back at him with a tired sigh. "After careful consideration, I've decided not to endorse this park."

Birdwatching

CHARLIE NEWMAN-JOHNSON

THE VIRGINIA SKY WAS uncommonly blue, flat like the too-still surface of a pond—and another dead bird fell like a rock out of it, nearly hitting Ari.

The sweet little thing looked peaceful, although its neck had been wrenched to an impossible angle by the impact. Ari knelt to look more closely. Spotted belly and a patch of red behind its head, and a long beak—a Northern Flicker. He wanted to reach down and pull its eyelids shut, but the thought of touching the dead bird made the hairs on the back of his neck stand up. He turned to tell the others.

Jen, in her flannel shirt and puffy vest, stood facing Nic, her arms crossed. Ari knew her as smiley and easy-going, but her round brown face was tight with frustration, her lips curled inward.

"...and so I just think that there should be more men in this hobby, honestly," Nic was saying. "Like, I'm all for women being into science and stuff, but we gotta make sure things are equal, right? How did the birding group around here get to have so many women?"

Jen's stink eye slid right off of Nic as he kept talking. Finally, she noticed Ari and walked over to see what he'd found.

"Another dead one," he said mournfully. He pointed to the Flicker, its empty eyes staring up at something beyond the frosty sky.

Jen exhaled heavily, her breath lingering like a ghost in the bracingly cold air. She bent to peer at it.

The day after Christmas held little significance for Jen, who wasn't particularly religious, or for Ari, who leaned toward Hanukkah if anything. The real holiday for them was the 2025 Audubon Christmas Bird Count, and they'd started their day bright and early outside of Staunton. Now, late in the morning, they sat in Natural Chimneys Park, binoculars held in mittened hands. A birding friend posted a Winter Wren sighting on iNaturalist, and they wanted to get it on the record for the official count, if possible.

Unfortunately, the Winter Wren was nowhere to be seen. Nothing moved in the park except biting gusts of wind. Ari thought he could almost hear a sound lurking below the bluster, quietly grating at his nerves, but he couldn't pick it out through Nic's incessant chatter. How he had gotten invited wasn't clear. In retrospect, the Audubon Club president's insistence on referring to Nic as an 'acquaintance' rather than friend should have been a red flag. Ari's friend Shruti had stayed home with a sick kid, and it seemed a shame to not fill the empty seat.

Jen prodded the Flicker gently with a stick, then turned to Ari, her face scrunched up in concentration. "Do you hear that?"

Ari prided himself on knowing most of the birdcalls of the valley, but he'd never heard anything like this. Guttural low notes and piercing high ones filled a rare gap in Nic's blathering. The sound made his teeth hurt. It drifted in from beyond sight with unreasonable clarity, as if whispered directly into the soul of the silent valley.

"I do," he agreed, nodding. "That's... a bit weird. I'm gonna try to Merlin it." He opened the Merlin app on his phone, but the bird stopped abruptly before he could press 'ID by sound.' "Dang, missed it!"

"It's probably time to move on to the next site anyways," Jen said. "We counted the first dead one by Churchville. Are we agreed on keeping that precedent?"

Ari nodded; Nic wasn't paying any attention. She made a note on their list of sightings for the day.

Natural Chimneys Park — 10:57 a.m. 12/26/25

- *Cardinal - 1 (male)*

- *Northern Flicker - 1 (dead)*

"This is weird, right?" Ari asked quietly, biting his lip. "If we don't count the dead ones, we've only seen... three. And two were in Churchville. Should we wait a little longer for the Wren?"

"What are you guys talking about over there?" Nic yelled from fifteen feet away. In the stifling stillness of the park, his voice felt like a transgression, and bird-startlingly loud.

"I think we're probably not spotting any wrens." She raised her voice enough for Nic to hear and said politely but firmly, "Nic, if you keep yelling, we're not gonna see much today. Let's go to the next stop and get a fresh start there, okay?" Without waiting for an answer, she turned for the Jeep.

"Can't scare dead birds anyways," Nic muttered as he walked by Ari.

***

Before long, they were rattling up the mountain in Jen's semi-reliable Jeep. Nic lounged in the backseat, packed in with the gear, loudly slurping from the Camelbak he'd brought instead of a normal water bottle.

"You know, birds are most active in the early morning, at noon, and at dusk," Nic provided graciously between slurps. "It's important to know when the birds are going to be out if you want to spot them. I'd consider myself a bit of an expert," he bragged, though Ari was pretty sure his swanky binoculars had never been used before today. "It's probably just the wrong time of day right now. That's all."

Ari, daydreaming, imagined Nic's awful hipster mustache turning into a squirrel and jumping out the window. Once it scampered well off into the woods, he took in what Nic said.

"Wait, I'm with you for early morning and dusk—but noon?" Ari asked, his voice louder in the closed car than he expected. "What kind of bird is more active at noon?" He uncurled the fists he'd made and laid his hands flat in his lap.

"Noon birds, obviously," Nic replied. His Camelbak made the loudest slurp yet. "How far is the next spot?"

No one answered.

"It seems like the closer we get to the mountains, the fewer birds there are," Ari offered hesitantly.

"Yeah," Jen agreed, her voice barely loud enough to reach Ari. "I've done this same route for the last six years, and it wasn't like this at all."

"Are we scaring birds away?" Ari asked, rolling his eyes meaningfully at Nic. Jen's eyes were on the road as she drove further up the narrow holler, her knuckles tight on the wheel. More quietly, he added, "Have you ever seen birds fall out of the sky like that?"

"Even with"—Jen tilted her head subtly toward the backseat—"we should be seeing a lot more. And—I've seen it once, maybe? Some crows were fighting with a hawk, and I think the hawk got one of them in the wing. It squawked all the way down, though, and died on impact. These..." she trailed off.

"Hey, you guys might include me in that conversation," Nic piped up. "It's rude to whisper."

***

Noon stop: Flagpole Knob. The hilltop was clear enough that they enjoyed a stunning view down to the southeast, the whole of the Shenandoah Valley laid out before them. Seeing it from above usually made Ari feel wistful, imagining all the people below who didn't know he was watching over their lives.

Today the view evoked the dream he'd been having every night for a week.

In the dream, standing on a hilltop a lot like this one, he looked toward the northeast. It started as a bright sunny day, but clouds gathered, and everything grew dark. He heard the same mysterious birdcall he now recognized from Chimney Rocks and the approaching *whoomph* of massive wings. Every night the sounds drew closer, and last night he was about to finally turn to see what was coming. He quaked from its titanic gravity; he'd been filled with anticipatory joy to finally see it, to finally know the shape of it! To finally behold and exalt it!

Just before turning, he'd woken covered in sweat. In the morning sun, the dream rapidly drained from him, leaving only dread.

Now, with the sun disappearing behind the clouds, and Jen standing to his left, he spun suddenly, expecting... something.

Instead, he saw Nic gesturing wildly.

"See, I told you!" he yelled triumphantly.

Ari turned again to look out above the valley.

"Noon birds!"

"He's kind of right, Ari," Jen said reluctantly. "The thermals start to pick up around noon."

High above the shadowed valley, an unsettling throng of raptors wheeled in eerie silence, forms too distant to discern without lenses. Jen, her face taut, pulled out her notebook and murmured, "How many do you count?"

The mood improved a bit with something to do. Nic and Ari reached the same count: fifteen birds of prey wheeling around on the thermals. Jen started a page in the notebook. They got out their binoculars to identify some of the raptors.

Flagpole Knob — 12:16 p.m. 12/26/25

- *Turkey Vultures - 8*

- *Black Vultures -*

- *Red-tailed Hawks -*

"Red-tailed Hawk on the edge of the pack," Nic said, somewhere to Ari's left. "Mostly turkey vultures, though. Oh man!! That's an eagle!"

"No way it's an eagle," Ari muttered to himself. He was unsurprised Nic would be the type of American who would see a Bald Eagle in every bird. "Nic, where is that one? Just curious," he asked more loudly.

"At the two o'clock of the group."

Ari tracked it down. The bird in question was, in fact, a Bald Eagle. His shoulders slumped.

Don't be petty. You don't have to like the guy, but it's still pretty cool to see a Bald Eagle.

"Hey, you're right!" Ari forced himself to say. "Good spot."

"What's it doing, though?" Nic replied.

Ari scrambled to track the Eagle as it plummeted groundward. He expected the bird to cunningly snatch a rabbit or mouse, but it pulled out of the dive early, leaving his field of view.

"Shoot, I lost it!" Ari lowered his binoculars.

Jen was busy recording their spots. "Nic, did you see what it got?"

"Well," Nic muttered, uncharacteristically quiet. "I think it caught another dead one falling out of the sky." He turned the focus on his binoculars, taking a few tries to dial it in. "Bright yellow... a Goldfinch, I guess?"

Ari said nothing, but he raised his binoculars again, training his gaze higher. A layer of clouds gathered like a shroud over the sun.

Every few minutes, another small bird fell from somewhere beyond the veil of cumulus. Each falling bird was deftly seized by a waiting raptor, which then alighted on the mountain's crags to tear into its lifeless prey with an unnatural, almost reverent precision.

The big birds weren't squabbling over the bounty, like they usually might.

They knew more food was coming. Ari couldn't help but think of feeding his fourth-grade classroom fish tank. What must it have been like, being one of those little fish fed from above by some unknowable thing? Did they see the humans above, or just the food as it slowly drifted down?

That awful birdcall again, louder this time, floating down from above. The unsettling sound came from somewhere to the south-west, growing inexorably closer. Under the seemingly random jumble of screeches and grunts, there appeared to be a deep rhythm to it. Ari found himself swaying. The rhythm pulsed with an unearthly cadence, teetering impossibly between three and four beats, sending a wave of vertigo through Ari as the world seemed to tilt beneath him.

He gritted his teeth and called up the Merlin app again.

After a brief lag, the app latched on to the birdcall. *Hearing a bird,* it read in the corner. As the call swooped and blared, the app flickered through increasingly outlandish matches. Great Blue Heron, Steppe Eagle, even Large Frogmouth. Ari had seen one of those at the zoo once and was pretty sure it was native to Asia.

The names flickered faster, suddenly in languages that weren't English. Then in other alphabets, characters, and symbols that Ari didn't recognize. The list of logged species grew unreasonably long. His phone became almost too hot to hold. The app crashed dramatically, re-opened itself, crashed again, and this time crashed his phone too. The birdcall finally cut off, with a final flourish more discordant than ever.

Ari raised a trembling hand to his left ear, his fingers brushing against a warm, creeping trickle of blood. The unnatural resonance still echoed in his skull.

"I guess to keep with the precedent, we'll count both the Bald Eagle and the Goldfinch?" Jen said, seemingly oblivious to the sound. She was focusing hard on her notes, fresh purpose in her rapid handwriting.

"Did you not hear that?" Ari asked her, amazed. "I can't even... I don't know what... I mean, I'm bleeding, Jen."

Jen smiled serenely. "I'm starting to like it, actually."

***

It wasn't far, as the Bald Eagle flew, to their next stop, but the drive took a while. Dunkle Hollow Road was the most direct route to High Knob, but calling it a road was generous. The dirt two-track hugged the side of the slope, winding in and out on the contours carved by streams that flowed long ago and would at some point flow again. This road would crumble away in less than a moment, as the old hills perceived time.

More than once, the right front wheel lost traction near the edge, and Ari's stomach lurched as the engine whined. He wiped the blood from his ear and checked his cell phone—still nothing. If they crashed, they would not be found for a long while. Jen was driving slowly, tense and silent. Ari didn't catch her blinking once. All around the trees creaked and groaned. The only other sound was something by Drake leaking from Nic's earbuds.

At last, Dunkle Hollow merged with a broader path, its rugged edges smoothing into something more tamed yet still dwarfed by the looming, watchful presence of the ancient mountains. The Jeep emerged from the woods next to a gorgeous mountain lake. The surface churned into little whitecaps in the increasingly heavy wind, growing thunderheads rushing overhead like freight trains. The forecast that morning had called for clear all day, but some kind of front was coming.

"Alright, gang, let's see if we can find some waterbirds," Jen murmured, her voice strained with feigned zeal, her shoulders sagging under the weight of the harrowing drive.

Nic had something to say, of course. "I'm not sure it makes much sense to look for waterfowl right now." He riffled through a field guide. "My understanding is they're most active when the fish are out. Morning and evening, y'know? They're probably taking a little siesta about now."

In unison, Jen and Ari got out of the Jeep, slammed their doors shut, and looked at each other. Jen grimaced theatrically, rolling her eyes, and despite himself, Ari smiled. Today wasn't what he'd been looking forward to, but it would certainly be a story worth telling to Shruti later. As Nic opened his door and sauntered out of the car, Ari made a show of fussing with his binocular lenses.

Once again, Nic was infuriatingly correct. A single Canada Goose sat in the middle of the lake, too lazy to have gone further south, but nothing else. Not a heron, or a duck, or even a cardinal. They sat on the cold rocky shore. Ari's turn to record, so he sat with his pen in hand, looking at the mostly blank page.

Skidmore Lake — 1:37 p.m. 12/26/25

- *Canada Goose - 1 (seemed anti-social)*

That damn phantom birdcall was back, and it was constant. Coming from all around, floating on errant breezes. It would get louder as an impossible puff of warm air tickled his nose, then louder still as a bone-chillingly cold gust smacked him from behind. He could feel that steady trickle of blood restarting, one that would surely cover his scarf in blood.

"Nic, what got you started birding?" Jen had to raise her voice to be heard clearly over the sound.

Ari knew her well enough to recognize the tone of voice she reserved for customers at her plant nursery day job.

"Y'know, I always felt like I had a lot in common with birds," Nic began. Ari thought about heckling but decided he was better than that. "Especially the big ones. Majestic, but it's gotta be a bit lonely up there in the sky, right? I'd been playin' a bunch of *Magic: The Gathering* earlier this year, to be honest with you, but it didn't feel right sitting inside with those huge nerds all the time."

"Better to do something real, like we're doing right now," Nic continued. "Just the three of us out here in the elements, communing with nature. I mean, what could be better?"

"I know what you mean," Ari started to say. He could be kind to Nic. He was an adult. "Games are fun and all, but—"

"I think I'm really gonna stick with birding," Nic interrupted, and Ari bit his tongue. He was an *adult*. "I just feel it, y'know? Maybe I'll even go to school for it or something. When you're good at something, you gotta follow that. Have I told you guys about the time that I met The Rock at the gym yet? You know, Dwayne Johnson. I knew he lived somewhere by Charlottesville, but..."

A frantic splashing cut through the air, followed by a guttural, strangled squawk, yanking their gazes back to where the Canada Goose had been bobbing. A huge eagle hovered in place, half of the Goose in each claw.

Without beating its wings, it glided silently toward them across the lake.

Nic, Ari, and Jen froze in place as the eagle drew nearer and nearer. A smell like formaldehyde emanated from it. Ari closed his eyes, bracing for the moment the massive beak raked across his chilly skin.

Then the wonderful, ethereal birdcall returned. Ari wasn't sure why he'd ever thought it was unpleasant. His gaze shot upward to the rushing clouds and to something he felt was even higher.

The eagle heard the call too. The massive predator took off abruptly, bits of goose guts dropping into the water, beating its massive wings as it flew toward the roiling clouds above.

"Yo, Ari, that was a Golden Eagle!" Nic exclaimed. "Write that down!"

***

High Knob Fire Tower would be their last stop, one more chance to survey the soaring raptors. Built on top of the mountain between World Wars, it was a sturdy stone building likely to last eons longer than anything in town. Above it, the sky filled with clouds so thick that Jen turned on her headlights.

Ari stepped reluctantly out onto the frosted ground. He felt a powerful urge to cover his head, but putting his winter hat on did nothing to quell it.

They started the hike up to the fire tower. Jen took the lead, and Nic followed on her heels, Ari lagging behind. A gnawing dread churned in his gut, pushing him back toward the safety of the Jeep, but the urge to protect Jen from Nic won out.

They were halfway up the hike when Nic, panting hard, insisted on a break.

Ari found himself impatient to get to the top. He hadn't wanted to leave the car, but now the wild sky above them was beckoning, and if Nic made them miss what was coming... *wait, what? What's coming?*

Nic was still struggling to catch his breath when he asked, apropos of nothing, "Jen, do you have a boyfriend?"

Jen's gaze, fixed longingly on the brooding sky, snapped back abruptly. Her wide, haunted eyes locked with Ari's for a fleeting moment, then looked right at Nic. Whatever she saw in his face, Ari couldn't know, but she turned and hiked off faster than before.

Nic tried his best to follow, but quickly his breathing became ragged. He slowed and Jen pulled away. Ari was about to step around him when Nic turned and said with a conspiratorial glance, "Is she always this rude?"

Ari stared at him hard.

Under different circumstances, Nic was probably Ari's type—a comfortable height, soft looking, and he'd be cute without the mustache, Ari had to reluctantly admit. Currently, though, Ari wanted to scream at him. *No, she's never this rude. Not to her wife, not to her friends, not even to a bad customer. Just to **you**, you absolute chode!*

A dead bird—could that iridescent blue really have been a Stellar's Jay? Here in Virginia, thousands of miles from home?—whistled out of the sky, almost sideways in the heavy wind, and crashed into the woods somewhere off the trail. The suddenness jolted Ari into motion.

"Go up please, Nic," Ari begged. "Or let me by. We're going to be late."

Slowly, Nic struggled his way up the hike. Ari stayed impatiently four steps behind.

As they reached the clearing at the top, the wind rose to a violent gale. The frigid air rushed around the old stones of the fire tower, moaning faintly as it curled through the staircase. The eerie sound was like someone getting news they'd hoped to never hear. Sprinting past Nic, Ari bounded up the stairs that wound around the tower.

At the top, Jen braced herself against the rail facing upwind, southwest along the ridgeline. Ari rushed to her side, desperate to ask if she was alright, but she barely noticed him.

"We made it on time," she said calmly. Her voice was mild and relieved.

Ari looked at the sky, and now he was calm too. They were here on time to Witness, and that was all that had ever mattered.

"Yes," Ari agreed. "Do you hear that?"

The shadow he'd felt in the sky earlier was now clearly visible, a darkness somewhere above the rushing clouds. The sound of every birdcall Ari could imagine tumbled, every song overlapping, faint but growing closer. A tweeting tower of Babel. Underneath everything was the sweet melody that had been growing louder all day. The swelling call harmonized with the other birdsongs and drew them together into one symphony.

Nic stumbled over to the railing next to them, his face a shade of purple that some corner of Ari found concerning. The rest of him was sure that it didn't matter much, though. Nic was screaming, the harrowing wind stealing his words away before they could trouble their ears.

"It's here," Jen exulted, and a hole opened in the clouds.

The sun blinded them for a moment. As his eyes adjusted, Ari saw an impossibly large flock of birds: every kind he'd ever seen, some he'd only heard of, and probably some that had no name.

In the middle of the flock was the most beautiful Thing ever. The hulking majesty of Its body iridescent in the sunlight like an oil slick, and It had... ten wings sprouting from it? Maybe twelve? Where Its beak should be was simply a hole, darker than the space between the stars. Did It have eyes? Ari couldn't make his own eyes focus on It clearly. Ari couldn't look away.

The Splendid Thing moved placidly through the wheeling flock of little birds. Any that touched the hole It had for a mouth passed right through It. Their wings kept beating for a few moments longer. Then they curled their wings to their bodies and simply fell.

Watching how long they took to fall, Ari realized that the magnificent Thing was higher than he'd thought. He'd initially guessed It was the size of a plane, but he revised that considerably upward.

Seconds after Its Gargantuan Presence passed directly overhead and blocked out the sun, the downpour of birds began.

As Ari darted under the roof of the fire tower, six or seven frozen carcasses struck his head and shoulders with staggering force.

Later, he would spend many days sitting in the dark for concussion treatment. He would struggle to answer the policemen's questions about what happened, but all of his injuries were consistent with a freak hailstorm. Eventually someone would decide that was a sufficient explanation for Nic, too. No one would think too hard about the birds.

In the moment, though, the pain was someone else's. He'd needed to grab Jen by the hand to get her under cover. They stood listening to the hundreds of dead birds slamming into the roof above them. Jen's shirt was torn, and a cut ran down her exposed shoulder. As the roof started to make ominous cracking sounds, the deluge stopped.

Ari surveyed the wreckage. The fire tower was battered. Jen slumped to the floor next to him, but she was not badly hurt.

Nic's left hand and forearm had made it under the roof, but the rest of him hadn't.

Ari's memory elided most of what it saw there, but he wasn't surprised to hear later that Nic died. When asked why he hadn't tried to save him, Ari would say he'd gone into shock. In his bed in the dark, he would often remember the feeling of being trapped in a remote corner of his brain, watching things unfold. He would never sleep well again.

That day, though, Ari ran back outside gleefully. Around him on the mountain, birds of prey descended upon their feast, ripping the little birds apart with beak and claw. The air was charged with Christmas morning energy. He didn't feel much like eating a songbird himself, but that was okay. All that mattered was watching the Wondrous Thing as long as he could while it flew northeast along the ancient ridgeline, high above the valley.

The Body in the Lake

LORI D'ANGELO

"THIS DOESN'T LOOK MUCH like a lake," Kate Calvert said to Sergeant Tom Barrett when she met him at the parking lot of what she was told was Shenandoah Lake.

What was supposed to be a boat pier was overgrown with weeds and plants, and Kate didn't see any water.

"Not everything is as it appears to be, Calvert. That doesn't look much like crime scene attire either," said Barrett, who was eyeing Kate's inappropriate sun-yellow strapless dress and flip-flops with alarm. "And, yet, apparently it is."

"In my defense," Kate said. "I wasn't expecting to come to a crime scene today, and I certainly wasn't expecting to bring my daughter."

When Kate had gotten the call that the Rockingham County Sheriff's Office needed her services as a psychic consultant, her first inclination had been to say no; in fact, she had said no. And she kept saying no until it was Barrett himself on the phone asking for her help. If Barrett, who had once referred to her psychic abilities as "that hocus pocus mumbo jumbo," wanted her assistance, she knew the situation must be serious. She had come for that reason. And because she needed the money. Five-year-old Erin stood behind her mother, clinging to the hem of her sun-yellow dress. In her matching Pac-Man short set, the little girl looked far cuter than Kate.

With her bare arms showing, Kate felt self-conscious, but she didn't have time to change or drop Erin off anywhere. She supposed that was for the best. Since she was in the process of divorcing her husband, using her mother-in-law as a babysitter was out of the question. She'd never really taken Kate's career seriously, anyway.

Though the temperature was at least ninety, Barrett was dressed in a full silk-blend black suit with a gray tie. He wasn't even breaking a sweat, while she could feel the droplets forming. Soon, they would run down her neck and back. His tie complemented his silver-streaked black hair, and his tight-fitting shirt highlighted his toned body. He looked like Tom Cruise after training for the latest *Mission Impossible*, only Barrett, who didn't try to hide his gray hairs, was aging better.

How was he not stifling in that outfit? The only kind of hot he was was the desirable kind of hot, she thought before admonishing herself. He was both too old for her and, considering the baby weight that she'd never lost, too fit. He probably weighed less than she did. She kept meaning to start on some regular exercise routine again, but something—her fog-inducing headaches, Caleb's unreasonable demands, her lack of money and her need to care for Erin—always interrupted. She occasionally walked the Silver Lake Nature Trail, but sometimes instead of walking she snuck into the Virginia Quilt Museum.

"I didn't realize I was supposed to dress for a church service," Kate said.

"More like a funeral."

Barrett's sense of humor was about as irreverent as hers.

"This your daughter?" Barrett asked, though the question was unnecessary. It wasn't like Kate was going to be carting someone else's daughter to a crime scene. Bad enough that she had to bring her own.

Kate nodded.

Barrett bent down and said in a voice more friendly than she had ever heard him use with her, "Hi, I'm Tom. I'm going to be working with your mother today. Nice to meet you."

"Nice to meet you, too, Tom. I'm Erin. Does my mom help you do important work?"

Barrett nodded solemnly. "The most important work. Your mom makes the community a safer place to live. Now, Erin, would you mind coming with me, so that your mom can do her thing? I'd like to show you around."

"Sure," Erin said. And, without hesitation, she took Barrett's outstretched hand.

"Calvert," he said, as he led Erin in the opposite direction, "look for the crime scene tape. You can't miss it."

As Barrett walked off with her daughter, Kate headed to the left. Then she saw the boat landing that was connected to the actual lake, which was smaller than it had once been. You could walk right into it. That was where the body was. He was young, probably around Erin's age. But, unlike Erin, he had ligature marks around his neck and wrists.

Kate studied the boy, her gaze lingering on his sandy blond hair and chocolate brown eyes. He still looked more like a little boy than a corpse, even after being submerged, so he likely hadn't been dead or in the water that long. Mercifully, the fish hadn't yet made a meal of him.

The difference between life and death was animation. Now, his eyes held no light. A sudden vision struck her—a fleeting glimpse of him running, alive with joy, before the stillness returned.

A child's death was harder than an adult's because it went against the natural order of things. One was supposed to be born, grow up, have children, then die. Not be born and quickly proceed to the unpleasant business of dying. This kind of crime seemed to go against the wishes of the gods.

Kate was still staring at the body, so she didn't notice Barrett's quiet approach from behind.

"I'm glad you got here before the ME's office took the body away," Barrett said.

"Did you ditch my daughter?" Kate blurted out because he had startled her, and she didn't like to be startled, and because she didn't know what else to say. He'd been gazing at her while she'd been gazing at the body.

But he took her prickly response in stride. "Yep," he said. "Left her on the pollinator trail near the dried-up part of the lake and told her to learn all about bees. The good news is you don't have to worry that she'll fall in.

Kate gave him a death stare.

"Relax," Barrett said. "I asked one of the deputies to show her a police car. She'll be talking about it for days."

"I certainly hope not," Kate said. She could hear Caleb's incredulous voice rising to near soprano pitch. *You took our daughter where? While you were doing what? What kind of mother are you?*

These were some of his favorite questions now.

"Hey," Barrett said as if sensing her uneasiness, "that was better than the other option."

"Which was?"

"Giving her the now-discontinued limited-edition *City of Harrisonburg Crime Scene Coloring Book*. I keep them on hand in case I ever need a laugh."

He unfolded a copy that he had neatly stuffed in a hidden pocket. His suit, she thought, was rather impressive with its fancy Inspector Gadget-like pockets. It hid not only his badge and gun, but also a notebook-sized stack of paper.

"Give it a look," he said.

Kate scanned the coloring book in disbelief. On one page, a police officer helped an elderly woman cross the street. On another, a body bled out on the sidewalk. A caption proclaimed in garish red letters, "Crime doesn't pay."

Kate shook her head. "Jesus, Barrett, whose bright idea was this?"

"The city's old communications guy," he said. "He was quite the character, apparently. Seemed to think that the police department's job should involve some kind of re-creation of *Dragnet*. For obvious reasons, he's since been replaced. This coloring book was his misguided attempt at community relations. If you should want a copy, I can score you a less wrinkled one. From what I hear, they're a bit of a collector's item now on eBay. You might be able to make a little money off of it. So what do you think?"

"Of the coloring book?" Kate asked.

"No, Calvert, of the body. You think he drowned?"

She shook her head. "I think it was murder."

"Because of the ligature marks?" he said.

"Not only because of that," she said. "It's just a feeling I get."

"That helps a lot," Barrett said.

"Those aren't going to be the only marks you'll find." Kate knew there would be other marks, like the one that Caleb left on her back when he "accidentally" slammed her into the metal cabinet that one time. He had told her, "This is going to scar. But, luckily for you, your clothes will conceal it, and no one's going to want to see your fat ass, anyway."

"Barrett, I think he was abused," she said.

"And the report from the medical examiner's office will confirm this?"

"Yes, the report will confirm it," she said. "I get the feeling that whoever did this has probably been messing with the boy in painful but barely noticeable ways for years. This time, that person just went too far."

More than a feeling. Kate was certain, but she didn't think detailing the flashes she had of scalding water, cigarette butts, and an iron would help until they had proof.

"Christ, Calvert," Barrett said. She could tell that this wasn't the news he hoped to hear, but this was what she *saw*.

"What leads do you have so far?" she asked.

She had nothing, but neither did he. There were no witnesses other than the fisherman who found the body.

"Has he been interviewed?" Kate asked.

"The deputies talked with him after they got the call, but it wouldn't be a bad idea for us to take a crack at him too, in case he's one of those weird serial killers who kills people and then hangs around pretending to be a helpful witness," he said.

"I don't think this is the work of a serial killer," she said.

"Why not?"

She thought of the ways that Caleb used to punish her and knew that this had been done to the boy. She heard a man's voice clearly in her mind: *I didn't want to hurt you. You made me do it. Say you're sorry.*

"This is personal," she said. "Whoever did this knew the victim."

"I think you're probably right," Barrett said.

"Giving up on your serial killer theory so easily? You don't want the guts and the glory?"

"Well, there's that and the fact that there's no missing person's report. If a family member was looking for the boy, there would be, but they wouldn't be looking for the boy if they knew he was dead."

"Barrett, does anything about this strike you as strange?" she asked.

"Does anything about this strike you as not strange?" he countered. "Boy all alone out here on the lake, and no one sees or hears anything?"

"No, I mean, look at him," she said.

"He looks dead," Barrett said.

"Aside from that. He looks well-groomed. He's wearing nice, brand-name clothes. On the one hand, it's like someone really cared for him," she said.

"And on the other hand," he added as if finishing her thoughts, "it's as if someone really didn't."

***

Barrett knew that Kate Calvert thought he was only working with her because he had to, but the truth was that it was also because he wanted to.

He hadn't taken much of an interest in women since his wife, Ginny, left him twenty years ago. But Calvert was different. She was beautiful without realizing it and charming without meaning to be. Though she beat herself up about her parenting skills, he suspected that she was an amazing mother, and her ex had a reputation for being quite the prick.

At the Dayton Redbud Festival in the spring, Barrett had even seen her ex in action.

Her daughter wanted a waffle hot dog, and Calvert's ex-husband had said no, because, "I don't want you to end up looking like your mother."

Calvert hadn't seen him, but after Barrett caught the devastated look on her face, it'd taken all his restraint to stop himself from punching the jerk right then and there. It was as if she'd been hit, and Barrett wanted to tell her that she was better off without her ex, but he didn't know how.

Instead of voicing his feelings, he did what he could. And what he could do was throw this job her way.

"Barrett, were there any identifying marks on the body?" Calvert said.

"You're getting ahead of yourself, Calvert. Remember, we don't have the ME's report yet. And besides, I would think you wouldn't need it. Can't you just touch the water and have a vision or something?"

"Barrett, you know that's not how any of this works. Sometimes my abilities are helpful, sometimes they're not, and sometimes I see nothing more than you see."

"Then why are we paying you the big bucks, Calvert?"

Calvert chuckled. "You must be thinking of someone else. Last I checked, my paycheck was barely enough to cover a portion of my mortgage. Of course, Caleb is supposed to help, but..."

Barrett could tell that Calvert was barely holding it together, and he wanted to get her mind off the ex.

"I think we can rule out tattoos as far as identifying marks," Barrett said. "But maybe there are scars, bone breaks, something that we could find and compare with known medical records."

"Or possibly moles, freckles, birthmarks," she said.

"There's another thing that makes me think that the killer was an amateur," Barrett said.

"What's that?"

"In addition to the ligature marks, there's the fact that the body disposal was the work of someone inexperienced. Based on the state of decomposition that the body is in, I don't think it's been out here long," he said.

"There's also the fact that this isn't a very good place to dump a body if you don't want it seen," she said. "There's lots of boaters and fishermen."

"Right. If you head down the road to Elkton, there's a public boat landing where you can easily dump a body, and the current will carry it downstream," he agreed. "Or, if you take thirty-three up the road a little ways, you'll be in Shenandoah National Park, and it would be easy to push the body off a trail where it might not be found for days. It might even get eaten by bears before being discovered."

"You've given this a lot of thought," Calvert said.

"It's kind of my job."

"How do you get so close to the darkness without letting it consume you?"

"Calvert," he said gently, "let's go talk to the fisherman."

"What about my daughter?"

"One of the deputies can take her back to the office where Bobby Jean can watch her."

Calvert groaned.

"What, you don't trust my judgment? She's more than qualified, watches her three grandchildren all the time. She's even CPR-certified."

"She sounds like grandmother of the year. No, it's not that," Calvert said.

"Then what? Remember, I'm not the psychic here."

"I'm pretty sure that woman really hates me," Calvert said.

"Really? Bobby Jean? She's never been anything but sweet to me."

"She probably has a crush on you, Barrett," Calvert said, and the shade of crimson her face turned filled Barrett with hope.

"Why don't you let *me* talk to her?" Barrett said, smiling.

***

After Erin and a knotty-haired Barbie doll from Kate's car were safely ferried away from the scene by Erin's new best friend, Deputy Martin, Kate and Barrett headed out to interview the fisherman. He was an out of towner from up North and staying at a Hampton Inn in Harrisonburg. The fisherman told them over the phone that he came down to the Shenandoah Valley every summer for the fishing. He was surprised to hear from the Rockingham County Sheriff's Office again given that he'd talked to them that morning, but he was glad to be of help.

When they got to the room, Barrett handled the introductions.

"I'm Sergeant Tom Barrett, and this is my associate, Kate Calvert."

Though it was only eleven a.m., the man, who exuded that specific air of competence and arrogance that made her think he was a doctor, was already done fishing for the day. And, based on the smell of his breath and how red he was in the face, he had consumed at least two or three beers.

When the man said his name was Dr. Todd Stone, confirming her suspicions, she wondered what kind of doctor he was. Given his current level of intoxication, Kate was glad he wasn't on the clock.

Stone offered them a drink, which they declined. Kate tried to keep the look of disapproval off her face, but she wasn't sure that she succeeded.

"The best time of day to fish this time of year," Stone explained, "is late night or early morning. After that, it gets too hot. You can't fish till an hour before sunrise, and you have to quit an hour after sunset. Some people like to fish at night, but I prefer the mornings. By nine a.m., I'm done for the day."

This, Kate thought with relief, at least partially explained his early drinking. She had endured her fill of mean drunks.

"How was the lake this morning?" Barrett asked.

"It was good," Stone said, "and it would have been a good day for fishing."

"If it hadn't been for the body," Kate supplied.

"Yeah, it had some mud and branches around it, and, at first, I wasn't sure what I was seeing. Then, suddenly, I knew. It was like something out of one of those crime TV shows," Stone said.

"What crime TV shows?" Kate asked, thinking he might mean something like *America's Most Wanted.*

"You know, like on *The X-Files*," he said. "You're just out there thinking it's going to be a normal day, and everything goes haywire."

"And what did you do when you saw the body?" Barrett asked.

"I phoned the police, of course," Stone said.

Cautiously, for she had a sinking feeling, Kate asked, "Did you do anything else?"

The man hesitated. Barrett reminded him that this was an official police matter, and so the man finally admitted, "Yeah, I posted some pictures on my blog."

Kate watched Barrett try to conceal his anger. "Would you mind showing us those pictures now?"

The man pulled out his smartphone and complied. Barrett muttered quietly about every idiot having a smartphone nowadays.

The fisherman asked them, "What, did I do something wrong?"

***

"On the bright side," Kate said as they returned to Barrett's car, "maybe someone will see the photo and phone in a tip."

"You mean like the guy who posted the comment, "'Cool! Where is this? I've never caught anything that big on my fishing trips,'" followed by the laughing emoji?"

"Maybe someone who knew the boy will see the post," Kate suggested, trying to quell his anger.

Barrett clenched his fists. "I think we need to try to see if we can find any other witnesses."

Kate knew he was right, but she dreaded walking around the lake in this heat, knocking on doors.

As if reading her mind, Barrett said, "I think we need to talk not only to those who live in houses along the lake, but also the fishermen who are out now. The lake is more than twenty acres. It's too big to walk around. Besides, part of the trail on the upper side is covered with rocks and tree branches, and you don't have the right shoes. I think we should take a boat."

***

Their boating options were limited because motorboats weren't allowed on the lake, so now here they were in a canoe. Under different circumstances, Barrett would have loved to be alone with Calvert on the lake.

"I think you should sit up front, so you can get a good view of the lake," Barrett said. Part of the reason was that he wanted to watch her. "Maybe you'll see a flash of light, and it will lead us in the right direction."

She made a self-depreciating joke asking if the heavier rider should sit in the back, but he didn't think it was funny. He hated that she felt that way about herself.

Though Barrett was trying to stay cool, the heat was also getting to him. Not as much as it was to her, though. He watched the sweat pour down her neck and her back before handing her a handkerchief.

"Well, aren't you a regular Cary Grant?" She took the handkerchief and wiped her neck.

"Okay, Madame Calvert, lead the way," Barrett said, trying to lighten the mood. He reached into his pocket once again.

"What now?" she asked. Her eyes were on the water. His eyes were on her.

"It's sunscreen, Calvert. Put it on."

"I can't reach," Calvert said.

"Then I will," Barrett said. "I expect that with skin like that, you probably don't tan too well. Looks like you might fry up better than some of the catfish out here. According to the sign, the lake is also stocked with crappie, musky, largemouth bass, and sunfish. You don't seem much like a sunfish to me."

"I don't usually tan."

"Let me put it on then."

She hesitated before agreeing, but she let him direct her toward the center of the boat. The touch of his hands on her shoulders felt electric. He didn't want to remove them, but he had no good excuse to let them linger.

Kate wasn't looking at him, so he couldn't judge her reaction.

"I think we're good," she finally said, indicating that they should move back to their respective positions.

"Hey, Barrett," she said, "I want you to turn the boat."

***

It was more than instinct that caused Kate to say this. What she saw was the boy—or a specter of the boy—beckoning them toward a house on the lake. The woman they encountered once they got there was elderly, cranky, and unlikely to be the boy's mother. For one thing, she was too old. Still, she could have information that might be useful. But how to pry it out of her? Based on her response to their presence, Kate didn't think she was likely to volunteer much. The first thing she said when approached was, "Well, well, what have I done to attract the attention of the po-lice?"

Even in plainclothes, Barrett looked like a cop. But he apparently hadn't met a woman he couldn't charm, even one who was old enough to be his mother, and Barrett was hard at work on that while Kate scanned the area for possible clues. Were they even headed in the right direction, or had she led them astray? In the moments after Barrett had applied sunscreen to her back, she felt so certain. Like she used to before Caleb had shaken her confidence. But maybe Kate was mistaken. Maybe the ghost had been nothing more than a heat-induced hallucination.

The woman's name was Vera King, and she'd lived on the lake for thirty years.

Kate said they were looking for some help.

"What kinda help?" Vera asked.

Kate wondered if she was naturally suspicious or if she had something to hide.

"Oh, you know, just an expert opinion." Barrett's tone suggested that he was talking to a trusted colleague.

Kate watched Vera relax. God, she thought. He's good. Kate wished she had his natural ease with people.

"Sure, I might be able to help with something like that," Vera said. "In fact, I'd be happy to. It used to be a lot safer out here, you know? Now, it seems like every time you pick up the phone or answer the door, someone's trying to scam you."

"We were wondering if you've seen anything suspicious around here lately," Barrett said.

"I don't know anything about those kids who've been making out over by the lake," Vera said defensively.

Barrett looked puzzled, so Kate jumped in.

"Oh, that," Kate said, as if she knew exactly what Vera was talking about. "I mean, what can you say? I mean, kids will be kids, right?"

"It's not like I watch or anything, but sometimes I can't help but see, you know?"

"Of course," Kate said, radiating empathy. "What we're looking for has more to do with a little boy. Have you seen any families around here, especially ones where maybe something didn't seem quite right?"

Vera looked thoughtful for a second, like she was about to say no, but then she hesitated and said, "Well, maybe. There were this one."

"What can you tell us about them?" Barrett said.

"I noticed the boy more than the man," Vera said. "The boy looked like an angel, blond hair, puppy dog eyes. But it was hard to get a good look at the man. He had on a hat and sunglasses and was wearing baggy clothes, but, well, he just seemed to me like a lost soul."

***

Once they were back on the boat, Barrett said, "That was some high-quality acting there, Calvert. You do any community theater that I don't know about? Like maybe down at ShenanArts?"

"You take classes at the local charm school?" she quipped back.

"I was their star pupil," Barrett said, deadpan. "But it didn't pay the rent. That's why I had to get a side job with the sheriff's department."

"What do you think, Barrett? Should we follow the lead she gave us?"

"You're the psychic," Barrett said. "You tell me."

Kate sighed, confidence still shaken by thoughts of Caleb. Sometimes, she couldn't remember who she had been before.

"She said she thinks we're looking for a man who seemed like a lost soul. I have no idea what that means, but maybe we should check out that church, the one with the white roof across the lake?"

"Good thing we're not paying her for information, because that's not much of a tip. But I guess the church is as good a place to start as any."

"Barrett, I have a bad feeling about this," Kate said. Then again, she didn't like churches in general. They tended to be as skeptical of her beliefs as she was of theirs.

Near the entrance of the church, they heard a noise, so Barrett got his gun ready, just in case. But they couldn't determine its origins—on a weekday afternoon, no one was there. Maybe it was another ghost like the vision of the boy she had seen on the water, Kate thought. Barrett called the number on the sign outside the church, but no one answered.

Once they were back in his car, Kate expected him to admonish her, but he didn't.

"I'm sorry that was a bust," she said. "But I think I have an idea. Do you trust me?"

"With my life."

"Okay," she said. "Here's what I think we should do."

***

Kate said that she thought the killer would return to the scene of the crime. "Remember what that old lady said about the guy who was fishing with a boy?"

"You mean how she said he seemed like a lost soul? Honestly, I think a physical description would have been more helpful. Like five foot six, two hundred and eighty pounds, or five foot eight, and a lean one-fifty."

"You mean you can't recognize a lost soul?"

"Can you?"

"I used to think I could," Kate said. "Now I'm not so sure. But it's getting late, and we can't expect Bobby Jean to watch Erin forever. Maybe we should head back."

"Let's not give up yet. I'll give Bobby Jean a call and see if she's willing to watch her for a little longer."

Barrett took a step back from the lake to make the phone call while Kate waited by the water.

"Well?" she asked when he'd finished.

"Bobby Jean said Erin's an angel, unlike her mother."

"You liar."

"What she actually said was that she'd be happy to watch Erin for as long as you need her to, that it would be a pleasure."

"Aw, really?"

"Really," Barrett said.

Kate and Barrett waited in the car for three hours. At first, they tried sitting with the windows down, but it was too hot, so now they had the AC on with the windows cracked so they wouldn't miss anything. There was nothing to miss, though, because they saw and heard nothing. No cars. No bikes. No people.

Then they heard a crunching sound, but all they saw was a fat white possum, startled by their presence.

"You know, I'm thinking it's possible that he could approach on foot," Calvert said.

"Or maybe he's long gone, back to whatever swamp of human darkness he crawled out of."

"I don't think so. People believe that water will wash away their sins. But it doesn't," Kate said as if recalling an unpleasant memory.

"You think he needs closure?" Barrett asked as he fiddled with a pack of gum.

"Yes."

"You know, he could approach from the other side of the lake. Rather than sitting here, I should walk down to where they found the body."

"You mean *we* should walk down to where they found the body?"

"It's too dangerous, I need you to stay here."

"You need a cover," she said. "We could be like the lovers that old woman mentioned, taking a romantic stroll down by the lake."

"Okay," Barrett said, thinking that maybe he was agreeing to the plan more easily than he should have. His pulse raced when she took his hand.

"Should we approach quietly, or?" she asked.

Barrett fought back the urge to kiss her as he watched, senses heightened, for any sign of movement.

"Shh," he whispered. "I hear something. Get behind me, Calvert."

The man and Barrett saw each other at the same time. He was lean and scrawny with pale skin, the type of guy who seemed like he had been bullied as a child. He fit the picture Barrett had of a weak man targeting the weaker.

"Looking for something?" Barrett saw panic on the man's face.

The man circled Barrett before charging at Calvert, purposely knocking her down. Barrett wanted to check on Kate, but he knew that she could hold her own, and he knew that this was what the man wanted. Instead he kept his eyes locked on his target.

The man started running. He was younger and fast, but Barrett, who lived his life at the gym, was faster.

He'd only managed to run a few feet when Barrett tackled him, pinning him to the ground.

"You killed the boy," Barrett insisted once he had the man safely cuffed.

"What boy?"

"Your son," Barrett said, bluffing as he cuffed him. "DNA doesn't lie."

Predictably, the man broke down. "I didn't mean to. It was an accident. I'm sorry."

Calvert, who was behind them now, said quietly, "What about the other times? The welts? The burns? The ones that healed and the ones that only seemed to."

The man's jaw dropped, and his eyes widened.

"Try not to scare the guy, Calvert," Barrett said as they headed back to the parking lot.

***

Once Barrett had the man in the car, he locked the doors but cranked up the AC. He didn't want to be accused of practicing cruel and unusual punishment, even if the suspect deserved it.

"Hey, can I talk to you for a minute before we head back?"

"Sure, Tom, what's up?"

"Look, I was wondering, after I get back to the office and process the paperwork and you pick up your daughter, could I maybe take you both to Kline's and buy you an ice cream?"

"I'm not sure they'll still be open then. And, besides, it's not like I need the calories."

"Please don't do that."

"Do what?"

"If I could get a hold of that asshole ex who made you feel this way about yourself, I might be tempted to commit a felony."

"That so?"

Barrett was struggling to keep his attention on her face, and he found his eyes wandering lower.

"Barrett, I don't mind if you take a sneak peek."

He moved to kiss her but stopped himself. "Oh, Christ," he said, "I just completed that sexual harassment training."

"Let me make this easy for you, Tom. I don't think there is any woman alive who wouldn't want you to kiss her."

"I don't care about the opinion of *any* woman. Only the opinion of one."

"In that case," she said as she moved closer, "is this clear enough for you?"

"It's pretty clear. After this, I'd like to..."

"Yes."

"You didn't even let me finish asking the question."

"I can see the future, remember? And when it comes to you, Tom, I very much like what I see."

Baxia Rolls

Catfishes, Casseroles, and the Demonic Fiddle of Staunton

FENDY S. TULODO

NO ONE REALLY TALKS about the hum anymore. It's just... there. Like the smell of burnt coffee inside the DMV or the way everybody in Staunton waves, but no one makes eye contact. People get used to weird stuff faster than they should.

The hum started five years ago, maybe six. Hard to say. It didn't start loud. Simply a low kind of buzzing that made your keys rattle if you stood near the back of Big Lots for too long. One of the teenagers working there thought it was "electrical reverb." A pastor claimed it was divine frequency. A dog ran in circles for four hours and wouldn't stop foaming.

But nobody ever found the source. So they ignored it. Covered it with asphalt. Paved over the hum.

Then Baxia rolled in.

You wouldn't expect a retired Mobile Legends hero to wind up in Virginia. Not voluntarily, anyway. But Baxia wasn't really the dramatic type. He liked snacks. He liked quiet. He liked things that made sense, which is a little ironic, all things considered.

When the game developers phased him out—right around the time new heroes got flashier and weirder—he bought a truck. Had it painted to look like his old shell: green, gold, a bit beat up on the sides. Called it **BAXIA ROLLS: Dumplings of Destiny**. It was a pun. He loved puns.

He didn't know Staunton. Didn't know about the hum or the fiddle or the town's weird reputation for… let's say "spiritual potholes." He just saw the parking lot, saw the traffic, figured people who buy knockoff batteries from Big Lots probably get hungry. Parked and started steaming.

First customer was a woman in a wide green coat carrying what looked like a ferret in a baby sling.

"You new?" she asked, squinting.

"Yeah," said Baxia. "Want dumplings?"

"You parked on the hum."

"Excuse me?"

"The lot. It hums. Like, spiritually. Bad things happen on that spot."

He blinked…

She thrust a casserole dish into his hands—still warm, tinfoil crinkling like a warning. "You'll need this." No explanation. Just the click of her heels walking away, leaving him stranded with whatever simmered beneath that shiny silver lid.

Inside the dish was something that smelled like peanut butter, pickles, and cinnamon.

Baxia made $42 that day, not counting the cursed casserole. Not bad. But right before he locked up for the night, the truck shifted. Not like wind. Not like a tire issue. It *shuddered*. Like something deep underground turned over and said **Huh?**

And that's when he heard the music.

Faint, scratchy, not quite a song. Only the first notes of something that didn't *want* to be played. And the bow—the glowing fiddle bow—was just… *there*, stuck underneath the rear axle like it had been waiting.

He didn't touch it.

Not at first.

Moonlight painted stripes across his sheets as he twisted in bed. The clock's ticking grew louder with each passing hour—a metronome counting down the night. He squeezed his eyes shut, but the darkness only played the day's mistakes on loop. Not from guilt or fear, simply... curiosity. So he brought the bow into the truck. It pulsed. Not menacingly. More like a forgotten memory trying to be remembered.

The next morning, a kid was waiting for him.

Skeleton hoodie. Dirty sneakers. Weird energy.

"You got the bow," the kid said.

"Excuse me?"

"I'm Madge. Last Fiddlekeeper. That bow is haunted. You touch it?"

"...No?"

"You *look* like you touched it."

"I sell dumplings."

Madge crossed her arms. "Great. A cursed food truck. That's new."

Staunton, as it turns out, has a long, mostly undocumented history of **spiritual instruments**. Not in the joyful church choir way. In the *this-fiddle-melts-door-knobs* kind of way.

The bow was part of a set. The fiddle itself went missing years ago, during a production of *King Lear* at the Blackfriars Playhouse where all the actors spontaneously developed nosebleeds at the same line. Doreen, the municipal ghost, had been trying to contain the whole mess ever since.

Baxia didn't believe any of it. Not really. But when his truck tires deflated again by themselves, and the Rite Aid sign started blinking in Morse code, he figured it might be time to listen.

Madge explained it like this:

The bow chose him. Not because he was noble or wise or particularly musical—he wasn't—but because **Staunton needed a distraction**. Some kind of spiritual sponge to soak up the weird. He was here now. He was weird-adjacent. Close enough.

And besides, there was a fiddle tournament coming up. Sort of a magical duel disguised as the Staunton Music Festival showcase. And Madge, being underage and slightly cursed herself, couldn't participate.

"So you want me," Baxia said slowly, "to play haunted fiddle at a demon tournament."

"Well." Madge shrugged. "Only if you don't wanna get possessed by Wednesday."

The Staunton Music Festival was a disaster before it even began.

The prize for the fiddle contest was a jar of moonlight sealed in salt, a coupon for three months of free septic maintenance, and **the favor of Doreen**—which apparently meant free parking in most downtown zones. The competition? Bad.

Like, aggressively bad. One guy played the spoons until they caught fire. Another girl sang in reverse. A man called *Percy the Possum King* showed up playing a hurdy-gurdy made of teeth (Baxia tried not to ask where from).

But no one had the bow. Not like Baxia.

He didn't *know* how to play, not really. He just mimicked the sound the hum made—scraping the bow across thin air like he was pulling notes from the static itself. Tried to follow the rhythm of the food truck's old fan belt. The result was... well, **unholy**.

In a good way.

The air vibrated. Dust rose from the grass like smoke. One of the judges turned into a goose briefly, then turned back and handed Baxia the prize.

Of course, that's when the fiddle itself crash-landed.

Dropped out of the sky like a meteor. Landed in the middle of the fairgrounds, right between the funnel cake tent and the Porta Potty line.

And *someone* picked it up.

No one saw who. One minute it was just there. The next, the music began again.

Only this time, it wasn't playful. It was old. Like cave-old. And angry.

The grass wilted. The moon blinked. People dropped their cotton candy and screamed for no reason. And Madge?

Madge ran.

"Fiddlekeeper's job is over," she muttered. "It's yours now, Dumpling Man."

Baxia stared at the fiddle bow in his hands. Felt its hum match the one under the parking lot. Maybe it *had* been calling. Maybe he'd just been the first to listen.

He took a breath.

Walked to the center of the fairgrounds.

And played.

Not well. Not confidently. But real. Honest. Messy. Alive.

The music didn't fix things. It didn't stop the wind or erase the clouds or make Staunton normal again. But it changed something.

Made the hum pause. Just long enough to matter.

No one told Baxia that the winner of the Fiddle Duel had to **keep playing**.

Not forever. Only whenever the hum got loud again.

At first, he didn't mind. People started showing up not just for dumplings, but for the sound—strange and wobbly and kind of like a banjo made of thunder. They called him "The Shell-man," which he didn't love, but okay. Better than "Soup Truck Goblin," which was the other nickname floating around town.

But the thing was... he could *feel* the fiddle now. Even when it wasn't in his hands. It hummed at his elbows. Buzzed behind his teeth. Like a bad radio signal caught in his bones.

And he started hearing other things, too.

Like the **catfish**.

The first time Baxia heard them, he was cleaning the truck. Nothing but a regular Thursday. Nothing demonic, no fairies or bleeding clouds. Just Lysol, elbow grease, and leftover bao filling. And then—

"Ssssstttaaaauunnnntoooonnnn," a voice said from the drain.

He froze. Stared at the sink. Waited.

"Daaaaiirrryyy Qqqquuuuueeennnnn."

It wasn't loud. It wasn't aggressive. Just... wet. Slippery. Like somebody gargled rocks and regret.

Baxia leaned in.

Something blinked at him. From the pipe.

He slammed the lid shut and ran into the parking lot.

"I thought the catfish lived in the creek," he said later to Madge, who had reappeared uninvited and was eating frozen peas from a bag with a spoon.

"Yup," she said. "But then they got kicked out. By the eels."

Baxia stared.

"Eels. Got territorial after the fiddle incident in '92. Long story. Short version: now the catfish are in the pipes."

"And... they talk?"

"Only on Thursdays."

He rubbed his forehead. "Why are they whispering about Dairy Queen?"

Madge shrugged. "Maybe they're hungry. Maybe they're cursed. Or maybe Dairy Queen's the next target."

Turns out, she was kind of right.

That night, the Dairy Queen exploded.

Not like boom, fireball, Michael Bay style. More like... it *unzipped*. The walls peeled inward. The blizzards curdled. The tiles vanished. And at the center of it all, floating three feet off the ground, was a man in a banjo shirt holding **the fiddle**.

Not *a* fiddle.

The fiddle.

The twin to Baxia's bow.

The air around him shimmered. Not like magic. Like **bad heat**. Like car hood on a July road trip kind of shimmer. He opened his mouth, and a **whole marching band of teeth** smiled out.

"I am Marvyn," he said. "I come for the encore."

Madge dragged Baxia into the bushes. They watched Dairy Queen finish imploding. No casualties, miraculously, unless you count the Peanut Buster® Parfaits.

"That's Marvyn," she hissed. "He used to be human. Sort of. Played a cursed violin at a fiddler's campfire in 1986 and never fully came back."

"What does he want?"

She gave him a look. "You, obviously."

Baxia stood. "I am not interested in him *that* way."

"No, dummy. You. The bow. The sound. He wants to finish the song."

"I don't even *know* the song!"

Madge pulled out a very soggy napkin.

"It's on here," she said. "Kind of. If you squint."

The napkin was from Hardee's. Smelled like ketchup and old fries. On it, drawn in smudged eyeliner pencil, was what appeared to be music. Possibly. Or maybe it was an ancient map. Either way, Baxia couldn't read it.

"You expect me to play *this*?"

"Not play," said Madge. "Translate."

"To what?"

"To *food*."

The air went stiff between them.

"Sorry," he muttered—too late, too hollow, the word collapsing under its own weight. "Did you say food?"

"Marvyn's cursed fiddle doesn't just want sound. It wants memory. Smell. Emotion. Like... like musical umami. You don't *play* the tune. You *cook* it."

So that's how the city of Staunton ended up with a **musical cook-off ritual** held inside a **flattened Dairy Queen**, with a retired Mobile Legends hero cooking a forbidden dumpling recipe to save the town from fiddle apocalypse.

Marvyn stood across the lot, tuning his glowing string instrument with a piece of someone's hair.

Baxia planted himself behind a portable burner, holding a single egg with a crack down the middle that **glowed faintly green**.

"Egg of Echo," Madge whispered. "Very illegal."

"No one's arresting me," he muttered.

"Yet."

He cracked the egg. Fire rose. The sky blinked.

And the cook-off began.

The rules were unclear. There was no judge, just sound.

Marvyn played notes that made potholes ripple and local pets howl.

Baxia fried dumplings that hissed in three different keys. One of them harmonized with a stop sign.

Marvyn bowed a glissando that made a nearby bird molt instantly.

Baxia flipped a scallion pancake that **sang** as it cooked. Not words. Simply... sorrow. Really crispy sorrow.

It dragged for an hour, and then the final round began.

Baxia zeroed in on his last ingredient. The casserole. The weird one. The one the lady gave him on Day One. Still in the fridge. Never spoiled. Still... **warm**. He didn't question it. Just opened the foil. Poured it into the pan.

It hissed. Then laughed.

No, really.

The pan **laughed**.

Madge gasped. "That's!—That's the forbidden binding mix. From the old chef-hexes."

"I just thought it was peanut butter and pickles."

"It is. But also heartbreak. And maybe a little necromancy."

The smell hit the lot like a punch to the nose. Marvyn choked mid-fiddle. His strings snapped.

Baxia flipped the mix. Played the bow.

One note. Pure. And everything stopped.

Marvyn dropped his fiddle.

The hum—beneath the town, under the truck, inside the drainpipes—**paused**, and the bow stopped glowing. A catfish crawled out of the busted Dairy Queen sink and saluted.

Baxia exhaled. Looked around.

Staunton had survived. Again. Somehow.

He looked at Madge. "So what now?"

She shrugged. "You win. For now. But Staunton's weird. You'll see. This town's like a haunted casserole."

He nodded. "Still warm. Still cursed. Still... delicious."

But Staunton wasn't done yet.

The next morning, Baxia made one decision. **No more magic casseroles.** Or at least... not without reading the ingredients first.

He sat cross-legged on the roof of his food truck, drinking slightly burnt coffee from a mug that said *World's Okayest Dumpling Dealer.* The town looked... mostly okay. Bits of Dairy Queen still hovered midair like confused ceiling tiles. The air had that aftertaste—like ozone and regret. But nobody was screaming, and the catfish had gone quiet.

For Staunton, this was peace.

And peace made him nervous.

"You know it won't last," said Madge, who somehow climbed onto the roof without using a ladder.

"I was enjoying the quiet."

"Don't get used to it."

She handed him *The News-Leader.* The headline read: **"Saxophone Cult Steals Mayor's Bones."**

Baxia sipped his coffee. "Okay. That one's not on me," he muttered, already sensing that something weirder was coming next.

"Yet."

He folded the paper and looked at her. "Madge... what *are* you? You're not just a dumpling enthusiast, right?"

She squinted at the horizon. "I used to be a cartographer for magical ley lines. Then a temp at a cursed JCPenney. Now? I freelance."

"At what?"

"Crisis. Mostly food-related."

They sat in silence.

Then something howled. Not a dog. Not a ghost. More like a haunted accordion being sat on by an emotional bear.

"I'll go check it out," Madge said, jumping off the truck with the grace of a drunk squirrel.

Baxia stayed put. His phone buzzed. A text from "**MAYBE PASTOR??**"

> heard you saved the town with fried grief. respect

> wanna guest star at the next sunday potluck?

He sighed. Even his phone was weird now.

Later that day, a **man with celery stalks for fingers** knocked on the food truck. "Can I get a triple dumpling special, no sauce, extra fate?"

Baxia blinked. "You mean spice?"

"No, fate. The extra destiny stuff you drizzled last week? Real crunchy."

He nodded slowly. "That was an accident. We're out."

The man sighed, fingers drooping slightly. "Fine. I'll just get a bao. But if it's not *mildly prophetic*, I'm yelping."

He left five dollars and a small glowing cube. Tip? The cube whispered his name. In his father's voice.

By Wednesday, the town adjusted.

The Dairy Queen was now a portal museum. Three dollars for entry, five if you wanted to poke the wormhole. Baxia's food truck line had doubled, even though half the customers were clearly interdimensional travelers. A teenager ordered noodles while levitating six inches off the ground and humming in binary.

Baxia got used to it.

Sort of.

But something gnawed at him. Not the catfish this time. It was the fiddle. The **song**. He could still hear it. Not out loud. But... in *dreams*.

And worse: it wasn't finished.

That night, Madge slammed a giant Tupperware on the counter. "Pack your knives, Shellman. We're going to Church."

"I don't do religion."

"Not that kind. This is **The Chapel of the Eight Cooks**. Only way to seal a half-played tune is to feed it to a choir of retired recipe spirits."

Baxia stared. "That's not real."

"It is now. Staunton Rules."

He sighed. "What do I need?"

"Your bow. Your bravest dish. And something you regret."

"I regret meeting you."

"Perfect. Bring that."

The Chapel wasn't on any map.

It sat behind the old bowling alley, through a curtain of discarded cheese curds and regretful Yelp reviews. Inside: eight stone pews, each shaped like a kitchen appliance. Ovens. Crock pots. One air fryer.

The ghosts floated near the ceiling, humming low and sweet like lullabies dipped in molasses.

Baxia stepped forward. Held the bow. Said nothing. He simply cooked.

He made dumplings with memory.

Scallion joy from his childhood.

Pork seasoned with jealousy.

Wrapper folds crimped with homesickness.

He added a drop of oil from that cursed casserole—the part that sang sorrow—and one sprig of laughing parsley (illegal in twelve counties and one dreamscape).

The ghosts descended. Tasted. Their eyes closed.

A harmony filled the chapel. Not a song. Not exactly. More like the feeling of finishing something. A final page turned.

A sigh.

The fiddle hummed once.

Then fell **silent**.

When Baxia stepped out, it was morning. Madge offered him a taco.

"I thought we were done with cursed food?"

"This one's just regular. Maybe."

He bit into it. Smiled.

"So," she said, "you gonna stick around?"

He looked out over Staunton. The fog had turned pink. A raccoon floated past holding a trombone. Somewhere, something mooed in iambic pentameter.

"Mm." A slow grin as he stretched out on the truck's roof cushions, the foam molding around him like they'd been waiting. "Could definitely live like this."

EPILOGUE

Inside the truck, the fridge hummed.
Behind the chili paste and old cabbage, sat a note.
Scrawled in messy handwriting:
The song's not over. Just paused.
PS: Loved the crispy sorrow. -M
Baxia closed the fridge.
Smiled.
And turned up the burner.

The Iron Gate

JAMES COLE

"So, is he dead?"

"No, thank heavens, they got him on an IV of TPA just in time."

I remained silent for a moment, agonizing over the informality of my previous response. To Aunt Rina's credit, she waited patiently while I mustered something akin to sympathy.

"Well, it's just one of those things..."

"Please, Roland, save that for when he actually passes away."

"Sorry, I—I'm glad to hear he's alright. So, what's the plan from here? Physical therapy? Assisted living?"

"Hard to say at this point, but we're going to start by moving him back into the house on Algernon."

At this, I pried a wider gap in my blinds, stared out at the crabgrass-tufted hillside across the street from my house. Beyond that was a little creek segmented by briar cataracts and lone limestone heaps, and beyond *that* another few hills, a gravel road, and finally a grave plot mowed into a slant rhombus demarcated by a fence of split timber. This created nesting backdrops which, overlapping crest-to-foot, led to the Pleinway family home moldering on its promontory above Algernon Road.

"Roland, you there?"

"Yeah, sorry, I just—when'll he be coming in?"

"We're going to try and move him out of the hospital before the end of the week. The doctors say—well, they say plenty, but I think it'll do him some good to return to familiar environs."

I *mhmm*'ed for the rest of the conversation, didn't even realize Rina had hung up until well after my phone screen went dark.

Naturally, it fell to me, the living relative closest in both relation and proximity, to help prepare for the old man's arrival. While Aunt Rina took care of the hospital hoopla in New York, I was sent out to canvas the ancient homestead. When my mother was still around, she'd periodically nudge me to swing by on my off days to make sure the place didn't collapse into a heap of mildew and splinters. On such outings—digging the filth from gutters, putzing about with an emphysematic mower, I'd dream fondly of the day when a stray cigarette defenestrated by a passing motorist would finally catch the dead dogwood and reduce the whole property to cinder. We had a history, me and this house, and not just from the chores. In fact, it's safe to say this house had a history with everyone in Weyers Cave, because, like any accursed domicile, it seemed to age as rapidly as its most infamous resident. And now, with that resident's brain partly obstructed by ischemia, who knew precisely how this illness would manifest on the sagging roof, the indolent eaves, the narrow windows impervious to warm light?

Dexter "Dex" Pleinway, my grandfather, was no one's favorite. He couldn't even be considered curmudgeonly charming, nor so expressively villainous as to warrant the occasional practical joke. His favored sin, my father used to say, was his staunch indifference to everyone and everything. We grandkids were often instructed to keep it down, keep it outside, keep it to yourself, whenever Grandpa came around. On Christmas, he would sit up in the attic by himself, and on Valentine's Day he'd lock himself in the bathroom doing Cupid knows what. The only time I could recall him ever seeming giddy was the turning of the seasons when birds migrated overhead. He'd sit out on one of his three porches and fire shells into the high-altitude vees, then make us kids run out into traffic to fetch his kills. He even kept a whistle which he used to command us like dogs.

One time, my cousin Theo, who'd just turned thirteen and learned to swear, told him to "get your own damn birds!" Grandpa fired a shot just over his head. I don't think he meant to hit anyone, but a couple of pellets ripped into Ranger, a Welsh Sheepdog and the only bright soul living under the Pleinway roof. The cousins and I cried all night in the laundry room, huddled over poor

Ranger, until the towels couldn't turn any pinker and his furry flank ceased its heaving.

In the years since, I've tried to find ways of explaining that to folks. Terms like "bastard" and "sonuvabitch" always seemed insufficient. It was not uncommon for a neighbor, their window shattered by lead shot or mailbox rear-ended, to come storming up to the family gate, stand there rattling against the cold iron, hurling accusations at a listless, lifeless house. Even if Grandpa were out on his porch, twelve-gauge in his lap, the shouts of: "Pleinway you ornery motherfucker, get on down here!" would dust right off him like dry pollen.

Three days after my call with Rina, I finally convinced myself to head up to the property to check things out. I'd started a round of weeding in the front yard when Dennis McElroy pulled up in his pickup.

"Lil' Rollie up and at it 'gain? Say, I thought you usually did your yearly penance 'round July when things really get a-sweltering. Don't tell me the old man's got you workin' early."

"And then some," I replied.

"No shit? I thought surely he'd be dead by now. No offense."

"If only we were all so lucky." I set the herbicide down and approached the gate. No sense yelling all that distance. "He'll be here before the end of the week. Had himself a nasty stroke, but they say he'll recover. Aunt Rina thinks he'd do better in the family home. Besides, I think it drives her and all the other kids nuts that we got all this land and no one to enjoy it."

Even this felt too sarcastic. I cast a cautious glance back at the house as it loomed with Virginia creeper spider-webbing down either flank, all varicose and deranged.

"Folk won' be too happy 'bout that," he said.

"Well, he'll move in on Saturday. Sunday's a good enough time for the torch-and-pitchfork crowd. Maybe they can carpool." I tried to laugh at my own little joke, but Dennis looked at me with all the severity of scar tissue. He wiggled his dip from one gum to another.

"People go a long way to keep livin' the lives they livin'," he said. "Sometimes they's extreme. You just be careful now."

And at that he pulled away. I lingered by the iron gate a little longer, felt a twinge. Cryptic warnings aside, I'd become so accustomed to the property's unique brand of unease, I was surprised to feel another chill walk its fingers up my spine. I told myself it was a perfect confluence of settings, and nothing more; the cemetery to one side of the road, the house on the other, and beyond that, the ancient Blue Ridge holding who knows how many secrets, gradually showing through like ribs of a carcass going lean.

✱✱✱

My fiancée kicked me awake.

"Roland, *Roland*," she said. She struck me in the ear with her pillow. "Your phone. How can you *not* hear that?"

"Hmmm, no, I couldn't possibly have any more sherbert... mhmm."

My faux sleep inertia didn't convince, and so I was struck a few more times. Shannon groaned, kicked off her covers, and retreated to the bathroom. My phone went dead, and I thought all would be well. After a few seconds, another call came buzzing in and I, slapping blindly at my nightstand, eventually answered.

"Hrm-llo?"

It was Aunt Rina again. This would make the fifth call since Saturday. First, the toilets wouldn't flush, then the stair runner was "dangerously loose," and I'd made at least three trips back to the property because some pipe or joist made too much noise at night.

"I know what it is that's been keeping us up all hours," she said. I had a smartass reply ready and waiting but put it away when Rina continued. "That damn front gate. I'm standing here in the dining room looking at it right now. The wind is stirring it and making it clang something awful."

"Rina, I checked the gate already. The hinges should be tight."

"Well, they aren't. It's driving your grandfather mad. He's been up in his room groaning every night since we got back. His doctors say—"

"It's not good for him, I know. Listen, I'll come by tomorrow and take the damn thing off if it's bothering y'all so much. But I promise it's not the gate."

"Roland, I'm watching it right now, and it will not stop."

"Goodnight Rina," and I hung up.

Shannon came out of the bathroom a moment later and face-planted into the space beside me. Muffled by the mattress, she said: "Whuff at ur Awn n'gain?"

"I don't know if I can keep doing this," I said. "At this rate, I'll die before Gramps."

"Whe one a' yew beher."

"Thanks babe," I said, smiling. "I love you too."

***

I spent the next afternoon with a can of WD-40 and an ache in my back. The hinges got another dose of oil. I replaced a few of the bolts, practiced swinging them open and closed until satisfied that, short of a hurricane-force wind, they would never again creak, crack, or otherwise disturb. I took a break to suck down some Gatorade and check my messages when Rina appeared on the front porch.

"So it's done? You wanna come in and tell your grandpa?"

"He going to look at me this time?"

"Rollie, don't be nasty. He gets enough of that from the neighbors."

Almost on cue, another van, busted up from years of field work, rolled down the road. It slowed to let two occupants, a husband and wife in their late seventies, glower not so much at me and Rina, but at the whole homestead, a look so hateful that I felt it might afflict my future children. Once they'd reached the edge of the cemetery, the husband hit the gas and sped off in a cloud of dust.

"Been getting that all week," I said. "You sure this is a good idea, him staying here?"

"Screw the whole lot of 'em," Rina said. "People get this story in their heads and can never shake it. It's a sickness of the community. I'm not sayin' your grandfather was a saint, but they had no right to chase him off his own land."

"Chase?" I said. My family always maintained that Grandpa moved up to New York to be closer to his brother. What a load of horseshit. If there was anyone Grandpa hated more than his brother, then he hid it well. Me and the cousins long speculated that Grandpa shot one too many birds and was wanted by the EPA for avian genocide. Another theory posited that he was actually in Witness Protection and his underworld associates had finally tracked him down.

"Come up here and sit in the shade a spell," Rina said with a wave. Once situated on a stool that canted to the right, Rina continued.

"Do you remember a young man by the name of John Crouse?"

I squinted. The name didn't so much ring a bell as crack a windshield. A sudden, almost drunken surge of nausea dropped into my lower stomach. Cursory eye flicks to the corners of the porch yielded no reachable vessels in case this sickness decided to ricochet off my bottommost end and rocket up wet and stinging.

John Crouse. A name, I realized, that'd undergone some suppression in the years since childhood. Back in the day, when we kids would spend summer Sundays making up games in the front yard, John Crouse would hobble down from Algernon Road in his blue overalls. He'd come up to the front gate and rattle it with his one good arm, the other curled up at his side. Rumor had it he suffered a stroke as a little boy, and so could not motivate the limbs on his left side, giving him a herky-jerky locomotion not unlike an animated corpse in some B-movie. Nowadays, I like to think I've overcome a lot of that ableist fear, but when you're a kid in rural Virginia—well, you soak up some of the local prejudice.

John was maybe twenty-one years old and hated my grandpa more than anyone else in the Cave. When we kids weren't around, he'd spend afternoons throwing rocks at the front of the house. Grandma would come out with a couple of pans, one as a shield, the other her bludgeon, and chase him out of sight. But when we would visit, John would come by just to play the menace.

"Hiii, Rollie," he'd say, leaning into the impediment to freak me out. He'd always reach his good arm over the iron spikes but could never quite reach the latch. "Whyn't you open up this gate?"

For years we'd run screaming from him, but as we got older, a bit meaner, taking on, I'm ashamed to admit, some of grandpa's people skills, we would taunt him, get close enough for him to reach for us over the gate before jumping back in the nick of time.

One summer, we used an unreeled fly rod to prod at him. So we'd go, in and out, back and forth, until John would get all red in the face and say: "Tell yer pa, I's come 'n' see him someday."

By this point, Rina could tell I'd made a wrong turn in the avenues of memory. A nudge on my knee brought me back.

"Yeah, I remember. He caught Carrie one day at the gate, said he wouldn't let her go until Grandpa came down. I ran up to get him, but he just sat in the attic and told me to leave him alone. I was worried John would hurt Carrie, but—"

"He was the only one who ever seemed to get under your grandfather's skin. Well, one day, when you kids were back at school, John tried to climb over that gate in the front. Normally, your grandma could chase him off with her pots and pans, but this time he seemed determined. Well, he was halfway over the gate when your grandfather came down with his shotgun, telling him to get off his property and all that. Well, you know ol' Dexter, more used to wingin' birds than bastards, he got a little tense with his trigger finger and hit John in the chest. It seemed a miracle he didn't die right then and there. John fell back onto the road and crawled back to his mother's home down Algernon. They said she found him dead on her stoop an hour later. Her hearin' was going bad, and so she didn't know he was pawin' at the door.

"Now, I don't need to tell you it's a stand your ground crowd in these parts, and no one was particularly fond of that poor Crouse boy, but most folks found this murder unforgivable. How long, they figured, till it was one of them that got blasted for givin' your grandpa the guff he deserved? And when the law decided this was an open-and-shut case of self-defense, well, that only stoked the fires. I guess the harassment got pretty bad. I was still in Harrisonburg at the time, so I didn't get all the details from your grandma. Either way, in a couple weeks' time they told me they was movin' and, well, here we are."

All this aligned with what little I could remember. That must've been twenty-three years ago. It seemed odd people would begrudge an old man, even one as repellant as my grandfather, after so many years. But then again, this was the shadow of Appalachia, where resentment pooled in the places between the hollows, stagnating into a spirit-souring something, and, hell, I've yet to meet anyone who is immune.

"I suppose that makes sense," I said. "Which only goes to support my former theory. Y'all should get him the hell out of here."

"Roland, please," she said. "His father, your great-grandfather, built this home. That *means* something."

"I'm just saying, the few lucid moments he's had have not been calm. I don't think he wants to be here, Rina."

"He's always that way. Just so long as folks leave him be, nothing will come of it."

I scratched my beard and cast an anxious eye across the road toward the polished headstones half-secreted in uncut grass.

"I better get down to the hardware store," I said. "Need a few things before I finish up here."

"You'll stay for dinner then?"

"What're we having?"

***

The path to Ms. Crouse's place lay fraught with toppled lawn ornaments. The whole yard looked like a mini-Katrina had blasted through, tangling hoses that hadn't been used in years, birdbaths broken at the stem, and more than a few smiling frogs that didn't look like they had much to smile about. A pile of mail almost shin-high greeted me. I suppose that explained the empty post hole by the road. While looking down at the warped envelopes, many the victims of April showers, I remembered the sickening detail about John's death. I imagined his blood pooling under my soles, claw marks in the door jamb, a splay of legs retroflected by fits of slithering toward an unrealized salvation.

"Yes?" a fragile voice asked. The door had opened, my finger hovered by the doorbell, and I gawked at it, not even remembering the act.

"Ms. Crouse?" As if there was ever any doubt.

After all the awkward introductions, I found myself seated at a tiny Formica table with a cup of pink Country Time mixed fresh and only partially dissolved. I tried to find a space to place my glass, but, as with most surfaces in the house, the table was hidden under a stack of catalogs too tall and teetering to serve as a coaster.

For the first few minutes, Ms. Crouse fidgeted with her hearing aid.

"So you were a friend of my Johnny?"

"Not exactly," I said.

She sprinkled some dry cat food into an already full bowl. In fact, bits of Meow Mix sowed the whole floor, skittering with each of Ms. Crouse's shuffling steps and making the whole kitchen smell like a pet shop.

"I guess I should've known that," she said, taking a seat across from me. "Johnny never had any friends."

"That's kinda what I wanted to ask about. I'm actually—" A strained pause. "I'm actually Dexter Pleinway's grandson." I waited for the usual look of disgust. "You know, Dexter from down the road?"

"Oh right, Dexter. He's coming by later to fix the sprinklers."

This furrowed my brow.

"No, ma'am, I think you're confused. Dexter is my grandfather. He only just moved back in last week. The big house down the road?"

"Yes, he's done some good work for me before. Even fixed my roof after Hurricane Camille came through."

She beamed at me. Until that point, I'd only seen Ms. Crouse from a downward angle, she being one of those unfortunate folk shrunken to child-like proportions in their advanced age. Her walnut-round face split by the disturbing width of her grin, which seemed imminent to tear further, revealing—what, more teeth? I shook, told myself this was just a byproduct of childhood anxieties. For a moment, I watched the food bowl, but no cat came.

"Ma'am," I said. "Does anyone ever come by to check on you?"

"Well, you know what, why don't we find out—" she stood, rounded into the cluttered den. Moments later I heard a rear screen door open and close. Courtesy kept me fixed in place for another couple minutes, but I had no idea when my hostess would return, where she was going, what year she thought it was. I put my glass in the sink and started for the door, confident I would learn nothing from the old coot. As I finished retying my shoes (Ms. Crouse, ironically, fearing I'd dirty her dirt?) the front door opened, and there she stood as though just coming back from the garden, hands all blackened and soil down her front. She saw me crouched, and her veiny eyes, a little yellowed at the edges, went wide with lunacy.

"Who the hell are you, and what are you doing in my house?"

"No, Ms. Crouse, it's me. Roland Pleinway. Remember?"

She moved as if to strike me. I threw my arms to shield my head, but, when no blow came, I looked back. Her fist still raised, her expression softened.

"Johnny, what are you doing with your shoes on in the house?" she asked. "I thought you was going out to look for work today."

"I uhh—yes, ma'am."

"And try not to drag your feet as much this time."

I skirted around her wagging finger, catching the front door with my heel and pushing my way to freedom.

"Yes, ma'am," I replied.

"And don't you go down to your daddy's place again. You know that only riles you up."

***

We finished eating around sunset. Aunt Rina had attempted to make Grandma's meatloaf recipe, but, with no one having gone grocery shopping that week, she was forced to make some... creative substitutions. I finished picking a whole clove out of my gums while Rina started clearing the table. We'd managed to get Grandpa down into his old chair at the head of the table, and, throughout the meal, he would give a grunt of *yuah* or *nyun* as Rina attempted to feed him. Although she left out the mouth-made propeller noises, I still think her game of *here-comes-the-airplane* was too belittling by half.

While Rina disappeared into the kitchen, I sat watching Grandpa, his eyes half-lidded, lower lip obtruding as though fresh from a tooth drilling. His time in bed had tousled what remained of his hair into a cottony crown. He occasionally swayed, opened his jaw in the likeness of yawning, but made no noise. Without his formal speech faculties, it was difficult to discern just how much he recognized. To be fair, though, he wasn't all that different.

"Grandpa," I said. "I don't know—it's Roland."

Silence, save the clinking of dishes from the kitchen.

"I went down the road today. I had a little chat with—well, I don't know what you'd call her. Your old friend? Neighbor? Ms. Crouse?"

His eyes flicked to me, exposing bloodshot crescents under the thinning brow. Rina hadn't bothered changing him out of his long underwear, an old prospector-style I didn't think could be found outside TV Land westerns.

"I wanted to ask about her. And about—"

"Roland, I made up the couch in the living room for you," Rina interrupted. She dried her hands with a dish towel. "While I help your grandfather back to his room, I want you to go out into the old shed and get his gun out of its locker."

"Gun? What the hell for?"

She gave me a glare of reprimand before continuing: "Honestly, it's like you haven't been listening to me at all. I told you we've been hearing all sorts of commotion around this old house. I'm pretty sure some of the local kids are all hopped-up on their parents' gossip and have come around at night. I'm pretty sure I heard someone trying to break into the shed, and I don't want them making off with any guns. And besides, if the folks around here think they can mess with our family's property, well—"

"I'm not going to shoot anybody," I cried.

"I'm not asking you to, I just want to make sure if anyone starts making trouble, we're... prepared."

I groaned, crossed my arms, felt all too like the disgruntled teenager spurning parental command. As Aunt Rina lifted my grandfather to his feet, a stiff wind ripped over the house, shifting the ceiling beams and sending tremors through the joists that made the whole property shudder. Grandpa stalled a moment, seemed to jerk like he might throw my aunt to the floor, made a long, frightened groan as though he'd felt cold metal gracing some avenue of flesh it shouldn't.

"And while you're out there, make sure nothing will make a racket. We were up all last night with that gate."

***

A gibbous moon shined that night. I'd tried calling Shannon to catch her up on the day's migraines, but, as always, my cell flickered in and out of service. The gale-force winds certainly didn't help. I'd spent about half an hour trying to make my lumpy upholstery comfortable enough for sleep and even managed an hour or so before the terror settled on my chest. It perched, superficial at first, but then winding deeper like a cord through my very center, causing arrhythmias of heart and lungs, jolting muscles, and a swelling of the tongue so that, as I tried to roll onto my stomach, my dreams turned to the image of a man standing in the corner of the room, a silhouette among silhouettes. As the entity approached, its spasmodic gait creaked like old iron, nearing, patiently, until bathed by a slant of moonlight and—

I bolted upright, sweating, my blankets in bundles around me. I kicked them from the couch and stood. Just a load of nightmare business, I reasoned, the result of stress and under-seasoned meat. All of it mere shadows of bad memories, all of it except the iron creak.

From the front-facing window, its sash made ashen with waxing light, I could see the iron gate to the property lurching to and fro with haunted oscillation loud enough to make me wince with each clang. I was surprised Rina hadn't been down already to chastise me for my shoddy work. Didn't matter how much oil I used, though, that much movement would make a gong out of any gate. To be preemptive and help my own passage back into slumber, I took the shotgun I requisitioned from the shed and started for the door.

I didn't bother putting on pants, and the night winds chased up my bare shins into a shiver against my tailbone. The weapon weighed into a pressure point between neck and shoulder. I never liked guns. Always too heavy, sensitive, prone to tipping over, going off, deafening your cousin in his right ear.

All of Algernon moved with the hither-thither of the wind. Trees whined as they bent, the grasses scintillated, and the house itself filled with air through perforations of rot and broken shingles, swelling and sighing like a bellow. This created a cantillation of ghostly whistles, all the dead things trapped in walls biding their time. When I reached the gate, the wind died and so too did the clanging.

I rested the gun by the stone wall and shook on my phone's flashlight. Its beam cast through the iron bars, creating shadows, and among the pattern of white-lit road and the blackness of the grating, another long shadow stretched out across the road. It so startled me that I dropped my phone. When I recovered it, the shape had vanished. I steadied my hand, expecting it to squirm back into the beam, presenting itself as another inky streak. Beyond, the cemetery showed no notions of life or unlife.

A couple of bricks from a porch remodeling project two-and-a-half decades now unfinished would keep the damn doors from swinging. I unlatched the gate and opened it wide, piling a few additional bricks to ensure it'd remain stationary even in cyclonic conditions.

Right on time, a gust howled through, throwing me off balance. The gun toppled, the shutters flittered, the dead poplar in the corner of the yard twisted opposite its aged bend, but for all the bluster those gates remained sandwiched between wall and brick-stops.

Satisfied, I gathered the shotgun and started back to the porch. I'd only made it a couple paces when I paused. A sound like a rake dragging through gravel was barely audible under the nocturnal noises. I turned around but saw nothing. On the first wooden step, the clap of something around the side of the house made my insides cinch. Another plaything of the wind? I couldn't keep falling for these haunted house clichés. Still, with my adrenaline so high, I figured I wouldn't be falling asleep any time soon. Might as well burn some of it off.

The sides and rear yard showed nothing unusual. Well, nothing unusual for that old place. I double-checked the well pump and the shed, chasing off a few cockroaches but nothing more. With things seemingly secure, I yawned, the stress-crash making that sofa seem oh-so-inviting, and circled back to the front. It was only in passing the right side of the house, gazing up at the vine on the trellis, the second story all in ivory with moonlight, that I saw...

"What the f—hey, you!"

Through the middlemost window, the one that led into my grandfather's room, there lurked the outline of a human head and hunched shoulders. Too tall, by my estimate, to be Aunt Rina, and too upright to be Grandpa Dex. The figure turned away from the window, disappearing into the blackness.

My attempts to dial 9-1-1 one-handed only distracted me while I bounded up the porch. In my rush, I missed the front door's raised sill and tripped chin-first onto the runner in the foyer. My phone skidded off under an end table. The shotgun landed next to me. Dazed but undeterred, I gathered myself and my weapon, headed for the stairwell.

"Rina! Rina, wake up!" But my shouts were drowned out by a chasing wind surging throughout the main hall. The ancient roof above us groaned, and the few hanging pictures clapped against the walls. Climbing three steps at a time, I bounced off the banister and banked right.

"Grandpa!"

After the initial shock of my crashing through the door subsided, I found the bedroom cool, still, a type of dark that my eyes, even adapted to night, could not penetrate. The sash was open, allowing a little breeze to tickle the curtains. Slowly, I placed the butt of the shotgun against my shoulder. Objects took gradual shape—the bed against the wall, a lamp, the rhythm of a key-wound clock. Though I did not see the entity, I could sense a third presence. It grazed my senses like a texture just beyond your touch, like a hum that moves even deaf ears.

"I saw you," I said. "Come out."

I shuffled along, shoulder blades following the uneven wallpaper. Whoever it was, they'd not get the drop on me. Once directly opposite Grandpa in his bed, I could see—no, again, it wasn't by sight, but something like memory, a human form at his side, upright but curled to one side.

"Don't...move..." the syllables extra deep as I leveled the gun.

The thing moved closer as if it didn't understand me, as if—as if it saw from across a crowded room, mine the only familiar face. My hands shook, my index finger heating from a trembled friction on the trigger. It finally stopped about five feet to my front, blocking my view of Grandpa in his bed, a curtain in the wind with the crooks of elbows sticking out, a little shake in its head from anticipation. Then, a drip, a few more, the metronome of liquid hitting the hardwood.

"Hiii Rollie..."

A few sniffles of suppressed laughter. The skewed shoulders bounced. All my passageways closed so that no breath, no air at all could go in, come out, until—

Bang. My right shoulder slammed into the wall behind me. A whiff of gunpowder and a flash briefly illuminated the figure in front of me. Then a groan, a wet wheeze of lungs shredded by lead pellets. I exhaled so long, so slow; I shut my eyes just so I could focus on it. When I opened again, the specter was gone. I stared straight ahead, down the barrel of the shotgun, to my grandfather's seizing body, his chest all bloomed with dark spots spreading across the white sheet. As he writhed, he tried to say something but only managed a few gurgles. By that point, Rina hurried into the room, flipped on the light.

"Roland, oh my God! Oh my—" She saw Grandpa going still, the smoke of the gun still drifting. "*Oh my God! Oh my God!*" Shrieking, she ran to the bed, never minding the blood that now saturated and dribbled off the sheets onto the floor. "Daddy? Daddy, can you hear me?"

I set the gun down against the wall. Outside, a dog barked. I could see yellow in the windows of our closest neighbors. Aunt Rina sobbed, her forehead pressed against the now limp arm. Everything sounded with such clarity while I sank to the floor, hands against my head. There was no more wind. In the distance I heard the iron gate clang shut.

About The Authors

James Blakey — "The Battle of Route 42"

James is the author of the paranormal thriller *Superstition* (Book One of the Secrets of Van Buren University) and three short story collections: *The Cat Who Loved David Duchovny, Fast Times at Spiro Agnew High,* and *The Five People You Meet in Atlantic City.* He is a three-time finalist for the Short Mystery Fiction Society's Derringer Award, winning in 2019 for his story "The Bicycle Thief." James resides in Broadway, Virginia.
Website: JamesBlakeyWrites.com
Instagram: @JamesBlakeyAuthor
Facebook: Facebook.com/JamesWBlakey
Twitter/X: @JamesWBlakey

Julie Cline – "The Train to Mount Jackson"

Julie Cline is an emerging writer living in Woodstock, in the Shenandoah Valley. She's a facilitator for the Writers Group for the Valley Educational Center for the Creative Arts (VECCA), and a regular attendee to the Rocktown Writers Guild. Ms. Cline is currently working on a manuscript in the magical realism genre, set in a post-apocalyptic world in which a middle-aged clerk rebuilds a life, assisted by a plumber, two small neighbor children, and a small fluffy dog.

Julian Close — "Talk to the Hand"

Julian Close has lived in Charlottesville since 1975. He graduated from Albemarle High School in 1987, studied Psychology at Davidson College, and received a Masters in Teaching from Mary Baldwin. He has worked in finance and investing, technical writing, and financial journalism, where he developed a passion for teaching essential investing skills. In addition to market analysis, Julian writes short fiction, novels, and drama.

James Cole — "The Iron Gate"

James Cole is a poet, author, and scientist based out of Morgantown, WV. Originally from Roanoke, VA, James attended the College of William & Mary and later the University of Virginia. After earning his Ph.D. in neuroscience, he went on to join the faculty of West Virginia University as an Assistant Professor. During his five years in Charlottesville, James served as a member of the Virginia Writers Club, Charlottesville Critique Circle, and founded the Charlottesville Poetry Critique Circle. His work has appeared in numerous publications including *Oddball Magazine, Carolina Muse, Artemis Journal,* and *Charlottesville Fantastic.* In 2019, he published his first poetry collection, *Crow,* come home, through VerbalEyze Press, and his second collection, *The Somatoliths,* was released by Gnashing Teeth Publishing in 2024. He is the cofounder and an editor of *The Rumen Literary Journal.*

Lori D'Angelo — "The Body in the Lake"

Lori D'Angelo is a grant recipient from the Elizabeth George Foundation, a fellow at the Hambidge Center for Creative Arts, and an alumna of the Community of Writers. She is associate flash fiction editor at *JMWW* and holds an MA from Pittsburgh Theological Seminary and an MFA from West Virginia University. Her work has appeared in various literary journals including *BULL, Gargoyle, Drunken Boat, Moon City Review,* and *Rejection Letters.* Her first book, a collection called *The Monsters Are Here,*

was recently published by ELJ Editions.
Website: loridangelo.com
Instagram: @lori.dangelo1
Twitter/X: @sclly21
Bluesky: @sclly21

Will J Fawley — "The Kite Mechanic"

Originally from Augusta County, Will holds an MFA from George Mason University, where he was assistant fiction editor for *Phoebe Journal of Literature and Art.* His speculative fiction has appeared in various journals and anthologies, including *Arlington Literary Journal, The Northern Virginia Review, Prairie Fire,* and *Parallel Prairies.*
Website: willjfawley.com
Facebook: facebook.com/willjfawley
Instagram: @wjfawley
Twitter/X: @willjfawley

K.G. Gardner — "Trail Angel"

K.G. Gardner has more than twenty-five years of experience as a business journalist, a career that has enabled her to indulge her curiosity and her passion for words. After writing and editing tens of thousands of news articles and producing a podcast under her legal name, she has returned to her first love, fiction. A native of New Jersey, she has lived in five cities on two continents. She lives in Charlottesville, Virginia, with her husband, daughter and two cats. When not writing for work or pleasure, she enjoys travel, yoga, gardening, and reading all genres of fiction.
Facebook: facebook.com/kristenhallam
Bluesky: @kristenhallam.bsky.social
Instagram: @kristen_hallam

Ginger Grouse — "Free Birds of Singers Glen"

Ginger Grouse is an anarchist, land defender, trail runner, and occasional blogger who writes short stories, creative memoir, and essays about the intersections of bodily movement, resistance, and decolonization. Ginger has spent many days running and riding their bike around the roads of Singers Glen, but knows nothing of insurrectionary plots among the region's poultry.
Substack: runarchism.substack.com
Instagram: @runarchist
Bluesky: @runarchist.bsky.social
Mastodon: @runarchist.kolektiva.social

Ember Rensel Heishman — "Wishing Home"

Ember is a Writer/Editor who has spent the last five years making the Shenandoah Valley home with her husband and two cats. She grew up in Pennsylvania's Allegheny National Forest and holds writing degrees from Messiah College and James Madison University. After six years of working with National Parks and their nonprofit partners, she started Ember Ink Writing & Editing, and she can now be found in her home office surrounded by green things, books, and half-finished hobby projects.
   Website: www.ember.ink
Instagram: @emberbrooks.books

Kurt Johnson — "Fore Ever on Ingleside"

Kurt Johnson is a career higher education administrator. His fiction writing craft has evolved from years of creating humorous rhymes for friends and family to dabbling in children's literature centered on the adventures of his cat. Now, he yearns to share more broadly his work in historical and fantasy fiction. He lives in the beautiful Shenandoah Valley of Virginia.
Amazon: amazon.com/author/kurtjohnsonwrites

Genevieve Lyons — "Real Mischief"

Genevieve Lyons wrote and illustrated her first book at the age of six, and she's pursued creative arts ever since. She has studied film photography and she considered a career in music performance, going so far as to pass conservatory-level music theory. Genevieve was too extroverted to spend hours in tiny practice rooms, graduating with degrees in Neuroscience and Biostatistics. She enjoys the connections between ideas, and making connections with others. Curiosity is a hallmark trait that drives her work as a public health statistician and as a reader and writer. Genevieve is a member of the Women's Fiction Writers Association and a local library writers critique circle. She lives in Virginia with her husband, children, three chickens, and a messy wildflower garden.
Website: genevieve-lyons.com
Substack: genevievelyons.substack.com

Charlie Newman-Johnson — "Birdwatching"

Charlie Newman-Johnson is a Midwesterner transplanted to Virginia (and recently re-transplanted to Seattle). He loves Virginia for its mountains—for their bike routes, for their metamorphic rocks, for their beauty. He and his spouse have a dog named Anela (Hawaiian for 'angel') and a cat named Ashmedai ('king of demons' in Yiddish). The pets get along, mostly.

Kent M. Peterson — "Past is Prologue"

Kent M. Peterson grew up in the Shenandoah Valley and still lives there. He is the co-author (with Jeff Simon) of the fantasy novel *Outlander,* as well as the author of *The Murdered Knight.*
Website: kaempii.wordpress.com

Bethany W Pope — "Not-A-Deer"

Bethany W Pope has won numerous literary awards and published ten novels and collections of poetry. Nicholas Lezard, writing for *The Guardian*, described Bethany's latest poetry collection as "poetry as salvation" ... "This harrowing collection drawn from a youth spent in an orphanage delights in language as a place of private escape."

E.G. Reger — "The Hunt for Monty Glassman"

E.G. Reger has been living and writing in the Shenandoah Valley her entire life. Her favorite things to write about include powerful friendships, eccentric characters, and the innate sanctity of baked goods.
Website: sites.google.com/view/egregerwrites
Twitter/X: @egregerwrites

Stephen A. Roddewig — "The Long Sought *I. batatas*"

Stephen A. Roddewig is an author residing in Arlington, Virginia. Though not originally from the Shenandoah Valley, he grew up in the shadow of the Blue Ridge Mountains, hiked countless miles on the Appalachian Trail, and would always stock up on bulk bags at Route 11 Potato Chips before visiting his grandparents. Naturally, he later attended James Madison University for his undergraduate degree (joining several other family alums) and has nearly completed his quest to tour every cavern in the valley, including his favorite, Shenandoah Caverns. You can find more of his speculative fiction and comedy at his website.
Website: stephenaroddewig.com
Instagram: @stephen.drinks.for.his.books

Rodman — "The Long Walk"

Rodman is a Virginia-based writer as seen in the *Alternative Liberties* anthology, the *Midnight Garden: Where Dark Tales*

Grow anthology, and *Andromeda Literary Magazine.* He is an avid watcher of 80s movies and fosterer of dogs.
Instagram: @ell.rodman.wr

Catherine Simpson — "Dam Negotiations"

Catherine Simpson is a writer and editor who lives in the shadows of the Blue Ridge Mountains with her cat and occasional creative muse, Mauka. She's currently working on a Southern Gothic novel about a secret society within a secret society, and her short story work can be found most recently in *Wallstraight*, a literary journal for weird fiction. When not drafting or knee-deep in track changes, Catherine can be found wandering, looking at trees, and daydreaming about her next project.
Website: CatSimpsonWrites.com
Instagram: @catsimpson_writes

Jake Solyst —"Fixer Upper"

Jake Solyst is a fiction and nature writer living in Charlottesville, Virginia. He writes stories about the mistakes, lost dreams, and silver linings of millennial life. He also covers environmental news for a nonprofit and serves as a contributing editor for the online literary magazine *Feign*.

Carol Steele — "Old Yeller Ain't No Dog"

Carol writes about events she hopes will never happen to her; her genres are mystery and horror. Holding her attention for first place in her life is her family, and in second place, she divides her time between writing and studying modern Western philosophy.
Email: CarolSteeleWrites@yahoo.com

Griff Thomas – "The Whitetail Whatchamacallit"

This selection was inspired by the author's grandfather Robert Sarrett, a wonderful storyteller who grew up in West Virginia. Griff and his wife of thirty-five years Amy, another inspirational story

teller, live in Stephens City. They have three grown daughters Zoe, Bronwyn, and Gemma.
   Website: WhatGreatLeadersKnow.com

Fendy S. Tulodo — "Catfishes, Casseroles, and the Demonic Fiddle of Staunton"

Fendy is a writer and content creator from Malang, Indonesia. His work blends local flavor with speculative strangeness, often mixing humor, mystery, and a touch of the absurd. When he's not wrangling words, he's composing music, chasing stories hidden in plain sight, or questioning why the rice cooker talks back.
Linktree: linktr.ee/fendytulodo

Matthew Turner — "Marigolds in the Mesozoic"

Matthew is a U.S. history teacher and artist who lives in Winchester with his beautiful wife and their sweet little cat. He especially enjoys both studying and writing about World War II and the Cold War, and as a reader enjoys science fiction and fantasy. He also enjoys traveling along with his wife. His favorite authors are Tolkien, Orson Scott Card, and Cixin Liu. This will be his first submitted work of hopefully many more!
Facebook: facebook.com/matthew.turner.376
Instagram: @matthewturnerart

Caitlin Woodford — "The Fractal"

Caitlin Woodford is a Pushcart-nominated writer of strange and speculative fiction from central Virginia. Her work has appeared in *The Foundationalist*, the *Charlottesville Fantastic* anthology, *Creation Literary Magazine*, and more. She was the winner of the Globe Soup 2024 Historical Fiction Challenge and a 2023 winner of the Writing Battle Short Story contest. When not writing fiction, Caitlin is a writer and editor for science publications, and frequently escapes to hike the Blue Ridge Mountains.
Website: caitlinwoodford15.wixsite.com/caitlinwoodford

Also from Whitaker Lyon Press

A Vampire at a UVA Sorority...

A 400-year-old Dragon Hidden in Shenandoah National Park...

An Enigmatic Tuxedo Cat on the Downtown Mall...

These are just a few of the characters you will encounter in CHARLOTTESVILLE FANTASTIC: ARCANE ECHOES FROM VIRGINIA'S HEARTLAND.

Twenty tales in total, each exploring the mystical essence of the region, revealing a place where the past, present, and future intertwine in unexpected and enchanting ways.

Some funny, some serious, all just a little spooky, there really is something in this collection for everyone. Whether you are a born and bred Charlottesvillian or a visitor looking for a book to give you a feel for the local culture, CHARLOTTESVILLE FANTASTIC is bound to capture your attention and spark your imagination. —**Samantha Koon Jones, Book Critic for *The (Charlottesville) Daily Progress***

CHARLOTTESVILLE FANTASTIC in eBook, paperback, and hardcover from your favorite book retailer.

Read an Excerpt from SUPERSTITION

A Paranormal Thriller by James Blakey

A mirror shatters. An umbrella is opened indoors. A black cat crosses your path. All omens of bad luck that no one takes seriously. But at Van Buren University when these and other superstitions are broken, students die.

***

Saturday 1:13am

Her headlamp illuminating the way, the college student trudged to the campfire circle and dumped another armful of sticks and leaves.

Satisfied with the pile, she rested on a boulder, her breath visible in the chilly air as she retrieved a bottle of water. To her right, an Adirondack 46er loomed. Above, a cloudless sky of stars twinkled, no city to drown their light.

Easier to try this at the nature preserve back on campus, but even at this late hour that risked awkward encounters with pot-smoking art majors or insomniac townies.

From her overstuffed green-and-gold backpack, she retrieved half a dozen copies of the college newspaper. She
crumpled the pages, placing them strategically amongst the
branches, then marinated the heap with charcoal lighter fluid.

She struck a match and tossed it. Orange flames erupted,
blinding her for a second, enveloping her in a wave of heat.
The hypnotizing fire reminded her of summer camping trips
with her father. *Should have brought marshmallows.*

Her phone chimed. Five minutes until the new moon.

She pulled out the shrink-wrapped lamb chops, on sale
for $9.99 per pound at Price Chopper. The student wouldn't,
couldn't, sacrifice a living animal for the power she craved.
Even the thought of touching raw meat filled her disgust. She
slipped on a pair of latex gloves liberated from biology lab, then
tossed the chops into the flames.

The scent of burning meat filled the air. She hoped to finish
before any bears or wolves arrived.

She retrieved the blue textbook, turning to the marked page.
Squinting at the diagram, then the sky, she oriented herself,
zeroing in on Orion's Belt. A couple of moon widths to the east,
she located Alpha Monocerotis.

Of course, that wasn't what the Picts called the star two
millennia ago when they ruled what today is Scotland. No
one knew their name for it. Almost all their knowledge had
been lost. One scrap that survived: their high priestesses wor-
shipped this star for luck.

No bars on her phone. Not a problem. The student pulled
the folded printout from her pocket, silently rehearsing the
spell. There wasn't a person alive who could reconstruct the
enchantment the way the Picts originally spoke it. Her new
friends on the dark web assured her that Modern English
would work fine, as long as it rhymed.

The past few weeks, she experimented with charms and
simple conjuring. Enough to prove to herself that magic was
real, and she possessed the power to wield it.

The phone beeped. *Now.*

She stood before the fire, hand raised to the sky, pointing at
the faint red star.

The paper rippled in the wind. She focused on the magic, emptying her mind of all other thoughts.

As she recited the words, all feeling receded, as if her consciousness left her physical form behind, merging with the fire, the star, the spell.

> *Goddesses of the Night, hear my plea*
> *Bring Success and Prosperity*
> *My offering to you, a favored sheep*
> *A promise to you, I will always keep*
> *To my endeavors great and small*
> *I call upon you, one and all*
> *With a whisper soft and a heart so true*
> *I conjure Fortune to come anew*
> *Bring me riches, bring me fame*
> *And banish all my doubts and shame*
> *I summon the forces of Star and Sky*
> *To grant me Destiny that cannot die*
> *By my will and desire so strong*
> *This Magic now shall not go wrong*
> *Bringing Luck to my life at last*
> *So mote it be, this Spell is cast.*

She became aware: clothes sticking to her sweat-drenched body, mouth dry, hair plastered to her head, heart pounding. She stumbled to the boulder, resting, regaining her strength.

An owl screeched in the darkness. Good sign? Owls were supposed to be magical. Or was that some Harry Potter nonsense?

The owl quieted. No crickets at this altitude. No sound but the wind and faint jet engines as red-and-green navigation lights hurried across the sky.

The student didn't look or feel different. No supernatural power coursing through her veins. No enhanced perceptions allowing her to observe a secret world. No ethereal light enveloping her.

How anticlimactic. What do you expect for $9.99 a pound?

No way to know if she cast the spell correctly.

No way to test if the magic was working.

No way to tell if this ceremony was a big waste of time.

Not waiting for any predators that caught the scent of the sacrifice, she doused the flames with three bottles of water. Buried the ashes with her collapsible shovel.

Only you can prevent forest fires.

She scoured the area, gathering any trash.

Leave no trace.

She slipped the pack on her back and began the four-mile hike to the trailhead. She stifled a yawn. At least it was downhill.

Thirty minutes on the trail and her mind was numb. Legs on auto. Step, step, step. Leaves crunching under her feet. Another three miles to go. All she wanted was to get back to her dorm, make a cup of hot cocoa, and crawl into bed.

Gack! A spider web across the trail on her face, in her mouth. She spit and raised a hand as the toe of her hiking boot caught a root. She pitched forward, losing her balance, falling toward the sharp rocks on this section of the trail. Arms flailing, she couldn't stop herself. In the darkness, her hand grabbed a branch, wrenching her shoulder, but arresting her fall.

The student righted herself, let out a deep breath, her palm scraped and scratched. Need to be careful. Could have broken a leg or worse. Been stranded with no way to call for help. And no one knew she was up here. Pretty lucky.

A smile spread across her face.

Pretty lucky.

"It works!" she shouted into the night.

***

SUPERSTITION (Book One of The Secrets of Van Buren University) by James Blakey and published by City Owl Press available as an eBook or in print from your favorite book retailer.